THE AFTERMATH | BOOK ONE

THE SHATTERED ONES

BRIGITTE CROMEY

Yarrow Leaf Press

Cover design by EAH Creative

Copyedited by Deborah O'Carroll

Formatting by M. H. Woodscourt

Published by Yarrow Leaf Press

ISBN: 979-8-9850208-2-3

www.wordsinmyblood.com

Dedicated to those who have hidden from others for fear of their own broken edges. May you take courage and trust that you really are worth fighting for.

And to Emmy, who started it all.

CONTENTS

THE
SHATTERED
ONES

THE AFTERMATH | BOOK ONE

No one ever cared much about this territory. The aliens didn't. Our new government doesn't. There's not enough water for agriculture, too much heat to make big settlements feasible, and the foliage routinely tries to kill you. The forbidding terrain has always been a refuge for lawbreakers and rebels, a place where criminals could operate unchecked. With humanity finally getting its sea legs back after years of oppression, the only people who care about this region are the people whose roots go too deep to ever consider leaving—or those with something to hide.

And me? I'm here because I have nowhere else to go.

Earth Defense Force Base 36
Gila River Valley
June 21

THESE BASES WERE ALWAYS the same. Same mismatched linoleum and tile floors, patched at weird geometric angles. Same scuffed and fading concrete walls. Same twisting corridors, smelling of dust and stale coffee no matter how recently they'd been cleaned. Same handwritten signs, scrawled in black marker and taped over what had once been "official" ones. To hear the older troopers talk, it had been like this in workplaces even before the world they'd known had abruptly ended. No matter how sterile and official a setting, the human touch always found its way in.

With the rise of Earth's new government, air conditioning had been reinstalled in the main base buildings. It didn't do much against the late-June heat, but I appreciated the effort. My screens took up a full corner of the Fishbowl, glowing cheerfully with the blue-and-white logo of the Defense Force as I flicked on the main fluorescent lights. The light reflected off the inside of the big hallway windows that gave the command center its name, casting back the image of a sleepy eighteen-year-old with dark curls and bronze skin who desperately needed the coffee in the thermos he was clutching.

A hiss came from the other corner of the room as the lights came to full strength.

"Turn those things off!"

I jumped and obeyed, sending the room back into dusk. "Deadeye?" I squinted through the gloom to see my tech specialist counterpart lying on the floor under her desk, a penlight clamped between her teeth as she fiddled with something on the underside of the desk. Carefully setting my things on my console, I picked my way across the dim room to crouch beside her. "What are you doing? Won't more light help?"

"Not worth making my headache worse," she grunted as the penlight slipped and fell to the floor, casting a shadow across her angular face and black eyepatch. I knew her name was actually Reneé, but her call sign suited her demeanor and appearance so well that most people used it instead. I'd asked how she lost the eye soon after our first meeting. After a long pause, she'd grinned and said, "Bear attack."

I hadn't bothered asking again.

"Here, I'll hold it." I picked the light up and held it so Deadeye could see the tangle of wires and lights running across the underside of the communications desk.

"Thanks, Gabe." She grabbed a pair of pliers, squirming hands and tool into the mess only to give a sigh of relief as another light illuminated her face. Wriggling out from under the desk, she dropped the pliers into a tote on the floor. "Sorry about yelling at you." I'd been told her accent was German, but the knowledge hadn't enlightened me beyond having a description to put to her voice. She pulled the eyepatch strap tighter around pink-streaked dark hair and explained, "It's a migraine day, and the lights weren't helping."

I offered her a hand up. "I'm sorry. We can keep them off." I looked around the room. In the emergency lighting, the Fishbowl was almost cozy. "Were you able to fix what broke?"

"This time." She crashed into her chair, its springs creaking in protest as she sank back. A booted foot landed on her desk beside her keyboard. "Sometimes, I wish it would just break and be done. The more times I fix it, the more times Regional Command blows off my request for a new one."

I went over to my own console, arranging my things neatly on the desk: Two color-coordinated notebooks, coffee with half-and-half but no sugar, a digital voice recorder, two pens, and a protein bar I'd been too groggy to gnaw through yet. The screens—stacked several high and arranged in a semicircle—lit up with a blank background as I put a flat palm on the login pad. I flipped open my blue work notebook and set it beside my keyboard as the surveillance system fired up. Connected to the satellite high over earth, the network of towers were our eyes and ears in the region. I'd always had a knack for getting systems like this to work; reason number one I'd been assigned here straight out of training.

I was reminded of reason number two as a tall, broad-shouldered man in his late forties walked in the door, snapping on the lights and swearing as both Deadeye and I yelled, "No lights!"

Captain Espinoza—our base commander—chuckled and turned off half the lights. He grinned at Deadeye as she sagged backward in her chair, wrapping her palms over her eyes. "You know, if you spent more time outside, the lights wouldn't bother you as much."

"Shut up, Bandit," she groaned. "We're not all born and raised desert rats."

Espinoza set his things down at his own, smaller workstation before coming over to me. He switched languages as he stuffed his hands in his pockets, fluent Spanish filling my ears with the sounds of my childhood. "Morning, *mijo*. How are things looking for today?"

I pulled up the weather report for the week and highlighted the part I knew he was asking about. "It looks good... well, about as predictable as it gets. There's a chance of a storm later today."

Espinoza nodded approvingly as he unfolded a navy bandana from his pocket and tied it around his neck. "Halo and I have to go on a supply run. We'll be okay even if it does storm, but I like knowing what's out there before it hits me."

I nodded, looking up at my displays. In this respect, he and I were alike. I supposed that similarity was one of the reasons he'd recruited me to this placement, after meeting me while teaching marksmanship at training. "I'll make sure to keep you updated as you go. At least it's a straight shot from here to Phoenix."

Deadeye spun in her chair to face us, having caught the familiar location in the stream of Spanish. "Hey, are you going north today?"

"Yes." Espinoza switched back to English as he said it, going to his desk and picking up his own coffee cup. His free hand tapped absently against the grip of an old handgun at his hip as he explained, "I have a meeting with Supply and Allocation, and we have to swap out the truck's power core." His amber eyes twinkled in a sun-browned face. "It was doing fine until summer hit, then everyone started using the air conditioner each time they took a patrol. I swear they're turning that thing down to sixty degrees."

I snorted back a laugh. It was warm in June, but I'd never been used to climate-controlled *anything* growing up. To me, even the shoddy air conditioning in the base was a little too cold.

"Well, do me a favor?" Deadeye's smile had a diabolical twist as she stuffed papers in a folder and skimmed it across the room at him. "Take *that* and stuff it up Supply and Allocation's nose for me."

I put on my headset, drowning out their ensuing argument with white noise. Settling into the rhythm of my work, I was able to sink into the streams of data as the others came and went, setting up workstations and checking in for daily assignments. After a few months of me being assigned here, the rest of the base staff were used to my ways, and were happy to leave me alone in my world of white noise, video feeds, weather overlays, and surveillance reports. From here, I felt like I could sense the heartbeat of the entire region— from the rugged mountains guarding the valley, to the glittering solar fields that ensured our survival, to the broken asphalt strips that were our lifelines to the outside world.

Deadeye had said it, and she was right. Not everyone was born here, and it took guts to stay. But me?

I rolled my neck from side to side and took a sip of my

already cooling coffee. There was a third reason the colonel at Regional Command had stationed me here; a lone rookie with a fearful streak in a base full of old soldiers. Even from behind a set of screens, in a dimly lit room at the center of a base long neglected, hardly anyone else on the force knew this desert like I did.

TWILIGHT CAME to the valley with a dusty purple sky, thunderheads illuminated in the distance by occasional flashes of lightning. My shift long over, I sat under a desert willow, recorder balanced on the cast-concrete bench next to me. Deadeye's German accent drifted from the device into the evening air as I transcribed my latest interview into my red notebook. I'd always had a fondness for stories, but collecting them from the squad members was a new pastime. Once I'd realized that the heroes of my childhood were achingly, genuinely human under their formidable reputations, I couldn't bring myself to let the old veterans' stories fade into obscurity.

No, Deadeye's not old. I corrected myself—and my notes. *She's not even forty yet.* Of the two dozen or so troopers assigned here, only Deadeye, Captain Espinoza, and our doctor Josephine Flores had been directly fighting this war since its inception more than ten years ago. All three of them had worked personally with the founder of the EDF; the powerful telepath who'd been the first to rally the struggling human resistance against the occupying xeno forces. They'd seen Shattered power wielded in battle, faced off against creatures that I could only pray to forget—

"C'mon, Gabriel, focus." I shook away my distraction,

crossed out a line, and backed the recording up a few seconds to try again.

Deadeye's voice repeated the last sentence. "—wanted us out of the way, once everything was said and done. Some of the new senators even wanted to court-martial Michael, on account of the lives lost once the dampening fields dropped and the population went ape."

"But he wasn't responsible!" I mouthed the exclamation even as my own voice came over the recording. Michael. It felt wrong for me to even *think* of a hero who'd saved humanity in terms of his first name, but Deadeye talked about him like he'd been a friend. "W-was he?"

"Of course not!" Deadeye's offense was as palpable now as it had been while she was telling the story. She'd stopped tinkering with her office chair to glare at me with her good eye. "The xenos were losing control of the fields—everyone could feel it. Or, you know, as much as you could feel anything back then." She'd given a fierce twist to the screwdriver. "You grew up under one—you remember."

I'd squirmed, the memories twisting in the back of my mind like a dream viewed through fog. While experiencing the population "going ape" from the inside, the stories of the fearless saviors of earth had been one of the only things that kept me going. "I just remember being really tired as a little kid."

"Be glad that tired was all you felt." I couldn't hear the creaking of Deadeye's chair through the recording, but her expression had been suspicious as she sat down. "We adults experienced it much worse. You'd know your friends and family were disappearing, but it was like you couldn't even bring yourself to care; not properly, anyway. That type of pain can't stay buried forever. *Everyone* knew when the fields finally went down, and I understand why so many people lost their minds underneath it all."

Yeah. I paused the recording and clutched my fingers around my pen. *And not everyone lost their minds in a "lay down and die" kind of way.* A flash of red splattered across the interior of my mind, a familiar scream lancing through the deepest parts of my memory. For some, the fields falling had meant a chance to regain power in the most violent way possible. I sighed and told myself out loud, "Of course they wanted *someone* to blame."

"It was just convenient to pin all the blame on Michael," Deadeye's voice said as I started playback again. "The Defense Force—all of us who he recruited to help him along the way—did what it needed to, but not everyone liked the cost that victory came with." She'd snorted and dropped the screwdriver into her toolbox. "Michael knew that everyone who'd fought with him would be in danger. He got word to us to scatter, so we did." The recording blurred into static for a moment, her next words almost lost in the digital filters I'd added to make playback clearer. "He died only a month later. The rest of his organization got rolled into the government's forces as the new Earth Defense Force." She sighed. "Some of us returned after a while. It was all we'd known, so it was hard to stay away." Her good eye had gone glassy, and she'd blinked hard a few times before confessing, "I don't even know how many of the others are still alive."

I switched off the recorder and set my notebook aside. Twirling my pen between my fingers, I stared at the western horizon. The sky had long gone dark, and the lights of one of our communication towers blinked in the distance on the far peaks.

They restored humanity's hope, and we just shoved them

aside. No one will ever know what they gave up so we could be free.

I scooped up my notebook as headlights shone against the side of the building. Gravel crunched under all-terrain tires as the truck's engine died down.

"Hey, *mijo!*" Espinoza called from the cab. "Come help us unload!"

I crunched through the gravel to the driveway and punched a button to let the cantilevered door to the vehicle bay swing up. Our driver, Halo, started up the engine again, and the truck rumbled through to its spot beside two others in the vast bay. Under the harsh overhead lights, they looked small and lonely in a space designed to hold over a dozen of the vehicles. Halo jumped down from the cab with several bags of groceries, briskly nodding at me as he brushed past. He wasn't wearing his body armor, and I stifled a snort of annoyance as he went inside. For someone who was so concerned about doing things by the book, he certainly didn't hesitate to bend the rules for his own comfort.

I stabbed the button on the door and ducked inside before it closed on me. One of the crew seats in the truck's passenger cab was unfolded, a man with white hair and a slim build standing up to pass groceries to Espinoza.

Espinoza handed me a box. "Here, *mijo.* Just stack everything over by the door for now. We'll get it after dinner. Oh, and..." He gestured to the new man. "Gabriel, this is Alexi Morozov. He's been reassigned here from Regional Command."

The newcomer extended his hand down from the truck bed. "Nice to meet you."

"Likewise." I reached up—and stopped. The white hair had been striking enough. Now, I saw that it was probably bleached, that Alexi was a lot younger than I had expected—maybe twenty-seven to my eighteen years—and that his eyes glowed an unearthly cyan color.

My surprise must've shown on my face, as both men started laughing. "Close your mouth, *mijo*," Espinoza said. "You act like you've never met a Shattered before."

I did what he said, not wanting to admit that's not why I'd been staring. A glance at the nameplate on his shirt confirmed the rest of my suspicions. The call sign was a name I'd heard before—a character out of legend.

Judge.

"I WAS on duty that afternoon. They told Tara what had happened to Caleb, and she just—" Josephine mimicked an explosion. Behind her, an isolation compounding cabinet hummed peacefully, filling the fluorescent-lit room with white noise in marked contrast to the story she was telling me. "The light came out of everywhere, all around her. I'd only been working with Shattereds for a few months, but I could tell power when I saw it."

"The commander couldn't stop it?"

Josephine gave me a dark-eyed corrective look. Even with me hunched over a notebook at the end of the workbench, the doctor and I only barely saw eye to eye. What she lacked in height, however, she made up for in dark curls and energy. "Michael was capable of processing immense amounts of information through his mind and was an expert at communicating over distance. His reflexes weren't that great, though. No," she sighed. "It was Judge. Right as Tara's vortex opened up, he threw a shield."

"Judge—" I checked in my battered red notebook. "Alexi… Morozov? Was he even there yet? I thought he joined later?"

Josephine brushed lint off the scrub jacket she was wearing over her uniform, a combination that warned she could just as easily end a life as save it. "He was there." She smiled affectionately. "He was all of sixteen, skinny as a beanpole, and cocky as hell. He got all the way across the hallway, opened the door, and cast the shield without anyone getting hurt."

"Wow." I whistled. "He's powerful, then?"

"Judge Shattered at an early age, and had a good grasp of his power from the very beginning. Russia fell early to the xenos, and there was more time for the dampening fields to affect the population." Josephine went back to what she'd been doing on the workbench, pouring white powder from a paper envelope into a glass beaker. "Once he cast the shield, Tara's vortex collapsed and she passed out. Michael let her go on the mission to rescue Caleb, once we figured out where he was. And you know, it's funny—" Josephine poured water into the beaker. Her small hands were as nimble and graceful as a dancer's as she swirled the mixture together. I glanced at the open door of a cupboard, the brightly colored dresses of folklórico dancers shining from a photograph taped to the inside of the door—reminders of a disappearing past. "With Caleb nearby, Tara had a better grasp of her power. It made the two of them unstoppable on the field."

"Wow." I closed my notebook. "So, between you and me?" I leaned against the workbench. "What happened to them? Now that the war's over."

Josephine wiped her forehead with her sleeve. "Judge stayed with the Force. Command sends him where his power can be used the most. Caleb and Tara went into the wind *when everyone else scattered." She frowned, dark eyes thoughtful. "All of them saw so much. Endured so much." Glass clinked gently as she picked up a stirring rod. "I can't say I blame them, if they just wanted to hide."*

I nodded. I couldn't blame them either. Hiding, after all, was what I'd done most of my life, too.

DINNER THAT NIGHT WAS GOOD, with the extra groceries brought from Phoenix. I flipped a grilled cheese sandwich off the pan onto a plate and turned off the electric burner. There had been quite a crowd around Judge earlier, but finally things had died down to just him, Deadeye, Josephine, and Captain Espinoza. The four of them lounged around the rickety table, teasing each other mercilessly and exchanging anecdotes in cheerful tones. I leaned against the kitchen counter, eating my sandwich and trying not to make it too obvious that I was listening in. My notebook sat in a pile of my other stuff at the end of the counter, and my hand was inching toward it when Josephine noticed me.

"Gabriel, *mijo*, come and join us!" She patted the table between her and Deadeye. "You don't have to hang back over there."

My face felt warm as Judge pushed a chair out with his foot, his unbuttoned uniform shirt flopping open to reveal a non-regulation T-shirt underneath. I tried not to stare too hard at the design, but it looked vaguely like a melon with a spoon stabbed into it. *What's with that?* I took the chair, nodding thanks quietly as Captain Espinoza asked, "When they gave you your assignment, did Regional mention anything about the Ridges?"

Judge smirked. "You mean, did they say anything about the Blood Angels?" I hadn't noticed before, but there was something unfamiliar about his voice. Thinking over his last name—Morozov—I remembered that my notes had him listed as being born in what used to be Russia. "According to them, I'm here to replace what's-his-name who left a few months ago." He raised an eyebrow. "But then, Regional Command isn't known for being forthcoming with their motives, and I'm not even sure they'd *know* the names of mountains outside of the Rockies."

"They only know that name because it's right outside their windows," I muttered, not that anyone heard me. I'd been to Regional Command once, when I was fresh out of training. The mountains in Colorado hadn't been nearly as pretty as the ones here.

"The guy who left was basically a grunt," Deadeye said, running a hand through her pink-streaked hair with a shrewd look at Judge. "Replacing him with you is a *serious* upgrade."

"That's what I thought, too, so I did some research." Judge's chair legs screeched on the tile as he pulled his chair closer. I winced at the sound, but no one else seemed to notice. "Some of the guys up there remembered me from a few years ago, and they let me look at some files that mayyybe I shouldn't have had access to." He winked at the others as they gave him exasperated looks. "In all their documentation, the Ridges came up a few times—way more than I would've expected for a miserable line of rocks that no one cares about."

I sat up indignantly. *I'm allowed to call it miserable, but no one else gets to.*

Captain Espinoza noticed and chuckled. "Don't mind him, *mijo*. He's just ignorant."

"Stupid," Deadeye supplied, swinging a foot up onto a vacated chair.

"Also arrogant," Josephine added as she collected our plates.

Judge threw up his hands, glancing my way. "You see? This is why I stayed away so long; this type of abuse!"

"Ah, you're confusing abuse with constructive criticism. Long on the criticism bit." Deadeye smirked at Judge before bringing the conversation to where it had originated. "We've been watching the Ridges—well," she corrected herself, "the Blood Angels *in* the Ridges—for months. They *seemed* content to stay festering in the mountains, but—"

"They're not anymore." I shifted uncomfortably in my seat as everyone looked at me, pulling a pen from my pocket and twirling it between my fingers. "They've been quiet, but they can never stay away for long. They've been extending their reach back into the city." The xenos had been bad enough—cold and scientific, inhumane in every sense of the word, and interested only in reaping humanity's stem cells, hemoglobin, and lymphocytes to further their own desires of immortality and conquest. The human gangs that'd gained power in the wake of their defeat were almost worse, operating with all the ferocity and none of the mercy you'd expect from another human being. "The EDF only knocked the Blood Angels out for a little bit. They've regained their strength."

Judge grunted with surprise. "Kid's sharp," he said to Espinoza. "That's exactly what I was about to say. Where'd they dig him up?"

"Gabriel was born here," Josephine said, squeezing my shoulder before taking the plates to the sink. "Just like Bandit and I. There's no one better than him when it comes to knowing this desert."

"That's right. And he's right," Espinoza agreed. "The gang's looking at shaking things up; maybe even challenging Regional Command for authority." He eyed Judge across the table. "And Regional is nervous enough about it that they decided to risk sending you here? That's enough to make *me* nervous. We all know how you get."

"What?" Judge asked innocently. "I'm not going to do anything stupid or foolish. I've learned that lesson already." His voice dropped, and the enthusiasm went out of his voice. "The xenos saw to that."

"We know. But at least we lived to talk about it." Deadeye gave him a sad smile and raised the dregs of her water. "Here's to those who didn't."

I joined them in the salute, downing the chlorinated water in a quick swallow. Even if I couldn't get used to the idea of using his first name, the fact remained—humanity would still be suppressed, oppressed, and literally bleeding dry if it hadn't been for Michael and the handful of others who'd first made the decision to fight for something bigger than their own lives. With that in mind, it was more of a mystery than ever why Regional Command now distrusted those who'd been closest with him.

The others seemed glad to have another member of their old crew back. The talk drifted from there, ranging from stories of the old days to plans for the future. Bandit wanted to get a water catchment system built into the side of the base, and the others were all chiming in with suggestions on other improvements. My hand soon cramped from writing out the stories circulating around the table, but worry had begun to stir in my stomach. From everything I could tell, the

Earth Defense Force leadership felt threatened enough by the members of the original rebellion forces that they had deliberately kept most of them out of action for years. Now, they'd sent Judge here to rejoin not one, but three of the original squad.

This can't be coincidence. I closed my notebook and left the kitchen as the others continued catching up with each other. *I need to get back to work. Command is worried about something in this region, and I need to know what it is.*

STAGE TWO

Earth Defense Force Base 36
Gila River Valley
June 23

"CAPTAIN ESPINOZA?" I stood by his desk, clutching a handful of printouts from my latest surveillance sweep. Around us, the Fishbowl hummed with transmissions, conversations, and the whirring of ancient computers. After the concerning news Judge had brought a few days ago, I'd spent hours searching through my systems for anything out of the ordinary. No one else had bothered to check on why I was spending so much time logged into the system, and the days had progressed along the lines of "business as usual."

Espinoza looked up from the report he'd been writing. He immediately set down his work upon seeing my face. "You know, I keep telling you, you don't have to use my title. My call sign is fine, or even my name."

I shrugged and held out the printouts to him. Using only

his call sign seemed disrespectful, and I knew we were nowhere near a first-name basis. "Would you mind taking a look at these? Something's not right, and I'd like a second set of eyes on it."

He grunted and took the printouts, looking up as the others broke into raucous laughter at some joke Judge had made. I shifted from foot to foot, stuffing my hands into my pockets to keep from fidgeting as Espinoza flicked through the papers. His amber eyes narrowed, and after a moment he looked up sharply. "Let's go for a walk."

He grabbed a broad-brimmed hat off his console and strode out of the room, calling to Judge, "We're going out for a sec. Don't break anything."

I hurried after him, barely catching Judge's sarcastic reply as the Fishbowl door closed behind us. Outside, the late June weather was doing its best to remind us why living here was only for the resilient or foolish. My eyes itched and the breeze stole all the moisture from my mouth as Espinoza headed to the benches under the trees. "All right," he said, glancing up at me from under his hat brim as he sat down in the shade of a palo verde tree, the sparse leaves and green-barked branches casting barely enough shade to make being outside bearable. "I know what you found isn't ordinary, but I can't tell exactly why. Suppose you walk me through it."

I nodded and took the papers, laying them out on the bench between us. "These are readings from the solar field between us and the Ridges." I pointed at the wobbly graph that I'd put together, going back a good six months. "Sir, I've only been here for a few months, but something seems off about the power usage. There's way more power being consumed than I expected, and when I looked at Tucson's demand, it doesn't add up."

"Right..." Espinoza shoved his hat back to rub his forehead. He looked up at the palo verde branches, as if the answers could be found in their pattern against the sky. "Could it be that they're using more power than usual? Maybe there's a drain of some kind because of a change in the population?"

I shook my head and shuffled through to pull out another report. "The program I wrote accounted for that." It had taken me hours, but I'd been pleased with how well my code had worked. "The population hasn't grown too much in the last few years, and the demand is consistent with what growth there was. I did think that maybe there was a problem with the power grid in the city, so I looked into the maintenance logs for the equipment."

"And?"

"Still nothing." I smoothed one of the pages against the bench. "I mean, sure, there are inefficiencies. The equipment is ten years old at best, and the rest of it's been repaired so many times it's barely recognizable. But even with bad equipment, the deficit's too big to just ignore." I frowned. "And I found something else, but you probably won't like it."

"Try me anyway," Espinoza ordered.

"Yes, sir." I pushed the power readings to the side and pulled out another printout. "While I was doing the check of the maintenance logs, I also did a check of the sensor stations. Just to be thorough." I lowered the paper, looking up at Espinoza. "Two of them came up static."

At this, Espinoza sat all the way up, looking at me urgently. "Which ones?"

"Twenty-three and..." I checked again, even though the numbers had appeared clearly in my mind. "Seventeen. The two on the far side of the dunes."

"By the Ridges. *And* the solar field."

I nodded, brushing sweat from my forehead. Even in the shade, the heat was enough to make my eyes gritty and my hair damp with sweat. "I ran a sensor scan with the satellite, to see if I could tell why those two stations went down. A dust storm, I thought, or maybe they've just reached their lifespan."

Espinoza shook his head. "I doubt that. Let me guess—"

"Strange activity between there and the Ridges, sir." I bit my lower lip as I produced another folded printout from my thigh pocket. "And there was this, too."

There was silence for a long minute as Captain Espinoza read through the report from the satellite. Finally, he set the paper down and looked out at the desert toward the west. "*Me lleva.* I thought when we kicked the xenos into orbit, we'd have seen the last of their pets."

I nodded, completely understanding his surprise and fear. Brutes had been the xenos' muscle—mindless, alien, predatorial monsters that the xenos used to keep the few errant humans in check. We hadn't seen any in years, and I'd been happy to reduce them to childhood nightmares. "I only picked up a few on the scan, but that's after seeing none for years."

Espinoza sighed, the lines on his face deepening as he said, "I'm glad I stuck to my guts and had us come out here."

"Why? Would the others panic?" I started stacking the papers, lining up the edges carefully by tapping them on the bench. "Surely they've dealt with Brutes before."

"No, that's not it." Espinoza flicked a finger at the sky. "The transmitter from Regional Command in the confer-ence room works two ways."

"They could be listening to us?" I swallowed hard, my

face going red as I recalled all the times I'd sworn at my equipment. "How often?"

Espinoza crossed his arms unhappily. "It's retrofitted xeno tech—I know Regional must have a way to activate it and listen in remotely. There've been too many instances where they've let things slip that they shouldn't have known."

"Oh..." I looked out at the mountains, imagining their jagged edges smoothing into the mountains grouped around Regional Command in Colorado Springs. "They must know about all this already, then. I wasn't exactly being sneaky with my investigation."

"They might not have thought to actually *look* at the reports, once you generated them. The power drain could be incidental or, like you said, bad equipment." He sighed. "But those sensor arrays are too important to leave down for long. We can't afford to be blind out here, especially with Brutes making a reappearance. I'll have to report it to Regional."

I offered him the stack of papers. "Want these?"

He sighed and took them reluctantly. "Might as well." Folding them unequally and stuffing them in his pocket, he cautioned, "Don't say anything about this to anyone. Well," he clarified, "don't say anything to anyone *except* Judge, Deadeye, and Josephine." He looked out at the desert, toward the Santa Cruz Valley and the accompanying city of Tucson—the reason our base existed. "Things are already on a knife's edge with the Blood Angels making trouble. We don't need anything else to worry everyone."

"Yes, sir."

SHIFT over and the surveillance desk in the hands of my

relief, I finally gathered my things and left the Fishbowl. I'd spent hours checking and double-checking my systems, trying to convince myself that the disturbing findings from earlier had only been coincidence. No matter what I did, things didn't add up, and the implications bothered me more than I wanted to face at the moment. It was almost midnight when I wandered past the kitchen, voices inside making me pop my head through the door.

"No, no, you idiot! You're rolling it too fast!" Deadeye exclaimed. "Go slow, don't tear it!"

Judge made a face at her from the other side of the counter. His uniform shirt was off, and his T-shirt dusted with flour as he gently tipped a long, flimsy cylinder of dough toward Deadeye. "I'm going as slowly as I can. It's just fragile."

"Strudel is *supposed* to be fragile, *dummkopf*," Deadeye huffed and smacked his hand away as I walked over. She blew a lock of hair out of her good eye and looked up at me. "Gabe, take over for this moron."

"Um..." I looked at the flour-covered counter with trepidation. "What do you want me to do?"

Deadeye waved her hand at the dough log. "Roll that as carefully as you can toward me." She picked up a baking sheet and held it at the edge of the counter. "Right onto here."

Gingerly, I obeyed. The pastry landed with a dull flop onto the baking sheet.

"Thank you." Deadeye slid the sheet into the oven, smiling as she asked, "Was that so hard?"

"Not that you gave me a chance to prove it or anything..." Judge sat on the edge of the counter, apparently unaware that the flour was leaving dusty marks all over his cargo pants.

"Shut up." Deadeye slung a wet rag at him before running more water into the mixing bowl in the sink. "Gabriel did a great job."

I brought her the other utensils as Judge started cleaning the counter. By the time everything was tidy again, the kitchen was filled with the smells of cinnamon and apples. The three of us sat in a row with our backs to the cabinets, Deadeye and Judge reminiscing while I listened. When they started talking about the old days, I sneaked up to grab my notebook. Deadeye gave me a long-suffering look but said nothing as Judge kept talking.

"And when Michael saw it, he laughed and said, 'You crazy Russian. Keep it. Make it fight for us.'" Judge smirked and leaned against the cabinet with his hands behind his head, a tattoo of a snake amid flowers twining in dark purple ink around his right forearm. "So I did, and I made it scout ahead for us. It absorbed so many attacks that would've hit us."

"That's amazing..." I scratched another note alongside what I had already written.

"What he's not mentioning is how he kept hold of the Brute even after we'd gotten what we were there for," Deadeye laughed as she adjusted her eyepatch. "Or how he marched it right into the Thunderbird, and kept it under control until we got to base, or how he lost control right after walking it into the bay, *or* how he passed out immediately after that."

"And then we couldn't get him to wake up." Josephine had come into the kitchen while Deadeye was talking.

"When I came into the bay with the gurney, they were still trying to get him to safety."

"Caleb had to kill the stupid thing *without* hitting anyone else," Deadeye added. "Accuracy isn't exactly a shotgun's strong suit, so he had to get really close and personal."

Judge chuckled. "When I finally woke up in the infirmary, Michael was sitting there with a face like he'd been sucking on a pickle."

"You got in a lot of trouble after that one," Josephine said with a motherly tone. "And did you learn *anything?*"

"Not from him!" Judge stretched long legs out with a yawn. "Caleb made sure I regretted it, though. Our next workout, he had me flipping tires for an hour."

"Ouch." I wasn't exactly in poor shape myself, but even the thought of that much tire flipping had me cringing.

Deadeye cackled. "I didn't hear about that part."

"I did, when he reported sick the next morning," Josephine said. She leaned over the counter and sniffed appreciatively. "What smells so good in here?"

"Some European thing Reneé makes," Judge answered. "I tried to help, but she said I wasn't gentle enough."

"You weren't." Deadeye slid the baking sheet out of the oven, the pastry now golden brown and gently steaming. "Not that I'd expect anything different of you. You can't even say 'strudel' properly."

I clicked shut my pen and closed the notebook. "If you don't mind my asking, how *did* you manage to keep something that big under control?"

Judge looked up from the floor, pure mischief on his high-cheekboned face. "Are you saying you want a demonstration?"

"Alexi," Josephine warned, "be careful."

"I won't hurt anyone," he promised as he got up.

I was beginning to regret asking when *something* grabbed my limbs. Terror shot through my veins as I realized I couldn't move anything but my eyes. A presence hovered in my mind, feeding my body instructions I couldn't possibly ignore.

Walk this way.

My limbs moved of their own accord, forcing me to walk with stilted steps toward the bowl we'd set to soak in the sink. Water sloshed over my hands as I grabbed it, as powerless to stop myself as I was to speak or resist.

"Keep that away from my strudel!" Deadeye yelled. "I worked too hard on this for you to ruin it."

Relax. I closed my eyes against the sensation of Judge's voice coming through my head, even as the same word drifted through the air. "I won't ruin anything."

"Enough already," Josephine said from the other side of the counter. "Let go of Gabriel."

"Pffft." Judge snorted. "Fine."

In a heartbeat, my muscles were free. The water sloshed into the sink, and I caught myself against the counter as my limbs remembered how to work together. Judge was doing the same thing at the other end of the counter, a cyan glow fading from his eyes. His face was flushed, and his breathing came hard and fast as he asked, "Demonstration enough?"

"Alexi, you scared him." Josephine crossed her arms and clucked her tongue. Her foot tapped the ground in a rhythm heard only by herself. "I said to be careful."

"I'm fine," I reassured her, my limbs still feeling uncoordinated. I looked up at Judge. "Can you do that with everyone?"

"Most people." He leaned an elbow on the counter, bowing his head over a closed fist as his breathing regulated.

"There's some resistance you can learn, with practice," Josephine explained, amusement written all over her face despite her tart voice. "Ways you can block out unwanted interference."

"Caleb was always the best at it. I could only control him one or two times out of five." Judge rolled his shoulders. "I'm out of practice. That should *not* have tired me out as much as it did."

"Tomorrow morning, you need to get into training." Josephine rounded the counter to take a plate of dessert from Deadeye. "Thanks, *mija*." She squinted at Judge. "You'd better rest up, buddy. It's rough out here, and we can't have you running on empty as often as you used to."

Judge accepted his plate with a rueful smile, and the conversation drifted from there. I sat cross-legged in the corner of the kitchen, quietly eating my dessert while I sorted through the last ten minutes. *I had no idea Shattereds could do that.* A shiver ran up my spine. *What else are people like this capable of?*

———

A FEW DAYS LATER, I was on duty in the Fishbowl when a warning message blipped onto my screen. Immersed as I was in a stream of data processing—I was still trying to suss out the reason behind the power drain on our solar field, a feat that was proving as frustrating as it was fruitless—it took me a lot longer than normal to notice what it said.

"That can't be right..." I muttered to myself as I brought

the message to full screen. A satellite map of the valley took front and center, and with a few commands I brought up the colored overlay to show the locations of all our emplacements —communication towers, water silos, vehicle stations, and power transformers. Looking over the portion of the map farthest west of us, my suspicions were unsettlingly confirmed.

Pulling my headset off one ear, I leaned back in my chair and twisted my head. "Captain Espinoza?"

"He's not here," Deadeye said from under her desk. At this point, I wasn't sure if she spent more time at her desk, or under it. "What's wrong?"

I glanced at the open door to the conference room, the communication transmitter barely visible in the middle of the table. *Even if they are eavesdropping, this is too critical to keep hiding.* "Relay 22 is out of communication."

She slid out from under the desk and came over to me. "Reboot. It could be a problem with updating the tracking data."

Suppressing a sigh, I did what she said. Rebooting the ancient system took over fifteen minutes, during which Deadeye departed to get a cup of coffee, the other members of the squad came and went, the air conditioner clicked on, and my unease grew exponentially. *This isn't a problem with the computer.*

When the system finally whined to life and I had restored the screen to the previous display, Deadeye slouched back to my corner and peered over my shoulder.

"See?" I pointed out the recently silent communications tower. "This one, 22, went down a little bit ago. And 23 and 17 died last week sometime, but I only noticed it a couple days ago."

Her good eye narrowed under her eyepatch strap. "Can we reboot them from here?"

I shook my head. "I already tried that. Whatever's wrong, it's hardware related, not software. We have to send someone out to fix it."

Deadeye gave a long sigh, studying the screens with a grim look. Finally, she ordered, "Call it in to Command. I'll go find Bandit while you do." She set her coffee cup on the edge of the console and walked off, kicking her chair under her desk as she went. "They're not going to like this, but we have to find out what's gone wrong."

A FEW HOURS LATER, I shouldered a backpack and walked out into the vehicle bay. The truck had just been refueled, and our driver Halo was doing his last checks over the outside compartments. Deadeye and Captain Espinoza stood outside the crew compartment, armored vests over their uniforms. Espinoza looked up at me from under the brim of his boonie hat as I approached. "Ah, *mijo*. You're ready?"

I scuffed a hand over the nameplate on the front of my armor. I'd worn the vest plenty of times during training, but until now I hadn't needed it in the field. "I think I'm ready." I patted my holster, where my regulation handgun sat below my hip. It wasn't anything special, but at least I could fire it with decent accuracy. "They told me to bring this."

"It's for the best." Captain Espinoza climbed into the truck bed, ducking his head in the low-ceilinged crew compartment. "I'd rather us be over-prepared than under-prepared." He opened one of the side compartments to stow a rifle with a beautiful scope attached. I climbed up after him, casting an admiring look at the rifle before refocusing on what I was here to do.

Like in the Fishbowl, the truck was equipped to interface with our surveillance system. Flipping down my seat and pulling out the screens, I logged in and was in the middle of booting up the software when Deadeye clambered into the truck and slammed the hatch shut. "Comms in, everyone," she reminded us as the engine rumbled to life.

I nodded over the noise of the truck. My earpiece was tangled in its own cord as I pulled it out of a pocket on my armor, and by the time I had it untangled and settled properly into my ear, we were well underway. With the noise of the truck lessened by the comms set, I was able to hear Deadeye, Espinoza, and Halo talking—well, joking. It never stopped amazing me how they were able to joke about anything. Even with the addition of armor and high caliber weapons to our usual patrol preparations, my stomach was a bundle of nerves.

All-terrain tires, a straight path, and a mostly intact road made the journey out to the dead zone shorter, but the drive still took us several hours. I hadn't brought my notebook or recorder, so I just listened as the others talked, keeping an eye on my screens the whole time. The data from the satellite and remaining surveillance towers gave me enough connection that it wasn't a surprise when Halo's voice came over the comms, "There's a storm coming up from the south."

Captain Espinoza looked over at me, and I gave him a short nod. "How's it look?" he asked.

"It's dark. Could be a haboob."

I rolled my eyes. Halo wouldn't know the difference between a monsoon and a dust storm if it smacked him between the eyes. I toggled the weather map on, a glowing red dot tracking our position along what had once been an interstate highway. As the software refreshed, I sucked in a harsh breath. A blobby weather pattern was emerging to the south of our position, green morphing from yellow to red as the radar predicted the storm's development. Within a half hour, it would be wrapped around the feet of the mountains, stretching toward the east as it plowed over us with driving winds, blinding rain, hail, and flash flooding. Even if we turned around now, we wouldn't be able to avoid getting caught.

"Damn. The monsoon's arriving early," Captain Espinoza said from behind me. I looked up to see him hanging on to a handle inset in the ceiling, looming over me as he bent to peer at the radar screen. "There's no way we're getting out of this one."

"Should we turn back?" Halo asked from the front.

Espinoza shook his head at the same time I did. "It's going to hit us no matter what, so we might as well push on. Let's just hope whatever's wrong with the relay is easy to fix."

The atmosphere in the truck was a bit more tense as we rumbled onward. I kept my eyes glued to the weather tracker as the storm gathered over the mountains, turning pink in the center of the predictive tracker. *It's going to be a strong one. Good for the desert; bad for us.*

As we got closer to the radius of Relay 22, I toggled over to check for whatever signal it might be broadcasting.

Nothing. Not even static.

"Any luck?" Deadeye asked from her seat, her face tensing as we went over a bump.

I pressed my mic. Everyone else's headsets had the channel open all the time, but mine was a much-repaired thing with a button that needed to be pressed in order for anyone to hear me. "Nothing. It's like it doesn't even exist."

She frowned, the pink streaks in her dark hair a bizarre hue under the orangey low-pressure cabin lights. "It could be a problem with the transmitter. Or the software... Either way, I think I'll be able to fix things." She glanced at the roof as thunder rumbled outside. "Of course, it'll be interesting if I have to do it in the rain."

The truck shuddered as we went over another bump, then shook violently. My eyes darted to my screen as a message popped up from the next closest communication relay. "There's something out there!" I yelled, fingers flying across the keyboard to pull up the report. "I don't know what, but—" My screen flashed and went dark, as an electrical pop sounded from the instrument panel between us and the cab. Overhead, the lights flickered with seizure-inducing rapidity before dying entirely.

Up front, Halo swore. "I've lost power! What's going on?"

"I don't know," I shouted. "But all my systems are down."

With a rush of sand and a cough from the engine, we slid to a halt.

"Gabriel, what was that you said a second ago?" Deadeye asked.

I slid the now-dead screens into their slots and undid my seat belt. "My systems are dead, but Relay 13 caught something nearby just before they went down." Now that the noise of the truck's motion was gone, wind rushed past and thunder rumbled outside as the storm got nearer. "It could've been an aberration caused by the storm, but—"

"Stay here," Captain Espinoza commanded, pulling his

bandana tight over his face and yanking his hat down over his forehead.

Deadeye shot out of her seat as he threw open the hatch, pulling open the weapons compartment and handing him his rifle before he vanished around the side of the truck. Wind blasted past us, the air heavy and charged with energy. Looking outside, I barely caught a glimpse of the creosote bushes thrashing in the wind before a wall of dust rolled over us.

Well, what do you know? Halo was right after all.

STAGE THREE

"WHERE'S ESPINOZA?" I screamed over the wind to Deadeye as the dust cloud swirled around us.

She stabbed a finger over her shoulder toward the back of the truck before prying open the access panel on the side of the passenger compartment. "Watching our six. Get out there!"

I started for the open hatch before retrieving a shemagh from the pouch on the outside of my backpack. The closely woven fibers blocked the dust, and I tugged it higher on the bridge of my nose before jumping out into the wind.

Captain Espinoza crouched in the lee of a rear tire, his handgun drawn. "What's happening?"

"Deadeye's trying to get it started again." I crouched next to him, the wind catching at the edges of my shirt under my armor and sending grit into my eyes. "She's rebooting. Looks like an electrical pulse fried everything." That part, at least, I had understood while I'd been getting my gear together. The rapid-fire German swearing that accompanied it had been a mystery.

Espinoza grunted and holstered the handgun, unslinging his rifle from over his shoulder.

"It could've been lightning, right?" I asked, glancing at the sky. In between swirls of dust, it was the sickly yellow-purple of an impending monsoon storm.

Espinoza didn't reply immediately, ejecting the magazine and swapping it for one painted lurid green. The sight sent a stab of panic through my stomach. Those rounds weren't to be used except on Brutes.

"C-captain?"

"*Mijo*, I've told you." Espinoza slammed the magazine into the rifle and flicked off the safety. The barrel indicator began glowing green. "Enough with the 'Captain.' Use my call sign." His eyes darted behind me, and with a yell, he swatted me aside and fired.

I tumbled to the ground and rolled under the truck, grabbing for my gun with shaking fingers. This was *not* the surveillance duty I was trained for. Fumbling the safety off, I squirmed to the edge of the truck and sighted on the first thing I could see emerging from the dust clouds. It moved with a lumbering sort of gait, too-long arms and disproportionate torso pinging every "wrong" filter in my mind. Every instinct I possessed screamed "run," but I tightened my grip and fired.

I remembered too late that standard service rounds didn't do much against the bigger Brutes. It roared in anger and charged, as three successive shots from Espinoza—Bandit—took it through the eyes.

"Get out of there!" he yelled over the rising wind. I took his offered hand and scrambled out from under the truck. The dust cloud pushed by the front of the monsoon was shredding to pieces in the driving wind, and the shapes of bushes and rocks could once more be seen through the darkness.

"How many are there?" Halo's voice came through our local comms—proof that Deadeye had managed to get *something* working.

Bandit's voice came from next to me *and* through my ear, the comm signal muffled in the wind. A twisting dust spinner skittered across the plain as he answered, "Just the one, so far."

"Keep your eyes open, but get in the truck if you can." Halo's crisp voice was mostly impersonal, but I could hear a trace of panic in his words. "I don't like the way this feels."

I don't either. I eyed the storm, my stomach twisting again as chain lightning ripped the sky apart. The first drops of rain began falling, splatting against the dusty ground as thunder crashed overhead. On the heels of the thunderclap, an unearthly howl split the air, a primal sound I'd been content to leave in my childhood nightmares.

The truck shuddered as we climbed aboard. A spluttered curse in German—or something—came from Deadeye's lips as she stabbed a button on the instrument panel. Outside, something howled in counterpoint to the thunder. Bandit braced himself against the side of the truck and sighted his rifle. "Contact! Four of them, on our nine!"

Halo's gun sounded from the driver's compartment, joined by Bandit's rifle as the truck shuddered again.

"I've got it!" Deadeye yelled. "Drive! Drive!"

The lights inside the passenger compartment flickered,

then stayed on, dimming as we lurched forward. I clung to the overhead railing, trying to get to a seat and strap in before something else crazy happened. Bandit left the hatch open and kept firing through it, the rifle muted against the sounds of wind, rain, and howling.

Halo's voice sounded panicky from the front. "Contact! At least five, at our three. They're trying to flank us!" The firing redoubled from the front seat as we skidded to a halt, followed by a strangled scream through comms.

Deadeye clapped a hand to her ear. "Halo!"

I couldn't help it. I ripped the earpiece out of my ear as his scream changed to a horrible gurgle. The truck rocked as something heavy climbed onto the roof. Deadeye grabbed her rifle and joined Bandit at the rear, both of them emptying rounds into the Brutes outside. Screeching came from outside; metal being torn by something far stronger than any human. I closed my eyes. *So, this is where we die.*

The howling suddenly changed pitch. Over the thunder, heavy gunfire sounded, and I opened my eyes as something smacked the outside of the truck with finality.

Curiosity overwhelming my fear, I joined Bandit and Deadeye at the edge of the truck bed. Over a dozen Brutes prowled around the truck, and beyond that—

I'd never seen anything like it.

Two people were running down the nearby hillside; one holding a shotgun, the other carrying a rifle similar to ours slung across their back. Both wore armor and helmets like the ones I'd seen in the footage of the EDF's early days. Rainwater dripped from their closed visors and reflected in their headlamp beams as they skidded to a halt, the angles of their heads showing they were watching the Brutes as closely as I was.

I grabbed for my gun. "We have to do something!"

Bandit's hand closed around my arm. "Don't worry, *mijo*." His voice was strangely filled with excitement as he reassured me, "We'll be all right."

Just as he said it, one of the Brutes howled and charged the mysterious pair. As if a spell had been broken, the others joined, extending their claws to rip into their victims' bodies. Instantaneously, a dome of glittering cyan light surrounded the strangers. The smaller figure raised their free hand, more energy gathering in their palm.

"Close your eyes!" Bandit yelled.

I obeyed, ducking to the floor. My world went white behind closed lids, and the howls from the Brutes abruptly silenced. Bright spots dancing in my vision, I stood up to see every single beast between us and our rescuers scattered brokenly across the ground. Deadeye threw the door open and jumped out, hurrying around the corner of the truck. The engine coughed to life as our rescuers ran over, the smaller one—I assumed a woman, based on her height— standing guard at the mouth of the truck as the taller one ran past.

"*Mijo*, get your comms back in!" Bandit ordered as he jumped out, clapping the smaller figure on the shoulder before disappearing into the rain.

Shaken into action, I fished for my comm set, jamming the earpiece into position in time to catch Deadeye saying, "—the gun and armor at least, even if there's nothing else we can do."

Halo.

The last of my shock disappeared into determination. Standing up, I popped the latch on the medical compartment, sliding the table out and locking it in place. Another compartment held all the things for a drip set, and meds that I didn't know how to use. Hopefully, Bandit would know what to do, to keep Halo alive until we could get back to base —my hands stopped against the bright orange package labeled "body bag" in a slot next to the table.

If there's anything left of him to save.

Thumping came from outside, and Bandit's broad-brimmed hat appeared around the door. He and the taller of the two strangers carried Halo between them, his face deathly pale in the cabin lights.

"He's alive?" I asked as Bandit staggered to lay him on the med table.

Bandit grunted a brief affirmative as the taller stranger ducked outside, disappearing into the rain. "Barely."

In my ear, Deadeye asked, "Are we good to go?"

"Need a few minutes," Bandit said, pulling his bandana down and pushing his hat back. Water dripped down his face as he grabbed a pair of trauma shears. "He went to grab their gear." He began cutting away Halo's bloody uniform, swearing quietly as the injuries became apparent.

I turned to the ruined door as our rescuer came into view, this time with two old-style backpacks. Throwing the packs to the floor, they gave the hand signal for "move out" before helping their partner into the cabin and slamming the door.

I pressed a hand to my mic. Rain pounded against the truck roof as I said, "Deadeye, we're clear to go." I eyed Bandit, who'd pulled out an IV start set. "But try not to bump too much."

"Roger."

The truck rattled as we got underway, bumps punctu-ated by Bandit swearing under his breath. I pulled the oxygen mask down from the wall and strapped it over Halo's face, turning the knob on the tank to start the flow. "How bad is it?" I glanced down at the bloody mess that had once been our driver's torso as he moaned faintly.

"It's not good." Bandit reached for a sealant kit, stopped, and shook his head. "I don't know if there's anything we can do."

"Let me help."

I looked up in surprise as the woman pulled off her helmet. Dark brown hair stuck to her forehead as she set the helmet down, wiping a dripping forearm across her face. I gulped. Her eyes were cyan—even brighter than Judge's.

"I didn't think you could do anything, so I didn't ask." Bandit's voice betrayed confusion. "You never could before."

She smiled sadly. "Times change. I guess we have a lot to catch you up on." Taking a deep breath, she stepped over to Halo, catching her balance as the truck hit a bump. The same cyan glow from before appeared, wreathing her fingers in soft light as she laid her hand over the horrible abdominal wounds. After a few tense seconds, the lines in Halo's face relaxed, and his breathing eased. "Thank God. We're not too late, yet."

"*Gracias a Dios,*" Bandit breathed. He looked up at her partner. "Bet that's come in handy a few times?"

The man snorted as he removed his helmet. Faint scar lines traced his face around silvery-grey eyes, a rueful smile appearing as he admitted, "With as much trouble as I've gotten into... yeah." The smile grew as he and Bandit hugged, thumping each other's backs happily. "Good to see you again, El Bandito."

"Just Bandit, now." He winked at me as he explained,

"They didn't want our call signs to be more than one word. Screws with their systems, I guess."

The man nodded, extending a hand to me. "Caleb."

"Gabriel."

I blinked hard, the pieces all coming together in a cacophony of "wake up, stupid."

Old style helmets and armor.

"Caleb made sure I regretted my actions..."

"...made the two of them unstoppable on the field."

Caleb and Tara?

Caleb laughed, and I realized my face had given me away. "I guess you've heard about us, huh?"

I nodded mutely, glancing at Tara. Her face was furrowed with concentration as she moved her hand along Halo's torso, cyan light pooling between her fingers and seeping into the wounds.

"Gabriel here, he's a real storyteller," Bandit said affectionately. I hunched my shoulders and tried to look unassuming as he added, "Always has a notebook or recorder on him. You've come up, a time or two."

"Oof. I hope that's a good thing." Caleb grabbed one of the overhead bars, his body easily compensating for the truck's bouncing. To my relief, he and Bandit started talking about the base, and who they knew from where. I did my best to get to work, buckling myself into my seat and pulling my screen down to check on my surveillance systems. They'd come up with the power being reset, but still weren't picking up anything.

On a whim, I checked for the relay that had sent the warning about the Brutes. With a sinking feeling, I saw that it, too, had disappeared from the readings as if it had never existed. *It could have been the storm,* I thought as we rumbled across a wash. *But even if it wasn't, we can't do anything about it now.* It didn't escape my notice that the relays going down were steadily creeping closer and closer to the base. *First the relays closer to the Ridges, and now these. Something—or someone—is doing this on purpose to knock out our communications.* I looked up nervously at Tara, who'd closed her eyes as she kept pushing blue light into Halo's injuries. *Intentional or not, we can't do anything about it for the moment.*

Eventually, I slid the screens away, the rattling becoming easier as the storm let up. The others kept talking, ignoring the bouncing floor as they swapped stories. I wanted to soak up every word, but my recorder was still at base and I hadn't brought a notebook. *Besides,* I told myself as Caleb started laughing at something, *it's better for them to have some time to adjust.*

Finally, I closed my eyes and drifted off, Tara's blue light the last thing I saw.

"WE WERE AMBUSHED by two packs of Brutes almost as soon as we crossed out of the dunes."

Bandit stood at ease in the meeting room off the Fishbowl, delivering our report to Regional Command. His uniform was still covered in mud and blood, and his bandana hung limply around his neck. His hat dangled by the stampede strap, and he hadn't put away his handgun. That last, more than anything else, told me how worried he was about what had just happened. In the center of the table, an image of the lieutenant colonel in charge of our region hovered against the hologram plate. I stayed out of range of the camera pointed at Bandit, listening quietly as he finished summarizing the abysmal failure we'd just encountered.

"Sergeant Watts will recover, but I'm not sure how long it'll take. Dr. Flores took over as soon as we got back to base, and we're having the Thunderbird prepped to fly him to the hospital in Phoenix."

The colonel sighed. "Thank you for the report, Captain. I know we'll want a full breakdown on what went wrong, but for now get some rest." He glanced at someone out of frame, nodded, and added, "We'll talk tomorrow. Good work, getting Watts back safely."

As the transmission blinked out, Bandit sighed. "Well, that went about as well as it could've gone." With a cautious eye toward the transmitter, he jerked a thumb out of the room. "Let's go get cleaned up."

I followed him out into the hallway, wearily scrubbing at the grime on my hands. "I won't say no to that." As the door closed behind us, I switched to Spanish. "You didn't say anything about Caleb and Tara."

Bandit shook his head, answering in the same language. "I need to talk with them first. I'm not sure where they've been, or if they want Regional Command to know they've resurfaced. Tara, especially." Concern crept across his face. "She's always been a wild card, even when Michael was still alive. Regional might decide she's too dangerous to leave free, since she and Caleb aren't officially part of the Force any longer."

I stopped in the hallway leading to the crew quarters. "They wouldn't lock her up, would they?"

Bandit shrugged and walked past me. "I don't know. I *do* know that she and Caleb need to be able to make the choice to stay or go for themselves." His voice hushed as I fell in step alongside him. "I hope they stay. Other than Josephine, there's no one else I trust more."

We rounded the corner toward the crew quarters as Tara approached from the other direction. She'd washed her hands and face, but her clothes were still covered in dirt and blood.

"How's Halo?" Bandit asked in English. Her head barely came up to his chest as he gave her a hug.

She rubbed a weary hand over her face, pale under her suntan, as he let her go. "Stable, finally. I'm glad medical tech kept advancing. Even with what I could do, those sealant kits came in awfully handy a few times. Josephine's with him now." She yawned. "It's been a long day."

I was reminded of Judge's weakness after demonstrating his power, and hurried to open the door to the living quarters. "Have you gotten some food yet?"

"Caleb brought me some after we got back. I'm all right," she reassured me as she looked around the day room, mismatched couches and chairs clustered in front of an entertainment system that only worked about half the time. It was late, yet plenty of people had chosen to stay up past their usual lights-out time. I suspected curiosity about our new arrivals was the cause, rather than worry about Halo's welfare.

The card games and conversations paused as we walked through, and Caleb stood from a brown-striped couch with an apology to the woman he'd been talking with. "How's Watts?" he asked as he opened his arms to hug Tara.

She leaned into him, resting her head on his chest. "I did what I could. They're moving him to Phoenix, but Josephine thinks he'll be all right."

Caleb nodded over her head. "Good for you. They've got us all set up with a room. You ready to go and rest?"

Tara stepped back and looked up at Bandit. "Will you come, El—Bandit?" Her bright eyes flicked around the room with a trace of suspicion. "We have things we need to talk about."

"Yes, we do," Bandit answered grimly. He looked at me. "*Mijo*, go clean up and get your notebook. I want you in on this."

STAGE FOUR

Earth Defense Force Base 36
Gila River Valley
June 27

CALEB AND TARA had been assigned a room originally intended to be an officer's quarters, back when this had been a Border Patrol facility. A full-sized bed took up most of the narrow bedroom, which opened onto a small living area and bathroom. Caleb and Tara's gear lay scattered across the bed, civilian clothes mixing with tactical equipment.

My hair damp from my own hurried shower, I sat down on the floor with my back in the corner of the sitting area. Caleb leaned against the wall next to me, reading from an old tablet computer. The sound of water running came from the bathroom, indicating where Tara had gone.

"Will she be all right?" I asked after a long silence.

Caleb looked up in confusion, and I pointed toward the closed bathroom door. Comprehension lit his eyes, and he nodded. "She has a huge reserve. Though she'll probably sleep like the dead tonight." He rubbed his face, and I caught sight of a silicon ring on his left third finger. "I know I'll sleep well."

I opened my notebook as unobtrusively as possible. "They made it sound like she was unusual, to be able to heal injuries along with—whatever that other thing was."

Caleb set his tablet down. "Not that unusual. Most Shattered powers come as complements to each other. When Tara Shattered, her power came out as destruction. When we left, she learned how to use it to heal as well." His grey eyes clouded with some emotion I couldn't place. "It helps make up for all the lives she's taken."

I was on the verge of asking more questions when Tara reemerged from the bathroom in clean uniform pants and a grey T-shirt. "I can't remember the last time we had *hot* water in the shower." She toweled off her shoulder-length hair, shaking it loose and tossing the towel into the bathroom as Bandit knocked on the half-open door. "Come on in!"

Bandit had also showered, his dark hair still beaded with water. Although he'd changed into clean clothes, he'd replaced the handgun at his waist. "Alexi sends his regards. We figured someone should be watching the screens, just in case something weird happens."

I winced as I stood up. That should have been my job. Bandit noticed my expression and shook his head. "Don't worry, *mijo*. I told you to be here for a reason." He gestured at the notebook I was holding, closing the door with his other hand. "I need you here to take notes that won't ever be logged by a computer."

Caleb stood as well, stretching before taking a seat at the table beside Tara. Even at rest, he conveyed a sense of quiet danger, like a coiled spring. He nodded at Bandit's statement before asking, "Does Regional know we're here?"

"Not at the moment," Bandit said. "But they won't stay in the dark for long. Everyone here's already seen you, and it's not like they're stupid. I'd be surprised if Regional doesn't know by tomorrow that you've resurfaced."

"We were happy out in the sky islands." Tara leaned an elbow on the table and balanced her cheek in her hand. Now that I knew to look, I noticed a ring matching Caleb's on her left hand. "There's an old adobe house out past the creosote flats, where the well hadn't even dried up. We had water, solar, and the adobe kept things cool..."

Bandit shook his head. "Stop it, you're going to make me cry."

"Cry or join us?" she asked, mischief dancing in her eyes. "It was a peaceful life, for the most part."

"And it would be still, if it weren't for the Blood Angels prowling around." Caleb sighed. "They'd left us alone for years, but I guess they found out who we were. I didn't want to kill them and bring the whole gang down around our heads, so we moved on."

"And that's when we realized there were Brutes involved too." Tara whistled softly. "Brutes, in a place where none had been in years. I suppose it was too good to last long, anyway."

"I hate to ask it," Bandit said, pulling a chair out and sitting. "But what are your plans now?"

They looked at each other, a question and response flitting between them as plainly as if it had been spoken. I wondered what it would be like, to be so close with someone that you could immediately tell their response to a question neither of you had asked out loud.

"If you'll have us, we'd like to stay," Caleb replied. "We'd rather not hide out in the desert if there's more trouble brewing for this region."

Bandit gave a sigh of relief. "Thanks. And on a more personal note, thanks. It's like I was telling Gabriel." He gestured in my direction. "I trust the two of you almost more than anyone else." He turned to me and asked, "*Mijo*, would you take some notes? I want to get some plans in order for the future, now that I know what type of team I have to work with. We need to get communications online, or we risk losing our grip on the whole region."

THE FOLLOWING DAY, Bandit gave his official report to Regional Command of Caleb and Tara's rejoining the squad. I was on duty in the Fishbowl, mapping terrain and sorting reports as Bandit opened the conference room door with the good news of their reinstatement. I turned in my chair, watching with amusement as Bandit handed them the printouts.

Tara smirked at Caleb as she saw her rank. Squinting at the paper, I could read the word "Captain" through the back of the page. "I outrank you? Since when?"

"Since Shattereds no longer have separate ranks," Caleb said, folding his papers and putting them in his pocket. "It's okay. I'm happy without the extra responsibility."

She laughed at that, going off to get acquainted with the rest of the base. Caleb stayed in the Fishbowl, looking at the various consoles and chatting a bit with Deadeye. Eventually, he came to stand behind me. "Can you tell me what I'm looking at?" he asked, pulling a chair over.

I nodded and turned to the screens, zooming the satellite

map I'd been examining out to a more easily recognizable scale. It was an image of the valley below the Ridges, near the dunes and close to where we'd had the encounter with the Brutes. I ran a finger across the biggest screen in a diagonal line.

"This is where our relays were—are," I corrected myself quickly. "They're still there, they're just out of communication. I'm looking at the terrain to predict a good way in and out, in case we get attacked while we're fixing them."

"You think they'll attack you?"

I shrugged. "Not sure, but I don't want to get caught off guard."

"I gotcha." Caleb looked around the mostly empty workstations in the Fishbowl. "How many of the staff here are good in a fight?"

I blinked. The question was not one I'd really considered. "I mean, everyone went through training, and we all know how to fire the service weapons, and there's almost enough armor to go around..." I knew I was starting to stammer, and my face warmed as Deadeye interrupted.

"Not many, at least not by our standards." She had slid her keyboard to the side, and was fiddling with a screwdriver inside the visor of a helmet. "As far as veterans of the first defense force go, there's Bandit, Judge, myself, and you and Tara."

I nodded. Everyone she'd mentioned had been part of the original group led by Michael, long before any mention of an "Earth Defense Force" was made. "Halo—the guy that Tara stabilized last night—he was pretty good, even if he insisted on checking the admin guidelines every time someone looked at him sideways." I smothered a laugh as I said it. We'd heard that Halo had come through surgery fine, but had been reassigned to Regional Command. In my opinion, trading him for Caleb and Tara had left everyone better off.

Deadeye didn't even bother hiding her laugh. "Yeah, he was a pain." She shrugged. "Everyone else here is okay, but they haven't faced up to much. This region *was* quiet."

"Right," Caleb sighed. He rubbed his face wearily. "Things were better in the desert."

"They always are," I muttered, turning back to my screens. *It's when you get tangled up with other people that things get complicated.*

"We'll have to up our training regimen. I'll talk to Bandit about that." He straightened up from the desk. "Did either of you happen to notice where Tara went?"

Deadeye laughed briefly. "Last I saw, Josephine was talking to her out in the bay. Something about Alexi getting out of condition and needing to be taught a lesson."

I spun around in my chair as Caleb exclaimed, "What?"

"Yeah." I could hear the satisfaction in Deadeye's voice as she said, "I think they were getting ready to spar."

Screens could wait. This I had to see. I slapped my palm against the reader plate and made for the door, Caleb close behind me. A second later, Deadeye followed, all of us hurrying down the hall. Shouts and exclamations drew our attention to the vehicle bay, and we pushed through the swinging door as a flash of cyan illuminated the ceiling. A cluster of people stood at the end of the bay, their backs obscuring the action beyond. As we approached, another flash lit up the girders and the onlookers gasped.

I clambered on top of one of the big air compressors and balanced against a support girder. My head cleared the crowd in time to see Judge shove a hand toward Tara, who was facing him across the lines marking our basketball court. Before I could blink, a wall of force erupted from his hand, knocking Tara back a pace. She growled and swirled a cupped hand, the motion sweeping pulsating blue light between her fingers. She threw the energy with a yell, and the wall dissipated.

Judge yelped, ducking to one knee and swiveling out of harm's way. His chest heaved under his sweat-soaked T-shirt. By contrast, Tara's face was barely flushed. *I wonder how long they've been going at it.*

Caleb hopped up beside me and leaned against the rusted steel pillar, watching with interest. "He's gotten stronger."

"Sorry?" I asked as Judge regained his feet and tried the same attack again. This time, it only took a second for Tara to dissipate it and shove him back the same way as before. "It looks like Tara's wiping the floor with him."

Caleb shook his head, amusement in his voice. "No, he's holding back. He's always liked showing off..." He nodded toward Judge as Tara backed to the edge of the basketball court. "Ah, here we go. Watch closely."

Judge straightened suddenly, exhaustion apparently gone. His eyes began glowing, and the onlookers started muttering. It took just long enough for their unease to change to wonder for me to realize that Tara was struggling in the grip of an unseen hand.

Caleb tensed in my periphery. His hand went halfway to the hilt of the knife at his belt before he stopped and crossed his arms.

Judge grinned triumphantly as Tara glared at him, checking the monitor on his wrist. "Doc, are we done here?"

In the corner of the practice court, Josephine checked a tablet. She showed the reading to Deadeye, who'd gone to stand beside her. "I think so…" She glanced up at Tara, who was still standing as if frozen. "Actually, see if you can hold her another few seconds."

Beside me, Caleb took a sudden breath, like something sharp had prodded him. I looked at him in concern, right as his grey eyes became illuminated with glowing cyan streaks.

I gasped and jumped back, just as Tara moved. Her hands arced through the air, blasting a wave of crackling energy at Judge. The crowd scattered amid shouts, and Judge's expression turned from satisfaction to panic. As the cyan energy washed over him, he ducked into a ball. A glittering shield blinked into existence over his huddled form.

Tara didn't lower her hands until the rest of the onlookers had dispersed, finally gesturing toward the open bay doors. The energy rushed outside and exploded with a thunderous sound over the driveway as Tara unstrapped her monitor from her wrist. "I think we're done here."

Caleb started chuckling as Judge's shield broke into tiny, flickering bits of light. The white-haired Shattered stirred and sat up, his face ghostly pale. "You got me good." He pointed at Caleb. "But that was still cheating!"

I didn't imagine it, then.

Caleb's eyes had resumed their normal grey color. His chuckle broke into full-bellied laughter as he jumped down from the compressor box. "It's not cheating on a battlefield, so it's not cheating here either."

I sat down with my legs dangling over the side of the compressor as Caleb pulled Judge to his feet and wrapped him in a bear hug. The hug quickly became wrestling, as Josephine, Deadeye, and Tara discussed the readings from

Josephine's monitor tablet. I leaned my shoulder against the pillar, content to watch from a distance. The easy interactions and cheerful companionship of these people warmed my heart in a way not much else did.

I wonder if, someday—no. I pushed the thought away before it had time to form. Scrambling to my feet, I turned to clamber down and head to the Fishbowl. *Don't get attached. They have each other, and there's no place for you among heroes.*

THE DESERT FELT OUR UNEASE. By the first few days of July, massive thunderstorms piled up against the distant mountains each morning. Afternoon heat lent them height, until they broke free of the sky islands and churned across the creosote flats to pound us with driving winds and heavy rain. It made things all the more difficult when it came to repairing our communications network. After Caleb and Tara's sudden reappearance, we had gone on several missions to bring the towers back online. One had been successful. Two had not. Brutes—the creature from my generation's nightmares and the veterans' pasts—kept appearing, and the most recent mission had seen us exchange gunshots with a Blood Angel patrol. Whatever my thoughts had been toward the gang before, I no longer doubted their intentions when it came to hostilities. After that, I practiced with the tower at the base, learning how to repair everything so Deadeye could be free to fight if needed.

That morning, we were back near where I'd first met Caleb and Tara; the spot where we'd almost all died under monsters' claws. Relay 13 had been constructed inside a fortified wall, which also enclosed a water station and small fuel tank. The entire compound had been trashed, the nature of the destruction suggesting more than mindless animal rage.

I balanced several dozen feet in the air, legs wrapped around a girder as I wired a new transmitter into the plastic housing. It wasn't the easiest thing, climbing with a tool belt and armor, but I'd managed to scale the tower without help. My balance had gotten better over the last few weeks, and I'd gotten stronger under Caleb's training.

If I'd been suspicious of human involvement from our previous encounters, the damage done to the tower confirmed things ten times over. While the tower was intact, the entire sensory and tracking array had been cleanly removed from its housing and was nowhere to be seen.

"It's just like 22 was," I said into my comms, looking down at the rest of the squad as they prowled the compound. The height didn't bother me as I said, "The tower's fine, it's just all the electrical stuff is missing."

The pink streaks in Deadeye's hair caught the sun as she shielded her eyes to look up at me. "Electrical stuff how?"

I grunted as I snapped the cover over the new transmitter. Comforted at the sight of blinking lights, I answered, "The sensors, the cameras, the transmitters..."

"Not that that's exceptionally scary or anything," Judge commented sarcastically. I could see him outside the perimeter fence, leaning against a twisted mesquite tree. His posture looked at ease, but I could hear the tension in his voice. "I didn't think Brutes were smart enough to disable specific parts of equipment."

"They're not," Bandit said from his vantage point on the

roof over the well. "They're still stupid, bloodthirsty animals. It's humans I'm worried about."

I fastened the last snap on the cover and sealed it shut with contact cement. If I ever came back to repair this, I'd have to break the cover off, but it was worth it to try to discourage tampering.

Below, Tara said, "People *are* what we should be worrying about." As I twisted to begin climbing down, I saw her come out from under the well enclosure holding a test kit. "This water's been contaminated."

A curse came from Bandit. "With what?"

"Don't know. We'll have to run more tests at base." She handed Deadeye the test kit. "This kit's only able to tell me it's some kind of phosphate-based poison."

"Scorpion spray," I muttered. Bandit looked up in surprise, and I repeated myself. "It's probably bug poison. My abuela used to use it, back—" I stopped myself. I'd almost broken my own cardinal rule, and around the people I wanted most to impress. *Stupid. Leave the past in the past.* "Never mind."

Bandit's eyes—the only part of his face I could see between bandana and boonie hat—narrowed with concern before he turned his attention to the desert. "Phantom, see anything?"

Caleb's voice crackled through my comm set. If I shaded my eyes and looked north, I could just see him crouched with a pair of binoculars in a clump of creosote. "Dust cloud over on the west side. I can't tell exactly what it is, but it's not right to just be wind."

I stopped and turned to the west, funneling my hands around my eyes. Dust spinners towered above the open expanse between us and the mountains, but this wasn't that.

I raised a hand to my mic as Bandit said, "That's a vehicle trail. Gabe, are you almost done?"

"I'm coming down." I dropped with a clatter to the corrugated metal roof of the awning. "The sensors are working, but I need to check from the truck to make sure they're in communication."

"Let's go, then," Bandit answered. "If it's the Blood Angels, I don't want to hang around to see if they want a fight."

I slid from the awning, grabbed my backpack from the ground, and ran for the truck. Judge abandoned his post and jumped into the driver's seat, bringing the engine to roaring life. Deadeye and Tara reached out helping hands to Bandit and I, and the four of us lurched toward our seats while Judge swung around to pick up Caleb. In the brief moment of stillness as he clambered aboard, an unmistakable howl sounded outside.

"Damn!" Judge exclaimed from the front. "Hold on!"

As we accelerated, I scrambled into my jump seat and buckled myself in. My fingers shaking with nerves, I pulled the surveillance system screens out of their slot. The robotic arm holding them vibrated with the urgency of the truck's movements, and I grimly rested my hand against the modified login panel. It took an agonizingly long moment for the software to wake up, in which Bandit and Deadeye balanced themselves against the hatch with rifles ready.

"Do we need to stop to make sure the relay's online?" Deadeye asked through comms.

"I don't think it would be a good idea," Judge answered. "That sounded too close. Gabe, what's our status?"

My fingers flicked across the keyboard, muscle memories guiding me faster than conscious thought. "I'm getting it now. Looks like the sensors are working." As soon as the software responded, I had the overlay pulled up, zooming in on our location and praying frantically for a reading from the tower we'd just repaired. "Right now, there's only one vehicle. Looks like the one we saw last week." A warning came across the screen, and I swiped it away before toggling the overlays to show heat signatures. My heart sank. "But it's followed by a pack of over a half dozen Brutes."

Caleb yanked a lethal-looking shotgun painted in old-style desert camouflage from the weapons locker. "What about the other vehicle?"

"I don't think we have to worry about them." I frowned at the screen as the overlays shifted. "They're turning around."

From the driver's seat, Judge said, "It *is* the same group from last week. I recognize the antennas on their roof—looks like they jimmied together parts from three different systems." His voice sounded almost disappointed. "Guess they don't want a fight after all."

I gasped. "The pack's not stopping. They led them right into us!"

"Helmets, now!" Bandit commanded. At the order, I yanked my earpiece out and pulled on the helmet I'd left next to my seat. Settling the headset cups over my ears, I made sure the mic was live and brought comms online as Bandit said, "Judge, stop the truck. Once you do, get on the roof and see if you can slow them down." He dropped his hat on the floor and clicked his helmet into place, his voice muffled through comms as he added, "Banshee, get under cover as soon as we get out there. Phantom, Deadeye, with me. *Mijo!*"

I jumped halfway through fastening the chin strap of my helmet, my eyes meeting his through his visor. "Sir?"

He stepped back to grab my shoulder. "You're our eyes. Watch our backs out there."

I nodded and settled my shoulders as well as I could under my seat belt and armored vest. We juddered to a stop, and Bandit threw the door open. "Go!"

The rest of the squad leaped out of the truck as one of the Brutes howled again. The backs of their helmets flashed in the sunlight as they disappeared around the edges of the truck, scattering to take cover in the sparse rocks and bushes at the foot of the ridge we'd been traveling along. More howls echoed against the jagged rocks, and my hands froze for a moment at the noise.

A gunshot from Deadeye's rifle called me to reality. I peered past Bandit as he stood firmly with his back to the truck, bringing his rifle to his shoulder. The ballistic protection in my helmet was old, but it muffled enough of the report of the gun that I wasn't deafened as he sighted and fired.

Wake up, Gabe! My thoughts sounded just like my father's voice for a moment—a baritone barely remembered and heard only in between sleep and waking. *You have a job to do.*

I took a shaky breath. "Three of them just broke off from the main pack."

"I got it." Tara's voice floated calmly through my ears. "Bandit, cover me."

"Copy." Bandit stepped to the side, barely out of sight from the truck opening. His rifle went off again, and one of the oncoming Brutes stopped moving on my screen. A blueish flash went across my vision, followed by something howling close by.

"Two down," Tara announced.

A shotgun blast sounded on the other side of the truck, and Caleb said, "One more."

"Not fair, you two," Judge whined. "I know you've spent the last few years fending for yourselves, but don't hog all of them!"

"There are five more, just off the truck's seven o'clock," I said into my comms, settling the biggest part of my consciousness into watching the heat blobs of the Brutes on my screen. Already, several were changing from hot red to cooler yellows and greens, their thermal images fading into death. Mindful that there could be more I wasn't seeing, I pulled the image out farther, just in time to see something erupt white-hot in the direction we had fled from. A split second later, the overlay blinked out of existence, leaving me staring at an old satellite image of empty desert.

"Guys, there's—" I began over the sounds of more gunfire, as the truck vibrated under the tremors from an explosion. The dying howl of a Brute counterpointed a roll of noise like thunder as the gunfire died out. I threw aside my seat belt, bolting for the open hatch and shading my eyes at the entrance. A cloud of smoke rolled up from the relay station, and I remembered the fuel tank that had been there to power the water pumps. Amid the smoke, sunlight played along the edge of the tower as it slowly toppled.

There was a gasp and curse from someone—I wasn't sure who, but the accent made me think it was Deadeye.

"What was that?" Tara asked, pulling cyan light into her palm from over a dead Brute. Around her, the remains of the five that had been hanging back from the others lay in a broken heap.

The truck rocked as Judge jumped down, landing with a grunt. "Was that the relay?"

I didn't need to explain, but the words spilled out in misery and disbelief anyways. "The Brutes were a distraction. The Blood Angels led them into us, then doubled back to the relay station." I leaned forward dejectedly, the weight of my helmet pulling my head down. "We've lost Relay 13 again."

STAGE FIVE

Barrio Santiago Hills
Santa Cruz River Valley
July 16

"WHY AREN'T we taking the truck?" I was aware of the whininess in my voice as I followed Bandit to the roof of the base a few days later, but I didn't care. Losing Relay 13 after putting effort into its repair had put a vindictive taste in my mouth toward the Blood Angels, and every moment away from my screens felt like wasted time.

Bandit didn't even bother turning around. "Too slow. I want to have some free hours at the Tucson base. And Logan says the Thunderbird's secondary power system has been giving him issues, so he wants to get it checked out."

The door squeaked miserably on its hinges as he opened it, letting in the golden morning light and the faintly acrid smell of damp creosote bushes. The white-coated roof still bore patches of wet from the previous night's storm, glistening like jewels as the sun crested the horizon.

The Thunderbird squatted in the center of the impro-vised helipad. The EDF had taken the earliest opportunity to utilize captured xeno technology, creating an aircraft that ran off rechargeable cores and could take off vertically. With its engines rotated to keep out moisture, it reminded me of a predatory bird hunched over something on the ground.

Logan, the pilot, came around the side of the aircraft with a clipboard in hand, calling a greeting as Bandit and I approached. He was about Caleb and Tara's age and had joined the EDF only a few years ago, but I barely knew anything about him beyond that. "Morning! She's all checked and ready to go."

"Thanks." Bandit set the box he'd been carrying into the belly of the aircraft. "Where do you want us?"

We got all situated in the passenger compartment of the Thunderbird, the arched ceiling and webbing very different from the passenger area of the truck. Luckily, the seat belts weren't too different, and the back was equipped with a surveillance station similar to the one I was used to. Connecting my helmet comms and getting the screens awake, I barely noticed as the pitch of the engines changed and we lifted off.

Once airborne, it took less than an hour for us to cut across desert and over the mountains between us and the city of Tucson. The rocky, cactus-speckled edges gave way to pines at higher altitude, providing the cooler temperatures necessary for the monsoons to form over their sides. Soon, the sky islands faded to desert, and the abandoned signs of civilization could be seen outside the tiny window.

I looked down at the derelict grid of streets and buildings as Logan swung into a wide bank over the city. White-painted roofs reflected the sun with blinding flashes of light, interspersed by terra-cotta tiles. Occasional patches of open space sprawled in tan and brown amidst the other buildings; the cavities where a home or business had been destroyed by xenos, riots, or both. The rains had been good here, I thought as I looked out the tiny window. The usually dry riverbed still held traces of water, and the foliage growing along the edges looked healthy and green. As we completed our banking turn over the Santa Cruz River, the Tucson base finally came into view.

My view changed from river to hillsides as Logan swung around to descend onto one of several helipads atop the flat roof of the main building—formerly a hospital, now the linchpin of the EDF in the Santa Cruz Valley. Once painted rusty pink, the four-story building and its associated tower had faded to white, and even the flag fluttering proudly at the corner of the roof did nothing to hide the facts of the matter. Just like Tucson, St. Augustine's was falling apart.

I'd only been here a few times. I'd grown up in the middle of the city, tucked in a pocket of greenery where the water flowed closer to the surface and humans held a truce with the desert. As a teenager, I'd left the crowded barrios, living on the edges of communities and trying to dodge anyone's notice. Luckily, Bandit knew his way around. Leaving Logan to oversee the Thunderbird's checkup and chat with the other pilots and flight mechanics, we headed for a stairwell in the main tower, our footsteps echoing on the chipped concrete steps. After four flights of stairs, I asked, "Where are we going? This isn't the way I took last time I was here."

Bandit glanced up at the ceiling. "We need to see the tech guys. They have a spare set of sensors, for us to take another shot at fixing Relay 22." He snorted. "It would've been nice to use them for 13, but..."

"Yeah." I swallowed hard, remembering the black-edged fireball that had consumed the tower *and* the valuable equipment I had just attached. "Too bad." I stuffed my hands in my pockets and followed him through twisting corridors, under ceilings lined with cracked pipelines and more cables than I could count. A thought jogged my memory, and I stretched my legs to come alongside Bandit. "Josephine said this used to be a hospital."

"Oldest hospital in the city," he affirmed, shifting the box in his arms. "This is where Josephine worked, before we realized what was going on. It was at the very edge of the dampening field, so she wasn't as badly affected when the xenos started ratcheting it down." He gave a short laugh as we passed an alcove filled with broken hospital furniture. "I'm sure they had a nasty surprise when she and most of the staff disappeared."

"Why'd they leave?"

"Setting up a clinic farther afield. Once I found out where she was, I joined her. There were more people than just civilians who were interested in her and her skills." Bandit opened a scuffed door and led me through to a workspace crowded with bits of equipment, computers, and boxes upon boxes of reclaimed junk. "Benny? You here?"

A lanky, dark-skinned guy with wild hair stuck his head around the edge of a towering shelving unit. "Carlos, my man!"

Bandit accepted the offered handshake, clapping the other man on the shoulder. I hung back at the edge of the work table as they exchanged pleasantries, until Bandit set the box he'd been carrying on the table. "Hey, Reneé sent you something. I don't know what it is, or where she got it, and I don't want to know."

The engineer popped the lid on the box. "Don't worry, it's not gonna hurt you." He whistled with admiration at the sight of the contents. My curiosity getting the better of me, I leaned over to see a glowing diode, a handful of wires, and a few instrument panels. "It's the guts of a xeno nav computer," Benny explained with a glance up at me. "I've got a side project I'm working on, and Deadeye said she could get me the parts I needed."

Bandit laughed. "She's like a pack rat, hanging on to all that old stuff." He shook his head, the brim of his hat exaggerating the movement. "You got the sensors?"

"Yeah, man. Regional flew them down the other day when the major came to visit." Benny pulled an equipment case from one of the shelving units, clearing junk from the corner of the workbench before setting it down. "And you didn't hear this from me, but there was a ton of back and forth between him and the brass upstairs."

"You catch what it was about?"

"Dude, I don't know." Benny showed us the array of tech inside a fabric-lined case. Like everything else, the sensors looked like they'd been "refurbished" about ten times before this point. "I'm the wrong person to ask, anyway."

"Benny, don't give me that. You hear *everything*, even from down here in the basement."

I stifled a laugh at the tone in Bandit's voice—like a world-weary dad.

Benny snorted as well, but said, "Okay, so maybe I heard something." He lowered his voice, caution creeping through it. "They're getting more worried about the Angels. A sensor drone flew out while they were talking, heading straight for the Ridges."

"Really?" I raised my head, forgetting that I'd been trying to keep a low profile. "That's an expensive toy to pull out for a scouting run."

Benny nodded. "Expensive, fragile, and irreplaceable." He raised an eyebrow. "Just the power supply is worth more than any of us make in a year."

"They really wanted to know what's out there, huh?" Bandit leaned against the edge of the shelving unit, resting his hand near his holster. "You hear if they found anything?"

Benny's eyes narrowed. "I don't know." Annoyance edged his voice. "I need to find out. Even if they're not saying anything, someone'll know."

"Well, do me a favor?" Bandit asked. "If you hear what they found, or even what they were looking for, get a message to us? I'm sure you and Reneé have ways to talk."

The engineer shrugged modestly. "We have ways." He frowned. "If I had to guess, I'd say they know what's out there, and they're just trying to find it."

"Sounds like it," Bandit agreed. "And they're nervous enough about it that they sent us one of the Shattereds from the old squad."

"That's right, I heard they sent Judge to Base 36. And—" Benny lowered his voice. "I heard Banshee and Phantom showed up."

Bandit cast a glance at the door. His voice was firm. "We're trying to keep that information as tight to the vest as we can. They weren't well liked, and I don't want to risk people with old scores to settle coming for them—or, well, for Tara."

"Hmm." The engineer took a long minute to adjust a

screw on one of the components. "Well, if things go the way Regional thinks they will, you'll need all the help you can get." He snapped the case closed, threading a plastic lock through the latch before handing it to me. "Good luck out there. If I hear anything, I'll be in touch." He flicked us a salute. "And hey, tell Reneé thanks for me."

LOGAN TOOK the opportunity of being at a larger base to have one of the flight technicians go over the Thunderbird's landing gear, so we ended up having a few hours after checking in with the rest of the staff. I was in the middle of reading a book swiped from a table in the cafeteria when Bandit's head appeared around the doorway. "*Mijo*, come on!"

Annoyed at being interrupted, I stuffed the book in my pocket. Down the hall we went, exchanging greetings with the other Defense Force members at the base. "Where are we going?"

"Grocery run," Bandit explained briefly in Spanish as we emerged into the sunlight. The landscaping around the old buildings had once been nice, but now the mesquite trees had grown overhead, their drooping branches tangling in overgrown bougainvillea vines and an ancient grapefruit tree. "And reconnaissance." He took a sudden left turn, making for the edge of the buildings where several trucks sat in an open-air bay.

"The market is that way," I said, pointing down the road. "Barely a mile. We're going to burn fuel for a mile of walking?" I knew I was being unpleasant, but I didn't care. This neighborhood was similar enough to the one I'd grown up in to send old memories hammering through my mind, and I wanted nothing more than to run back to the Thunderbird and hide behind my screens.

Bandit examined a handwritten logbook, scrawling his signature to sign out a key. "This neighborhood doesn't have what I'm looking for." He pointed me to one of the smaller vehicles. "Hop in."

"You're joking."

"No, *mijo*, I'm not." His eyes were kind under his hat brim, and for a moment he reminded me of my barely-remembered father. "Come on."

I yanked open the passenger door with a growl and sat on the cracked seat. It was quiet for a bit, as Bandit navigated past the river and deeper into what had once been a thriving city. The desert had taken its due; cracking the roads and walls, eroding the paint off structures, and reducing vegetation to crisped husks alongside buildings. Eventually, the sadness of the derelict buildings seeped through the windows enough to dilute my surly mood, and I asked, "Where *are* we going?"

Bandit slowed almost to a stop before crossing an intersection, eyes flicking down the deserted road. "I wanted to see how the city's doing *away* from the base."

"Looks the same to me," I said, looking out the window. "Same empty blocks, same buildings baking under the sun, same everything."

"I expected better of you, *mijo*." Bandit didn't bother hiding the disappointment in his voice as he pulled the car into an abandoned parking lot. "You're good at picking out details; it's why I brought you. What's not right about this neighborhood?"

He's right, I reminded myself. I got out of the car and followed Bandit along the empty street, looking carefully around the area. *Memories aside, this* is *the region you're supposed to protect.* The market had taken up residence inside the empty shell of a warehouse. I could see the bulk of the building in the distance, but the farther we walked, the more the "wrong" filter kept pinging in my brain. By the time we'd reached the edge of the warehouse lot, I had put my finger on it.

"The kids are all gone. There's no one outside." I looked at the sky from under the brim of my hat. "It's full daylight, though. The sun could be keeping everyone inside."

Bandit shook his head, his own face concealed behind his trusty bandana. "They're used to the sun just like we are. And it's monsoon." He flicked a casual gesture at the southeast, where giant cloud towers had piled up at the edge of the mountains. "It's not so hot it'll kill you. They're not inside because it's hot. Think again."

I sighed, not wanting to acknowledge what he was implying. The evidence became even more stark at the sight of paint splashed across the side of a building, spelling obscene threats in lurid red. I closed my eyes, the memories I'd barely held at bay overtaking my mind.

Red splatters against a wall.

Breaking glass.

Gunshots.

Yelling.

I took a deep breath. "They're scared."

"Exactly." Bandit's hand went briefly to his handgun, as if reassuring himself it was still there. I wondered if it would've been a good idea for me to bring a weapon as he said, "I talked with some of the others while you were reading. The commanders all say the city's fine, but the rest of the staff made it pretty clear they're barely holding their own." A chill went through my stomach despite the heat as he added, "There've even been Brute sightings in the city, and every time it's in conjunction with gang violence." Bandit frowned at the graffiti as we passed it. "I knew the Blood Angels were crazy, but I didn't think they'd bring monsters into it."

We reached the market and soon had everything from our list, though Bandit made irritated noises at how much a few of the items cost. We'd gotten almost everything from Josephine's list, and were walking toward the entrance when Bandit caught sight of a booth hung with bandana pennants. He gave a half-laugh. "Josephine mentioned this lady had come back into business." He raised an eyebrow at me. "Do you remember marshmallows, *mijo*?"

I shook my head at first, the denial changing to a nod as the memory filtered back. "You cook them over a campfire, right?"

"Yeah." Bandit glanced at the list, sighed, and said, "We can do without another package of tortillas. It'll make Josie's day if we bring marshmallows instead."

The candy seller was a short native woman, her eyes almost as black as her glossy hair. Her booth was filled with the heavy smells of hot sugar and decorated with bright colors. A line of cheap cloth bags filled with candies sat on the converted plexiglass display case, others lining the counter beside her work space. When Bandit asked her about the red-painted threats, her gaze dropped to the stained concrete floor.

"The Force can't be everywhere," she whispered in English. "And they never come to this side of town. Besides, our enemies aren't aliens and monsters anymore, they're our own people."

She suddenly went silent, pushing a paper-wrapped package across the display case at Bandit. The market went quiet, like the terrible stillness just before a storm, as a trio of men in their thirties stepped through the open warehouse door. Red bandanas wrapped around their wrists and necks, and their postures indicated that they had no expectations of conflict in this building. Fear clawed through my heart, and I instinctively froze as still as the civilians.

Bandit's hand touched my elbow. "*Mijo*, let's go."

You're with one of your childhood heroes, I sternly told myself, settling my shoulders and keeping pace with Bandit as he walked straight toward the three men. *There's no need to be afraid of them anymore.*

"Morning!" Bandit said cheerfully as we approached.

I wasn't sure if it was his posture or the deadly cheer in his words, but the gang members jumped and clustered together like schoolchildren caught in misbehavior before regaining their confidence. One of them swaggered up to Bandit, saying in Spanish, "Espinoza, my man! I didn't expect I'd see you around here." His eyes flicked to me, standing a few feet away. "Aww, and you brought your kid. Though, he's a little young to be yours, isn't he?"

Bandit shifted a package from one arm to the other. "Hey, Beto. Just getting stuff for the base. You know how it is —it's hard to get good tortillas unless you make them yourself, and I'm no good in the kitchen." He settled his weight, balancing the bags on his left hip while his free hand dangled alongside his handgun. "I didn't expect to see you here, either. Shouldn't you be out threatening ranchers or something?"

A flash of anger—and annoyance—crossed the gangbanger's face. "Times change, you know. The Angels have bigger priorities in this city."

"Oh?" Despite the animosity rolling off the men, Bandit's voice remained light and friendly. "I'm sorry, I didn't realize you'd taken up community service." His posture shifted a bit, and all three men tensed. If I hadn't been so close to bolting myself, I might have laughed. "Since you're taking such an interest, I don't suppose you'd know anything about the communication towers going down out in the creosote flats?"

I wished I'd had a camera. The look across the gangster's face—pride and false innocence all mixed with deceit—was practically poetic. "I don't know, man. It's dangerous territory out there, and I hear all kinds of things might be prowling—more and more all the time. Those things can take out a car just like that." Beto snapped his fingers, the innocuous gesture somehow threatening. "If I was an annoying halfwit like you, I'd stay out of things."

Bandit shrugged. "Annoying's not the worst thing I've been called. And it'll take more than a few monsters to worry me." He shifted his weight again, easily stepping around the Blood Angels to walk toward the door. I followed, nervous about exposing my back to the gang members. "Thanks for the information. I'll be sure to return the favor sometime."

The Blood Angel's retort from behind sent a chill down my spine, the harsh words pulling half-buried memories from deep inside my head. "Don't underestimate us. The Angels have been waiting long enough for the EDF to take the hint and clear out. Our patience is running out, Espinoza, and we're not going to back down until we get what we want."

Bandit didn't turn around. "I know. But that's not going

to scare me off." He kept walking, passing me one of the bags. "Let's go, *mijo*," he said in quiet English. "Don't turn around. They're only waiting for a chance to start something."

I took the bag and slung it over my shoulder. No more words came from behind us as we walked away from the market, though I felt the eyes of the gangbangers on the back of my head from hundreds of feet away. Finally, I glanced back with a deep exhalation of relief. The warehouse shimmered in the sunlight behind us, its parking lot lifeless. "I don't think they followed us."

"They didn't have to." Bandit finally shifted a bag to his free hand. "They said what they wanted to, and so did I."

"You sounded like you knew them." I didn't even try to keep the accusatory tone out of my voice. After having spent my teen years trying to dodge gang conscription *and* keep myself alive on the margins of society, I wasn't about to soften my suspicion. "Before all this, I mean."

"If you're wondering if I ever ran with them, the answer is no." Bandit ducked his head to pull his bandana over his face as a hot gust of wind sent dust spinners whipping down the street. "Did you?"

Fair is fair, I guess. He has a right to ask.

I glanced at the warehouse, like even talking about the Angels would bring them down on us. "After the fields collapsed and the riots died down, a lot of guys my age joined them." I lifted one shoulder in a half shrug. "I hid instead. There was an abandoned library with a back room, and—" *Enough, Gabriel. No one wants to hear about that.* "How'd you know them?"

"The gangs have been here since before the xenos." Bandit tipped his face toward the eastern mountains, squinting at the thunderheads building over their rocky peaks. "But nah, they never tried to recruit me. Back then, no one wanted the son of a Border Patrol agent anywhere near their turf."

I nodded. In this area, the Border Patrol was still either revered as heroes or reviled as government oppressors—a distinction I'd never cared about, given the lawlessness of the last eight years. They'd disbanded, along with most government agencies, in the wake of the rolling blackouts that heralded the first dampening fields. "Is that why you joined the Force?"

"Indirectly, I guess. The EDF—well, the baby version of it—started *after* the invasion, and Josephine's the one who got me in with them." Bandit laughed. "Too bad you don't have your notebook on you. This is one she'll never tell properly."

Curiosity wriggled through my stomach, driving away the nerves of being in my old hometown. I slid the groceries to a more comfortable spot on my shoulder and checked my watch. "We need to get back to St. Augustine's. Will you tell me on the flight home?"

Bandit gave a resigned sigh. "Sure, *mijo*. But don't tell Josie it was me you heard it from." The edges of his eyes crinkled in a smile. "She'll hate me if she finds out I said anything."

STAGE SIX

Earth Defense Force Thunderbird
Over the West Silver Bell Mountains
July 16

I CLICKED ON MY RECORDER, even though I wasn't sure it would pick up anything over the background noise in the Thunderbird. After recording the date and time, I clipped it to the webbing between us and flipped open my notebook. Up in the cockpit, Logan had his own connection to the satellites and didn't really *need* my help getting us home. After once more warning me not to tell Josephine, Bandit leaned against the wall and began.

"We still aren't sure when the xenos showed up. Michael didn't even know, and he understood the situation better than any of the rest of us. All I knew was that rule of law was quickly disappearing, and law of force was replacing it." He frowned and tugged his bandana loose, wiping his brow and stuffing it into his pocket. "I guess I was about thirty-two at the time. By the time we really started scrambling, the first dampeners were going up. It took the xenos a while to tailor the specific frequencies, and at first it was causing people to go crazy. The Blood Angels really started getting traction then, as those of us less affected got organized."

"Had Josephine already started her clinic?"

Bandit nodded, pulling off his hat and setting it beside him. "She and a few others ganged up to clear out pharmacies. She took a bullet through the shoulder one of the times, and that's when I joined them."

"Did you know her already?"

He laughed. "Know her? We grew up together, and she tagged after me like she was my little sister. She was all braces, glasses, and elbows—and six years younger—but she wouldn't leave me alone. She wanted to get out of the barrio, and so did I."

My writing slowed on that sentence. *No wonder we get along. That's what I wanted, too.* "Was it hard?"

"Growing up, or getting out?" He stretched long legs out along the floor of the compartment before answering the question. "Both were tough. I joined the BP once I got old enough, and got my marksman's instructor patch." He laughed softly. "No one cares where you came from or who your parents are when you can put five rounds in the same hole on the target. Josie had it harder than me—her older brother was a gangbanger who kept coming and making trouble for her and her parents."

"I didn't know." I stopped writing, frowning at the page. "I wonder if I knew him."

"This was when the Blood Angels were barely starting out, so I doubt it. He disappeared during the occupation, anyway." Bandit made a noise halfway between frustration and a sigh. "Josie knew that studying hard was her only way out, so she joined me in paramedic training, then followed it up with pharmacy school. She graduated with honors, but right as she got settled at the hospital, things ended. Blackouts in the middle of summer, thousands dying in the heat, the government buildings getting overrun..." He sighed and looked up at me. "You sure you want to hear about this?"

I nodded, scratching out a misspelling and rewriting the last few words. "I knew most of this already." I did, too. It was in the training curriculum for new Force members, introduced as more and more new recruits came in with birthdays too close to the beginning of the invasion to remember it. Not that I needed a reminder of the violence that had happened after the fields dropped. "How do the Blood Angels fit in?"

"They'd been around, but law enforcement kept them in check. After the dampening fields started going up, a few smart ones set up shop far outside the city centers. They liked harassing the few others who stuck it out; ranchers and homesteaders and whatever. I was patrolling the outside of one of the depression zones, and ran into a bunch of the Angels roughing up the daughters of a cattle rancher." Bandit's eyes softened around the edges, though I wasn't sure why. It wasn't like these were *nice* recollections. "I ran them off."

The Thunderbird bumped over a patch of turbulence, and I glanced at the screens out of habit. The clouds we'd been watching all morning were building into a proper storm. For Tucson's sake, I hoped it would prove a very wet storm. The desert needed all the help it could get. "Why?" I stopped and clarified, "Things were falling apart. Why'd they decide to make life hard for the people around them, when bigger things were happening?"

Why? The question stretched out in the back of my mind, wrapped in the voice of a hurting child. I hadn't meant to attach such meaning to the simple question, but suddenly I *needed* to know what Bandit thought. *Why, when their own lives fell apart, did they still choose to hurt others?*

"It's not exactly a new response to crises." Bandit crossed his arms over his chest. "Everyone could feel the situation spiraling out of control, not just those of us who knew why it was happening. When you're under pressure like that—" He blinked, his eyes staying closed a fraction longer than normal. "Situations like that show the best or worst of people. Some of us responded by trying to protect as many lives as we could, which is how the Defense Force started in the first place." His eyes tracked downward, and his fist tightened against the edge of his holster. "Others reacted to the loss of control by exerting force of their own."

I nodded silently. He was right, of course, but hearing him say it was reassuring in its own way. Before I had time to let the truth settle through my heart, Bandit continued the story.

"Anyway, I thought my running them off would be the end of it, but two days later, they got me right outside of the clinic." He rubbed the back of his head, wincing. "I woke up miles away, out in Cochise Stronghold."

I whistled. The name was legendary—a place long deserted and abandoned to the few people determined to make it on their own. "What'd they want with you?"

Bandit shrugged, the nonchalance at odds with his words. "I still don't know. Ransom, I guess, but they never got that far. A few days later, they put a bag over my head, marched me to the freeway, dropped me and my stuff, and left." He smiled proudly. "Josie had figured out what happened and raised hell with my superiors. When screaming in their faces didn't produce the effect she wanted, she went to the clinic and loaded up with enough stuff to make an addict drool. With that in play, the gangsters were happy to do whatever she wanted."

The Thunderbird dipped again, and I swore under my breath as my pen left a messy line across what I'd just written. "She paid them off? Josephine?"

"Don't underestimate her," Bandit said, understanding the incredulity in my tone. "She's not above skirting the rules when it benefits everyone. How she secured the supplies for the clinic was *highly* illegal, though now it's just smart survival practice. And her history with the Blood Angels meant they didn't make her disappear. Santana—their leader then—wasn't stupid, and the meds she brought probably saved the lives of his men." Bandit sighed, shifting position against the wall. "He wasn't a bad guy—tough, but fair. He just reacted badly to the loss of control." He shook his head, the silver hair at his temples briefly catching the light. "I'd rather deal with him than with the current generation of gangsters any day. He'd *never* have pulled a stunt like leading a pack of Brutes down on his enemies."

"That reminds me..." I reached over and clicked off the recorder. "You said Brutes have been showing up in the city, always during Blood Angel encounters?"

Bandit turned to face me. "Yeah, that's what the St. Augustine's staff said. The Angels have been using them as muscle, kind of like how the xenos did." He arched an eyebrow. "'Pay us, or we'll turn loose the monster.'"

"Okay. So that's a definite connection. But what I want to know is, where are they getting the Brutes?" Bandit frowned, and I hastened to explain, "What if they're not just —I don't know—catching them?"

"What else could it be?"

I slid from my seat and sat cross-legged on the floor next to him, bouncing my pen against my knee. "I went back a few months and checked every anomaly, every interaction with the Blood Angels, and every instance of stuff going missing or getting damaged." I pulled my notebook down and flipped several pages. Bandit's concerns over getting eavesdropped on were rubbing off, and I hadn't wanted to trust a computer with my findings. "If you look back for about a year, there are different industrial things that went missing. Solvents, chemicals, stuff like that." Bandit's posture straightened as I added the last piece of information. "Nine months ago, a cache of xeno tech slated for destruction went missing instead. And now, the solar field's experiencing drains that don't match up with normal usage."

"Like they were building something, and now they need to power it." Bandit's tone deepened. "Toward the end of the war, Central Command did get sloppy with how thoroughly they destroyed xeno facilities." His eyes sharpened, and he swore. "The Ridges. I'll bet there's still a cloning facility out in the Ridges."

"What?" I looked up from my notes. "I was guessing!" My heartbeat sped up, nerves tingling all up and down my spine. "The xenos were able to clone?"

"Yeah." Bandit made a disgusted face. "Where do you think so many Brutes came from in the first place?"

The words rebounded through my head as the Thunderbird's engines shifted pitch. Logan's voice came through our comms as we started descending. "Home sweet home."

A FLURRY of unloading and debriefing swept us up as soon as we landed, and I didn't have time to ask Bandit any of the questions bouncing through my head. Once dinner had been cooked, eaten, and cleaned up, I retreated to my room. I'd planned on writing out Bandit's story, but my thoughts kept running in circles—Brutes, Blood Angels, old memories, Brutes again—until I slammed the notebook to my bed with a huff. No sooner had I done that than a knock came at the door.

I opened it to see Judge leaning against the wall outside. Bandit had given up on trying to get him to button his uniform—or wear it at all—and today his T-shirt was green and said something about cabbages.

"What's up?"

"Came to see what you were doing." Judge took a bare step into the room, and I scrambled to close my notebook. He tilted his head, a smile spreading across his face at the sight of the sketch I'd drawn amid my circling thoughts. "Is that a Brute?"

My shoulders fell, and I stopped trying to hide the drawing. A hunched creature, something between the trolls from my favorite books and an ape with cougar fangs, lay in smudged pencil across the blue lines of the notebook page. "I thought maybe if I drew it, it'd stay out of my head."

Judge's eyebrows drew together over the page as he examined the sketch. "That—is the *worst* drawing I've ever seen." His shoulders shook in a quickly building laugh. "You should stick to stories."

"Shut up!" I grabbed the notebook, laughing despite myself. He had a point; my skills were nowhere equal to depicting a nightmare incarnate. "Why are you here, anyway?"

Judge's laughter subsided, but the twinkle stayed in his cyan eyes. "Josephine lit a fire outside to cook those marshmallow things you and Bandit brought back. Want to join us?"

I flipped the notebook closed and tucked it under my arm, hesitating a moment as my responsibilities pressed against my shoulders. "Who's in the Fishbowl?"

"One of the others. I forget their name." Judge sauntered down the hall. "It's covered for tonight."

I'D EXPECTED it to be blisteringly hot outside. Most summer nights never really cooled off, and the day had been well over a hundred degrees. However, the storm from earlier had blown itself out over the mountains, coating everything in a layer of moisture and bringing the temperature down to a manageable level. Lightning still flickered over the rocky edges of the far sky islands as Judge and I approached the fire ring. Deadeye's pink hair caught the light as she crouched next to Josephine, both of them with marshmallows impaled on wires. Tara leaned into Caleb's shoulder, the light dancing across her face as she joked with Josephine. My footsteps slowed as I watched. *They're so happy together. I shouldn't intrude.*

Before I had time to slip away, Tara looked up. "There they are!"

Within seconds, I'd been pulled over to the fire and a piece of heavy-gauge wire stuffed in my hands.

"It's easy, look," Josephine said, demonstrating. "You have to keep it far enough back that it gets toasted, but not so close that it burns..." She sighed as Judge pulled a flaming marshmallow out of the fire with a grin. "Well, everyone has their own preference. Here." She handed me one of the bags we'd brought from the market.

I knelt next to the fire, the heat warming my face as the others talked. *Guess they don't mind me being here.* The tension gradually lightened from inside my chest, and soon I was able to laugh along with the rest of the squad. No one seemed to mind when I pulled out my recorder, balancing it on my knee to capture the banter.

After a while, the fire had died down and most of the marshmallows had been eaten. Everyone sat with their feet pointed toward the fire, leaning back and talking comfortably with no mention of how late it was getting. I sat on the edge of a bench alongside Judge, watching him idly casting shield bubbles around individual coals. Across the fire, Tara leaned forward with her elbows planted on her knees.

"Bet you can't make it airtight."

"Can *you?*" he retorted.

Tara's brow furrowed in concentration. A blue spark shot from her fingertip toward the coals, evaporating the moment it touched an ember. She laughed and sat back. "I guess not." With Caleb's arm around her shoulders, Tara looked more like a high schooler with her first boyfriend than a powerful Shattered. "I'll leave it to you."

She looked up at Bandit as he finally joined us. He was wearing his uniform shirt with his captain's insignia attached, meaning he'd just come from talking with Regional Command —probably briefing them on the altercation we'd had with the Blood Angels in Tucson. Logan followed him into the firelight, his pilot's flashings shining silver against one shoulder. The others made space for the newcomers around the fire,

Josephine extending the bag of marshmallows toward Logan by way of welcome. "Hey, welcome to the party!" She turned to look up at Bandit as he sat next to her. "How was your debrief?"

"Concerning," he said, undoing the top button on his shirt. He leaned forward to stir the fire, the flames casting flickering light over his face. "They're worried. An official order just came down from the Springs—they're recalling the enlisted ranks from Base 36 to the Santa Cruz Valley."

Silence reigned for a long moment, before Deadeye broke the stillness with a deep sigh. "I wondered. The techies told me Regional sent a drone to scan the Ridges, but they didn't know why or what was found."

"Whatever it was, they must be worried enough about the civilians that they want us back in the city," I said, trying to tamp down my dread at the idea of being reassigned permanently to Tucson. "And the Blood Angels were way too confident in the barrio we visited,"

"What barrio?" Josephine asked.

"The Vistas."

Josephine rolled her eyes. "It's not like that neighborhood would have *improved* over time. Regional's worried enough that they're recalling everyone?"

"Not everyone," Bandit said. "Just enlisted, which is everyone except the five of us." He pointed at Judge, Deadeye, Tara, and Caleb, who all nodded grimly.

"And me." Logan looked up from a marshmallow, his face somewhat guarded in the firelight. "They seem to think you still need a pilot, even with three-fourths of your personnel being reassigned."

"Niiice." Deadeye high-fived him. "Always nice to have someone else who knows his way around those stupid modified engines." She winked. "We'll have to make sure you get a call sign to match all the rest of ours."

Logan shook his head, a grin crossing his face. "I'm good. I'd feel silly using one when everyone's just used my name for so long." He rolled his eyes. "Besides, only fighter pilots feel the need to have a cool nickname."

"Whatever name we use, I'm glad they let you stay," Josephine said. "We've already had one medical evacuation from this base, and with me leaving as well..."

Bandit interrupted her before she had time to finish the sentence. "Actually, the colonel wants you to stay; you and Gabriel, both." He glanced at me as he finished the sentence, and the knots in my muscles tightened.

"Well, that must be an error on their part." I stared into the fire to hide the frustration welling up inside of me. "I wasn't part of the original force. I'm nowhere close to the caliber of soldier they want here."

"You have areas of expertise that no one else here does, *mijo*," Josephine said kindly, reaching over and patting my knee. Some of the tension across my shoulders lessened as she reassured me, "They'd be crazy to reassign you."

Deadeye spat into the fire. "It's all fine, but what are we supposed to do here? We can't present much of a threat to anyone with only eight people."

Bandit shrugged. "Someone has to maintain the solar fields. And they told me to keep the comms towers up, even if that means taking offensive action."

Caleb snorted. He'd been quiet through the whole discussion, but I'd noticed his eyes flicking from person to person as we talked. "Nice. They're *finally* letting us be proactive after slashing our numbers? Do those corner cutters in Colorado even know what things are like down here?"

"I think it's safe to say, no," Bandit admitted. "This region was never high on their priority list."

"Things were better in the desert," Caleb muttered.

I couldn't help my nod of agreement—even after the reassurance of being allowed to stay with the squad, the urge to hide instead of facing the trouble was a powerful one.

"I don't mind the smaller group, actually," Josephine said. She gestured at everyone—even Logan and I—with one graceful sweep of a hand. The movement brought to mind colorful skirts and folk music as she said, "We've all faced tough situations before, but at least now we have each other at our backs. With the others gone, we can go back to being more like a family."

Everyone nodded. *I* nodded. It was almost too much to have hoped for, being allowed to stay. *I'll probably never be one of them, but it's nice to be wanted.* I picked up my recorder and quietly turned it off. Whatever else happened in this conversation, I wanted the mention of family to be the last thing on the recording.

"What about the Brutes, though?" I asked as I slid the small device into my pocket. "Not that I'm disagreeing with their orders, but..."

"It's still a concern," Bandit agreed. He leaned forward, bringing everyone's attention in with the intensity of his voice. "I went over the reports like you suggested, *mijo*, and I'm convinced now."

"What's this?" Caleb said. "New information?"

"Gabriel pointed it out this afternoon, and I'm willing to bet it's what Regional sent the drone to find." Bandit sighed.

"Remember that one facility we hit, right after the first dampener went down?"

I didn't know what he meant, but everyone else apparently did. Judge and Tara both sat bolt upright, a flicker of light running through Tara's eyes. Deadeye frowned around her eyepatch strap, one hand going to a spot on her ribs. Logan and I exchanged a single confused look as Caleb answered, "Yeah, I remember. Before then, 'Grey Goo' only referred to a video game." Even though his voice stayed even, his shoulders had gone tense. "*That's* what's in the Ridges? Cloning?"

Bandit nodded seriously. "The force got lazy with destroying all the xeno tech. I'm sure there were entire facilities that no one ever discovered. If the Blood Angels found one..."

Logan looked up at the roof, where the edges of the Thunderbird's wings could be seen silhouetted against the sky. "It didn't take much to change their shuttle engine design, once we understood the principles." His eyes narrowed in calculation. "We even modified their radar to create our sensor systems. It wouldn't surprise me for someone to have rebuilt or modified a cloning array."

I shifted in my seat, fidgeting with a piece of the marshmallow wire to conceal how hard my heart had started pounding. "*That's* why they've been hitting our communication. A tower going down is a lot easier to ignore than packs of Brutes appearing where none were before. If we can't get the sensors up, we'll be blind."

"It won't be the first time." Even with tension running through every line of his body, Caleb still sounded as comfortable as he had been when talking about how to get the perfect golden crust on a marshmallow. "We went without sensors or comms for most missions in the old days, until the techies figured out how to link us all through Michael's helmet."

"We do have to do something about this, though." Deadeye tossed a wood chip into the embers. "It's no good for us to sit here and wait for the next load of monsters to show up."

"Ah, Reneé, you're being too pessimistic." Judge wagged a finger at her. "Have you forgotten who you're dealing with?" He struck a heroic pose, the posture incongruous with the cartoon drawing on his T-shirt. "We're the heroes who saved Earth. We can deal with a few Brutes."

"Shut up, Alexi. No one needs reminding." Tara threw one of the empty marshmallow bags at Judge, who scorched it with a cyan flash.

"Like it or not, our orders are clear," Bandit said. "Our priority *has* to be those towers and the solar field." He looked over our heads, toward the solar field and the Ridges. "If something happens to the power, thousands of people in Tucson will die."

Everyone nodded as the fire flared up, their expressions ranging from resigned to determined. For the first time, I wondered if they really wanted to be here at all, or if—like me—they would've rather been allowed to disappear into the desert, never to be seen again.

They want me here, I told myself as the conversation turned to talk of logistics. *If there's a chance this could become like an actual family, I'd be stupid to leave.*

Earth Defense Force Base 36
Gila River Valley
July 22

THE BASE FELT BIGGER with everyone gone. Bigger, cleaner, calmer—all things I would have enjoyed, had I not known why it was like that. The others felt the same way. Over breakfast one morning, we decided to move our belongings into one row of adjacent rooms. Setting my running shoes next to the box containing my extra socks, I shut the closet doors and sat cross-legged on the bed. The single overhead lightbulb cast the room in weird shadows, unfamiliar even though the layout was identical to my old room.

Reaching for the notebooks lying in a tidy stack on the nightstand, I stopped. The recorder light blinked once as I clicked it on, taking a moment to clear my throat—and my head.

"It's been almost a week since everyone left, and I honestly don't know how I feel about it. Logan's settling in well with everyone, Deadeye and Judge bicker all the time, and Bandit's helping me with my marksmanship, but..." I swallowed hard and rubbed my eyes. *Come on, it's your own log. Don't lie to your own log.*

"With more people here, it was easier to fly under the radar. I liked that. I was good at it—I've always been good at it. But now, there's nowhere to hide." I rubbed a closed fist against my chest, wondering why it was getting so tight. "I—I didn't realize how much it would mean, being around them. They share their jokes, and teach me stuff, and don't look at me weird when I ask them to tell their stories." The tightness in my chest spread up to my throat as I said, "It's not going to last—it can't— nothing does. And I know I'll get hurt when it all falls apart."

After Abuela died, a back room of an abandoned library had been home. I'd gotten used to it, felt safe there. Then, I trusted the wrong person and I'd gotten hurt again.

I bent my head over my crossed legs, my torso making a cave over the recorder. "It would make things so much easier to cut it off now and leave. I could survive on my own—I've done it before. I just *don't want to.*" Admitting it felt wrong, like I'd betrayed some part of myself. I balled up a fist against my mouth, stifling the tears that threatened my voice. "I never thought I'd find anyone who cared about me. And now, it's—I don't know, like—"

"Gabriel?"

I jumped, the recorder flying off the bed as I bolted to my feet. Josephine stood in the doorway, the knob still in her hand.

"I'm sorry, I don't think you heard me knocking."

I scrabbled for the recorder under my bed. *What did she hear?* "No, sorry, I was just—"

"It's okay." There was no way she hadn't noticed the tears on my face, but her voice stayed neutral as she asked, "May I come in?"

"Um, sure!" I scrambled to my feet and pulled out my only chair. "Have a seat, I guess?"

"Thanks." She sat down, an interested look spreading over her face as she looked up at the shelf of books over my desk. The overhead light filled her dark brown eyes with amber flecks, casting shadows over the wrinkles at their corners as she tilted her head. "I've never heard of some of these. *Oath of the Outcast?*"

I nodded, relief settling my nerves. If there was one thing I could safely talk about, it was those books. "It's one of my favorites." I pulled the book down and wiped the cover. The mist swirling on the cover of the book looked as otherworldly as the story within had felt. "Found it at training. No one else wanted it, so..."

While the other recruits had been making friends and enemies, I'd disappeared into the pages of words. Just like all those months in the back room of the library—I'd survive the day, knowing the stories would be there at the end. *Even if some days were harder to survive than others.*

"You collect more stories than just ours." Josephine's voice broke me from my teeming thoughts. "I love that."

"I guess so." I set the book back on the shelf. Clearing my throat, I asked, "Was there something you needed?"

Josephine pursed her lips. "I *was* going to ask for your help with lunch. Then I caught the tail end of what you were saying."

Oh.

I sat down on the end of my bed, embarrassment making

my skin prickle. "I didn't realize I was talking so loud," I muttered.

"You weren't." Josephine ran a hand through her hair, catching a few strands and tucking them behind her ear. "My hearing's gotten a lot better after exposure to the others' Shattered power for so long." Her eyes narrowed. "Gabriel, what's going on?"

My throat tightened a little as she said it, and I looked away. "I'm just—afraid." *Don't lie to her. You owe her the truth, at least.* I took a deep breath, returning her gaze with nerves churning my stomach. "My parents disappeared when I was little. I have no idea what happened to them, but I'm assuming the xenos were involved. My grandmother raised me after that, until the dampeners fell and the riots started." I squeezed my eyes shut on the image of blood spattering the wall of my childhood room. "I hid under the bed while she was murdered." To my dismay, my voice cracked again. "I—I was a *coward.* I was ten, I could've done something, I should've—"

Josephine interrupted me with a gentle hand on my arm. "You were ten." Tears sparkled in her eyes. "You were not a coward; you were a child. And by hiding, you survived." She swallowed hard. "Your grandmother, she hid you?"

I nodded, not trusting my voice.

"Stay there." Abuela's voice, bereft of its usual warmth. "Cover your ears. Close your eyes. Whatever you do, don't make a sound."

"When I finally came out, everyone was gone." I took a deep breath, counting slowly to four in my head as I inhaled and repeating the count as I exhaled. "After that, I was on my own." I crossed my arms, the action more like a barrier than a display of confidence. "I've gotten used to it—it's safer, and the only person who gets hurt is me." *Most of the time.*

"Ah, I see." Josephine's hands were small enough that it took both of them to wrap around one of mine. "*Mijo,* we understand. Bandit, Tara, Caleb—all of us have lost people we care about." She sniffled, letting go of my hand to wipe her eyes. "None of us had the families we hoped and prayed for. We had to build them ourselves. When you decide it's worth it to trust us, we'll be here. Okay?"

I looked at the floor. "I guess so." *At least, it's worth thinking about.*

"Good." She stood up, pulling me with her. "Come on. Let's make lunch."

———

A FEW DAYS LATER, I huddled next to Deadeye in the tiny square of shade cast by an industrial air conditioning unit, squinting at the glare off a blindingly white rooftop. Relay 15 had been built at the edge of a cluster of buildings —once warehouses belonging to a shipping company. The long line of the interstate carved a line through the desert, shimmering in the heat as thunderheads built across the plains. Benny at St. Augustine's had tipped us off that the Blood Angels planned to take out the tower in order to secure a faster route from the Ridges to Tucson—a concept that absolutely no one was thrilled about. Bandit's jaw had been set as he gave his orders. "Regional Command says 'protect the towers,' so that's what we're going to do. They might not give a damn about this region, but I still do."

Deadeye slouched alongside me in the shade, her helmet

visor open and a tablet balanced on her thighs. On it, the reading from Relay 15 quietly pulsed and shifted; an early warning system for this stakeout mission. She pulled her helmet off, wiping her forehead with the edge of her sleeve before continuing the story she'd been telling. "—study anything I liked. That's how it worked then—if you got high enough scores on the entrance exams, they'd waive your tuition fees and all you'd have to pay was room and board."

"Sounds amazing." I paused writing to sip from my hydration pack, looking across the warehouses. Even with sunglasses on, the rooftop shimmered and danced in the brilliant sunlight. I felt bad for Bandit, lying on his stomach across the way in what *had* been a shady spot before the sun moved. He'd muttered something about having the perfect vantage point from where he was, so I didn't push things, but I could only imagine how hot he was getting. Returning to the story, I asked, "So, with your tuition paid, what did you study?"

Deadeye's smile went lopsided and sheepish. "Well, it was going to be art."

"Art?" I set down my pen to look quizzically at her. "But you're so good with mechanical things."

"I said it was *going* to be art." She sighed and looked out at the desert, where the road disappeared into heat waves. "My parents insisted it wasn't a good career option. They always got what they wanted in the end, so I didn't fight it." She ran a finger down the side of the tablet. "I ended up with a dual degree in computer science and mechanical engineering. It took an extra year, but it was worth it to be able to fix both software *and* hardware."

"I'm sorry you weren't able to study what you wanted." I gave her what I hoped was a supportive smile. "But your background *has* saved us every time something breaks."

Deadeye snorted. "Good old German engineering strikes again. Ach, why couldn't my people have been renowned artists instead?"

A thought struck me. "Well, maybe you can actually help me with something." Flipping pages in my notebook, I found my horrible Brute drawing and turned it to face her. "I *was* trying to sketch one of the Brutes, but Judge told me I needed to stick to stories."

Deadeye handed me the tablet, swapping it with the notebook. The corners of her mouth twitched as she looked at my sketch. "Alexi's a moron, but he's right about this one." She sighed and held out her hand. "Give me the pen."

I handed over the pen, switching to my recorder while we kept talking. After a few minutes, Deadeye turned the notebook back to me. "There, I fixed it."

I suppressed a shudder. She'd taken the basic shape of my drawing and fleshed out the deep-set predatory eyes, broad shoulders, squat neck, curving fangs, and hunched back of a Brute with enough realism that I immediately closed the book. "That's it, all right."

Deadeye put out a hand. "No, no. Wait. It needs something still."

I handed over the book once more, checking in with Bandit and Logan through comms while Deadeye worked furiously. "There," she repeated, flipping the notebook to show me. "Now I'm done."

I snorted back a laugh. She'd added a frilly tutu and bow to the monster. "I don't think the xenos would appreciate your treatment of their mindless muscle."

"Well, they're long gone." Deadeye raised a sardonic eyebrow. "If they wanted a say in things, they shouldn't have left."

"Look alive." Logan's voice came through comms. I couldn't see the Thunderbird, but I knew he was nearby and watching through his own systems. Knowing he was there, that we had a lifeline, helped settle my rush of nerves as he said, "Contact, coming toward you from the interstate. Looks like a truck."

Deadeye shoved the notebook at me and took the tablet. "Contact confirmed," she said after a moment. "It's the same type of vehicle from before."

"Any Brutes?" Judge asked, his voice drowsy enough that I wondered if he'd been napping.

I held my breath as Deadeye flicked through readings from the tower. Relief washed over my limbs as she said, "Not this time. Looks like it's just the one truck. Ten hostiles at the most?"

"Their vehicles are smaller than ours," Logan said. "I'd say eight."

"Be ready," Bandit said. "Things could happen fast."

Deadeye and I moved into position on the rooftop, Deadeye taking the safety off her rifle. As I knelt beside her, picking up the tablet and checking our surroundings, I couldn't help but notice she sighted awkwardly with her good eye. The question came before I could stop myself. "So, how did you lose the eye?"

Her smile was pure mischief. "Running with scissors."

Before I could express my exasperation, a dust cloud swirled as the truck came to a halt near the relay. Blood Angels piled out of their vehicle, their bearing suggesting they weren't expecting any resistance.

"Judge, give them a warning," Bandit ordered.

I could practically see the confusion in Judge's face from

across the rooftop. "Sir? Just a warning?"

"You heard me."

Judge growled. "Yes, sir." A cyan glow built over the building opposite us, and a flash of light streaked to hit the ground amidst the Blood Angels. Quick as a thought, one of them darted forward, a hand going up to sling a bright blue lightning bolt toward Judge's position. The others scattered, running from the truck toward the sensor tower with the sunlight glimmering off their weapons.

"Dammit." Bandit groaned. "I hoped they'd take the hint."

His rifle sounded across the rooftops, and an armored gang member fell with a distant cry. My jaw dropped as he downed another figure, then another. *His accuracy is incredible.*

"That won't do them much good," Deadeye commented softly to me as one of the distant figures ducked behind the truck. "Look."

Cyan lit the air. The Blood Angel tottered from behind the vehicle, their arms stiffly out in front of them.

"Braiiins," Judge intoned, the drone in his voice turning to a yelp as someone got a bead on his position. The blue light wreathing the Blood Angel disappeared, and they staggered and fell as Deadeye's rifle cracked off a shot. Judge yelped, the sound more frustrated than pained. "Oh, come on! I had him!"

"Stay focused, you idiot," Deadeye snapped.

"*Mijo*, how many more are there?" Bandit asked, his voice tense with concentration.

I crouched as Deadeye fired again. Flipping through overlays and pressing my thumb into my mic button, I said, "There's only a handful left. They're trying to retreat to the vehicle."

Bandit's acknowledgment was lost in another round of gunfire, and I frowned as a warning flashed red across the tablet screen. *Power surge?*

I didn't bother keying my mic, yelling over the gunfire, "Deadeye, is the tower okay?"

"Looks fine," she shouted, ducking as a shot whined overhead. "Why?"

"Something's wrong—it's saying there's an electrical—"

My words evaporated into an earsplitting crack as another bolt of cyan lightning streaked from the clear sky, arcing between buildings and sending a jolt through my chest. My mouth opened in a scream I couldn't hear, ears deafened as a tremor went through my body. It felt like hours before I could sit up and look over the edge of the roof, skin tingling with residual energy as my hearing returned. In between the ringing in my ears and a stream of curses from Judge, Deadeye yelled, "They're at the foot of the tower!"

Another lightning bolt crackled across the sky, and Bandit's rifle sounded again. Across from us, Judge appeared over the edge of the rooftop, his form enclosed in a glowing shield. His hands came together before turning outward to release glistening pinpoints of light.

My immediate hope turned sour as the lights shot over the heads of the Blood Angels to form a sparkling square of light on the pavement—the same pattern we used to mark landing zones for Thunderbirds. "What are you doing?" I yelled, forgetting that he couldn't hear me without my mic turned on.

Deadeye ducked to swap an empty magazine for a fresh one. "They're running!"

Uncertainty coiled in my stomach. "They had the upper

hand with that lightning; why are they running?"

She gave me a brief, satisfied smile, jerking her head toward the glowing square. "They think we called reinforcements."

I set aside the dead tablet as the last of the surviving gang members made it to the truck, which pulled away in a flurry of dust. Finally turning on my mic, I said, "They're getting away, sir. Are we pursuing?"

"Let them go," Bandit ordered. "I'm not interested in killing them all." His sigh of relief was audible even through comms. "I don't think they'll be back. Not for a while, anyway."

THE TOWER HAD SUFFERED a blown-out solenoid, which I easily replaced with a spare from my tool kit. Logan brought the Thunderbird all the way down into the landing zone Judge had marked out. He congratulated us as we approached. "They didn't slow down until they got out of range of the Thunderbird's sensors. It was a good idea, throwing down the landing zone, Alexi."

"Thanks." Judge sounded equal parts pleased and annoyed. "Not that I had any warning I was being sent into a Shattered duel."

"None of us knew they had a Shattered on their side, either," Bandit said as he climbed into the Thunderbird. "Now we know, and now we can be prepared."

"A lightning wielder," Deadeye commented as we got underway. "That's a new one. Shattered subtypes usually come in pairs, right?" she asked Judge.

He'd forsaken the jump seats to lie on the floor, clasping both hands behind his head. "You could say that. But it's usually more like one subtype shows up in different ways. And it takes a while to develop. Why?"

"Nothing." Deadeye set her helmet on the floor and ran her fingertips through her sweaty hair. I made a face as I did similarly, unsticking my hair from where the helmet had plastered it to my skull. "Just, I wonder what else that one is able to throw at us."

They got into an argument over Shattered abilities as Logan turned the Thunderbird for home. I tuned out the rest of the conversation, logging into the screens to check for myself that the relay was still up and working. By the time my worries had been allayed, we were descending onto the helipad at Base 36, and Tara's voice greeted us through comms.

"Heard you did well. Josephine's got a special dinner for you."

Cleaning up the Thunderbird and our gear took only a few minutes. I made sure to clasp Logan's hand in thanks for the quick exit. "It was such a relief, knowing you were only seconds away with our getaway car."

He shrugged, stuffing his hands in the pockets of his flight suit. "It was nice to be out in the field for once. I'm glad I can be of help, but it gets old only flying errands between here and Tucson."

"I can teach you how the screens work," I offered as we followed the others downstairs. "With fewer of us here, it's a good idea for someone else to know their eccentricities."

Logan smiled gratefully. "I'm game. It'd be nice to have something else I can do around here."

"I'm on screens tomorrow," I said. The door at the bottom of the stairs opened to let a swell of music into the stairwell. "If you're not busy, can we start then?"

"Sounds good." He went toward the living quarters while I stuck my head into the kitchen. A wave of delicious smells hit my senses—fresh tortillas and *birria*, by the looks of things. Caleb and Tara were dancing in the space between table and counter, all beaming smiles and joy-filled eyes as Josephine turned up the volume on our old sound system.

"Smells good in here," I said over the music, laughing as Caleb spun Tara into his arms.

"Good!" Josephine flicked a hand at me. "Go, go! Get showered and changed!"

I closed the door on the merriment and went to obey. As I stood under the shower, the sounds of music and laughter filtered through the walls as the others gathered to celebrate our victory. It sounded like home.

It was *a victory, even if we only scared them off.* I discarded my uniform in favor of gym shorts and a comfortable, soft T-shirt. *We deserve at least one moment to celebrate.*

As I went down the hall toward the celebratory dinner, an unexpected thought pulsed through my mind, cutting through the optimism brought on by success. *They lost this one, but they've* never *taken defeat on the nose.* Examples from my teenage years flickered through my head. *What will they do now, to ensure they never lose again?*

STAGE EIGHT

JOSEPHINE WAS A BETTER cook than I'd ever expected to find with the Defense Force. My cooking abilities were less impressive—my abuela hadn't had the chance to teach me much, and the fractured nature of my adolescence had seen me eating more nutrition bars instead of real meals than I liked remembering. When I wasn't on Fishbowl duty, I could often be found around the kitchen, learning from Josephine and Deadeye as they worked together to feed us.

Today, it was tacos. We'd gotten halfway through a bowl of *masa*, and the tortillas were piling up alongside our makeshift press when the hallway door slammed open.

"An emergency beacon went off at the Gila River chemical plant," Judge announced. "Something broke the fence."

I dropped a ball of dough back in the bowl and grabbed a towel. I hadn't gotten over my nerves after the victory at

Relay 15, and the quiet days since had only amplified my anxiety. "And we don't know what?"

"It's in the radius of what used to be Relay 23." Judge made a face. "All we know is that something got in there that shouldn't have."

The door banged behind me as I went to grab my gear. *I have a terrible feeling about this.*

WE ALMOST EMPTIED THE BASE. Deadeye swore a blue streak when Bandit ordered her to stay behind with Josephine and Logan, but reluctantly settled down to control comms from the Fishbowl. I buckled my seat belt and put on my helmet as we rolled out of the driveway, the weight of a rifle leaning against my leg reminding me how little this resembled the job I'd been trained to do.

Regional Command thinks you're good enough to stay, I reminded myself, looking across the cabin at Tara and Caleb. They were still wearing the armor from the night they'd arrived—while old, it was still in better condition than some of the stuff the rest of us had. The sight of the old EDF logo on their helmets was enough to remind me of how far everyone around me had come to reach this place. *These are your heroes, and they're letting you fight alongside them. The least you can do is try to live up to it.*

Our journey was tense, but short. The chemical plant several miles from the dry Gila River had been shut down fifteen years ago, but the government had seen it reopened once order was restored. It was mostly automated production now, guarded by a powerful electric fence and concrete barriers.

I frowned at the last reading we'd gotten; from a tower

whose radius overlapped the one belonging to the downed communications relay. "The last sensor report shows Brutes, sir."

Bandit's voice fuzzed through my helmet comms. "I wonder if that's all it is."

"I doubt it, sir," Tara said as she checked over her rifle. "Brutes are too stupid to target a place like that without some kind of other interference."

We swerved past something, the momentum making my seat belt pull tight against my armor.

Judge swore before saying, "There's a truck there. Looks like the same type we've seen before."

Tara reached down for her helmet. Caleb did likewise as he undid his seat belt and stood up, easily hanging on to the handles in the roof. His eyes sought me out from behind the narrow slit of his visor. "Ready, Gabriel?"

I logged off the screens and stood up, slinging my back-pack over my shoulders and picking up my rifle. *They think you're good enough to fight alongside them,* I reminded myself. *You don't have to be afraid.*

"Just stay close," Tara said, patting my shoulder as she joined Caleb. "You'll be fine."

I took a deep breath as the truck skidded to a stop. Caleb threw the hatch open, jumping from the truck and running toward the shipping containers on either side of what had once been the gate. Tara and I followed, and I dove behind a rock just outside of the gate, which had been ripped free from its hinges. A Brute corpse lay nearby, its wrinkled skin riddled with bullet holes. *Someone let it destroy the gate, then killed it.*

Before I had time to look anywhere else, Bandit said, "I don't know if they've seen us yet. They're probably inside."

"Be careful," Deadeye warned through comms. "If they're trying to sabotage production, things could be extremely volatile."

Caleb leaned around the edge of the container, gesturing toward the center of the facility. "The office and controls are that way, I think."

We edged past the broken gate, my ears straining for any sounds from the electric fence. I didn't hear anything, meaning it had most likely been disabled. *I'll have to fix that after we've dealt with everything else.* Beyond, the concrete walkway sloped down into a subterranean basin filled with tanks, snaking pipelines, and catwalks. Steam vented from the tops of several release valves, and I hoped it was indicative of business as usual and not a malfunction.

"Keep going," Bandit said. His armor made his broad-shouldered frame even bigger, and his visor caught the sunlight as he looked up at the steel framework between the biggest tanks. He pointed at a platform between two storage silos. "I'm getting up there so I can see better. Banshee"—Tara turned as he said her call sign—"with me. If you have to scorch anyone out, try not to hit anything that looks important." Their feet clattered briefly on the metal as they climbed out over the sunken work area, disappearing behind one of the tanks.

"Movement. Over there." Caleb's voice was level and calm as he pointed a gloved hand across the facility. I squinted through the conduits to see a few figures going back and forth from a shipping container to the truck Judge had mentioned.

"What are they taking?" I asked, shifting my feet to crouch behind a guardrail. I looked down to see a large white tank, rounded on the ends and displaying a four-colored placard. "Deadeye, the numbers on this tank are four-zero-zero, *O-X-Y*. The four's in the blue square."

"Chlorine," Deadeye responded promptly. I didn't stop to wonder why she knew this. "Compressed liquid or gas."

"I can see the label on one of the bags they're moving from here," Tara said through comms. "If it's in bags, it's probably powder or tablets. Water purification, maybe?"

"So, they're stealing, not sabotaging," Judge said. "Should we try to stop them?"

"Get to the control room," Bandit ordered. "We'll cover you from up here. Make sure everything's okay with the compressors. I don't want this place to blow up in our faces."

"Copy that," Caleb muttered. He led the way along the concrete walkway toward the control room; a metal box at the convergence of several catwalks over the sunken work area. "For the record, sir, I don't like this."

I thought Judge was about to say something snarky, when a snarling mass of muscle knocked him sideways to the concrete. I jumped backward as Caleb swung his shotgun up and fired twice, sending rounds right into the skull of the Brute. It snarled and went still, sliding away from Judge.

"What happened?" Bandit shouted.

"Brutes!" Caleb replied, as the echoes of the shotgun faded into the tangled metal. Shouts echoed across the compound in response, as the men near the truck ran for cover.

Some sixth sense made me turn to see an armored figure perched on a girder overhead. "Above us!" I yelled, dodging behind the corner of the control room.

Judge rolled to a crouch, sending a streak of blue light directly at the man far above us. He fell with a thin scream, and I winced at the sound of something hitting the ground below. Snarls filled the air, and my vision filled with flickers of movement as Brutes converged on the downed man.

His scream died out as the control room door crashed open, and the doorway filled with several armed men. Crimson bandanas around upper arms immediately proclaimed their allegiance, and any thought I'd had of trying to negotiate vanished as one unleashed a torrent of extremely hostile Spanish.

I'm not hiding from you this time.

I drew my handgun and fired, the rounds hitting one man in the chest and another in the upper arm. Judge's hand clamped on my shoulder and dragged me back as another gang member shoved past his wounded comrades to spray the area with bullets. We backed onto one of the catwalks as the Blood Angels dragged their wounded inside, howls from the Brutes below us piercing through my mind to my instincts.

Run. Run!

"Get back!" Caleb shouted.

The three of us scattered along the various catwalks, hiding behind whatever cover we could find as the Blood Angels kept shooting from the safety of the control room. Sighting down my rifle, I fired at one of the larger Brutes. It roared and reeled backward, predatory instinct in its eyes as it looked up. I stumbled backward to the next walkway as the Brute jumped toward us, catching the metal tube ladder and scaling it with more nimbleness than I had expected of a monster that size. As its feet hit the catwalk, it froze, cyan light pulsating around it. I looked over to see Judge, one hand outstretched as he slowly backed away.

"Don't shoot," he ordered. Danger lit his eyes as he said, "Watch this."

With stiff, puppet-like movements, the Brute turned and began lumbering toward the control room. Snarling, it grabbed the doorframe and ripped it away from the wall, taking the door with it and sending the whole configuration spinning down to the factory floor below. The Blood Angels froze inside the box-like room, one of them crouched over a still figure whose chest was soaked in blood. With a pang of regret, I remembered the placement of my earlier handgun shots.

Don't think about that now.

Judge pressed a button on the side of his helmet, and his voice floated across the air between the catwalk and the control room. "Run now, or I let the beast loose."

One of the men looked around in panic before swinging his gun up and unloading a burst of ammunition into the Brute. The monster swayed and fell, and I caught a flash of color as the gangsters pulled their wounded out of the control room. Judge collapsed to one knee, a hand going to his helmet.

"Judge!" I vaulted over the railing and jumped down to the walkway he'd been standing on, my rifle smacking painfully against my side as I landed. "Judge, you okay?" Somewhere above us, more gunfire sounded as Bandit and Tara focused their attacks against the men near the truck on the other side of the compound.

"I'm okay, Gabe, I just—duck!" Judge threw out a hand, a wall of force slamming me against a tank as one of the Blood Angels fired around the edge of the control room. The bullet pinged off the tank beside me, ricocheting down into the tangled conduits.

An ominous hiss filled the air as Caleb's voice came through comms. "They're retreating to the truck," he announced. "The control room's secure, but I can't tell what's supposed to be blinking and what's not."

"I'd say blinking is a bad sign," Tara answered. Glancing up at the vantage point she and Bandit had found, I glimpsed a flash of energy streaking toward the ground. A Brute howled in pain, and I wondered how many were lurking between the pieces of industrial equipment.

"Gabriel, go see what you can do," Bandit ordered. "Judge, keep pressing the Angels back."

My footsteps pounded against the metal stairs as I hurried to the control room. Caleb stepped aside to let me look at the control panel, keeping a watchful eye on the bloodstained ground below the walkways. I bit my lip. Amid the flashing warning lights, one stood out. "Coolant malfunction..." I looked over the rest of the warning lights with concern. "The compressors to keep the gas condensed are offline. The pressure's building up in the tanks, and the temperatures are rising."

"Can we fix the compressors?"

"I don't think so." A gunshot punctuated Judge's words. "I'm right above them, and there's coolant spilled all over the ground."

"If that stuff meets any organic compounds, it could explode," Deadeye said. I'd almost forgotten she was there. "You're out of time."

"Get to the truck," Bandit said. "We have to get clear of this place before it goes."

"What about the Angels?" Tara asked.

"Leave them."

I surveyed the control panel as the lights continued blinking. *There must be something I can do.*

Caleb's hand on my shoulder pulled me away. "Come on."

Reluctantly, I stepped back and picked up my rifle. Outside, Bandit and Tara came hurrying along one of the main walkways toward us, Judge backing up behind them. The angle of his helmet showed he was watching not only the Blood Angels, but the Brutes below. I barely had enough time to wonder why the monsters hadn't attacked us yet when there was a metallic screeching, tearing sound, followed by a bang as a tank at the far end of the compound ruptured. An eerie green-yellow fog filled the air, drifting toward us as the wind shifted.

"Run!" Caleb shouted.

I followed him along the catwalks to where the metal met concrete, bending over and clutching my knees as a wave of the gas washed over us. Coughing and sputtering, I staggered toward the ruined gate, my lungs feeling like they were burning from the inside out. My ears filled with coughs as the others experienced the same sensation. I staggered out of the gate, Caleb pulling me the last few feet. Once outside, he also doubled over in a fit of coughs.

Only Judge seemed unaffected. He pushed Tara out of the facility, propelling her toward the truck before running into the gas cloud. "Get to the truck!" A glittering wall of force burst from his hands, spreading to push away the impinging gas.

I took a breath of blessed fresh air, my lungs protesting every moment. Only then did I realize that the sound of coughing hadn't disappeared from comms. Beside me, Caleb straightened with a gasp, panic lacing his voice. "Bandit!"

"He's over here!" Judge yelled. His energy wall flared, then grew brighter, pushing the gas farther into the facility.

The chlorine swirled inside the shield, the clearing air revealing Bandit sprawled where the catwalks met the raised concrete walkway. Another burst of coughs came through our comms as he struggled to his feet.

Caleb and I both pushed past Judge toward Bandit, but our feet had barely touched concrete when howls erupted from the work floor below us. I could see at a glance that Judge's shield had pushed most of the gas down, into the nest of tanks and pipes. Several Brutes' forms could be seen, thrashing in agony. My heart stopped as one burst up and out, gas trailing from its shoulders and head as it lunged over the edge of the walkway and seized Bandit's leg in massive jaws.

Bandit screamed, a gut-wrenching sound that sent shudders through my stomach and froze my feet to the ground. Caleb sprinted past me, skidding to a halt as the Brute released its jaws and turned on him. The force of the shotgun blast, point-blank under its chin, sent it dancing crazily over the edge and back into the gas. Dashing over and wrapping my hand through the straps at the shoulders of Bandit's armor, I dug in my feet and dragged him toward the truck.

The ground shook under another explosion, and Tara yelled something in my ears that I couldn't make out as Caleb covered my retreat. The force wall expanded, shimmering in blue light to cover most of the facility under a glowing dome. More gas erupted against the inside of the shield, showing a weird green color against the blue of Judge's power.

"Get him to the truck," Judge gasped as I dragged Bandit past him. "I can't hold this forever."

"Copy." Caleb grabbed the other side of Bandit's armor,

and between the two of us, we were able to haul him over to the truck.

I looked down at Bandit's leg as Tara helped hoist him into the passenger cabin. His uniform pants were a tattered mess, each movement sending more blood trickling down his leg. He groaned as we lifted him to the med table, coughing into life with a painful grimace behind his faceplate. *"¿Qué sucedió?"*

"Shut up and breathe. Just breathe." Tara undid his helmet and pulled it free. Bandit had gone pale behind his tan, his eyes clamped shut in pain.

Caleb thumped Tara's shoulder. "Do what you can. I'm getting us out of here." He jumped out of the truck and commanded, "Gabriel, help her. Judge, get in the truck." His voice dipped a little. "Try to hold the shield as long as you can."

"I'll try." Judge's voice was strained as he backed up to me and clambered into the truck, the shield now encompassing the entire facility. "It's getting harder to keep it up."

"A few minutes. That's all I'm asking."

The truck started with a rumble, and I lurched forward to lock the bottom portion of the hatch shut. Bandit stirred on the med table, coughing fitfully as Tara rested her hand on his chest. I pulled the oxygen mask out of its compartment, sliding it around his face and asking Tara, "What else can I do?"

She nodded at the bite injury, the blood beginning to pool around Bandit's leg as the truck picked up speed. "Put pressure on that. I'm going to try to put him to sleep."

"Guys, what's going on?" Deadeye asked. Her voice shook with panic, and I could only imagine what she might have heard.

"A lot." I pulled a package of gauze from a compartment and pressed it into the wound on Bandit's thigh. Blood soaked through almost immediately as I said, "Bandit's hurt bad. The Blood Angels sabotaged the chemical plant, and the tanks started rupturing." My voice broke into coughing, throat still feeling like it was coated in broken glass. I cleared my throat a few painful times before explaining, "We all took hits from the chlorine gas, and Bandit got chomped by one of the Brutes."

A scuffling noise came through my ears, and suddenly Josephine's voice asked, "Bit how badly, and where?"

"Right thigh, and it's bad. I can't get the bleeding to stop."

"Hold on. I need to check something."

Deadeye's voice came back, asking Caleb questions about the circumstances of the sabotage. As he answered, I looked back at Judge, who'd remained standing by the hatch as we sped away from the chemical plant. His hand was tense and white-knuckled around his handhold, helmet rolling back and forth on the floor next to him. His cyan eyes glowed faintly, and beads of sweat were starting to show at his temples as our distance increased.

I interrupted Caleb's explanation, keeping my hands pressed into the blood-soaked gauze as I glanced at the facility. Under the shield, the poisonous green cloud was beginning to spill over the sides of the sunken area. "Are we far enough away to drop the shield?"

"I'm finally tracking your position again," Deadeye said. "Given the wind, I think it's safe."

Judge sighed with relief, and the shield winked out of existence. Almost immediately, a plume of flame erupted from the facility, dirty brown smoke rolling into the sky and mingling with the newly freed yellow-green cloud. A few seconds later, the sounds of the explosion reached my ears.

"Dammit," I whispered, tearing my eyes away from the scene to add another layer of gauze to Bandit's leg. "Judge, you good?"

There was silence from the back of the truck, and I looked up as Judge toppled to the floor. Tara flinched and swore. "Take care of him, Gabriel. I've got this." She swapped her hands with mine, pushing cyan light through her bloodied palms.

I scrubbed my hands against my pants before kneeling next to Judge and turning him over. His head flopped against my arm, a line of blood trailing from his nose. "He's out cold," I said, feeling under his armor for the pulse in his neck. It beat reassuringly against my fingers, steady and strong. "I don't think he's hurt, though."

"Burned himself out," Tara said from behind me, her voice distracted. "It's not the first time. He'll be all right after some rest. Deadeye, was Josephine checking on something?"

"She was—hold on, she's back."

The comms rustled again as I pulled Judge to lie on his side with his back against the wall. Josephine's words came fast and breathless as she demanded, "How's Carlos? Is the bleeding going down?"

"It's going down, but..." Tara's sharp intake of breath told me more about the situation than anything I'd seen. "It's still faster than it should be. I'm doing what I can, but it's not—"

"Copy that," Josephine interrupted. "I went and checked some of the later reports on the Brutes. There's something in their teeth that's an anticoagulant."

"Like snakes," I added under my breath, certain that no one would hear.

"Yes, like snakes." Something rustled across the microphone, and Josephine sniffed. "I checked the list of supplies on the truck; you don't have anything that'll reverse those effects, and I doubt your power can stop systemic hemorrhage. Get him here as fast as you can."

"Drive fast," Deadeye said, muffled in the background. "There's a storm coming."

STAGE NINE

Earth Defense Force Base 36
Gila River Valley
July 29

WE BARELY BEAT the oncoming storm, screeching into the bay as the first spatters of rain hit the dusty ground. The others were waiting, loading first Bandit, then Judge onto stretchers and rushing them into the medical bay. Deadeye took barely a look at Caleb, Tara, and I before confiscating our armor and ordering us off to the showers. The water stung at first, but afterward felt glorious on the exhausted muscles in my back and shoulders. Putting desert-dwelling scruples aside, I didn't get out of the shower until the water ran cool.

With damp hair and clean clothes, I joined the others outside the window of the infirmary. Tara paced back and forth, her wet hair loose and dripping on the collar of her dark grey shirt. Caleb leaned against the wall where it met the window, watching intently as Josephine—her sleeves pushed to her elbows and hair messily caught in a clip— stabbed a set of IV tubing into a bottle of milky white fluid. She hung it alongside several others on a hook over Bandit's bed, tracing the tubing first into a box on the wall, then into a catheter taped down on the inside of his arm.

"She said it was good I was able to slow the bleeding." Tara stopped pacing to join us at the window. "It gave her time to get the drips ready."

I nodded, looking over at Judge. Deadeye and Logan had put him in the bed alongside Bandit's. Only one bag hung from the hook over his head, and a monitor cuff wrapped his wrist below his IV site. Asleep, his expression was much less cocky than I'd ever seen when he was awake. "What about him?"

"He'll be fine." Caleb snorted. "He put too much juice into the shield. He's always had difficulty knowing his own limits."

After checking something on the IV set, Josephine marched over and yanked open the door. A stray curl had popped loose from her hair clip and bounced over her eye as she snapped, "I told you, there's nothing you can do right now! Go away, and let me work!"

I jumped as she slammed the door. "What's gotten into her?"

"She and Bandit have always been together," Caleb said. "I'm sure she doesn't mean to be unkind." He pushed away from the wall. "Let's get some food and let them be. We can't really do anything for them now, anyways." He looked down at Tara, whose jaw was set and eyes narrowed. "And you need to eat. We can't have both you *and* Alexi burned out."

As worried as I was, the suggestion was sound. We retreated to the kitchen, where Deadeye plunked us down at the table with bowls of noodles and sauce. I ate without really tasting the food, my worry fighting against exhaustion. Across the kitchen, Deadeye clattered pots and pans together, the sound filling the silence as we finished our food. Swallowing my last bite, I asked, "Who's watching the screens?"

"Logan," Deadeye said. "He's not you, but he's pretty good." She dumped a bowl into the pot of soapy water, saying, "He's got enough experience from the Thunderbird systems that he can let us know if anything happens that shouldn't. Not that we'll have a whole lot of warning, with the towers going dark."

Something in her tone made me look up. "Did another one get taken out?"

"Yeah, right after you started coming back; Relay 4, just on this side of the dunes. I didn't want to say anything until after you'd rested. It's not like we can do anything about it, anyway."

I pushed my bowl aside and dropped my head down on the table. Over my head, Tara asked, "Did you already report to the guys in Colorado?"

"Not yet." By Deadeye's tone, I knew exactly why not. With Bandit out of action, there was a chance we could *all* be recalled to the St. Augustine's base, leaving the solar fields and water stations unguarded. "But we'll need to. They know about the chem plant going offline, and they're already asking questions."

Caleb sighed. "I'll talk to them." His chair screeched against the floor as he stood up. "We have to tell them *some-*

thing, and we'll see if hearing it from me will be enough to calm them down for the time being."

As the door closed behind him, the two women started laughing. "He's going to hate this," Tara commented. "Mark my words, they're going to put him in command until Bandit's better."

"Him? Not Logan?" I asked. From what I remembered, pilots automatically had captain ranking, and Caleb was just a lieutenant.

"Trust me," Deadeye said. "It'll be Caleb, even if Logan does outrank him."

"Or Tara?" I looked at her. "Aren't you technically a captain?"

Both Deadeye and Tara cackled. "Me?" Tara wheezed. "Command? *Perish* the thought. No—" She wiped her eyes. "They're too smart for that. Trust me, it'll be Caleb."

"He's good at command, even if he hates it." Deadeye ran a wet cloth across the counter before slinging it into a bin marked "dirty" in the corner of the room. "Even back in the old days, Caleb did whatever he could to avoid that type of responsibility."

"Including volunteering for crazy dangerous missions and solo work," Tara said as she got up from the table. "That *never* came back to bite us."

"He ended up with the most days spent in sickbay out of all of us, and that's even with Alexi burning himself out every other mission," Deadeye laughed. "Command knows how he feels about being in charge, and I'm certain they'll take the opportunity to stick it to him." She flicked the lights off and eyed the clock. Between getting home and cleaning up, it was almost eight. "Bed? Cards? I feel like Josephine'll murder us if we go too close to the infirmary right now."

I wasn't really up to playing games, but I knew I'd only sit in worried solitude otherwise. As we passed the Fishbowl, Logan waved us inside. "They're going at it in there."

"Who are?"

As we stepped inside, it became clear who "they" was referring to. From inside the conference room, we could hear shouts—and it wasn't just the colonel's voice. With a conniving look, Deadeye opened the door a crack, all four of us clustering around the slim opening.

"They're working themselves up to kick us out of this entire region. I don't care what protocol says; they'll keep sending those things at us in greater and greater numbers." Caleb's voice held an edge of anger as he insisted, "We know they're trying to take control of Tucson, sir, but if we don't do something about their base in the Ridges, this problem is only going to get worse!"

"We're well aware of the situation, Lieutenant Fletcher." The colonel's voice was as dead and official as ever, the patronization in his tone sending my hands curling into fists. "We're working on restoring order in the Santa Cruz Valley first, then more resources can be put toward the Ridges. Trust us, we're working on it."

I peered around the edge of the door as Deadeye inched it open. Caleb's silvery eyes blazed with fury as he addressed the projection in the center of the table. "They're intent on removing us from this region, and they don't care how many deaths it'll take to do it. We're already flying blind, and the dead zones are growing by the day. 'Working on it' just won't cut it."

I thought a sigh came from the colonel, or maybe it was an aberration in the transmitter. "We sent a request for improved armor and helmets for your squad. Hopefully, it's enough to avoid any more casualties from incidents like this one. We'll let you know when they arrive." The tiny bit of personality vanished from the voice, and he concluded, "Thank you for your report, Lieutenant. Rest assured, we'll do all we can to ensure your and the rest of the squad's safety. Hold the line until further notice."

Caleb swore as the transmission cut out, before realizing how far open the door was. His face reddened as he saw us in the doorway.

"Nice mouth you've got, there," Tara said. Pushing the door all the way open, she went and leaned against his chest as he hugged her.

Looking at the rest of us over her head, Caleb asked, "How much did you hear?"

Deadeye kicked a chair out from under the table and crashed into it, pulling off her eyepatch and rubbing both eyes. "We heard enough. 'So sorry your commander got hurt and could've died; here, have a new toy to make up for it!'" She snorted and looked at Logan, her bad eye tracking wildly out of sync with her good one. "Bet you wish they'd moved you to St. Augustine's too, huh?"

The pilot shook his head, both hands in his pockets as he leaned on the door frame. I hadn't been sure how he'd like being stuck here, but he did a good job blending in. He'd learned the screens after only a few days of training, his humor matched the same dry sarcasm that the others spoke with, and he even got along with Judge. "You're outnumbered," he said, a calculating look in his light brown eyes. "And I can fly more when I'm stationed here. Besides"—he raised an eyebrow—"Josephine cooks a lot better than anyone else on the Force."

"Sure your family doesn't mind?" Caleb asked.

I looked up in surprise. *Does he have a family?*

Logan smiled distantly. "My wife and I talked about it. She and our daughters are safe for now, but they won't be if we can't take this gang down." The smile vanished, and his voice turned serious. "She knows this is the best way to end things quickly and keep everyone safe."

All of us nodded, the conversation abruptly shifting as Josephine walked into the Fishbowl. Her hair sprang out in curls around her face, and nervous energy charged her words. "Tara, are you here?"

"I'm here." Tara stood on tiptoes to plant a kiss on Caleb's cheek before brushing past Logan and I. "What's going on?"

"He's started bleeding again. I could use your help."

The words put an even greater damper on the already tension-filled evening. As the two women departed, Logan returned to the screens and Deadeye walked off, muttering about "at least one of us getting a good night's sleep."

Caleb shut the rest of the equipment down and turned to me. "Want to get some air?"

WE ENDED UP OUTSIDE. The storm had blown itself out a long while ago, leaving the air heavy with moisture. Flipping down the back hatch of the truck, we sat with our feet dangling over the side and looked out at the mountains far across the valley.

"Are you okay?" Caleb asked after a while. "You've handled everything pretty well so far, but I know it sneaks up on you."

And he would know that, too, I thought. Neither he nor

Tara was past their thirty-fifth birthday, but they would still remember a time "before."

"I joined the Force so I'd never have a reason to be scared again." I shivered, my stomach churning at the memory of the blood spurting out of the chest of the Blood Angel I'd killed. "I shot someone for the first time today, and it made me realize nothing is different." My hand closed into a fist, as if I could punch away the fear. "I'm still scared, just now I have a gun in my hand."

"Oh." Caleb shifted to face me. "That was the first time you've killed someone?"

I ducked my head. "The noise he made—I don't think I'll ever stop hearing it."

The motion-sensing floodlights clicked off, leaving us in darkness. Outside, the desert glowed under the light of a full moon. Finally, Caleb sighed and said, "That memory—it'll be there in your head each time, for a long time. But you'll get used to it." His expression—or as much as I could catch in the dim light—had softened with sympathy. "You have to remember it was him or you, *and* you're still alive to help others because of the quick action you took."

"Like what you said about Tara, the day we met," I remembered. A shiver ran up my spine as a Brute's howl echoed across the vast valley. "You said her healing helps make up for the lives she's taken."

"Something like that," Caleb agreed. "At least, it's how I'm able to stay sane after how long I've been fighting." He closed a fist, looking out at the desert. "No matter how bad it gets inside my head—no matter how many deaths I've racked up—I make up for it by saving as many other lives as I can." He smiled, and I glimpsed a bit of the strength that lay behind his eyes. "Most of the time, that means I watch Tara's back, so she can heal those who need her the most."

"She's incredible," I agreed, glad the conversation could take another direction. "What's it like, being married to someone that powerful?"

Caleb shrugged. "It doesn't really impact our relationship. We grew up in the same community in Appalachia, and got along great long before there was any hint of romance *or* Shattered powers. And it was a good thing, too." The corner of his mouth twitched. "Our families were proud of the old blood, and determined that we'd be the next generation to preserve it. I think they got more than they bargained for, when it turned out that the same blood is what made Tara Shatter as hard as she did."

"Fascinating..." I pulled my legs up to sit cross-legged, pulling my recorder out of my pocket and showing it to him. "Do you mind?"

He chuckled. "Josephine told me you collected stories. Go ahead, if you want. It's not like it's an interesting one, but..."

"It's a story no one else has," I said, my nerves driven away by how strongly I believed what I was saying. "If I don't collect them, they'll disappear forever."

Caleb nodded, a funny look in his grey eyes. "Do you want me to start over?"

"No," I answered, clicking the button to start recording. "Keep going. Does the old blood make people from Ap—" I paused on the unfamiliar name and tried it again. "—Appalachia stronger when they Shatter?"

"That's my guess. Tara had a sister who Shattered first, and she was just as powerful if not more." He waved away my questioning noise. "We never had a chance to find out for sure. She died only a few months after."

"I'm sorry." I meant it, too. Family was a rare enough commodity that anything breaking it was a reason for sympathy. "Is that what made Tara Shatter? Losing her?"

Caleb shook his head. "It was long after the xenos had taken over. I wasn't there when she Shattered, and I had no idea how being close with her would change *me* until much, much later." He shifted again, his eyes taking a faraway cast as he explained, "There was this one mission we went on. We were short on medical supplies, and the government had a supply depot in one of the cities. It wasn't legal, but by that point they were independent in name only. All of us knew the xenos were pulling the strings, and not always from the shadows." He rubbed the bridge of his nose with one finger. "We tried to stay out of the dampening fields, but it's hard to avoid when the place you're aiming for is right in the middle of one of them."

Caleb fell quiet, looking outside at the desert as an owl hooted. The thin scars on his face were silverish in the light reflected from outside. Having now seen the size of a Brute's claws up close, I knew they must've come from something else. *What happened to you?*

Finally, he said, "Sorry, I'm trying to think of how to describe it. You know how the fields felt, right?"

I nodded, making sure the recorder could pick up my words. "They dropped when I was little, but I remember being really sleepy as a kid." I was glad that was all I could remember, at least of *that* aspect of the xeno occupation.

"Shattereds had funny responses sometimes," Caleb explained. "Tara, especially. And at this particular facility, she was having a really hard time keeping things under control. She almost brought the building down on top of us when she lost her grip."

I winced. From the tiny bits I'd seen, I knew I didn't want to experience a Shattered losing control.

Caleb nodded. "You understand. So, the commander yelled at me to do something." He chuckled softly, leaning against the side of the truck with his arms crossed. "I think he meant, 'calm her down,' not 'boost her.' I still don't know how I did it initially, but now I've got enough experience amplifying her abilities that I can choose when it happens."

"Your eyes never turned," I pointed out.

"No," he agreed. "And I don't think they ever will. After that, they put me through the same tests they did with new Shattered recruits, just to see if—" His voice dipped, so little that if I hadn't been paying attention, I wouldn't have caught it. "If I'd had the same capabilities, we'd have known. As far as we know, I can only boost Tara; no one else."

He fell silent again. I didn't bother hiding the fact that the recorder was still on. Somehow, I didn't think he minded.

"It's not all battles and pain, you know," Caleb said. "The war has impacted most of our relationship, but I would've still loved her even without the conflict." A cool breeze washed across us, bringing with it the smells of damp earth, creosote, and—from somewhere far away—a hint of jasmine. "She's so energetic and outgoing. Growing up, she was always keeping up with the rest of the boys, even though she was smaller and scrawnier than the rest of us. Even without power, she could never sit on the sidelines if someone needed help. Neither could I—and it's what drew us together."

A rueful smile crossed his face. "I didn't want to come back. After how they treated Michael and the rest of us, I didn't want to give anyone on the Force the time of day. But she convinced me. Said that while we were safe and happy in our little desert paradise, we had to make sure others could enjoy the same happiness and safety." Caleb looked straight at me, the silver light from outside reflecting in his eyes. "When she put it like that, I couldn't say no. But then"—he grinned—"I've never been able to say no to her."

STAGE TEN

Earth Defense Force Base 36
Gila River Valley
July 29

BANDIT'S CONDITION GOT WORSE. According to Josephine, his blood was still refusing to clot like it was supposed to. That night, Logan and Caleb flew to the hospital in Phoenix to pick up a medication to rebuild the clotting factors the Brute's saliva had destroyed. Watching the Thunderbird disappear off our radar, I felt profoundly unsettled, as untethered as I'd been in the first surviving year by myself. *They'll be back. Don't worry.*

A noise from my elbow startled me, and I looked up in surprise as Deadeye set a cup of coffee next to my keyboard. Her face was creased with sleepiness around her eyepatch, she was wearing sweatpants, and her choppy dark-and-pink hair was definitely unbrushed.

"Why are you up?" I asked.

"I could say the same to you." She dragged a chair over

and sat back, sipping her own coffee. "Are you even supposed to be on screens duty tonight?"

"It's supposed to be Judge's night." I picked up my mug and looked into it with a sigh. We'd been out of fresh groceries for about a week, and somehow, I doubted that Caleb and Logan would have time to get any. Black coffee was okay, but I missed half-and-half. "But with him burned out, I figured I'd let him sleep instead."

"How nice of you." Deadeye put her pink-socked feet up on the edge of my desk. "Guess I'll stay up with you." She cast a crooked smile in my direction. "I can't sleep when anyone's out on a night mission. It was the same in the old days too."

I would've been fine, but it was nice to have company. We ended up talking most of the night, until the Thunderbird touched down on the roof. Going upstairs, I squinted against the early morning sunlight as Caleb jumped down from the aircraft. He handed me an insulated box. "Take that straight to Josephine. They said to keep it as cold as possible, but their refrigeration plant wasn't working and we didn't have any ice to put it in. She'll need to administer it immediately."

"Copy." I hurried down the stairs to the infirmary, pushing the door open with my shoulder.

Once inside, I stopped and smiled. Josephine had pulled a chair over to the side of Bandit's bed, and fallen asleep with her head pillowed on crossed arms. At some point during the night, he must've woken up and noticed her. One of his hands lay barely touching her elbow.

Going to the door, I closed it loudly enough to let Josephine wake up naturally. Her head popped up in a tumble of dark curls, and she pushed them out of her face before squinting at the clock. "They're back already?"

I set the carrier box down on the work table across the room. "The fridges broke, and they didn't have any ice packs to send with it. Caleb says they got it here as fast as they could, but it needs to be given now."

A very unladylike word slipped from Josephine's mouth as she stood up, pulling her hair into a ponytail. "I wish they'd given me a little more time. Whatever." She went and washed her hands in the corner sink, asking, "Can you open it for me?"

"Sure." I flicked my pocket knife out and cut the seals Regional had placed across the edges of the box. Inside, a trio of small glass vials sat nestled in crumpled paper, the rusty powder inside reminiscent of the chile-lime salt that came with fruit. The vials fit easily in my hand, and I brought them over to the compounding cabinet next to the sink.

Josephine had already put the rest of her supplies into the old piece of equipment, and was sliding her hands through the connected gloves. Unwrapping syringes and alcohol swabs, she craned her neck to look at Bandit as something started beeping. "Will you go turn that off?"

I looked back. "Um..."

"Push the button that says 'silence alarm.' It's fine."

I wandered over and searched the monitor panel for the silence button. As I found and pressed it, Bandit's eyelids flickered, and he turned his head. "*Mijo.*"

My eyes widened, and I sat down in Josephine's vacated chair. "You're awake?" I said in Spanish. "I thought—" I looked at Josephine, deep in concentration over in the corner.

"She took me off the sedative." Bandit winced and

added, "And the pain meds. I don't think we had much on hand. If I need it, Tara can put me to sleep."

"Right..." I looked down. "I'm sorry. If I'd been a little faster, or if I'd noticed, or—"

"Hey." Bandit's hand came down to rest on my wrist. "This couldn't have been avoided. I knew my helmet seal wasn't good, and I still dawdled after the tank ruptured. There's no one to blame but myself. Besides," he added, "Judge said you went back for me. That's the most I could ask of anyone."

"Anyone would've done the same."

I'd forgotten Caleb spoke Spanish. He came to stand at the end of the bed, arms crossed. For someone who'd been up the whole night, his eyes were still bright and his posture straight. I wondered how long he'd be able to keep up the pace he'd been setting. "Regional sends their regards."

Bandit snorted sarcastically. "Oh really? Is that all they sent?"

Caleb raised an eyebrow. "They sent some pretty sweet armor—chest pieces, back plates, inner jackets, helmets, comms, everything. Picked it up in Phoenix." He shrugged. "The helmets are even bio-compatible, not that we use bio interfaces anymore."

Bio interface?

I gave him a quizzical look, and he explained, "All of us from the original force have them." He nodded toward Bandit before tipping his own head sideways and pointing to a spot behind his right ear. Halfway hidden in his light brown hair, a piece of circuity could be seen embedded under his skin. "Between his fancy helmet and these, Michael was able to see through our eyes and hear through our ears on missions. It's how we kept comms in places without towers."

I nodded, still unsettled by Caleb's usage of their old commander's first name. I was about to ask more questions when Josephine came over, holding an IV bag filled with bright red fluid. "Ready?" she asked.

Bandit eyed the bag as she attached the tubing into the machine on the wall. "I guess." We resumed talking about the features of the new armor Regional had sent down, as the antivenom slowly drained into Bandit's bloodstream. About half an hour into the infusion, I noticed his jaw tighten.

Caleb noticed as well. His posture shifted from relaxed to tense as he asked, "You okay?"

"Fine." Bandit sucked in a sharp breath.

I looked up at the monitor over Bandit's head. "Um, Josephine? Is that supposed to..."

"Oh no." She dropped the notepad she'd been writing in and rushed over, stabbing a button on the screen and leaning over Bandit. "Carlos? Carlos!"

"Josie, what's happening?" Bandit blinked hard as the numbers began flashing red on the wall. One arm thrashed, jerky and uncoordinated. "Something's wrong!"

"Hang on to him!" Josephine yelled as she ran toward the cabinet where she kept our meager drug supply. "Someone call Tara!"

I grimly held on Bandit's arm, a blur of Spanish coming out of my mouth. "Hang on, it's going to be okay. You're not going to die from this, it's okay, it's okay." I bowed my head, willing the words to be true as Caleb yanked open the hallway door, yelling Tara's name.

Bandit's breathing became more rapid as his face grew

paler. His free hand grabbed the front of my shirt. *"Mijo? Don't let Josie—"*

His words trailed off, and he lapsed into unconsciousness, eyes flickering behind closed eyelids as Tara crashed through the door. "What happened?" she demanded.

"It's the medicine," I said, willing my voice to stay steady. I still sounded like a scared kid. "I think he's reacting to it."

"Damn right he is." Josephine hurried over with a syringe filled with clear fluid. Twisting it into the tubing snaking from Bandit's arm, she injected the contents while the rest of us held our breaths. "He got bit by a rattlesnake when he was a kid, and the body never reacts well to similar antivenom after the first time." She took a deep breath and unscrewed the syringe, swapping it out for another, larger one. "This was still worth that risk, to save his life. I just hope..."

"It's working, whatever you did," Tara said, brow furrowed as she planted both blue-glowing hands against Bandit's chest. She looked up at the monitor. "His pressure's going back up."

"Keep an eye on him." Josephine's boots clomped on the floor as she went to the med cabinet.

"I'm going to put him under, so you can do whatever you need to without him panicking." Tara moved her hands to either side of Bandit's head, blue light pulsing from between her fingers. Her voice went soft as she whispered under her breath, "Don't leave us now, El Bandito."

I pulled my chair over and sat down, trying to keep as quiet as possible. The numbers rose and fell on the panel behind Bandit's bed, matched by his breathing. Eventually, things calmed, and Josephine left after being bullied out by

Tara. As the door closed behind the doctor, Tara's cyan gaze turned on me. "You too."

"I'm fine!" I insisted. "I want to stay."

"No, you've been up all night watching the screens. So was Deadeye." She threw her hands in the air. "I don't know what's with everyone in this squad. None of you have an ounce of common sense or self-preservation."

I had to smother a laugh. She did have a point.

"Go to bed. Seriously." She stamped over to the door and gestured expansively through it. "If not for yourself, then do it for all of us. We can't keep fighting if we're dead on our feet from exhaustion."

I made for the door, Tara closing it behind me with a decisive slam. Once out in the hallway, the exhaustion hit like a ton of bricks. I dragged myself to my bedroom, going into the sleeping quarters as Judge was coming out. He waved cheerfully as I went past. "Thanks for taking the screens last night. Anything happen I should know about?"

I stopped with one hand on my door frame, words pouring out in a frustrated, stressed-out torrent. "I don't know what an INR is, but Bandit's skyrocketed during the night and he started bleeding again. Logan and Caleb had to fly up to Phoenix to get him some medicine. *Then* he reacted badly to it and almost died again." I glared at the ridiculous goose cartoon on Judge's shirt. "Nothing happened on the screens other than seeing another pack of Brutes. I'm going to bed."

I closed the door on his questions.

———

ALMOST A WEEK LATER, Judge's voice echoed around the

inside of a metal bowl as he menaced Tara with a spoon. "Join me, and together we can rule the galaxy!"

We were cleaning up from dinner, which for once had included all of us—thanks to Deadeye's ingenuity with a set of cables and a disused monitor, we could pipe in the feed from the console in the Fishbowl.

"I'll never join you. You're the reason my father is dead!" Tara's voice cracked with laughter as she staggered against the cabinets, dropping a butter knife as Judge laughed maniacally.

"You pathetic fool!" His Russian accent became more pronounced. "You think your father's dead?"

I leaned toward Logan as we finished drying the plates. "What are they even talking about?"

He immediately dropped the plate into the sink. "Hey, stop!"

The activity a few feet away stopped as Tara slid to the floor laughing.

"What?" Judge demanded, moving the bowl so his voice took on more of an echo. "How dare you interrupt a Sith Lord?"

"Just hold on a sec. Gabe." Logan looked at me. "You don't know what they're doing?"

I shook my head. "Should I?"

"I can't believe it," Deadeye commented, leaning on the outside edge of the counter. She looked at Bandit, still sitting next to Josephine at the table after being told firmly to stay put. Almost a week after his injury, he was starting to move around a bit better—if a little slowly after the blood loss and subsequent allergic reaction to the medicine that had stopped it. "Kid's never heard of Star Wars."

"Star Wars? Is that what this is supposed to be?" One of

Judge's T-shirts had pictures from the films, but the exposure hadn't made me any wiser. As far as I knew, it was about aliens and battles, and we'd already had enough of those to last several lifetimes.

Tara grinned. "You're saying he doesn't know—"

"Shut up," Judge hissed, giving her a hand up. "I guess we know what we're doing tonight."

"I don't know... I never liked those movies."

Everyone turned to Bandit with outraged faces. The innocence on his face was just a little too perfect, and the outrage shifted to laughter.

"You had us going for a moment, there." Deadeye came over to the table and helped him up.

He hopped a bit on his good leg before leaning on her shoulder. "It wasn't entirely a joke; I couldn't stand the newest ones."

Caleb flapped a hand in Bandit's direction as he finished putting away silverware. "We don't talk about those."

An hour, two bowls of popcorn, and a lot of Germanic utterances later, we were set up in the living area outside the corridor of bedrooms. Our old speakers gave off tinny sounds, and the picture on the TV was not nearly the quality I'd come to expect from modern technology, but the enthusiasm of everyone else was enough that I could ignore these deficits. I flicked my eyes over to the screens, angled somewhat away from us and set to flash red upon the detection of abnormalities.

If there could be any night without an interruption, let it be tonight, I prayed as the opening titles began scrolling across the screen, accompanied by blaring trumpets and orchestral music. Around me, the rest of the squad had settled in; Caleb's arm around Tara's shoulders, Deadeye sprawled on her stomach with her elbows under her chin, Josephine sitting attentively close to Bandit, Logan in a chair with half an eye on the screens, and Judge taking up most of a couch all on his own. This—all of it—was brand new to me, but they seemed as comfortable as if they'd done it all their lives.

And maybe they have. Maybe this is what families did, before.

I'd barely settled into the unfolding story when a new scene dawned, a sandy landscape stretching as far as the camera could see. I sat upright. "Hey, that's the dunes!"

Judge and Deadeye exchanged mischievous looks, and Judge shook his head. "Nah."

"Well, where does it take place, then?" I pointed. "I *know* those mountains."

"I don't know, Gabriel." Caleb winked. "This all takes place in a galaxy far away."

WATCHING movies became a standing activity most evenings. In between the quiet evenings, we lived in fear of the red-flashing screens. The continuous fighting was exhausting, yet with the exhaustion came the relief that our new equipment and armor were working. For me personally, it also came with the reassurance that my combat skills weren't nearly as bad as I'd feared.

With Bandit still mending, Caleb was forced to take the controls, both in our interactions with Regional Command and the continually escalating encounters with the Blood Angels. There were several mornings when I walked past his desk, only to find him slumped dejectedly over a stack of forms needing to be signed, or angrily deleting lines in a report normally filed by Bandit or Josephine. Finally, after Deadeye almost got flattened by a gigantic Brute while trying to repair a damaged water pump, Caleb had had enough. One afternoon, he disappeared into the conference room and stayed there for several hours. The others noticed his absence, and it was no surprise to me that everyone "just happened" to be in the Fishbowl when he finally emerged.

I spun around from monitoring the screens as Deadeye asked, "What's going on?"

Caleb looked at all of us—some busy, others pretending halfheartedly, and Judge not even trying. "How long have you been lurking out here?"

I didn't bother trying to lie. I'd been on duty, anyway, and had a right to be in the room. "An hour or so," I said as I turned to clear a message from the screens. "They've been taking bets on how many people you were cussing out."

"Three." Caleb shoved a pile of stuff out of the way and sat on the corner of Deadeye's desk. "And it was only a little bit." He glared at Judge as the Shattered sighed and passed a wrapped candy bar to Tara. "Knock it off, you two. We have bigger things to worry about."

Tara unwrapped the candy, speaking around a bite. "Like what?"

"I was talking with some of the guys over at St. Augustine's." Caleb cast a quick glance at the conference room before going over and shutting the door. "Not everyone there is happy about how Command's handling the whole Blood Angel situation. Some of them also noticed a shift in the Angels' targets, just like we did. When I explained our hunch about the cloning facility, it was like the lights went on in their heads."

Bandit frowned, shifting his bad leg. "They notice anything odd out there?"

Caleb nodded as he resumed his seat. "Chemicals going missing—acids and bases, salts. Stuff like what we used for shocking pools back in the day."

Logan raised an eyebrow over the edge of his tablet. The back was covered in pink and purple stickers, left over from a trip he'd taken to visit his family in Tucson. "Even if they *didn't* discover a cloning facility, the Angels could do a lot of damage depending on what they got their hands on. Some of that acid is no joke. Anything else missing?"

"Sugar, also." Caleb shrugged. "All kinds—honey, agave, corn syrup. Not that anyone had a whole lot lying around, but what was there is completely gone. Um..." His grey eyes searched the ceiling tiles before he added, "Even stuff like flour and *masa*."

"Cell generation needs fuel..." Josephine mused, clasping small hands under her chin and looking thoughtfully into the middle distance. "They could be using it to feed their tanks. What's St. Augustine's think about it?"

"They agreed that just trying to fight the Blood Angels off isn't enough. While we're chasing our tails, they're laughing at us." Caleb slid from the desk and walked over to me. "We're going to set up an operation to try to take out as many of them as we can. Gabriel, can you pull the map back to show the whole region?"

I turned to the screens and did what he'd asked. As the others gathered around us, Caleb tapped two fingers against a spot in the center. "There's a railyard up here, where supply trains go through from Phoenix to Tucson and beyond."

Deadeye scowled at the screen, the creases around her eyepatch suggesting she was getting another of her headaches. "Have we been losing supplies off those trains?"

Caleb nodded. "Regional seemed happy to let it be, and focus their manpower on trying to stop thefts in the cities, but they're getting frustrated too."

"It's about time," Tara scoffed.

"One of the St. Augustine's guys has connections with the Blood Angels. He's going to let it slip that some valuable stuff is being moved up to the Picacho industrial yards, and that for a certain price he'll make sure it stops *before* its destination."

I put an elbow on my desk and cupped my hand around my chin. The railyard was adjacent to a number of manufacturing plants, so it would make sense for cars journeying that direction to carry valuable parts and materials. *It's a good target, no mistake.* I looked up at Caleb. "What's to stop them from raiding the factories?"

"You could intercept them farther down the line," Logan suggested behind me. "Come up with a reason for the train to stop earlier."

"That's exactly what we'll do," Caleb agreed. His fingers traced a line down from the volatile chemical and steel plants to an overgrown forested area. "The train will stop at these warehouses. A team from St. Augustine's will be in the warehouses, and we'll be in the trees. Between the two of us, they'll have nowhere to run."

"Regional approved this?" Bandit asked, concern deepening his voice.

"We presented them with a plan that they could just rubber-stamp. They're smart enough not to argue with something we handed them." Caleb's eyes took on a steely glint. "They also told us to capture if we can, but we have the green light for lethal force if it's needed."

STAGE ELEVEN

BANDIT WAS NOT PLEASED. Upon testing, his leg still gave out at inopportune times, and Josephine forbade him from doing anything more than monitoring the screens. He lurked unhappily in the background as we prepared for the sting operation, checking our gear and offering advice when asked.

The day of the mission, we assembled in the bay long before daybreak. Outside, the air was already warm—the monsoons growing fewer and farther apart as August straggled to a close. Bandit limped over from exchanging words with Judge to check my armor and helmet. The new equipment had once been pristine and polished, but we'd taken Logan's suggestion and painted the rigid pieces to match the desert surrounding us. Deadeye had taken things a step further and stenciled an eagle clutching a snake on the sides of our helmets—homage to the original Defense Force unit that Bandit had once been part of.

Overhead, air whooshed and dust flew past the bay doors as Logan took off, headed to Tucson to rendezvous with the crews tapped for our backup. *I hope we won't need them.*

"Nervous?" Bandit asked me in Spanish.

I tugged a strap tighter around my midsection. "I'd be stupid not to be nervous. There are a lot of things that could go wrong with this, but the risks don't outweigh the benefits."

"That's a very logical way to think of it." Bandit picked up my helmet and rotated it, checking the inside display. Setting it down, he put a hand on my shoulder. "But it's still okay to be nervous."

Before I could think any better of it, I hugged him. He stiffened at first, then brought his arms around me in a brief embrace. "Easy, *mijo*. It's going to be okay."

The others almost certainly noticed us hugging, but were kind enough not to comment. As we clambered into the truck and slammed the doors, the overhead lights cast everyone's faces with a peculiar glow. After how many deployments we'd been on, there was no reason for this to feel any different from any other day. Yet somehow, I felt lost being on a mission this important without Bandit at my back.

I fitted my headset over my ears, sinking into monitoring the screens and listening to the others chatter. As we rolled away from the base, everyone fell into discussing how awake —or not—they were.

"You sure picked a good day to use up the last of the coffee, Reneé," Judge accused Deadeye from the driver's seat.

She was sitting across the truck from me, cradling a thermos like it was her firstborn child. The look on her face was pure mischief as she took a sip, exaggerating the slurp so it came through comms. "I was up first. You snooze, you lose."

"You could've shared. I had to go talk to Josephine and get a caffeine patch instead." From the whining in Judge's voice, I assumed this was a low blow. I rubbed my temples under my headset. The lack of caffeine was starting to get to me as well, but I'd sooner chew off my own arm than make Judge feel like he had an ally.

"She just doesn't like you." Tara crossed one leg over the other, managing to give the appearance of lounging even in her tiny jump seat. "She shared with me."

"What about him?" I asked over Judge's muffled exclamations, gesturing at Caleb. Like me, he had his screens pulled down and was talking into his mic. No sound came to my ears, so I assumed he was communicating with the St. Augustine's team. "I know he doesn't drink coffee, but what's keeping him going?"

Tara's face took on a shuttered expression. "He's solar powered."

"Yep," Deadeye confirmed, with another slurp from her thermos. "He doesn't need anything but adrenaline."

I cast a glance over at Caleb. The immediate responses from the two women told me there was a story there. I wasn't sure if it was something I'd want to hear, though. From some things the others had let slip, it was apparent that Caleb and Tara's path to this point had been filled with rocks cradl hard moments. With a sigh, I returned my attention to the surveillance screens. With dawn rapidly approaching, we needed to get into range of the remaining comms towers before the desert woke up.

PICACHO PEAK LOOMED in the distance, a jagged tooth poking into the dusty sky. We'd hidden the truck in one of the abandoned warehouses to the northeast of the train tracks, alongside the pair of vehicles brought by the St. Augustine's squad. From the introductions and conversations, I gathered that the rest of my team were held in awe by the others. They were veterans, after all, and most of the newcomers had only joined the EDF after it was rolled into the government eight years ago.

An hour of planning, strategizing, and syncing of communications later, we hiked into the pecan grove south of the rail line. The irrigation channels between struggling trees were choked with vegetation, which had crisped up nicely with the waning of the monsoon. Tara and Deadeye sang under their breath until Caleb shushed them, and from there the only sounds were the tramping of our feet, crackling of undergrowth, and occasional commentary through our helmets as the St. Augustine's teams got into position.

Once we'd gotten a few hundred feet from the rail line, Caleb stopped. Switching our channel to a local-only one, he gestured at a tumbledown shack that had once housed a water pump and controls. "Here's a good spot. Find cover and get comfortable." He turned his head toward the warehouses, visible over a low berm covered in dead grass and tumbleweeds. "Make sure you have a good line of sight on the area of engagement."

Judge's Russian accent came through the comms as sardonic as ever. "I didn't think anyone was proposing today.

Aren't you already married?" He ducked one of the punches Caleb threw, sidestepped another, and bounced away on his toes. "I'm kidding, I'm kidding." He stepped behind a tree, the sparse foliage casting dappled shadows across his helmet and armor. "There. Will this do?"

"Stand still, and you'll be fine," I said, throwing a pecan shell at him.

"Assuming you can stand still," Tara said. She hunkered down behind the irrigation pipes jutting from the ground. "And shut up. No one wants you clogging their comms."

I knelt behind the shack, pulling out a tablet computer and syncing it with the truck's surveillance. Luckily, the towers this far east hadn't been tampered with, and I was able to pull data from their sensors directly into my computer. The warehouses showed up as glowing white boxes surrounded by desert, the figures of the St. Augustine's team members appearing as purple silhouetted blobs. Caleb crouched alongside me, asking, "Are they all set across there?"

I nodded, moving the display so he could see it. "Want me to overlay it into our helmets?"

"Sure."

I toggled the feed into the displays in our helmets. Now, the other Defense Force members' locations could be seen past the berm; hiding in the warehouses and railcars, and out of visual range down the tracks in each direction.

"It sure is nice to have a proper communications setup," I commented, meaning every word. This, now. *This* was what I was trained to do.

Caleb clapped my shoulder approvingly. "Thanks for monitoring it for us." He pressed a button on the underside of his helmet, and his voice vanished from our local channel.

I settled into my position, reminding myself to stay alert as the sun rose higher into the sky.

Time passed slowly. Most of the others eventually found spots in the shade of the few trees that still had healthy leaves, lying down and trusting to their comms for early warning of intruders. The late-August heat, though nowhere as brutal as early summer temperatures, made any time in the sun miserable. I kept to the shade as much as I could as the sun moved from east to west. *Still no train.* I shivered despite the heat, and checked my screen again. *And no sign of the Blood Angels.*

Deadeye moved over to crouch next to me, squinting through her faceplate at the tablet I held out. "What's taking so long?"

"Logan radioed in a while ago. The train had mechanical problems leaving the station. It's delayed." *And I hope that's all it is.*

My attention quickly shifted, as a blip appeared on the screen in my hands. A moment later, everyone else saw it as the signal bounced into their helmets. A convoy of trucks sped toward the railyard, two breaking off to the north and south while three more approached the warehouses. Just as they did, the faint hooting of a train horn sounded somewhere in the distance.

"Look alive," Caleb ordered through comms. "Gabriel, does anything look weird?"

"Nothing at the moment," I said, checking again to be sure. "Each truck has four people in it, so twelve here and four each north and south." I frowned inside my helmet. "I don't see any Brutes. Could be it was too difficult to wrangle them this far east."

"We'll have to hope that's what it is," Caleb said. As he

did, the train came into view, metal screeching on metal as it slowed to a crawl and stopped before the warehouses. One of the cars had a bright blue graffiti tag splashed across the side —the symbol the Blood Angels had been told marked the valuable cargo. I could see in my helmet as the other EDF troopers stirred, readying weapons and moving to good vantage points.

I stuffed the surveillance tablet into my backpack, slinging the pack to my shoulders and tightening the straps. Around me, the others underwent similar preparations; Judge tightened his helmet and gave a thumbs-up, Tara adjusted a setting on the monitor built into her forearm armor, and Deadeye pulled her rifle free from the strap around her shoulder.

Whoever was controlling the train was a master. The decoy car stopped just in front of the warehouse where we'd hidden the trucks. The three vehicles we'd been watching skidded to a halt amid clouds of dust, and as the haze drifted away, Caleb snapped, "Now!"

We broke cover, pelting down the slope and vaulting over the irrigation ditch at the foot of the berm. As our heads crested the rise, the truck doors slammed open, and armed figures poured out of the passenger compartments—many more than the twelve I had predicted. I skidded behind a utility box at the top of the berm and flopped to my stomach, readying my rifle as dust swirled in the wake of the Blood Angels' deployment.

"What happened to only four in each truck?" Deadeye spat.

"Gabriel, what's going on?" Caleb asked, his tone deadly calm.

I blinked hard at my helmet display. The heat signatures

definitely belonged to the gang members, but there were far more than twelve figures around the railcars. "I—I don't know. They've doubled in numbers." A spray of bullets sent up a line of dust on the berm, and I ducked farther behind the utility box. Elsewhere, gunshots sounded as the crews to the north and south of us engaged the two outlying vehicles. "It's like the sensors couldn't even see them."

Deadeye cursed as a pair of black-helmeted men began hauling open the door of the blue-painted railcar. "Well, seen or not, they're here now and not happy to see us." Her rifle coughed, and one of the Blood Angels went down. The other dodged to the opposite side of the railcar, and more gunshots sounded from the St. Augustine's squad in the warehouse.

Rounds ricocheted between trucks and train cars as the rest of the squad pressed forward, driving the Blood Angels toward the train. One managed to make it to the decoy car, but a well-aimed blast of energy from Judge sent them toppling backward to the ground. Purple silhouettes fought red-orange blobs all along the railroad line, gunshots muffled by my helmet. I turned my head, keeping track of the others as Caleb and Deadeye advanced to the foot of one of the now-abandoned trucks.

Caleb was out of breath, but his voice remained crisp as he ordered, "That group there; see if you can take them alive. I don't want to kill unless we have to."

"Copy that."

I looked back as Tara set her rifle to the side. Kneeling behind the berm, she whipped off her gloves and planted both hands on the dusty ground. The earth trembled as rivulets of blue light flowed down her arms and into the earth, a spiderweb of fissures appearing around her kneeling form. Another shot whizzed past my head as the tremor passed through the earth and into the area below us, where several of the Blood Angels had taken cover between the railcars. In a split second, blue energy erupted from the ground beneath them, knocking all four off their feet and sending them ungracefully to the dirt.

Judge sprinted to come alongside Caleb and Deadeye, holding up a hand and yelling, "**Sleep!**"

The Blood Angels slumped over as a shower of blue sparkles fell on their heads. The shaking in the earth subsided, Tara's voice tense as she commented, "Do you always have to broadcast what you're doing? This isn't D&D, you know."

"Maybe not, but it's still fun. Try it sometime." Judge knelt over one of the downed gang members, sliding a set of tough plastic cuffs out of a cargo pocket and snapping them around their wrists. He rolled another of the Blood Angels over and lurched back, a curse splitting our comms. "Phantom, this one's a Shattered!"

"What?" Caleb's head snapped around. "Conscious?"

Judge's smirk was practically audible as his confidence returned. "Nah, she's asleep. I think it's the one who was throwing lightning at us a few weeks ago."

"I'm sure Regional will be interested in hearing about that," Tara said as she joined me atop the berm. "Gabe, is that all of them?"

I shook my head. "There's another group that made it into the boxcar next to the decoy." I peered around the battlefield. "The other team's working on restraining another four over on their side, and to the south there're a couple running this way. If you get to the end of the decoy car, you might be able to—hang on." My voice jumped up an octave. "Guys, look at the end of the train."

Helmeted heads snapped toward the direction I'd indicated, as the running forms of the Blood Angels disappeared from our displays.

"What the hell?"

"They're gone!"

"They're not gone." A shotgun blast, muffled through Caleb's microphone, punctuated his words. "The scanners are lying. Everyone, move in on that location!"

Deadeye finished cuffing the downed Blood Angels as Tara and I slid down the berm, running toward where a road crossed the tracks on a concrete bridge. Judge mimicked our movements, his helmet swiveling as he hopped over rails to draw near the train cars. I risked a quick backward look to see the rest of the St. Augustine's team converging on the boxcar where the remaining Blood Angels had taken refuge.

Judge reached the spot where the Blood Angels had disappeared from our scanner vision, ducking into the space between two boxcars. "I don't see anything; they must've gone aro—" He leapt back with a yell, a Brute slamming against the shield he threw up.

My heartbeat pounded in my ears as we scattered to the sides, Tara and I scrambling up the embankment leading to the road. We'd only gotten a few steps up the slope when a brilliant flash of light lanced across my vision. My ears filled with screams as both Tara and Judge collapsed, clutching their helmets and crumpling to the ground. From the higher vantage point, I saw Caleb also reel backward a pace, before recovering and pumping several rounds into the Brutes now spilling from the train cars under the bridge. A knot of dread twisted in my stomach.

It's been a trap all along. They knew we were here.

My breath caught as Tara started sliding down the embankment. Catching a hand on her armor, I rolled her to her back and dragged her to a level spot farther down the slope. Shots came from below, and I pulled my rifle free to sight and fire at the few Blood Angels I could see among the train cars. One fell, another was yanked down by a Brute that had broken off from the pack, and a third slammed a glowing fist into the side of the boxcar. Blue light erupted from inside, and I gasped as the implication hit me.

"There's another enemy Shattered down there!"

"No kidding," Deadeye gasped. "And here I thought they only had one on their side. Get Tara into cover, you idiot, before you both get killed!"

Jarred into movement, I hauled Tara into the shelter of a concrete barrier below the overpass. Her head lolled back against the barrier as I propped her up, eyes open—and glowing from within. A chill ran through my stomach as I scanned the battlefield. Judge was also glowing as he lay in the open at the foot of a boxcar. Just as I was about to say something, another person in desert-colored armor jumped over the junction between railcars, pulling Judge to safety as a pair of Brutes converged on them. A spurt of bullets and unearthly howling later, and both of the monsters lay dead on the tracks.

On the other side of the cars, the forms of the first St. Augustine's squad could now be seen engaging the few remaining Blood Angels hand-to-hand. Brutes milled back and forth between the cars and the walls of the overpass, snarling and attacking anything humanoid. I stayed behind the barrier, taking shots where I could be sure not to hit anyone friendly.

Tara stirred and grabbed my arm. "What's going on?"

"Enemy Shattered," Deadeye shouted, a howl from a Brute cutting across her words, echoing through comms *and* the surrounding air. "Another one. Glad you're back up. We need you!"

Tara winced behind her faceplate, scrambling to her feet and surveying the battle. Her hands described a similar motion to one I'd seen her use in training, bolts of energy shooting from each fingertip to strike eight Brutes between the eyes. They howled and dropped stone dead, and Tara staggered back a pace as another massive one wheeled in our direction.

The enormity of the situation struck as I emptied the last few rounds from my magazine into the Brute, my rifle clicking uselessly as it stormed toward us. "Tara, run!" I screamed.

We managed to get out from behind the barrier as the Brute jumped over it, the overhand sweep of its arm catching Tara across the back. Her surprised scream ripped through my heart as she pitched forward, the Brute's claws scraping her armor. Quick as a thought, she caught her balance, spinning to project a shield into its face.

The tiny glimpse of hope I'd had vanished as the monster smashed through the glowing wall. Its claws caught under Tara's helmet, ripping it off and knocking her backward as I struggled to free my handgun. *No, this can't be happening!*

Tara's head smacked against the ground, a gasp escaping her as she locked eyes with me. Terror filled my veins, mixed with longing for something—or someone—as the Brute roared and raised its claws for another blow.

Do something, you coward, do something!

I threw out a hand as the Brute's claws came down. "TARA!"

My arm shook as something both warm and freezing poured down it. A hum built in the air and a shimmering blue bubble formed around Tara, milliseconds before the Brute smashed into it. A shockwave ran through my bones, shaking me to my core. The beast dropped with a coughing snarl as one of the St. Augustine's troopers took it down from the top of the overpass. The last thing I remembered was the dusty ground rising up to meet me, strangely soft and somehow tinged with cyan.

"Gabriel?"

———

I WOKE up in the medical bay, Tara lying on the cot next to me. Caleb looked up from a tablet as Josephine came in. "I thought you might be awake." She bustled over and checked a wall display, then a device on my wrist. "How do you feel?"

"I'm fine, I think." I put a hand to my head, wondering if I'd told the truth. Something felt *weird*, like things had been pushed or pulled inside my brain. "Is Tara okay?"

"She's fine." Caleb set the tablet down on Tara's bed, the faint wrinkles around his eyes more pronounced and his voice tired. "She needs to sleep; she hasn't burned out like this in years."

"What happened?"

"That's what I'd like to ask *you*." Caleb turned to face me, planting his elbows on his knees. "Do you know what you did?"

I shook my head, the funny feeling lingering even as the drowsiness wore off. "It was cold, and—and hot!" I struggled to my elbows as the memories came back. "It stopped the—" I looked in shock at the device on my wrist. "I'm one of *them?*"

"Tara was in danger, and you did the only thing you could think of. Or not think of." Josephine slid a finger along the wall display, dancing lines jittering up and down as she scrolled through the readings. "You Shattered, *mijo.*"

STAGE TWELVE

JOSEPHINE INSISTED I spend the night in the medical bay, just to be sure everything was okay. That night, long after she'd fallen asleep in a little alcove off to the side, I stayed awake, blinking at the ceiling and trying to process. Finally, I pulled my notebook over from the side table where Caleb had set my things, flipping it to a blank page and clicking open my pen.

I'd been writing for a while, pouring every broken, jagged edge from inside my mind onto the paper, when Tara stirred and rolled over. Pushing herself to one elbow, she looked around the dimly lit room in confusion. "What happened?"

"You're awake." The words came out hushed and relieved. "Are you all right?" I set my pen and notebook down.

"I—I think so." She rubbed her eyes as she sat up. "Whew, it's been a loooong time since that's happened. I guess I can't really tease Alexi about it anymore." Her posture stiffened as she looked at me properly. "Gabriel." Her voice went soft. "Your eyes."

I sucked in a harsh breath, one hand going to my face. Swinging my legs out of bed, I scrambled over to the sink where Josephine scrubbed her hands before working in the compounding hood. My legs wobbled, and I clamped a hand on either side of the sink to stay upright.

"No."

A stranger's face looked back at me; a version of myself I barely recognized. Same dark curly hair. Same bone structure. Same bronzed skin.

Cyan eyes.

Shocked, I looked away, taking deep breaths as my stomach churned. Somehow, I *felt* Tara stand and cross the room, and wasn't surprised when she put a hand on my back.

"You Shattered." It wasn't a question.

I looked up to see Tara's face reflected alongside mine, her eyes shining the same luminescent blue-green. "I'm not going to be able to hide this. Everyone will know."

"And they'll never look at you the same again." Tara turned me away from the mirror and helped me to my bed. "You'll get used to it. How do you feel?"

I took inventory as I sat down. "Physically, I think I'm fine. Mentally..." I bent my head, the feeling of being pushed and pulled still lingering. "It feels like my head's been rearranged."

"I'm not surprised." The mattress shifted as Tara sat next to me. "Do you want to talk about it?"

WE TALKED ALL the way into the early morning hours, until Josephine woke up and ordered us back to sleep. By the time I woke up again the next morning, I was less scared and a little more settled. Still, it was a surprise to lift my head from washing my face, only to see uncannily bright eyes staring at me. Once showered and dressed, I stayed near my bed in the medical bay, flipping through pages of the notes I'd taken while Tara explained things the night before.

"*Mijo*," Josephine murmured, coming in from outside. She picked up the monitor cuff I'd removed from my wrist during the night, and set it on a shelf above my bed with a sigh. "Logan just got back from Tucson and we're all eating breakfast. You should come."

I shook my head. "I'm fine. I'm not even hungry."

"They all asked where you were."

"It's fine, really." I turned a page with more force than I'd planned, my hand smacking against the opposite side of the notebook. "I just want to be by myself."

"Okay," she said, reluctance clear in her voice. "If you really think that's best, I'll let you be."

The door closed behind her with a subtle click, and I returned to my absent-minded study. I'd finished going through the messy pages of notes once and was starting on them again when the door slammed open. Assuming it was Josephine, I opened my mouth to snap at her when someone yanked me over backward. I yelped and fell off the bed, landing hard amid a tangle of blankets.

"Someone said you were brooding in here," Judge said in my ear as he trapped my head in the crook of his elbow.

"Get off!" I choked, slapping his arm and squirming around to jab him in the ribs.

With a snicker, he released me, offering a hand up. "Don't be so upset. It's not the end of the world."

"It's easy for you to say," I muttered, glaring at him. Not only was his T-shirt a cheerful blue color, but the design was a stupid monster eating a cookie. "Didn't you Shatter when you were, like, eight?"

"Fourteen." Judge raised an eyebrow. "And my aunt and uncle thought I was possessed." He slung an arm around my shoulders and pulled me toward the hallway. "Sitting in here and moping isn't going to make it go away, so you might as well come be with the rest of us."

I scowled, but I knew he was right. Groceries were low again, but Deadeye had managed to make pancakes. I was beginning to think she could take the contents of a bare fridge and still make something delicious. The air in the kitchen was filled with the smells of warm batter and sugar, and the sounds of banter across the table were more soothing than anything I could have imagined. As I accepted a plate from Deadeye, and a bowl of prickly pear syrup from Logan, I briefly forgot how different things were.

It wasn't until after the meal was over that anyone said anything. Bandit limped over to the big chalkboard on the wall, examining our daily chore list and divvying out the various tasks as everyone cleared their plates. "Deadeye, you're mopping today."

"Sure." Deadeye flicked a piece of pink-streaked hair out of her face. "It's not like I've done it three days in a row or anything."

Bandit raised an eyebrow. "You wanted to scrub toilets?"

"Mopping's fine."

"Right." He made a mark alongside the list on the chalkboard. "I'll do the toilets."

Josephine pursed her lips. "Your leg—"

"It's fine. I need to move, or I'll go crazy." He put his initials alongside the word "bathrooms." "Logan, you and Caleb decide who's taking the Fishbowl and who's taking the bay and the Thunderbird."

The two men eyed each other, their similar builds and haircuts making them look like siblings for a second. Finally, Caleb sighed. "I'll take the Fishbowl. I have to draft a 'full report' for Regional Command about yesterday."

"I don't envy you," Logan said. His empty plate was pushed to the side, and he was working on a calculation for something. He shoved Judge away as the Shattered's elbow landed a little too close to his sheets of math. "When I was standing by with the reserves, they were all talking about how Command was just waiting for the plan to fail." He emphatically underlined a sequence before giving Caleb a matter-of-fact look. "Better make that report sound as good as you can."

"I mean, we *did* still capture a bunch of them," Deadeye groused. "That's gotta be worth something."

Tara dropped her plate into the sink as I ran hot water over the dishes. "What are you going to tell them about Gabriel?"

I stopped halfway through scrubbing the syrup bowl as everyone looked at me. Caleb frowned and leaned against the edge of the counter. "If they find out he Shattered, they'll probably reassign him to training."

Training.

The word sent a shiver up my spine just at the thought. The EDF training base was in the vast wastelands farther north, where the wind went right through your clothes. I was born and raised in the desert—the cold up north had been the worst thing I could imagine.

"That's true—"

"That's *ridiculous*," Tara insisted, talking over Bandit. "There's no reason for him to leave when Alexi and I are here. What better training could those idiots give him?"

"Tara, I didn't say I agreed. I just think they're likely to order it if they find out," Bandit said, shifting his weight from his bad leg to his good one. "For right now, let's see if we can phrase the report to leave out what happened to Gabriel."

"I can make it sound like someone else cast the shield over Tara," Caleb said slowly. "But a lot of the St. Augustine's guys saw what happened. Not to mention that if someone tips off the Blood Angels, we'll have more than one party interested in knowing about a brand-new Shattered."

The scrub brush slipped from my fingers and into the dishwater. I looked over at Tara, frightened at the feeling of my own life twisting free from my control.

"We won't let anything like that happen," Bandit said, reassuring both me and the rest of the squad. He slapped the counter decisively. "Tara, Alexi, consider yourselves off chores and Fishbowl duty until further notice." He nodded toward me as Judge pumped a fist in the air. "You too. If we can prove to Regional that you're receiving training here, maybe they'll let you stay once they *do* find out what happened."

"Yes, sir." I fumbled for the scrub brush. "Starting when?"

"Starting now, idiot." Judge plucked the brush out of my hand and tossed it back into the soapy water. "Let's go. Leave this to the ungifted losers."

I dried my hands as Deadeye commented, "At least we

don't have to spend half the day asleep after we come back from a mission."

"Ignore him," Josephine told her, linking arms and pulling her away. "He's just happy."

Happy? I looked at Judge, who was practically bouncing as he grabbed a handful of rags from under the sink. *I don't understand him. How can he be happy about this?*

LOGAN HAD OPENED the bay door, and morning sunlight streamed into the space as Judge tightened the strap of his monitor cuff around his wrist. I narrowed my eyes at the device on my own wrist, something both he and Tara had reassured me would track the ebb and spike of my power. Data brought more understanding, they'd said, and for that reason I'd agreed. *I have to understand this power if I'm going to be able to use it.*

Judge wadded a rag into a ball. "Catch."

The fabric flapped against my hands as I caught it, worn-out fibers straggling out of the material. "Okay. Now what?"

"Tie it around your eyes."

"What?"

"Just do it."

With a sigh, I shut my eyes and tied the fabric tightly around the back of my head. "Ready, I guess."

Something knocked me backward off my feet, and the air left my lungs with a whoosh as I hit the concrete. I stumbled to my feet and pulled up the blindfold. "What was that for?"

"Ah, ah, ah." Judge motioned with his finger. "Blindfold down. I'm going to do it again, and I need you to try to block it."

"How?"

Judge sighed. "Picture a bubble around yourself, and push it toward me—or toward where you think the attack is coming from. Ready?"

I ground my teeth and slid the blindfold over my eyes. *This is ridiculous.* "Ready."

I hadn't expected anything different the second time, and I wasn't surprised to find myself hitting the ground again. The pattern repeated, both Judge and Tara explaining the concept in different ways with no success until hours had passed. The farthest I got—or so they told me; I couldn't see a single thing from behind the blindfold—was a shield that lasted for a split second before dissolving. Finally, I yanked the blindfold off and threw it down. "This isn't working," I spat. "There has to be a way to do this without me breaking all my ribs from you throwing me around."

Judge ran a frustrated hand through his bleached hair. "I know! This was the only way I could learn, okay?"

I grabbed my water bottle. "I'm done." Anger bubbled to the surface, and I snapped, "I didn't want this in the first place, and it's obvious that I can't do anything like what the two of you can do."

"Gabe—" Tara began to say.

"Forget it!" Ripping the monitor off my wrist, I threw it onto the ground and kept walking into the desert. Eventually, I stopped under a gnarled mesquite tree. The craggy bark left scrapes across my knuckles and a deep ache growing in my arm as I slammed a fist against the trunk. *I need to get all this out of my head.* Patting my pockets, I realized I'd left my recorder in my other set of pants.

"Great. Just great." I slouched against the tree, watching the birds in the undergrowth until my mind cleared. The helpless feeling from the moment I Shattered hadn't gone away, and once the frustration and anger had faded, it returned in full force. Sinking down against the trunk, I leaned my back against the rough bark and rested my head in my hands.

I'm one of them now. One of them, and—I opened my eyes and stared up at the sky—*I'm still as scared as I was before.*

NO ONE SAID anything about the disastrous training session at dinner. If I had to guess, I'd say Tara had warned the others to leave off the topic for a while. We watched another movie from Judge's collection that night; a ridiculous comedy about an intelligence agent turning on his superiors and leading them on a merry dance between continents. The antagonist was similar enough to one of the Regional Command lieutenant colonels that I couldn't help but laugh, and it was possible to forget how *wrong* things were until bedtime.

Setting my things down on the bedside table after saying goodnight to the others, I changed out of my uniform and into gym shorts. Even with summer winding down, temperatures inside the base were warm enough that sleeping with a shirt on left me waking up sweaty in the middle of the night. Sitting cross-legged on my bed, I closed my eyes and took a few deep breaths, measuring them with four counts in and four counts out.

With my eyes closed and everything quiet, it was almost like I could hear what everyone around the base was up to. With a smile catching at the corner of my mouth, I let my imagination run free, picturing each of my friends in turn.

Logan talked to his wife and daughters tonight. I'd

covered the Fishbowl just for the excuse of being in the room while he'd been on the radio. He'd had to raise his voice in order to be heard over the squealing of two little girls, and his face had stayed cheerful even after cutting off the transmission. *He's sleeping now, and he'll probably sleep well after hearing from them.*

Bandit's in the Fishbowl tonight. I sighed, thinking of the chair that sat in front of the screens. Judge and I normally fought over who would get the chance to sit in Deadeye's chair when we were on screens duty, instead of the official— but less comfortable—desk chair. *I hope his leg'll be okay.*

Josephine's asleep; Caleb and Tara, too.

The images snapped into my mind as if I'd taken a photo —Josephine curled under a brightly colored blanket covered with embroidered butterflies, Caleb asleep with his arm around Tara. I snorted back a laugh at the mental image of Deadeye rummaging around in her corner of the Fishbowl, looking for something and upset that she couldn't find it. Shaking the pictures from my head, I reached for the light switch.

Everyone else is going to sleep. I should, too. I yawned even as the thought came. Pushing my worries aside, I lay down and tried to relax. Sleep claimed me even before I'd had the chance to worry that it might not.

My head pounded with pain, sending me awake with a stab of confusion. I was certain someone had yelled my name, but the room remained quiet and dark. Groping for my watch on the bedside table, I muttered, "It's only five o'clock, who—Aagghhh!"

I clutched my forehead and gritted my teeth through another wave of pain. Dropping my watch, I tumbled out of bed and into the hallway, the cooler air outside bringing clarity to my sleep-befuddled mind. *Where's this coming from?*

In the darkness, it was even easier to keep track of everyone in the base. I didn't stop to wonder how I knew where everyone was as I padded down the hall. *Deadeye's asleep, Caleb's taken over the Fishbowl, Bandit's asleep, Logan's asleep, Tara—*

Another jolt of anger and fear wracked my mind, and I stumbled into the wall. This time, I knew who it was. *Tara.* Sliding down the wall to sit on the floor, I tried to breathe normally. *What is this? What's going on?*

As the wave subsided, I staggered to my feet and down the hall, opening the door to her and Caleb's room. "Tara?"

A rustle came from the bedroom, and a muffled whimper. More pain washed over me, mixed with overwhelming loss. The edges of the furniture stood starkly against the walls in a wash of cyan light. Throwing caution to the wind, I pushed open the bedroom door as the light emitting from Tara flared.

Uh-oh. I stumbled to the bedside and grabbed her arm. "Tara, wake up!"

She screamed, sending a shockwave through my bones. A scene flashed into my mind—*a blond-haired man with cyan eyes, the Defense Force insignia emblazoned on his shoulders; Josephine, her face concerned and becoming panicked; blue energy shooting out into a vortex, spiraling up toward the ceiling before splashing against a glittering shield.*

Loss.

Grief.

Anger.

Helplessness.

"Tara, please!" I shook her shoulder. "Please wake up!"

Loss grief pain anger helplessness loss grief anger loss anger loss anger—

I closed my eyes, reaching as hard as I could with every bit of my concentration toward the source of the emotions overwhelming my mind. Cyan light streaked across my vision, and I yelled, "Tara, WAKE UP!"

The torrent of images stopped as she gasped awake, screaming, "Not again!"

I jumped as the door slammed against the wall and the room flooded with the light from a flashlight in Bandit's hand. "What's going on?" he yelled.

"I don't know!" The words burst out of me before I had time to think. "I don't know what I'm doing! Something woke me up, and now I'm here, and *what was that?*" Tears dripped down my face, and I slid to my knees alongside the bed. My shoulders shook as I cried, "I didn't want this! I didn't want *any* of this!"

Silence fell for a long moment, then the bedframe creaked as Tara came to crouch next to me. Bandit knelt on the other side, the flashlight falling to cast a cone of light across my knees. Their arms wrapped around me, her bent head and his broad shoulders creating a space in which I felt safe enough—finally—to let the walls fall.

"I'm sorry," I sobbed, panic and anger driven into helplessness. "I'm trying so hard, but everyone expects me to be some kind of superhuman. I don't know why any of this is happening, and now I'm stuck with this power that I can't even use! I hate all of this!" I broke into tears again, pulling my knees to my chest and crying until my eyes burned.

The others only settled around me, drawing the circle tighter against the darkness outside the room. Eventually, my sobs turned to shaky breaths, then died out altogether. "Sorry," I muttered, my embarrassment turning to confusion. "You're not angry?"

"Angry?" Bandit asked with a hushed voice. "Why would we be angry with you?"

"Well, I just—" I lowered my head. "I just—"

"You don't think all of us had those thoughts at one point?" Tara shifted to sit with her arm around my shoulders. "Wondering how we ended up where we did, and hating every moment of it?"

"No one expects you to live up to our legacies. Most of us wish they didn't exist in the first place," Bandit added.

The light clicked on in the living room, casting Bandit's face into shadow. "You're not going to drive us off," Caleb said from the doorway. I swallowed hard against the lump in my throat as he said, "This is home for us now, and it wouldn't be the same without you."

I'd thought I was done crying, but their words sent more tears to my eyes. *I didn't think anyone would actually want me.* Wiping my face with the back of my hand, I asked, "What about what just happened? I couldn't do anything about that—whatever that was."

"Yeah, what *did* happen?" Bandit asked, looking over at Tara.

Tara sighed. "Just a nightmare."

"It was awful." I shuddered and wrapped my arms around my knees. "What—what was I seeing? Who was that person?"

All three of them looked at me sharply, Tara most of all. "What did you see?"

I explained as well as I could, starting with how I'd been able to tell who was asleep or awake before I went to bed.

When I described the blond man I'd seen in Tara's nightmare, Bandit stopped me.

"Sounds like Michael." He shifted with a grunt to sit with his back against the opposite wall. "Tara, you were dreaming something that actually happened?"

Tara squirmed against the bed. "It was that day when Alexi contained an overload."

I think Josephine told me about this. I looked up at Caleb. "Something happened to you, didn't it?"

"I was escorting an engineer from a safe house to a place where the Thunderbird could pick us up, and we bumped into a xeno patrol." His face tightened, and he tugged the cuff of his shirt farther down his wrist. "The engineer got away. I didn't."

"And when Michael told me about it, I lost control," Tara said. "If Alexi hadn't been there, the whole roof would've probably caved in." She looked straight at me. "You saw all that?"

I nodded, certain now. "It was like I *was* you."

"You were both glowing when I came in," Bandit said. "That part was weird."

"I couldn't tell you how it happened." I shivered despite myself. Whatever happened from now on, I promised myself, I was going to start wearing a shirt to bed. This was much more vulnerability than I'd *ever* planned on.

"I don't expect you to know how. Right now, your power only works on instinct." Tara pursed her lips. "But what you said about being able to feel where all of us were is something we can work with. We'll have to see about that in the morning."

"About that..." Caleb said. "It's almost five thirty. It *is* morning."

"To you, maybe," she said sourly. "I think there's still time for a nap."

"I'll let you sleep." I stood up, my knees aching from how tightly I'd been holding them. "Sorry, again."

"Hold on," Bandit said, awkwardly getting to his feet. Shaking off a helping hand from Caleb, he wrapped me in a tight hug. I wasn't exactly short, but he towered over me—affection, guidance, responsibility, and care knitted into every fiber of his being. Even with me being shirtless and vulnerable, it felt safe. Comforting, even. I had to close my eyes against another rush of tears as Bandit began, "Gabriel, I—"

"It's okay." I slipped out of his arms and cleared my throat. "Thanks, all of you." I looked over at Tara, hope stirring somewhere deep inside. "We'll see if I can get a handle on this thing."

STAGE THIRTEEN

Earth Defense Force Base 36
Gila River Valley
August 28

I SLOUCHED ONTO THE CONCRETE. "I don't think I can do this."

"Try it again," Tara said. "What did you do in the moment?"

My temples ached from being compressed by the blindfold, and I wiped sweat off my forehead only for more to instantly form. "I can't remember."

"Did you see anything when things changed?"

"Blue." I took a drink from my water bottle, the tepid water not nearly as refreshing after sitting in the heat for hours. "Just blue light, like everything else with this *stupid* power." I capped the water bottle with a sigh. "I can't replicate it. It was instinct."

"Okay, well, let's try something different," Tara suggested. She paced to the center of the basketball court and sat down, pointing at the concrete in front of her. "Have a seat."

The concrete floor felt dusty against my fingertips as I first knelt, then sat, feeling utterly lost and alone. *I have to be able to learn. If I can't learn from them, someone will find out and they'll send me away.*

"This is the difficulty we have when people Shatter," Tara explained. "Because every single person breaks in a unique way, their power is expressed differently. We have to work around it." She looked up at Judge as he slouched over and sat a few feet away, his dejected posture matching how I was feeling. "Alexi's forte *is* shields, and keeping things out or in. When I first Shattered, I could only destroy things, but over time I've learned to mend them."

I nodded. "Like how you sealed the blood vessels in Bandit's leg."

"Right." She shifted to sit cross-legged. "All of us are able to do some universal things, like a shield or an energy bolt. But a lot of our abilities are unique to the person."

I snorted. "Why didn't we do this from the start? This is *way* more helpful than tossing me on the floor a bunch."

"Sorry," Judge remarked. Somehow, I didn't think he actually was sorry. "Being thrown around was the only way I was able to learn. You should've seen what our trainers did to *us*."

"He's not you, and we're not them," Tara admonished. "He doesn't have to learn the hard way just because you and I had to." She handed me the blindfold again. "Let's try something, all right?"

With a cautious look at Judge, I accepted the blindfold and wound it around my eyes once more. Tara's voice came as if from far away. "Okay, now take a deep breath and focus only on my voice." As I obeyed, she asked, "What's the last thing you remember about the moment before you Shattered?"

I struggled to remember. Strangely enough, the blindfold did help. "Th-the Brute ripped off your helmet, and you were in danger."

"Okay, that's what *happened*. What did you *feel*?"

I frowned under the blindfold. "Scared—no, terrified." I thought harder, trying to picture the exact moment the energy had surged down my arm. "I wished I could've said goodbye to—wait a second!" I sat bolt upright and ripped off the blindfold. "That wasn't me, that was *you*!"

"That's right." Tara knelt in front of me, putting a finger on the space right between her cyan eyes. "Right as you Shattered, you tapped into my emotions."

"Really?" Judge's tone, for once, wasn't laced with sarcasm. "You mean, just like—"

She waved him off. "Not exactly." Tara returned her focus to me, cyan eyes sharp and attentive. "Last night, you knew where all of us were, without hearing or seeing us?"

"I guess so, yeah... It was like seeing through the screens." I rubbed my forehead, the dull ache of a tension headache building behind my eyes. "I thought I was imagining it, but..."

Tara pulled me to my feet. "I want you to put the blindfold back on and start walking—slowly—toward the other end of the building. Think of it like walking through a dark room, and try to use the same type of senses. When you know where we are, stop and point."

"Okay." I let her wrap the blindfold around my eyes and took a deep breath. *It's just like the screens.* With that image in my head, I took a step forward, then another.

All of a sudden, it was like I'd added the sensor overlay to my mental image of the practice court. There was Logan, walking toward the kitchen. Tara was over there, by the compressor box. And Judge... I spun in a careful circle. There he was, by the basketball hoop. *You're not taking me off guard anymore, buddy.*

I took another few steps into the practice court before breaking into a sprint, launching myself at Judge before he had time to react. His shout of laughter sounded in my head as well as my ears as we both tumbled to the floor. A flurry of elbows and fists later, my blindfold had been pushed up from one eye and Judge's T-shirt yanked out of his waistband as we tussled across the floor.

"Okay, okay!" Tara laughed as she emerged from behind the compressor. "Break it up!"

Breathless and laughing, I let go of Judge and pulled the blindfold all the way off my head. "I think it worked."

He was laughing as well, punching my shoulder one last time before agreeing, "I'll say. I guess training just got more fun."

Two hours later, Caleb's voice came from the direction of the truck as we were finishing a round of blindfolded hide-and-seek. "Are we in kindergarten?"

I dropped the blindfold, turning to look up at him as he climbed to his usual spot on the compressor. "I don't know. Are we?"

"Don't laugh too hard; this is the best way to get him used to what his powers feel like," Tara said as she and Judge emerged from their hiding spot and came to join us.

"Oh yeah?" Caleb jumped down from the compressor. "Try it with me."

"Okay!" I pulled the blindfold back over my eyes. "No cheating from the peanut gallery."

"We'll stay right here," Tara promised. "I want to see this."

Someone new. Let's find him. "Let me know when," I said. I turned toward the basketball court, measuring my breathing. In and out, four counts each.

"Okay," Tara said from behind me. I could still feel her and Judge, now sitting shoulder to shoulder on the compressor box like birds on a power line. "He's ready."

The humming of the equipment filled my ears as I tried to focus on Caleb.

Nothing.

I frowned around the blindfold. "He's still here, right?"

"He's here," Tara answered. "Remember, it's like your scanner system."

Right, I reminded myself. *And you can't always find what you're looking for by looking at a satellite image, or in infrared. Try something different.* I squinched my eyes tighter, streaks of blue beginning against my closed eyelids. *Something different.*

Then, a split-second flash of something—fear so potent it froze my blood. *Someone's in trouble!* I didn't bother saying anything, my feet moving on their own.

"Whoa!"

I smacked into Caleb, who'd been standing mere yards away. He stumbled back but caught me. "Hold on, hold on! It was just me."

I yanked the blindfold off and shoved him back in the same motion. "That was *you?*" I stared at him, worried now. "Are you okay?"

He nodded. "Don't worry; it was on purpose."

"You're sure?"

He raised an eyebrow, silver eyes glittering. "Do I need to do it again?"

A shiver crawled up my spine. "Please don't." I held out an arm and showed him the goosebumps that had arisen despite the heat. "That was *terrifying*."

"But you were able to target it?" Caleb asked, tugging his long sleeves farther down his wrists as Tara and Judge slid from the compressor.

I nodded, still unsure if I was glad or upset that whatever he'd done had worked.

"That was incredible," Judge said, his usual cocky attitude dampened with admiration. "I knew you'd gotten good at masking, but he couldn't see you *at all* until you let it drop."

My jaw went slack, and I had to remind myself not to swear. "You knew he could do that?" *You knew all that was inside his head?*

Tara shrugged, much more nonchalant than I'd expected. "He got good at keeping Alexi out, so I figured he'd be equally as good at keeping you out." She checked her watch and said, "I think that's enough for one morning. Let's go see if Josephine wants help with lunch."

The others agreed, trailing off after her toward the door to the kitchen. I cleaned up the water bottles and other junk we'd scattered around the practice court, my head still spinning after the insane morning. Try as I might, I couldn't shake the nauseating feeling of terror that had surged out of Caleb.

Maybe he can turn it on or off, and maybe it was deliberately played up. I shivered again, my own memories rebounding through my head with the sounds of breaking glass and screaming. *But even if it was, no one knows what fear like that is like without having lived through something horrible.*

BETWEEN PRACTICE SESSIONS and occasional missions out of the base, I slept like a log most nights over the next two weeks. As tension-filled as our first practice sessions were, even I had to admit they were producing results.

My saving grace was the rest of the squad's response to my new abilities. "Empathic, huh?" Deadeye asked. "Fantastic. Now I know exactly who to talk to when I'm grumpy for no good reason."

"We think there'll be more than that," Tara said. "He has to get comfortable with what we're working with for now."

"Plays a good game of hide-and-seek, I'll say that much," Judge laughed, digging into his dinner. "Any requests for movie night tonight?"

That night, our animated movie was interrupted by a fuel tank near a water station exploding. Everyone else suited up and responded, exchanged volleys with a few Blood Angels, narrowly dodged a Brute pack, and returned in bad spirits. I hated being left behind, but someone had to keep an eye on the screens, and Logan had taken the Thunderbird to Phoenix for maintenance.

"If they keep doing this, there won't be a region left to lord it over," Deadeye groused over cups of hot chocolate once everyone got back. The others had gone to bed, leaving Josephine, Deadeye, and myself to debrief—or in Deadeye's case, vent. "I'm not even sure if they care at this point. They'd be happy to see the entire EDF dead."

"And for all Regional says they're on our side, I'm not seeing anything from *them* beyond this constant 'hold the line' nonsense." I cast a suspicious eye at the screens in the corner of the kitchen, warning them to behave. Training that morning had been hard, and I wanted to sleep through the night without any issues. "It's like nobody cares about this region beyond it being something to fight over." I flicked the end of my pen, making it spin on the cover of my notebook. "Don't tell Tara or Judge, but I wish I had their type of power. This empathy thing isn't any good against an enemy who has us outnumbered and outmaneuvered, especially when our hands are tied."

"Don't give up," Deadeye said, spooning up the chocolate sludge from the bottom of her mug. "There won't always be a need for people who can break things, but there'll always be a need for those who understand exactly what someone's going through." Her face took on the expression that I could only dub the "interested engineer" look. "It'll be interesting if your power becomes telepathy, like Michael's."

"That doesn't sound fun." I made a face as Josephine shot a warning look across the table at Deadeye. *I wonder what that's about.* "All I can do is catch the emotions that people leave lying around." Saying it that way sounded so effortless, and never mind the fact that it'd taken days to even get that far. "If they're trying to keep me out, I'm completely oblivious to what's going on in their heads."

"Well, it's also possible that it could develop in other ways than this." Josephine collected the cups and took them to the sink. Her tone screamed that she was desperately trying to change the subject. "Shattered powers come in pairs; primary and secondary, usually opposites of each other."

"Like Judge," I commented. "Keeping things out with shields, or breaking into other people's minds." I frowned. "Those don't make sense together, though."

Josephine raised her voice over the water running into the sink. "It's not usually intuitive, but there's always a link somehow." She shut off the water and turned to face me again. "With him—don't tell him I said this—I think it's control, whether over a specific area or someone else's mind."

"Makes sense, I suppose." I thought back to what Bandit had said. *I guess everyone reacts differently to their lives going out of control.* "Does the secondary usually take a while to develop?"

Deadeye nodded. "I know you've heard everyone mention it before, but Tara wasn't able to heal when we were all with the Defense Force the first time."

"When *did* she learn it?" I asked, flipping my notebook to a blank page. "Do you know how it happened?"

They both shook their heads. "No, but I can tell you about something else," Deadeye said with a laugh. "Did you ever hear the one about how I got the base's sound system to play only polka music?"

———

A FEW DAYS LATER, Tara decided to switch things up with our training session. I knew I should've been nervous, but I was only excited as she and Judge exchanged an intense look across the practice court.

"You sure?" Judge asked, something grim in his manner checking my enthusiasm.

Tara nodded. "Go for it. I want to see how he'll do."

I dropped my water bottle, raising my hands in anticipation of blocking the force attack I was certain was about to hit me. After almost two weeks of practice, I knew I could at least manage a shield. *Go on, try it.*

Judge turned on his heel and raised a hand in my direction. Quick as a thought, light exploded toward me with a sound like a thunderclap.

I yelled as I threw a shield between us, my yell turning triumphant as Judge's fireball fizzled out against its glowing surface. "Ha! I gotcha!"

"That?" Judge raised his other hand, his face deathly serious. "That was a distraction."

What? No! I swept a hand in front of me, power gathering between my fingers. Judge snapped his fingers, and an iron force grabbed my limbs. My head filled with pressure, the sense of something twisting into my mind both unsettling and uncomfortable. The energy disappeared as my hands fell to my sides, bound with invisible cords. My muscles quivered as I fought to break free, Judge's voice echoing through my head.

Gotcha, Gabe.

Tears came to my eyes, and I would've fallen but for the iron grip holding me upright. I'd felt Judge's presence before when he'd demonstrated his abilities, but this time it *hurt.*

Get out!

The hold on my mind twisted even tighter, and I caught a glimpse of the iron will that lay behind Judge's cocky exterior. **Make me.**

Furious now, and more than a little frightened, I grabbed the thread of emotion that marked his presence. Following it toward him was easy, but soon my senses ran into something like a slippery wall. The pressure inside my head increased, and I would have screamed but for my jaw being sealed shut.

A frustrated puff of air escaped my lungs, blue flaring behind my eyelids as I pushed with all my strength toward Judge's mind.

Let go of me!

My vision changed suddenly and a cityscape glittered below me, my vantage point an overpass high over the ground. I rubbed my face under my visor, swearing before Michael telepathically ordered me to keep my language to a minimum. It'd been three nights in a row of missions like this, and my power was flickering at the lowest ebb I could still function under.

Dizzy and nauseated, I forced myself to focus as more Brutes than I could count poured out of the mouths of alleys and the abandoned buildings surrounding the road-way. One of them scaled the overpass with uncanny speed and accuracy and grabbed one of the other EDF troopers with a sickening crunch. Her scream reverberated through all of our minds, sending another wave of nausea through my body.

"Judge, get that one!" Michael yelled. His thoughts ebbed across to my own mind, painful and shocking all at once as I realized how panicked he was from the other side of our link.

I frantically flung out a hand, energy shooting from my fingers and streaking to hit the Brute in the neck. It dropped the other trooper with a growl and spun to charge at me instead. I dropped my rifle and threw both hands up, my shield disappearing as the Brute crashed through it. Terror freezing my feet, I ducked and turned away, covering my head as a trio of gunshots sounded over my head.

"Get up!" Bandit shouted. He stood over me with his handgun, shots sounding again and again as Brutes dropped one after another. I scrambled to my feet and stood back-to-

back with him, feeling safe for the first time that night with him between me and the Brutes.

Judge's voice filled my mind, anger crackling through our link. **Get. Out.**

The bonds around my limbs fell away, and my knees hit the concrete with a jarring thud. Catching myself on my hands, I dry heaved several times before my body stopped rebelling. Across the practice court, Judge was only just getting to his feet, his face white. Behind him, Tara stood as still as if one of us had frozen her in place.

Catching my breath, I struggled to my feet. "Alexi, I—"

"Shut up." He stalked past me, his emotions a cold barrier as he yanked the kitchen door open, then slammed it closed behind him. My heart sank as the echoes died out in the bay, leaving only the sounds of my heartbeat pounding in my ears.

Tara's voice interrupted my swirling thoughts. "Wow. It's been years since I've seen him like that."

My stomach was still twisted into knots. "Tara, what did I just do?"

She put a hand on my elbow, guiding me to sit at the foot of the compressor box. "I'm not sure, exactly. All I saw was him grabbing you, then both of you collapsing."

I explained, barely certain of my own memories as I described what I'd seen when I broke through Judge's barriers. "I wasn't trying to break into his head, I swear," I finished. "I just wanted him out of mine. I didn't mean to hurt him."

"I'm not sure you did," she said, handing me my water. "If I had to guess, I'd say you scared him."

I looked at Tara in surprise. Sitting side by side, the top

of her head only came to the bottom of my ear, and my legs were a good four inches longer. "You're kidding."

"Nope." She pulled her legs in to sit cross-legged, facing me earnestly. "Gabe, all of us have moments of darkness in our lives. You probably saw one of his."

"Oh." I looked at the floor, clutching my water bottle hard enough to make it crinkle. Josephine's words from the other night came back to haunt me. *He hates being out of control.* "I guess I should apologize."

"Once he cools off, I think he'll realize you had no idea what you were doing. But you *should* talk to him." Tara brushed her hair away from her face and added, "Now, I am curious. Do you think you can do it again?"

"What?" I said, my voice going squeaky with surprise. "I don't know if I *want* to!"

Tara gave me a stern look. "Gabriel, this is the second time you've seen someone else's memories without trying. I want to see if you can do it on purpose." She held out a hand, forestalling the arguments building up behind my tongue. "Trust me. I'll bring to mind a memory—a *happy* one, okay? —and you see if you can push past and see it for yourself."

With a sigh, I set my water aside. "Okay."

"Deep breath. Close your eyes if you have to."

Obeying, I sought out Tara's presence from behind closed eyelids. Following her emotions, I imagined touching her shoulder.

I walked barefoot through a sunlit glade, trees with black-speckled white bark reaching over my head to cast dappled shadows across my face. The handle of a basket was rough against my palm as my feet padded along the cool, leaf-lined path.

"Tara, come on!" A young girl appeared from around a

rock with a brilliant smile, her faded white cotton dress melting into dark blue around the hemline. "It's just up here!"

I hurried to follow, eagerness lending my feet extra speed and grace. The trees made way for a sunny meadow, tangled bushes stretching above my head. Red berries hung from the thorny bushes, like jewels strung on a necklace. The first few berries went into my mouth, bursting with tartness and warm from the sun. As the next handful went into my basket, blue mist swirled around my vision and I fell out of the memory.

"Berries..." I said. "Picking berries, and—was that your sister?"

Tara's eyes lit up. "Sofia, my older sister. You saw all of it?"

I nodded. "It was like I was riding around inside your head. I could think for myself, but feel through your senses."

"*That's* interesting," she said. "Michael was able to do something similar, but he gained access through thoughts, not emotions." She quickly added, "But we don't have to get into that. Want to try again?"

I rubbed my face. "Actually, can we take a break? My head's hurting."

"Sure." Tara nodded toward the pocket where I kept my recorder. "Want me to tell you about that day? You can add it to your story collection."

She understands. "If you don't mind." I pulled out the device, putting it between us while Tara's voice painted a place where the trees weren't thorny and the mountains were green. By the time she was done, the sun was slanting into the bay, and we went our separate ways to shower and change. With my head still spinning at the new developments, I didn't even realize I had left my recorder in the bay until after I'd showered.

Still barefoot and with damp hair, I went outside to find the red light still holding steady on the small device. "That's funny. I thought I turned it off."

Uncertain if I'd recorded hours of dead air, I turned off the recording and returned to my room to transfer all the data to a tablet. Skipping forward in the recording, I went past my conversation with Tara until jiggling bars appeared near the end of the recording. The timestamp showed it had happened *after* I'd left to shower.

I pressed play.

"How's he doing?" Caleb's voice asked.

"Better than I could've expected," Tara said. *"He has so much potential."*

"How much potential are we talking?"

Judge's voice came through next. He must've gone outside once he was sure I'd hit the showers. *"He was able to follow my emotions back to gain access to my mind."*

"You're kidding?" Caleb's voice strengthened. I guessed they had been standing near the compressor, possibly even over the recorder. *"I know I'm able to block you, but—"*

Judge's next words were a bit muffled—I assumed he'd stepped farther from the recorder—before his voice came back clearly. *"—to practice keeping me out. He's new at it, and this memory thing makes me nervous. I know he didn't mean to do it, and I overreacted, but I haven't had anyone else in my head for years."*

"Not since Michael died, anyway," Tara said. I envisioned her leaning against the compressor between the two taller men. *"I know everyone keeps trying to tell him they're nothing alike, but you know what'll happen if Regional Command finds out how similar their powers are. The EDF has been without a strong commander for so long, they'll*

jump at any chance of someone who could do what Michael could."

"Well, there's another thing we haven't thought about," Caleb said. *"If he's really like Michael, it means he'll eventually be able to access our thoughts as well as emotions. You really want that again?"*

Tara took a long time to respond, and for a moment I wasn't sure they were still there. Then, her voice came through again, somewhat daunted but resolute. *"Even if we don't pursue things like that, it'll happen without our control."* She sighed. *"All it'll take is another nightmare for him to learn more than any of us ever planned."*

"I know I scared him by how I reacted." Judge actually sounded upset, something I'd never expected. *"I shouldn't have stormed off—he just caught me off guard."*

"We going to tell the others?" Caleb asked.

"What, that the kid might be about to gain access to all their darkest secrets?" Judge scoffed. *"Would you tell them something like that?"*

"Not when you put it that way," Tara retorted. *"But we have to tell them something."*

"Well one thing's for sure," Judge said. I could practically see him shiver dramatically. *"Even if he does have power like Michael did, I'm never letting anyone else into my head again."*

I paused the playback, not wanting to hear their final decision. "Telling me their stories is one thing," I muttered. "They can pick and choose what I find out. This, though..." I went through the recording again, stopping once more before the end. *If even Judge is so nervous about me being in their heads, I don't know if it's something I want to attempt.*

STAGE FOURTEEN

*Solar fields near the Central
Arizona Project
Colorado River Valley
September 15*

"GABE?" Logan stuck his head out of the Fishbowl as I walked past with a load of sun-dried laundry. "Is Deadeye out there?"

I shook my head and peered around him into the Fishbowl. Deadeye's desk had become so concealed by cases of equipment that I couldn't tell if she was there or not. "I thought she was tinkering in her lair."

"No, she left." He stepped back from the door, heading over to the screens. "Someone's on the line from Tucson for her. Some guy named Benny?"

I set the laundry basket down inside the doorway. "Oh, I know him. Well, kind of. I'll talk to him if you go find her."

"Copy that." Logan passed me the headset before leaving.

I adjusted the microphone. "Benny? This is Gabriel."

"Hey, man!" The St. Augustine's engineer's voice was loud in my ears, urgency crackling through every word. "I was looking for Reneé, but I guess you'll be good. It has to do with you, anyway."

My notebook was in my room, so I grabbed a printout from the edge of the desk and flipped it over to take notes. "I sent someone to find her—she'll be here in just a sec. What's up?"

A FEW MINUTES LATER, the whole squad had gathered around the Fishbowl. My pen drummed a nervous rhythm against my leg as I explained, "It happened barely an hour ago. The convoy up to Phoenix was hijacked, and the Blood Angel prisoners escaped."

Everyone groaned.

"Now do you believe me?" Deadeye asked. "I swear, they're *letting* stuff like this happen."

"Why didn't anyone tell us?"

I shook my head. "It just happened. *Regional* barely knows about it."

"These are the ones we captured at Picacho, right?" Logan asked.

"Right," I confirmed. "Their two Shattereds and a handful of others."

Judge's cyan eyes narrowed. "How'd this engineer know to call us?"

"He owes me favors," Deadeye said. "And he likes having the inside scoop on everything." She chuckled. "I never know where he gets his information, but he's almost always reliable. He probably hears the cockroaches talking."

Caleb shook his head. He and Tara had been outside, catching a quiet moment before Judge had gone to find them. "What's Tucson's response going to be?"

Logan snorted. After finding Deadeye, he'd stayed to hear the full conversation between her and Benny. "They're calling Regional to get further instructions."

"And we all know what that's going to be." Deadeye contorted her face and said, "'Hold the line.' Which, for us, means 'do nothing.'"

Everyone laughed, but the laughter wore thin over the building tension. "Benny felt the same way," I said. "He's getting pretty pissed with how Regional is handling this conflict."

"Can't say I blame him," Bandit said. Stubble scraped as he rubbed a hand across his face. "I'm pretty pissed, too. If they hadn't given up on the relay stations, we'd still have a way to see where the escapees had gone." His fist tapped the outside of his holster. "Or even an opportunity to recapture them, so they couldn't mess with us anymore." He sighed. "With the desert gone dark, there's no way we can find them before they make it to the Ridges."

Tara's head went up, and the worry speeding from her made my heart race in response. "They were there." Cyan light flared in her eyes as she looked at me. "They're not stupid—they'll know you Shattered. They're going to take that news right back to the rest of the Blood Angels."

Fear twisted through my stomach.

"We knew it couldn't stay a secret forever," Caleb reminded her—and me. He wrapped an arm around her shoulders, looking at the rest of us resolutely. "You're right, though. I think it's safe to say we're an even bigger target for them, now."

———

"I HOPE you told them exactly where they could put their input," Deadeye's voice crackled in my ear as I finished wiring a new control box to one of the solar arrays. The repairs to the solar field west of us were minor, routine things, but we'd arrived at the location ready for anything. The transformer towers and giant power lines rose like sentinels in the distance; a lifeline for the entire Santa Cruz Valley. The setting sun gilded the edges of the massive metal beams, the last bits of sunlight fading from the solar field as we continued our work.

"I told them," Caleb said.

"And then he told them again, a different way," Tara added.

"Just in case it didn't sink in the first time?" I asked with a laugh.

Caleb snorted—a bit uncharacteristic, but then I'd felt how frustrated he was during his conversation with Regional. With Bandit finally back on his feet, Caleb had told Regional in no uncertain terms that he was handing command over. They hadn't been happy about it, but he'd left nothing to the imagination with how creatively he'd spelled out his resignation.

I refocused on my work as the rest of the squad kept talking. We were deep in the dead zone, so our conversation was limited to local comms—and it had been *hopping*. I wasn't sure if everyone was nervous after the news about the Blood Angels, but everyone had been ridiculously chatty even *with* Judge and Logan back at base with colds.

We finished our maintenance and rendezvoused at the truck, parked in a cluster of white-painted utility buildings at the edge of the solar field. The sun had dipped behind the horizon, and evening shadows were growing around the feet of the buildings as Bandit hailed us from the roof. Between his long-range rifle and a portable infrared scanner, he was the best early warning system we had at this point. "All finished?"

Deadeye opened a side compartment on the exterior of the truck, setting down her toolbox and pulling off her helmet. "Done."

I joined her, unloading tools into the truck. "It won't boost the efficiency, but at least we're not deteriorating anymore."

Tara leaned against the side of the building, picking thorns out of the soles of her boots. "I'm not deteriorating. You, on the other hand..."

"Hey now, that's not nice," Caleb admonished. Even standing right next to him, it was difficult to pick out any more emotion than vague amusement. "Gabriel's the only one who's *not* deteriorating. All the rest of us are falling apart at the seams."

Bandit grunted. "That's rich, coming from someone twelve years younger than me."

"How's it looking from up there?" Deadeye asked, the laugh in her voice suggesting she'd deliberately changed the subject.

There was a pause. "It's been quiet, but..." Bandit paused, and I caught a stab of confusion from him. "There's something northwest; looks like a dust spinner or something."

Tara and Caleb exchanged looks, definite alarm sparking from Tara. "Nothing else on your scanner?"

"Nothing." Bandit said. "Just this dust."

"It's not a dust devil," I said, sliding my visor down to cover my face. Something felt *wrong*. "The evening's too cool, and there's no wind."

No sooner had I said it than my vision filled with dizzying white light. A shock went through my chest, and the helmet dampeners barely contained the noise of an explosion. Bandit's gun sounded once, twice, three times before he yelled, "Contact! Truck, just off the northwest edge of the field. Multiple hostiles engaging from around the buildings and inside the field!"

I grabbed my rifle, glad I'd carried it with me while we worked. The staccato sounds of consistent gunfire came from the solar field as I ducked around the truck. "They're trying to pin us down!" I yelled, peeking around the corner before a dangerously close shot whizzed past my helmet.

Deadeye darted around the other end of the truck, diving into cover behind the building adjacent to the one Bandit was perched on. She shut her visor before firing her own rifle at the enemies between the two buildings. Out by the solar field, Tara's power flared, her shield making a pool of light around her. Bandit's gun went off again before he gasped, "They have a bead on my position. I'm coming down."

"Better not." Caleb's voice had stayed level even through the sudden attack. I took advantage of a brief lull in the gunfire to scramble alongside him. He gestured toward the edge of the building, and I generated a shield over both of us as we crept to the corner. "We can't see a thing with Tara casting stuff around everywhere. Are they showing in infrared?"

All was silent for a moment, the gunfire resuming as our enemies pressed closer. At last, Bandit said, "They're showing, finally. I don't know why they didn't before. There's a pair coming around the side of the building, and another two in amongst the solar panels."

Deadeye popped around the side of the building, fired, and dropped back. "One less, now," she exclaimed. "Any by the truck?"

"Two more by the truck, I—augh!" Unearthly lightning illuminated the sky, and Bandit exclaimed something utterly untranslatable in Spanish before saying, "I'm on my way down. That was way too close for comfort."

"One of their Shattereds is here!" Tara said. "The lightning wielder! They're in between the solar panels."

"One?" Bandit asked. "Or both?"

"Hard to tell," she grunted. Another flash lit the sky before she answered, "One, both. I'm not sure."

"Tara, be careful," I warned as I sent a trio of rounds at the exposed legs of someone creeping through the solar field. "We don't know what they're capable of, and I think tonight's the wrong time to find out!"

"Take care of yourself, Gabriel," she snapped, a burst of Shattered power driving a man into range of Caleb's shotgun. "I'll handle them."

Before I could reply, a low hum built in the air, setting my teeth on edge. One of the transformers exploded with a spurt of white light and a noise like thunder. Blinded, I lost control of my shield. No sooner did I realize it had gone than Caleb doubled over, his gun hitting the dirt as he crumpled to the ground. A wordless scream echoed through my mind, the gunfire halting briefly as a pair of people darted around the building. I blinked away the bright spots in my vision as Caleb's boots disappeared around the corner.

"Caleb!" I bolted around the corner, my instinct to fire

on the Blood Angels dissolving in panic at the sight of his limp form bookended by two people who radiated hostility. One had a hand clamped around his armor, and was dragging him toward their truck. "They've got him!" I yelled into my comms, raising a hand to cast a misguided bolt of energy toward one of the Blood Angels.

Across the field, I felt Tara's shriek in more than my ears —echoing through my mind the same way it had in her nightmare. Blue light flashed across the field to strike each of Caleb's captors' helmets. In the distance, a Brute howled as a shockwave went through the earth. The ground heaved under my feet, and Caleb fell to the ground as the Blood Angels dropped on either side of him.

The side door at the foot of the building slammed open, and Bandit shouted, "Deadeye, Gabriel, cover me!"

Shaking away my panic, I raised another shield over myself, laying down covering fire as Bandit hauled Caleb back around the corner and toward the truck. His voice crackled with fury as he ordered, "Deadeye, Banshee, keep them back. *Mijo.*" His voice softened a tad as he boosted Caleb into the passenger compartment. "See what you can do for him."

I whipped around the edge of the building and sprinted to the truck, switching places with Bandit as Deadeye yelled with triumph. It looked like Caleb had regained his senses— but only partially. His movements were uncoordinated and jerky, tremors shaking his limbs as his hands went frantically to his helmet.

"Hold still; let me help." I swung the half door on the truck bed closed as Bandit left us, running toward Tara. The sounds from outside diminished as my fingers found the release on Caleb's helmet. His hair was sweat-soaked, silvery eyes blurry and unfocused, and emotions a churning mess behind mental walls. I dropped the helmet and reached out to grab his shoulder. "Caleb?"

He yelled and shrank back, as the wall dropped and a memory slammed into me.

Panic.

Fury.

Terror and pain.

Lightning shot through my veins, a scream ripping through my throat as the pain went on, and on, and on—

"Oh no," I whispered, my hand reflexively tightening on his shoulder. Cyan light swirled into the corners of my vision, and I pushed it toward where I could feel Caleb caught in a nightmarish web of terror. As the light poured into him, he took a shuddering breath.

The pain faded.

I snatched my hand back, staring wide-eyed at Caleb. "What—what *was* that?"

Tara slammed the hatch open, her voice a barely contained yell. "Gabriel, move."

"I don't think he's hurt—oof!" The wind escaped my lungs in a gasp as I hit the wall, thrown off my feet by the force Tara slammed in my direction.

Across the truck, she planted her glowing hands over Caleb's temples. He slumped over into unconsciousness and she rolled him to his side, a glittering shield forming around both of them.

The truck rocked as Bandit climbed up, clicking his mic on and saying, "Deadeye, they're running. They got to their truck, but there's a pack of Brutes on their tail."

"Copy," Deadeye said. "Let's get out of here."

"What happened out there?" Bandit asked as I buckled myself in next to him.

I looked helplessly at Caleb. "I think one of their Shattereds hit him with a mental attack. Like what Judge can do, but worse. Th-they were trying to capture him." I shuddered. "Or maybe it was me they were after." I dropped my voice to a whisper, phantom pains still running through my limbs. "There was a memory in his head when I grabbed him; what —" I stopped as Bandit shook his head.

"Not here, *mijo*." He looked sympathetically at Tara, who'd slouched against the wall alongside her husband. "I'll explain back at base."

CALEB STILL HADN'T WOKEN up by the time we got home. Tara asked for help getting him to their room, then shut the door in our faces. Confused and worried, I returned to the bay, cleaning and putting away Caleb's weapons and armor in addition to my own. While I worked, I could hear— or maybe feel—Bandit explaining something in hushed, concerned tones to Logan. Dinner was tense and worried, and not even Judge's jokes could lighten the mood. That night, I couldn't sleep.

They were after me. This happened because of me.

The scream I'd heard kept echoing through my head, despair and terror reverberating past the Shattered parts of my mind. Eventually, I went up to the roof, lay on the helipad, and stared up into the sky for over an hour before sleep finally claimed me.

I didn't get the chance to pin Bandit down until the next day, after chores and workouts had been done. Tara was nowhere to be seen, so Judge—still congested, but no less sarcastic—and I spent the morning practicing shields and pummeling the snot out of each other. As we finished, Bandit wandered out into the bay, tossing me a water bottle. "Let's go."

We ended up at the picnic table outside. The morning sun was taking its time with its climb into the sky, and the air was barely comfortable enough to be outdoors. Doves cooed in the palo verde branches, and far overhead a pair of buzzards wheeled in the first updrafts of the day.

I clicked on my recorder, opened my notebook to a brand-new page—one not covered in scribbled notes or doodles—and waited for Bandit to speak. I could feel him testing out ways to begin the conversation, the uncertainty coming through ever more clearly after weeks of practicing. Finally, he said, "You might not want to write this one down."

I looked down at the blank page. "If we only remembered good stories, we'd have no reason to push through hard things. They targeted him because of me." I clenched my hand around my pen. "I have to know what I caused."

Bandit sighed. "All right, if you insist. Don't blame me if it upsets you."

"I'll be fine," I promised, meaning every word. Enough of Caleb's pain had hit me that I knew I *needed* to know what had happened. *Especially since it was my fault.*

With that, Bandit tugged his hat brim down and set aside his water. "This has happened before—Caleb's memories coming to the surface. Last time I remember, it happened while we were infiltrating a high security xeno facility."

"What kind—" I began to ask, biting off the words as Bandit waved his hand wearily.

"They all blurred together after a while, okay? I want to

say it was one of the testing sites. We breached in through the roof, and cleared out the handful or so of guards in the first few rooms. They're built like labyrinths, those places." He traced callused fingers through a blotch of water left on the tabletop. "Things were normal until we blew down the next door. I didn't realize we'd gone the wrong way until we got into the room." He swallowed, his face tensing.

I set my pen down and waited.

It was September, and the monsoon long over, but a few clouds still drifted over the distant sky islands. Out on the plains, the dust spinners were growing, stretching to touch the milky blue sky like sentient beings. A brief wind blew across my face, ruffling my hair and bringing the smell of verbena from the flower bed by the front door. As I was about to turn off the recorder, Bandit said, "We were at war. It was a war waged in shadows, but it was desperate and bloody nonetheless. When you're that deep in conflict, you don't care what you do in order to come out on top, and they'd started getting desperate."

He clenched a fist, revulsion as plain in his voice as it was in his emotions. I squirmed uncomfortably as he explained, "I'd been in a few places like that before, on other missions. No matter what, it always smelled of blood, electricity, and cleaning solutions from when they'd mopped up after dismembering someone." He returned his gaze to me, eyes sorrowful. "I swear, I didn't know it was there, and I know Michael didn't either."

His words started coming out in a rush, so fast that my pen could barely keep up. "We'd been in facility after facility. Nobody expected this to go any different. And Caleb's always run point; his reflexes are too good to waste. He was first in. As soon as I realized what that place was, so did

Michael. I could hear him yelling Caleb's name, yelling for someone to get him out of there." Bandit shook his head. "I'll never forget that look on his face. He just"—he snapped his fingers—"collapsed. Staring into nothing, shaking like a leaf." He looked beyond the trees, amber eyes staring out at the desert—or past it, into memory. "We couldn't get him to move. I think he passed out."

My hand ached from trying to keep up with Bandit's dictation. I shook out my arm, asking, "Okay, that's what happened yesterday too, but why?" The memory of the terror flooding out of Caleb sent my stomach churning. "He's so calm, but you have *no idea* what type of fear he's hiding."

"There's a good reason for it, *mijo*." Bandit's sigh carried the weight of years spent fighting. "Back at the beginning of all this, Caleb was leading a resistance group under one of the fields. The xenos attacked and wiped it out; captured him and a bunch of the others." He wiped his forehead with his sleeve. "That's how Tara Shattered."

I frowned. "This is a different time from the time Josephine told me about, then." Understanding came as rapidly as a lightning bolt. "Is that why Tara was screaming, 'not again' when Michael told her what had happened?"

Bandit nodded. "They only had him for a few days the first time, before Tara ripped down an entire facility to rescue him."

"That does sound like something she'd do." I underlined a few words, the next question stopping halfway out of my mouth. *I have to know.* "H-how long was he a prisoner the second time?"

Bandit's voice hushed. "It was almost two weeks before we found a way in." His shudder ran clear through the Shattered edges in my head, making my skin crawl. "We're still not sure what they did to him during, or why they let him live. He usually sleeps for days after one of these episodes, and never says a word about it afterward." The broken note in Bandit's voice vanished, replaced by adamance. "And don't you go poking around either. Some memories are better left buried."

"I *didn't* go poking around. It was there in his head, and when I grabbed him, it was there in *my* head." Pages rustled as I slapped my notebook closed. "I don't go looking for darkness in other people."

"It touches all of us, *mijo*."

"I know." I stabbed the "off" button on my recorder and stuffed the device back into my pocket. "And I'd happily do without that part. It's just..." I stood up, craning my neck to look up at the palo verde branches. Their vibrant green bark and feathery leaves made a beautiful pattern against the sky, hushing my voice as I said, "Staring down the darkness makes it easier to see all the things we stand to lose."

STAGE FIFTEEN

Deep in memory
Gila River Valley
September 22

"TARA?" Neither she nor Caleb had been seen since the skirmish at the solar field two days previous. After my conversation with Bandit, I understood why. *They've been so kind to me. I know I can't help, but I need to check on them.* As soon as Bandit and Josephine had left with Logan for the supply run to Tucson, I'd gone straight to Caleb and Tara's room.

Right as I was about to set my gift on the floor and walk away, the door opened. "Gabriel? Is something wrong?"

"Sorry to bug you." I held out the book I'd brought. "I just thought, if you're going to be keeping to yourselves, you might want something to read."

Tara's expression softened. "Thanks. Actually..." The door swung farther open. "You might be able to help me."

I stepped inside. "Is Caleb—"

"He's sleeping." Tara closed the door behind me. Exhaustion lined her face as she corrected herself, "Or, well, I put him to sleep."

She must be so tired. "How can I help?"

"I'm not sure if you can do this," she said, sitting down at the table. "But do you think you can *push* a memory into someone else's mind—overriding whatever else is in there? Like when you see our memories, only in reverse?"

I blinked hard and looked at the tabletop. "I'm not sure." *They've helped me so much. I have to try.* "I think so?"

"Would you try?" Tara laid a hand palm up on the table, the simple gesture weighing my shoulders down with responsibility. "If it works, I'd like you to try it with Caleb. He's—" Her eyes filled with tears. "It's bad, this time."

I took the seat opposite her, trying to settle my mind. Finally, I closed my eyes and put my hand in hers. Blue washed across my mind, and I guided it toward Tara.

The sun beat warm against the back of my neck as I ran down the cracking sidewalk, skidding on gravel as I rounded the corner toward Abuela's garden. A faded blue gate heralded my arrival, an unruly bougainvillea nodding against the red brick wall. I stumbled over the cinderblock threshold to stand amongst a handful of citrus trees. My abuela looked up from a basket filled with cherry tomatoes at the other end of the garden, her brown face breaking into a beaming smile. "¡Mi angelito! ¿Cómo estás?"

I ran on short legs to hug her. The apron over her clothes was dusted with flour and she smelled like fresh tortillas and sunshine. "I brought you something." I fished in my pocket to pull out a piece of quartz. "It's a diamond!"

"You're my diamond, mijo." Her soft hand brushed curls

away from my forehead as she accepted the rock. "Come on, let's stick this in the windowsill."

The memory dissolved into sunlight as I let it go, bowing my head over Tara and my joined hands. Though long ago, the memory of my grandmother's arms around me was one of the things that had never faded or become tainted by fear.

"She called you her angel?" Tara asked, her voice soft.

"My name," I explained. "Gabriel? God's messenger?" I let go of her hand, my knee bouncing under the table. "That was from when I was really little, before things got really bad."

Tara nodded. "I think I could tell that. But more importantly, I saw and felt all of it. Gabriel—" She stood, clasping her hands across her middle and twisting her silicon wedding ring around and around her finger. "I have to wake up Caleb. I can't keep him asleep any longer without burning myself out, but I don't want a nightmare to be the last thing he remembers. I don't know if it'll work the same with someone who's not expecting it, but—"

"I'll try." I stood up, drying sweaty palms against my pants. "The same memory?"

"If you can do it again, yes." She paused with one hand on the bedroom door, her energy drained into concern. "I hope this works."

The bedroom was dark and still, even the overhead fan turned off. Tara clicked on the bedside light, revealing Caleb sleeping peacefully. Or, well, somewhat peacefully. His eyes flickered behind his eyelids, and his shoulders twitched like he was in a nightmare. He was wearing a faded green T-shirt, and I frowned at the sight of circuitry inlaid under the skin of his left arm, running from the inside of his wrist toward his heart. *So that's why he always wears long sleeves.*

"We think they were trying to augment humans," Tara said, noticing my stare. "He doesn't remember, or at least he says he doesn't." She sighed. "The doctors said trying to remove it ourselves would leave him with nerve damage and unable to use his hand, so we decided to leave it in." My sixth sense told me that she had tried to argue, but was resigned by this point. She flexed a hand, light dancing between her fingertips. "When I wake him up, do the same thing you did with me."

"Same way?" I asked, still hesitant. *He might not want me messing around in his head.*

Tara nodded. "He might fight you. And there'll probably be nightmares that'll try to pull you in." Her cyan eyes were intense and determined as she said, "Push them back if you can. That's why we're here."

I took a deep breath and knelt next to the bed as she placed her glowing hands around Caleb's temples. As the light washed over his face, I put a hand on his arm, focusing as hard as I could on the sunny memory.

Caleb. Caleb, wake up.

Something twisted through my head, like Judge but not quite. Fear and anger pulsed back at me, hostility and helplessness trapping me behind a slick wall.

I'm not leaving you in there. I gathered every bit of adamance I had. *There are better things in life than the darkness attacking you.*

Just like I had when escaping Judge's hold, I slammed against the wall until it weakened, then broke. A brief stab of pain jolted through me as Caleb's arm tensed under my hands. *Caleb, it's me!* Like sunlight breaking through storm clouds, the memories flooded through the breach in Caleb's defenses, warmth and comfort mixing with the images of a blue gate and bougainvillea. His arm slid from my grasp, and he took a deep breath.

I opened my eyes to find Caleb blinking in confusion, looking from me to Tara and back again. "Gabriel?"

I couldn't help the sigh of relief that escaped me at seeing his face smoothed from the tension that had been there a moment ago. "Welcome back. You okay?"

He sat up halfway, bracing himself on his elbows and rolling his neck. "Yeah... Yeah, I'm okay." He twisted to look up at Tara, voice filled with wonder. "That's the first time in forever that it hasn't hurt to wake up from one of those."

"Don't thank me; thank him," Tara replied with a nod in my direction.

Caleb blinked, the last few shadows fleeing his eyes as he said, "Thanks, Gabe. It took me a second to realize it was you..." His brow furrowed. "That *was* you, right? Whose memory was that?"

"Mine," I said, pleased that it had worked at all.

"Your own memories?" His eyes widened. "They're still there, right? I didn't take them?"

"I—I don't think so," I stammered, doing a quick mental inventory.

Sunlight.

Blue gate.

Bougainvillea.

"No, they're still there," I said with relief. "I just wanted you to feel something other than..." I waved vaguely at him. "All that."

He slid his legs over the side of the bed and stood up, rolling his shoulders. "Well, thanks to you, all I remember is Tara putting me under."

I gave him a searching look at the lie slithering behind his words. *Maybe he doesn't want Tara to worry.* Before I could decide what to say, Tara smiled and gave me a thumbs-up behind his back. *I guess it's better that way.* I returned the smile and followed them out into their tiny living area. "I came to bring you something to read, before I knew what was going on. I can still leave it if you want."

"She doesn't read much," Caleb said with a loving look at Tara. "I'll take it, though."

"Will you come for dinner?" I asked, going past them to the door. Now that he was awake, I didn't want to disturb their private time. "The others will probably wonder where you are."

The two of them exchanged looks—Tara's questioning, Caleb's reassuring.

"We'll be out in a little bit."

I WASN'T EXPECTING them to actually appear, but appear they did. About an hour later, Caleb and Tara came to join Deadeye and me in the kitchen. Technically, Judge was supposed to be cooking, but Deadeye had heard his menu plan and pulled the "age" card. Sulking, he'd gone off to watch the screens for the Thunderbird's return.

"What's going on here?" Tara asked as I dumped a pile of grated potato into a clean towel. I hadn't understood what we were making, but I trusted Deadeye's instincts.

"*Kartoffelpuffer,*" Deadeye said from the stove, her German accent coming out strongly in the single unusual word. "The others got delayed coming back from Tucson, and we're out of almost everything."

"Interesting..." Caleb prodded the mass of damp shavings with one eyebrow raised. He'd kept his short-sleeved shirt on, leaving the augmented part of his arm exposed. "So, is this dinner or a snack?"

Deadeye clanged the spatula against the frying pan. "Depends on how many we make, *without* all of them going missing!" The last part she all but shouted, as Judge slunk past. "You're supposed to be watching the screens!"

He switched on the monitor in the corner of the room, slapping it when it refused to cooperate the first time. Sitting back on his heels, he stuck his tongue out at Deadeye. "I can watch just as well from here."

I wrapped the towel around the potatoes and squeezed the extra liquid out into the sink as Tara and Deadeye started arguing with Judge. Despite the sharp words and insults floating through the air, the only thing I could sense was genuine happiness and enjoyment of each other's company. *There could be some good points to this power,* I thought as I began adding eggs and flour to the potatoes under Deadeye's half-distracted instruction. *I get to feel it when other people are happy.* I glanced over at Caleb, leaning against the fridge with amusement in his eyes as he watched the mayhem. *Well, almost. I need to talk to him sometime when Tara isn't around.*

The pancakes never really made it to the table. Deadeye gave up on keeping us away from them, transferring the new batches straight to our plates. We'd almost used up the last of the batter when a blip onscreen warned of the Thunder-bird's imminent arrival.

"Don't all crowd to the rooftops," Deadeye warned with a steely look at Judge. I was certain she could communicate more with one narrowed eye than I could with an entire transmitted memory. "There're still dishes to be done."

"I'll help, if anyone else wants to go help unload," I offered, turning on the water in the sink.

Judge slid off his seat on the counter, stuffing his hands in his pockets as he slouched toward the hallway. The feelings drifting from him implied that he was interested in scoping out the groceries before anyone else had the chance. "I'll go."

"I didn't mean you!" I called after him. "You're supposed to be on screen duty!"

Caleb laughed and came to drop his plate in the sink next to me. Up close, the circuits under his skin had a definite metallic sheen, and I wondered if he could feel them moving against his muscles. "I'll help too." He grinned. "Maybe they bought something fun, since they knew they'd be back around dinnertime."

I could almost picture the Thunderbird overhead, circling once before touching down. I'd never understand how Logan managed to eke so much precision out of such a large vehicle. The ceiling shuddered as the landing gear impacted, and I stepped up my pace with the dishes. A few minutes later, Judge's excitement carried far ahead of his and Caleb's footsteps as they came downstairs.

"Better start drying these plates," I said, interrupting Tara and Deadeye's conversation. "Josephine and Bandit brought dinner."

"Yes!" Tara exclaimed, grabbing a dishcloth and a plate out of the drying rack. She'd barely finished the first plate when the door crashed open to admit Caleb and Judge, both carrying armloads of bags. "Did they bring anything good?"

"Tacos!" Judge said, setting his bag on the table and carefully removing a large glass bottle filled with blood-red liquid. "And *agua de Jamaica*."

"You know you butchered that pronunciation, right?" Caleb asked from the fridge, unloading bottles of milk and a box of eggs straight into the shelves.

I was certain that Judge deliberately exaggerated his accent as he said, "I don't know, and I don't care. All I know is that it's delicious."

"It *is* delicious," Tara agreed, taking the last plates from me and heading to the table. "I'm assuming Logan and Bandit are securing the Thunderbird?"

"Yeah. Josephine brought a bunch of stuff for the med cabinet. She said she'd have to log them immediately, so we could eat without her."

We hurriedly set the table and passed around the bags of food. Bandit and Logan came in around the time I'd finished my first taco, Bandit's face looking worn out and worried under his hat brim. He sat with a sigh in the chair Caleb pushed out for him, accepting a plate from Deadeye. "Feels good to be home. It's way too chaotic, going to Tucson these days."

Tara raised her glass in his direction. "Thanks for your sacrifice. We all appreciate it, especially after the week it's been."

Everyone nodded, most with their mouths full. Bandit hung his hat off the edge of his chair and ran his hand along his hair. "It *has* been a week. And I don't know as it's going to get any better from here on out."

The food lost its appeal as I realized what he was saying —or not saying. The others didn't even need to be empathic to pick up on things. Deadeye set her knife and fork down. "What happened?"

Bandit pulled a folded paper out of a pocket, smoothing wrinkles and water damage from its surface before sliding it toward her. "St. Augustine's passed this to me."

Deadeye snatched the paper, pulling it over to our side of the table. "A wanted poster? Really?"

I leaned over to see my own face staring back at me—the photo taken right after initial training was completed. Seeing the version of myself from the beginning of the year, I was struck by the fact that more than the eyes had changed in the last few months. "That's me, all right." I lifted the paper out of Deadeye's grasp and passed it to Tara. "Wish they'd used a nicer photo, though."

Tara snorted at the joke, then scoffed as she saw the writing—both Spanish and English—under the photograph. "They've put a bounty on him. What is this, the Wild West?"

"I mean, kind of." Judge paused mid-bite to point out, "Most of the old westerns were filmed south of here."

"Shut up." Tara threw her napkin at him. "You're worth a lot, buddy," she informed me.

"Fantastic," I groaned, not wanting to look at Caleb. *They* were *targeting me. I knew it was my fault.*

Judge glanced at the paper as Tara passed it to him. "This says they want you alive." He looked around the table, the corner of his mouth ticking up in a mischievous smile. "Any takers on how long before the *next* targeted attack?"

Josephine had come in while we were talking, taking a seat next to Bandit. "I'm not sure, but they're upping their game. St. Augustine's guys lost a whole squad when the Blood Angels lured them into a warehouse by the old air force base. They barely had enough time to realize it was a trap before the exit blew up and a pack of Brutes were let loose inside."

I flinched and put a hand to my head at the sudden fear that stabbed through everyone.

"They're trying to take all of us out." Deadeye sat back in her chair and crossed her arms. "And Regional Command says...what?"

Logan snorted. He hadn't spoken much since getting back, but I could feel his worry—for his wife and daughters, if the flashes of children's voices in his head were any indication. "They say they have the situation well under control, and the Blood Angels are nowhere near as dangerous as we think they are."

"And you trust them on this?" Judge said.

"I don't trust anyone who doesn't acknowledge the possibility of their own failure." Logan's brown eyes narrowed as he looked at his empty plate. "They never have a plan in place for the day it happens. And when it does, they'll blame *you* for everything going wrong."

"Sounds about right." Deadeye put her elbow on the table and leaned her chin on her arm. "We knew they were spineless, but I'm beginning to wonder how invested they are in this region."

"Well, one thing's for sure." Caleb slid his chair closer to Tara's and put an arm around her. She leaned into his shoulder as he said, "As long as the Blood Angels have the ability to make more Brutes, they'll keep throwing them at us in greater numbers. The only way we're going to get anywhere close to knocking them out is taking down their facility—not that anyone but us sees it that way."

I STAYED quiet through the rest of dinner, thinking hard and trying to ignore the emotions drifting from my squadmates. Sleeping that night wasn't easy, as nightmares of Brutes tearing through armor mixed with the screams I'd heard in Caleb's memories. Starting awake in the darkness, I closed my fists around the edge of my sheets. Shuddering, I sat up and leaned against the wall behind my bed.

If we can't get an edge on this fight, nightmares like these will become an everyday occurrence. I took a deep breath, in and out for four counts each. My sixth sense told me that everyone was asleep except me and Caleb, on duty in the Fishbowl. *I need to apologize.*

Sliding out of bed and padding down the hall toward the Fishbowl, I found Caleb leaning back in Deadeye's chair in front of the screens, the book I'd lent him open against his knee.

"Judge and I steal her chair, too."

Caleb looked up, chuckling as I pulled the other chair over. "Don't tell her I did as well." He closed the book and set it to the side. "What's up?"

I sat down, giving him what I hoped was a no-nonsense look. "I know you lied about not remembering anything until Tara and I woke you up."

His surprise reached past his mental walls, followed by resignation as he admitted, "Yeah. It did help with the pain, but I still remember." He bowed his head, rubbing his temple where one of the scars cut across his face. "I remember too much."

I grimaced, thinking back and realizing I'd felt that scar— maybe even the moment he'd received it. "I'm sorry," I whispered. "They were after me, and got you instead." I closed my eyes. *Surely he'll be angry now that he's had time to process.*

"Hey." Caleb shifted in his chair before his hand landed

on my shoulder. "It was a mistake on their part. This wasn't your fault."

I shied away from his touch. "How can you say that? They attacked us because of me! This happened to you because of me!" My breathing came faster and faster, guilt tangling with the power in my veins and demanding to be released as I spat, "This is why I spent so much time alone. Getting tangled up in other people's lives only leads to everyone getting hurt." I clenched my hands again, light beginning to shine from between my fingers. "This is *my fault.*"

Caleb's hand weighed down my shoulder once more. "Gabriel." His voice stayed level, commanding, as he said, "Breathe. This is a really bad place to lose control."

Breathe.

Breathe.

I took a shaky breath, willing the churning energy to subside. *One, two, three, four.*

Caleb nodded. "Good. Again," he commanded. "Breathe."

Eons later, my heartbeat slowed and the churning in my veins stopped. Caleb's hand never left my shoulder, until the heaviness had gone and I could breathe easily once more.

"Sorry," I muttered. On the heels of the guilt came embarrassment. "I just—"

"Don't worry." He let go of my shoulder and scooted back, bending to retrieve his book from the floor. "It's just a technique. I do it too, you know—" He tapped his temple. "When things get too dark in here."

The scream from his nightmares still echoed through the edge of my mind, turning my throat raw at the recollection. My own voice came out hoarse. "How—" I stopped and tried again. "I know what you went through—Bandit told me, and I saw it in your head. How are you able to keep fighting after all that?"

Caleb stayed quiet for a moment. When he answered, the conviction rang through his words so strongly that the screaming in my head subsided. "What happened to me shouldn't happen to anyone else." He met my eyes unflinchingly. "That's why I fought then, and it's why I keep fighting now. I have the ability to protect others from the horrors I went through, and I'm not going to let the pain stop me."

STAGE SIXTEEN

EVEN WITH EVERYONE'S nonchalant response to the bounty on my head, I could tell the tension in the base had ratcheted up. I was taking my turn watching the screens—not that it really mattered, with more than half our system out of commission—when Judge spun me around in my chair. Well, Deadeye's chair. I'd stolen it again.

"You can't hide behind your screens your whole life, Gabe."

Annoyed, I yanked my headset down and glared at him. "I wasn't. Besides, didn't we decide today was a no-practice day?"

I knew the answer even before he said it. "Ahh, I said that so I'd have time to set things up." He grinned, hooking a thumb toward the door. "C'mon, I have something cool planned."

Tossing my headset at Logan, I followed Judge—not into the bay like I'd expected, but out into the empty desert behind our water tanks. Tara and Caleb were moving the last of a row of target dummies into place; crude things constructed of old tires and other bits of junk. I stopped and looked at Judge with confusion. "I can't mind meld with a tire."

"I never said you were going to." He grinned. "You're going to blow one up. We all need a chance to let off some steam."

"Okay..." A grin ticked up at the corner of my mouth. The idea of doing something without witnessing someone else's traumatic memories *was* refreshing. "How?"

"You've seen the vortexes we've done in the past?" Tara said, walking over with Caleb close behind. After our conversation the other night, he'd seemed like his normal self again. Or, maybe, I'd felt more normal around him.

"Yeah—wait, I can do those?"

Judge tugged the edge of his sleeve straight over his bicep. He was wearing the cabbage shirt again. I still didn't understand his explanation of why it was funny. "Probably. Almost all Shattereds can. Picture summoning a fireball, but instead of centering it on your hand, quadruple the size and center it over the target."

I took a few steps forward, eyeing the dummies and feeling for the energy swirling inside my soul. "What if it gets out of control?"

"That's why the master of all things shields is here." Tara elbowed Judge. "Ignore us. Just focus on what you need to do."

Inhaling deeply, I reached out for the power I felt when summoning a fireball. As I let the held breath go, the now-familiar warmth rushed down my arm. *No, not that.* I glared at the target dummies and raised both hands, their lumpy figures overwritten in my head with the monsters from my nightmares. Light blasted out of my palms toward the sky, swirling into a vortex of crackling cyan energy. I felt the others' surprise, but the majority of my focus was taken in controlling the exhilarating amount of energy pouring through my veins.

"Let it go!" Tara yelled behind me.

Gritting my teeth, I obeyed. The energy collapsed inward before exploding outward, sending broken bits of the dummies slamming into the shield Judge threw around us. I could even feel Caleb's excitement and awe as Tara said, "That's it!" She paused. "That's your first time doing that?"

"I think so—I mean—I don't think I've ever done that before." I shuddered, feeling like I'd been hit with a shock-wave. "Is it always that hard to control?"

"Always."

"Nah."

The two Shattereds answered in unison, Tara glaring at Judge before repeating, "*Always.*"

He sighed. "It usually gets away from you the first time. I figured it would, but you actually managed to keep it under control." He raised one eyebrow. "Want to try again?"

I frowned. Now that the initial adrenaline rush and accompanying emotions from everyone had died out, there was something niggling at the back of my mind. "Sure, but..." I looked at the sky. I couldn't see anything except a couple of buzzards wheeling in the updrafts. "Are we expecting visitors or something?"

I could tell we weren't, even before Caleb answered, "No. Why? Is something out there?"

Taking a few steps into the desert, I closed my eyes and pictured the satellite view of this area. Something pulsed against my mind; a presence not belonging to any of my squadmates. Certain now, I pushed a little farther, expanding my mental image to show me exactly where—or what—it was.

Hostility.

Bloodlust.

I yelled, shutting out the foreign emotions and whipping a hand up. A howl filled my ears as a crackling bolt of energy shot out of my palm, streaking across the desert to slam into the charging Brute. It dropped, skin smoking as it shuddered into death. I winced as the feel of its death reverberated through my mind, scarcely noticing as Judge and Tara ran past me. Now that I knew what Brutes felt like, my senses could pick them out—and our odds weren't good.

"There's a whole pack out there," I gasped. *That's too many. I can't take on that many.* My heart rate sped up as terrifying images of my friends dead around me filled my mind. *If I fail—*

Caleb steadied me with a hand to the shoulder. After a brief spurt of surprise at the initial attack, he'd calmed enough that all I could feel was—well, calm. His demeanor washed across to me as he asked, "Where?"

"There." I pointed at a palo verde, sticking out of the wash that ran perpendicular to us. "And there." My finger moved downstream, where the banks rose higher. "And there —Tara, watch out!"

She'd walked a few steps toward a mesquite thicket that suddenly burst into snarling life. One of the Brutes crashed into her shield, another falling to a burst of blue fire. "I'm okay," she gasped. "Get a shield around the two of you!"

Raising the shield *and* keeping everything around us in focus was more difficult than I expected. As the glowing field winked into place, a stab of pain went through my right eye and into the side of my head. *Keep it together. They can't see anything until it attacks them.* Grinding the heel of my hand into my temple, I squinted through the pain and kept yelling directions to Tara and Judge. Once they'd recovered from their surprise, they followed my lead, blasting the Brutes out of the undergrowth one after another. The ground soon became littered with corpses, each death sending another shock through my mind.

Beside me, Caleb's mind churned with frustration at not being able to help. He'd kept his hand on my shoulder, whether to stabilize me or to reassure himself I wasn't sure. As another Brute twitched and died, the pain in my head strengthened to dizziness. I doubled over, my knees hitting the ground as my breakfast attempted to escape my stomach.

From somewhere above us, gunshots sounded, and a thread of relief found its way through my mind as I realized it was Bandit, up on the roof near the Thunderbird. Elsewhere, I could feel Judge's cocky determination as he slammed another pair of Brutes to the ground with a wall of light, and Tara's almost feral anger as one of Bandit's shots took out her last opponent.

Another wave of pain and dizziness struck, and I closed my eyes against the overwhelming input from beyond the shield. *I'm sorry. I can't hold on to it.* Caleb called my name, concern leaking out of him before even all sounds faded and the tide of emotions ceased.

MY VOICE GRATED HOARSELY as I blinked my way back into life. "What happened?"

"Hey." Caleb handed me a glass of water with a flexible straw in it.

Craning my neck, I sucked down a few mouthfuls before leaning back against the pillows of the infirmary bed. The reflections cast by the stainless-steel bed railings made the ceiling tiles dance and shiver like they were underwater. Wincing at the dizziness, I asked, "Is this what burnout feels like?"

He set the glass aside, looking at me with a funny expression in his silvery eyes. I tried reaching out to see what he was feeling, but everything felt empty. *Empty. Is it gone for good?*

"Tara says you burned out, and she should know." Caleb glanced at the monitor behind my head. "Josephine knew you were waking up. She went to grab you some food."

"I don't know if I can eat anything." I closed my eyes as the ceiling swam.

"Trust her," Caleb said. "She knows what will help you recover the fastest."

"Is everyone else all right? Tara and—"

"They're fine," he reassured me. "Once everyone else heard the noise, they came to help. Bandit took out about five from the roof after you passed out, and Logan took care of the rest." He laughed faintly. "I had no idea he was so good with a rifle. Bandit might be out of a job if we keep him around."

I opened my eyes at the reminder. "Are *you* okay? Didn't the shield drop when I fainted?"

"Yeah. Don't worry, Logan covered me while I pulled

you inside." He shifted in his chair to show me the handgun strapped to his thigh. "But I'm staying armed from now on. Just to be safe."

"I don't blame you." The dizziness had faded to a faint swimmy sensation, and I felt safe sitting upright. "I don't know what happened. How'd they sneak up on us? Did they even show up on the screens?"

"They did, for a minute." By the look in Caleb's eyes, I knew what he was about to say before the words left his lips. "Someone shot out our receiver while we were distracted. And the tower at the mouth of the wash is also gone."

"Dammit." I slumped over, holding my head in both hands. "Are there *any* left?"

"Reneé said you'd ask that. The only towers left are out by Picacho and toward St. Augustine's." Caleb sucked in a deep breath, the type that makes you realize how close someone is to panicking. "All we have now are the little scanners in the truck. Doesn't matter where we go now—we're going to be blind as bats out there."

———

IT TOOK the rest of the day and that night before I was able to rejoin the others. After being cleared by Josephine the following morning, I walked down the hall—and right into an argument between Judge and Deadeye.

"—wasn't my fault they didn't show up on the screens," Judge spat. "I was busy trying to keep all of us from getting chewed to pieces. If you have a problem with it, *you* figure out a way to see them!"

Deadeye slammed her cup down on the table. My power had regenerated while I slept, and I could tell there was more than anger riding behind her words as she yelled, "Not all of us can wave our fingers at something and make it go away. You're just lucky it was you and Tara out there, and not any of the rest of us!"

I kept my head down, trying to shut out the flying emotions as I poured a cup of coffee and rummaged in the fridge for half-and-half. The argument continued behind me, ending as Deadeye stormed out and slammed the door behind her.

Judge didn't seem too pleased to have won. His irritation came plainly through the edges of my mind as he hunkered over his cup of coffee.

"Okay, what's going on?" Josephine asked as she came in. "Reneé looked pretty mad just now."

I decided it was safe enough to let myself be seen. Popping up from the fridge and leaning against the counter, I listened as Caleb explained, "She's mad about the attack yesterday."

"No, she's not," I said, surprising even myself. "She's scared." As I said it, the pieces fell together in my mind, putting words to Deadeye's emotions. "She didn't realize they were coming, and she's afraid that she could've lost one of us."

The others stared at me with amazement.

"I'd forgotten you could do that, *mijo*—tell us *why* someone is acting a certain way," Josephine said.

"He could do that even before he Shattered," Bandit corrected her. "Now, he's just always right." He pushed his chair back and left the table, pausing by the counter to clap me on the shoulder before following in the direction Deadeye had gone.

Everyone fell silent for a moment as the echoes of the door closing faded out.

"I didn't mean to make her worry," Judge said, still staring into his mug. The cheerful character on his shirt looked out of place with his demeanor as he confessed, "I guess I should've tried to get everyone inside, instead of charging ahead."

"We were taken off guard," Tara said from the stove. "And you've *never* defaulted toward caution." He conceded with a sheepish laugh as she reassured him, "No one expected they'd try to get us this close to base." She tapped my shoulder and handed me a plate of eggs, *nopal*, and beans. "Sit. Eat. You'll need every bit of your energy."

"Um, right. Exactly why is that?" I asked as I sat in Bandit's vacated seat. A flicker of evasion came from the other end of the table, and I glared at Judge. "And don't try to dance around it, either."

"Towers are down across the region," Josephine said, putting her elbows on the table and rubbing her forehead. Her curls had sneaked out of her ponytail and bobbed alongside her face as she lamented, "We can't even get weather updates from the satellite. Now, Regional Command will probably send us a new receiver for that—"

"Yeah, heaven help us if they don't have a reliable way to send us new orders..." Logan said from the corner of the room. An array of electronic components lay spread out on the folding table in front of him. Some of the pieces I recognized as parts of the scanner system. "Trust me, they'll replace it in a few days."

"Yeah, well, even with a new receiver, our scanners are toast." Caleb pointed to the jumbled stuff Logan was working with. "We won't know if we're about to be attacked unless you're able to warn us."

I swallowed a bite of breakfast. "Me?"

"You were able to feed us the location of the Brutes yesterday," Judge said, draining his coffee. "That's better than any scanning array."

I blinked hard, looking at my plate without appetite as a suspicious exchange came through from the other side of the table.

Curiosity.

Caution.

Insistence.

Looking up, I caught an intense look on Tara's face before she moderated her expression. I sighed, my shoulders dropping. "You don't have to try to hide it from me. I *know* my abilities are becoming more similar to Michael's as time goes on, and if Command finds out, they'll try to make me into Michael 2.0." I shook my head. "It's not the big secret you think it is."

Busted.

The sudden thought—and it came from Caleb, which made it funnier—was so clear that I started laughing in spite of myself. "Don't worry; I've known for a while."

Tara's sympathy came through in more than just her words. "Sorry for keeping it from you. He was a hero to so many; we just didn't want you to feel like you had to match him."

I shrugged, swallowed a mouthful of food, and said, "I understood. And I *wasn't* planning on trying to match his abilities, but now I guess I have to."

"Well, Reneé kept his old command helmet," Josephine

said. "It's in the Fishbowl somewhere. We could see how far the ability extends."

Logan looked up from his work in the corner. "She did? I thought all that stuff was decommissioned and scrapped."

Everyone laughed. "She's such a pack rat," Tara said. "She probably has a whole xeno ship's worth of tech hiding in her corner."

Logan set aside the parts he'd been fitting together. "That helmet was one of a kind. I'll bet you could use it if we updated the software; your powers *are* similar enough."

"I don't know," Judge said. He ran his hand across the back of his head. "The connection only worked because of the bio interfaces we all got fitted with."

Caleb and Tara reached back to the same spot behind their right ears. "I hadn't thought of that," Tara confessed. "They turned these off when he died. I don't know how to reactivate them."

"And I don't want to try." Judge's fork scraped across his plate. "I break into everyone else's heads; I don't want anyone breaking into mine." He cast a glance across at me, and I fought the urge to squirm under his scrutiny. "Not even you, kid."

STAGE SEVENTEEN

LOGAN'S PREDICTION about Regional Command's response to the destroyed receiver was right on the nose. Within a few days, a crew came to repair and replace the damaged components, installing a brand-new scanner array, receiver, and transmitter atop the building. I hid in my room the entire day, alternately reading and testing out my newly expanded senses. I'd been worried that the burnout from a few days ago would impact my power, but my sixth sense still reached outside the confines of the base. By the end of the day, I'd gotten comfortable enough with the new ability to emerge from my bedroom with some interesting information.

"Did you know the javelina have been using the wash as their own personal highway?" I asked as all of us assembled for movie night. "There was an entire family of them this afternoon, just going along as happy as could be. They didn't even care about the workers on the roof."

"That's kind of cool," Judge said, smacking the top of the ancient disc player. "Now, if we could only point them toward the Brutes and say, 'charge'—" He laughed and ducked a pillow that I flung at him, retaliating by knocking my feet out from under me with a well-placed shield bubble. I grabbed the pillow and hurled it at his ribs before yanking him to the ground.

"I'd say it's an opportunity for fresh meat," Bandit said, raising his voice to be heard over the sounds of us tussling.

Beside him, Logan pulled another pillow from the couch and thumped me over the head with it. "We could easily get them from the roof. Too bad javelina tastes terrible."

"Not if you're careful with how you butcher it..." Josephine corrected. "My grandfather always made it into chorizo."

"And it was the *worst* chorizo I'd ever tasted," Bandit laughed. He prodded Judge and I with his foot. "Hey, knock it off!"

We let go of each other as the movie started, Bandit and Josephine arguing over whose grandparent had been a better cook as the main titles rolled. I watched the movie with only half my usual attention, my senses keying in on more than just friendly banter in Bandit and Josephine's conversation. *There's something else there.* A pattern emerged as I thought over their interactions from the last few weeks. *I can't say for sure, but something's up.* I looked around the room as the movie ended and everyone began heading toward bed. From what I could remember, Deadeye had known Bandit and Josephine the longest. *I'll ask her.*

Kneeling next to Deadeye as she shut down the media

system, I asked, "Can we talk?" I glanced over my shoulder at Josephine, remembering the unearthly good hearing she'd admitted to having. "Outside?"

Deadeye unplugged the speakers. "Sure." Her eyes flicked to the ceiling. "It's a good night. Let's go up on the helipad."

Outside, the air was beginning to cool after the heat of the day. Deadeye sat at the end of the painted *H*, her pants and boots blending with the black paint as she stretched out her legs. "What's on your mind?"

I fidgeted with a pen from my pocket. Now that I was on the cusp of the question, I found myself reluctant. Instead, I settled for, "Josephine mentioned you kept Michael's command helmet." The name still rattled funny through my head, but I was determined to get used to saying it.

"Think you're going to try using it?" Deadeye sat up straighter, her voice changing to "interested engineer." "I didn't think you *could* without a bio interface, but if you want to give it a shot..."

"I wanted to take a look." I sat down next to her, bracing my hands behind me and looking up at the sky. "The others seemed to think I'd be able to fill in for the missing comms network if we could get it to work—well, Josephine thought so, at least." I stuffed the awkwardness back. *No way except asking directly, I guess.* "Were she and Bandit ever a couple?"

Surprise jolted from Deadeye. "Sorry?"

"Well, they seem so close, and I could never figure out exactly what they were to each other. And lately..."

"Well, lately, they've been acting lovey enough that you don't even have to be an empath to pick up on it," Deadeye answered dryly. She leaned back on her elbows. "I'm certain they've loved each other in some way or another since long before the Force disbanded. They've just never acted on it."

I didn't say anything in the hope that she'd continue. After a long moment, Deadeye sighed and said, "Bandit was married, back in the day. Not to Josephine, though—someone else, a rancher's daughter." She shifted, looking up at the sky. "He saved her and her sisters from the previous generation of thugs."

"He mentioned something about them roughing up some girls." I bounced the tip of my pen against my thigh. Now that I thought back, Bandit's voice *had* been nostalgic when he'd mentioned it. "He married one of them? That must've been right before—" I stopped as Deadeye nodded.

"I think they'd been married for about a year when the first dampening fields went up. And the baby was about two years old when I first met Bandit."

My pen clattered to the rooftop. "Baby? He has kids?" Something uncomfortable stirred in my stomach. *No one keeps their family a secret. Something must've happened to them.*

"*Had*," Deadeye corrected. Her voice *and* emotions took on a hard edge. *Bitterness.* "Bandit lost his wife and son in the riots when the fields dropped." She looked up at me, her good eye brimming with loss. "Cruz would've been about thirteen now, if he'd survived."

Unexpectedly, the images surged in—

Blood splattering a wall.

Screams from outside.

Glass breaking.

Fear freezing my muscles in place; dust tickling my nose as I buried my head in my arms.

"There's nothing for you here!" Abuela's voice, suddenly cut off in a cry of pain—

"Gabriel!"

Deadeye's voice snapped me into reality. Regret replaced the horrible memories, and I immediately grabbed her arm.

Sunlight on poppy petals.

Mango paletas.

Rain on a rooftop.

Her shoulders relaxed, and I sat back on my heels. "I— I'm so sorry." I let go of her arm. "I didn't know that would happen; I promise."

"It's okay." She shivered like a horse trying to rid itself of pestering flies. "I'm not mad, I just—" She reached out to put an arm around my shoulders, but I shied away from her touch. Her voice softened. "You lost someone in the riots too, didn't you?"

I blinked away the memories as they threatened to come out in tears. "My grandmother. She hid me under my bed, told me not to make a sound, and tried to stop them from coming in. I have no idea what they were looking for in our house, but they killed her." I took a heavy breath; in four counts, out four counts. "After that, I was on my own."

I heard her sigh in more than my ears. "No wonder you're jumpy any time the riots are mentioned."

I pulled my feet in to sit cross-legged, trying to restore order in my mind. "I wanted the Force to station me far, far away from here so I'd never have to relive those memories. But then I met Bandit in marksman training, and he convinced me to join him here." The pieces arranged them-selves in my mind, information old and new coming together in a clear picture. "I guess I remind him of his son."

"Guess so." Deadeye's boots scraped as she lay down,

tipping her chin toward the stars. "Anyway, that's why he and Josephine never went any farther than friends. At first, it was because of Maria. Afterward, I'm pretty sure neither of them wanted to risk it." Her voice hushed. "Why would you want to tangle your heart into something that could break it?"

"Yeah, that's something I apparently haven't learned either," I muttered. At her questioning sound, I sighed and explained, "I stayed away from as many people as I could, after Abuela died. The one time I made friends, they turned on me. I kept to the edges, didn't talk to anyone, and listened." I retrieved the pen I'd dropped earlier, closing my hand around it and stuffing it into my pocket. "I wrote down the stories I heard, including the ones about all of you." I turned my face away from her, even though I knew she couldn't see my expression in the dark. "You—all of you—were my heroes. Then, I actually *met* you." A shudder crept through my voice. "And before I knew it, I'd let myself get attached."

"Hey." She sat up to put an arm around my shoulders, and this time I didn't shrug away. "That's not a bad thing."

"I tried for so long to keep myself closed off, but now my heart's tangled into all of you." I blinked away unshed tears. "I don't know what I'd do now if something happened."

"We've all faced that potential over the years. Trust me, the exchange is still worth it." Deadeye tightened her arm around my shoulders, and her chuckle sent warm streaks through my heart. "I'm just happy you're tangled up with us."

"Yeah." I looked out at the vastness of a desert night. "Me too."

———

WITH THE TOWERS DOWN, watching the screens was less of a full-time job. We still kept someone on them at night in case something happened, but during the day the job of watching our six was left to me. Now that I'd gotten better at it, keeping track of the comings and goings around the base wasn't as daunting a task as I'd originally thought. We had a few run-ins with Brutes or the Blood Angels over the next two weeks, but nothing major enough to cause us more worry.

I should've known something was up.

That day, Josephine headed out with Logan on the weekly supply run. Ordinarily, one of us would have gone with her, but a ruckus at a water treatment facility had kept everyone up most of the night. That morning, Deadeye was fiddling with the command helmet and I was monitoring the screens with about half my usual attention when Logan's voice crackled through the speakers.

"Fishbowl, this is T-1. Do you copy? Over."

My notebook and pen went skittering off the desk as I almost jumped out of my chair. *Something's wrong.* I jammed my headset over my head and adjusted the microphone. "Fishbowl copies. What's going on? Over."

There was a heart-stopping moment of static, in which I cleared all the overlays from the screens to bring up the Thunderbird's tracking signature. They were in the dead area between us and Tucson, moving at about half their usual pace. Deadeye stopped her work and came to lean on the back of my chair as I toggled the mic on. "T-1, I have you tracking over the Midway Wash. Is something wrong? Over."

When the transmission returned, Logan's voice was cut

with so much static, I could barely understand his words. Deadeye muttered something and fiddled with a knob on the comms panel, and the static cleared enough for us to hear, "—crossed west of Highway 85—electrical problems with the main engines, and have switched to reserve—battery won't last. Over."

I willed my voice to stay steady as I asked, "What type of electrical problems? Over."

"—sudden power surge, thought it was lightning."

Deadeye wrapped her hand around my wrist, sending a confusing tangle of memory flooding toward me.

Dust storm, Brutes, electrical pulse, Shattered lightning from a clear sky.

I nodded up at her, trying to quell the panic rising in my throat. *We've had something like this happen before.* "T-1, can you make it back to base? Over."

Static.

"T-1, do you copy? Over." I looked up at the screens again, my heart sinking at the sight of the red dot remaining stationary on the monitor. Closing my eyes, I projected my thoughts as hard as I could through the base.

Guys, Fishbowl now!

Deadeye's knee buckled, and she grabbed the edge of my chair in shock. "Did I know you could do that?"

I gave her a "not right now" look as Judge crashed into the room, a glowing energy ball cupped in his hand. "What's going on?"

Deadeye pointed to the screen as the rest of the squad ran in; Bandit and Caleb dressed like they'd been working outside and Tara clutching a batter-covered mixing spoon. "The Thunderbird's gone down."

Everyone's sudden dread punched through my stomach.

Both Tara and Judge swore, eyes fixated on the screen. Bandit went white under his tan, hand going to his holster before coming away shaking. Caleb frowned and crossed his arms, the scar lines on his face deepening with concern. "Where?"

I pointed. "Just before the wastelands. Logan said he was having engine trouble and switched to reserve power. The main systems got fried by an electrical overload." I winced and put a hand to my forehead as the aftereffect of the news hit everyone in a churning blend of anger, fear, and worry. "That's all I got before the radio cut out as well."

Bandit recovered the fastest. His voice came out deadly crisp as he ordered, "*Mijo*, I need exact coordinates sent to the truck's nav system. Phantom, Banshee, Deadeye, get geared and report to the bay in five minutes."

"Copy that," Tara said, heading for the door with Caleb at her heels.

Judge shifted his weight to follow. "Me too."

Bandit stopped him with a hand to his chest. "Stay here with Gabriel."

Both of us started talking simultaneously.

"I can take care of myself!"

"I'm not going to be on babysitting duty!"

Bandit shook his head. "I'm not leaving him here alone," he told Judge. "I'll bet any odds you want that this is the Blood Angels' doing. If we take him out there, we could be playing right into their hands."

He switched to Spanish as he turned to me. "Gabriel, I know you can take care of yourself, but I don't want to risk losing you to an ambush. Stay here, and keep your senses sharp." His amber eyes commanded me to listen, the authority coming through so strong that I froze in my seat. "Don't do anything stupid."

My shoulders slumped. "I'll stay," I promised.

"*Gracias, mijo.*" He turned and walked out, pulling his hat off his head as he went.

Alone in the Fishbowl, Judge and I exchanged rebellious looks. "I don't want to be here any more than you do," I reminded him.

"I know." He slumped into a chair, running both hands through his bleached hair. The roots were growing in dark blond, and the change removed much of his usual confident aura as he said, "I know having Caleb and Tara together on the field is a better option, and Reneé can fix almost anything, but—"

Helplessness. Frustration.

I sighed. "I know. Watch the screens for a sec, okay?"

Even with all the lights on, the empty base felt creepy and dark as I went to the kitchen. The smell of chili greeted my senses as I opened the door, an abandoned bowl of corn-bread batter sitting on the counter alongside the stove. I dumped the batter into a pan, put it in the oven with a timer, turned down the heat on the chili, and started a pot of coffee. Once the coffee was finished, I filled two mugs and went back to the Fishbowl. Judge had taken over my chair, sitting hunched before the keyboard in a stew of black guilt.

"Hey." I set a mug down at his elbow. "This wasn't your fault."

"Yeah, I get it. No predicting it. It could've been any of us."

By the twist in his mouth as he said it, I could tell it was a quote from some previous experience. I reached cautiously toward the memory, hovering just out of reach behind his emotions. His cyan eyes narrowed, and the memory vanished. "Stay out of my head, Gabe," he warned.

"Sorry." I backed up to sit in the chair he'd vacated.

"Trust me; it's better for both of us if you keep away." He took a sip from the mug, surprise jittering from him as he stopped and looked at me. "You remembered how I like my coffee?"

I sipped from my own cup. "I know how everyone takes their coffee. Though, to be fair, I knew that even before I Shattered."

"Yeah?"

"Yeah."

He snorted. "That's pretty cool, kid."

Without another word said, we finished the coffee and stayed put, tracking the progress of the truck as it raced toward what we could only assume was a crash site. Even with the speed at which they were traveling, it still took more than an hour for them to reach the spot where we'd lost the Thunderbird's signal.

I refilled the coffee cups and checked on dinner, returning as the radio came to life.

Tara's voice was the epitome of cold professionalism. "Fishbowl, this is G-5, do you copy? Over."

"We copy," Judge said, craning his neck to look at me as I came over. "What's it look like out there? Over."

"We reached the site. They were able to make an emergency landing without too much damage to the Thunderbird." There was a break in the transmission, like Tara had paused to take a deep breath. "There's no sign of either of them, but there are tire tracks going toward and away from the crash site. Over."

I wasn't sure if the sinking feeling in my stomach was

coming from me or Judge as he asked, "Are there signs of a fight? Over."

"There's blood on the ground by the left landing leg. Can't tell whose it is, or how it happened. Bandit found some more by where one of the vehicles stopped. There were a couple of Brutes lingering around, but I think the blood drew them, not the other way around. Over."

"Check, G-5. Can Deadeye get the Thunderbird in the air again? Over." Judge's hands tightened around his coffee cup as we waited for Tara to respond. "This isn't good."

I pulled my arms tighter against my ribcage, wishing for the weight of my armor against my shoulders. "I wonder where they've taken them." I knew I didn't need to spell out who exactly "they" were.

"If we'd had scanners up in the area, we might've known. But now..."

Whatever he'd been about to say was interrupted by Tara's voice. "Fishbowl, Deadeye thinks she can reset the control panel and get the engines working again. We'll update you on our progress every half hour, copy?"

"Copy. We're standing by for updates." Judge sighed. "Keep your eyes open for more intel. Fishbowl out."

WE SAT by the console more or less in silence, the quiet only broken by the every-half-hour reports from the ground team. The more they looked, the clearer it became; Logan and Josephine had vanished, along with their captors. Finally, word reached us that Deadeye and Bandit were coming back with the Thunderbird, leaving Caleb and Tara to bring the truck home.

I stood up, my joints stiff from the hours of tense waiting. "They'll be hungry." I checked the clock. It was long past sundown. "I'll go finish up dinner."

"They'll be here in about twenty minutes," Judge said from behind me. "Better hurry."

The food didn't exactly need tending. I just wanted to stay busy. I'd been keeping the chili at a bare simmer and the cornbread covered in foil on the counter. Setting bowls, spoons, and plates at the end of the counter, I moved the food over and was wiping down everything for the third time when the roof creaked with the Thunderbird's landing. A few minutes later, footsteps sounded down the metal stairs. I started toward the hallway, only to stop before opening the door.

I'd never felt Bandit this upset before.

Pulling my hand away from the door handle, I returned to the kitchen, mentally tracking Bandit as he went first to his room, then out to the practice range. *There could be monsters out there,* I thought, focusing my senses on the area around the base. Nothing tripped my radar, save a coyote whisking out of range down the wash. *I guess he's okay by himself.*

The thought was confirmed as a cluster of shots rang out, then another. Sorting through Bandit's emotions, I could tell he was taking shots at one of the dummies Caleb and I had rebuilt—and that it was settling his mind the way writing settled mine. *He's got his handgun. And I'll know if anything attacks him.* As a stab of grief and anger went through my—his—mind, I decided to leave Bandit alone.

Deadeye came down from the roof around the same time as Caleb and Tara pulled up in the truck. "Where's Bandit?"

Deadeye demanded as she came in with Judge on her heels, her pink-streaked hair straggling around her eyepatch strap. The light had gone out of her good eye, leaving it hollow and sad.

"Outside." Another series of shots went off as I pointed in the direction of the range.

"Makes sense," she said. "And the others? I heard them come in."

"We're here," Tara said from the door to the bay with Caleb behind her. "Saw some Brutes, but it was easier to outrun them than fight."

Judge stuffed his hands in his pockets. "You backed down from a fight? You?" He shook his head. "You must've missed us."

Tara's face held a stoic expression, but I wasn't surprised when she burst into tears. Like a pin popping a bubble, it took only that moment for everyone to let their guards down. Tara rushed into Deadeye's arms, both of them weeping as Judge wrapped long arms around them. Caleb stayed by the door for a fraction of a second longer, before coming over and laying a hand on Judge's shoulder.

I blinked hard and clutched the edge of the counter at the intensity of everyone's sadness. Tara must've noticed, too, because she disengaged from the tangle of comfort to reach out a hand. "Gabe," she said, her voice choking with tears. "C'mere."

Rounding the counter slowly, I took her hand and stepped closer to the others. Together, we made a circle within a circle; Judge, Caleb, and I a protective wall around Deadeye and Tara. After a long moment, the tears began dying out, grief tempered by the comfort of being together.

"We'll be okay," Deadeye assured everyone as she let her arms slide from around Tara. "We'll be okay, and"—her determination filtered through my mind—"we'll find them. This isn't the end for us."

STAGE EIGHTEEN

Earth Defense Force Base 36
Gila River Valley
October 9

THE FOLLOWING DAY, Judge and I were out sparring in the practice grounds behind the bay. It was a good distraction, especially with Tara warning us to keep our thoughts out of each other's heads. Judge had shoved me back several paces with a force wall, and I was gathering a ball of light to hurl into his face when a sudden flash of surprise from inside the base caught me off guard. I let the energy dissipate, my shield dropping as Judge yelled and slammed me backward again.

I hit the ground in a cloud of dust, the wind getting driven from my lungs as his face morphed from triumphant to concerned.

"I gotcha—Gabe?" He dropped his own shield and came over, offering me a hand up. "You okay? I didn't mean to hit you that hard."

I took his hand, brushing dust from my shirt as I staggered up. "I'm fine, it's just—" I shook off the dizziness that came from overusing my abilities. "I think something's happened inside." I frowned, zeroing in on who it was that I'd felt. "Deadeye's in the Fishbowl, and something just surprised her."

Worry flashed from Tara, and she set down the camera she'd been using to record us sparring. "Surprised like how?"

"Ask her," I said. "She's coming out."

Just as I said it, Deadeye appeared in the bay doorway, a sudden breeze flicking her bangs across her face. "Guys! Regional just called. They got a ransom demand from the Blood Angels!"

WE CROWDED into the conference room, and Bandit brought up the transmission. He was more in control of himself than he had been last night, but hurt and worry still trickled out of him like a cracked glass leaking water. "Regional got this just now." He glanced up at me before playing the transmission. "They're asking a lot of questions."

The video flickered up onto the screen, a hazy picture painted in muted tones on the glass. Two handcuffed and blindfolded figures sat side by side in an empty room, their builds and clothing confirming identities even before the camera zoomed in on their faces. From offscreen, someone said in English, "No more messing around, Earth Defense Force. Turn over the Shattered operative Gabriel Mendoza, or lose your doctor and pilot to the monsters." As if cued, a Brute roared somewhere in the background, and Josephine flinched. Bandit's breath hitched as the offscreen speaker continued, "Meet us at the coordinates contained in this message. No tricks. No extra hands, or snipers in the sky. Just an even exchange—one Shattered for two Defense Force troopers."

The camera swung dizzyingly around to show a man's face, encased in an old-style helmet with his face obscured by a red bandana. "Don't test us on this, Regional Command. You know this is a fight you won't win."

The transmission blinked out of existence, leaving a blank sheet of glass balanced in the center of the table. Everyone held their breath, eyes darting around the room as we waited for someone to speak first. Finally, Caleb said, "Guess they want Gabriel bad enough that they've upped the ante. Sir?" The question was directed at Bandit. "What do you want us to do?"

Bandit heaved a deep sigh. "Regional Command says wait. They're developing a team response to this, and they want us to stay out of it."

"Stay out of it?" Tara said what I was sure everyone else was thinking. "They're our people, and we're being told to stay out of it? Are they even coming up with a plan?"

"That's what they said." Deadeye shoved a tablet across the conference table at Tara. "And they're extremely curious about Gabriel." A spark flickered in her good eye. "They didn't realize we had a new fully trained, extremely powerful Shattered here."

I snorted despite myself. "The bounty on my head didn't tip them off?"

"Apparently, they've forgotten how to read."

"Or they don't consider what goes on in the barrios worth their notice," Bandit said. "It wouldn't be the first time they'd missed something right under their noses because it wasn't part of official channels."

"That still isn't an answer," Judge argued. "You said what Regional Command wants us to do, but what are we going to do?"

I could feel indecision warring within Bandit as he stared for a long moment at the empty transmission screen. At last, he said, "We have to wait until Regional comes up with a plan. I know!" He held up a hand as Tara and Judge both opened their mouths to protest. "I know. I want to go after them just like you do."

"What if we came up with a plan?" I suggested.

Caleb crossed his arms and leaned against the wall. "You wouldn't suggest that unless you had something in mind. What's your idea?"

I took a deep breath. "Well, first, where's the location they outlined for us?"

Bandit pointed toward the Fishbowl. "It'll be easier to put it on the screens out there."

We trooped out, Deadeye logging into the screens. Adding a set of coordinates, she let the software zoom in. A giant white scar came into focus across the landscape, and I frowned in recognition. "The Ajo copper mine? No one's used it in decades."

"It's a good place," Tara said with grudging admiration. "Wide and open. Nowhere we could hide."

Deadeye pursed her lips. "Not exactly. Industrial mining ended decades ago, but some companies reopened production in the last twenty years."

"They got desperate, huh?" Judge asked.

"Well, wiring doesn't make itself." Deadeye carefully manipulated the overlays to refine the image of the crater. Now that I looked closer, I could see what she was pointing at. "They didn't have access to heavy equipment, so they did things the old-fashioned way. Satellite doesn't pick it up, but there are tunnels all over the place. I think *that's* why the Blood Angels picked this spot. They probably have the hostages nearby, but underground."

Bandit's amber eyes narrowed, calculating. "Underground... And there's no way our scanners on the truck can find them."

"They can't, but I can," I chimed in, moving over to take the mouse from Deadeye and lean on the desk with one elbow. Bringing the map out to a view of the whole mine, I pointed at the western edge of the crater. "If we get in behind here, we might be able to sneak a small team through the city. If they get down into the tunnels, they can get the hostages out before the exchange is supposed to take place."

"You think your range extends that far?" Tara asked, a faint sense of hope stirring in her words.

"Not from the other side of the mountains. But if I can set up somewhere above the crater, I could guide the rescue team from there." I minimized the images on the screen and turned to face all of them. "It'd be well inside my range for finding people, but outside of comms range from the truck."

Caleb swore quietly. "It does us no good if you can see them, but can't tell us where to go."

I steeled myself against the emotional pushback about to be unleashed. "I'd have to use the command helmet. And the rescue team would need to have their bio interfaces reactivated so we could talk mind-to-mind."

Judge shook his head, his eyes and emotions unreadable. "No. No way. Count me out."

"Alexi," Tara said quietly. "He's not Michael. He's not *anyone* from training. Gabe isn't going to hurt us." She looked over at Caleb, and I could almost see the agreement passing between the two of them.

Caleb nodded briefly. "We'll do it. The two of us; we'll let you into our heads."

———

AN INTENSE CALL with Regional Command, a sleepless night, and a nerve-wracking flight to Tucson later, Caleb and I sat in a white-painted room somewhere deep in the St. Augustine's base. Deadeye had proven an acceptable substitute pilot, seeing us safely off the Thunderbird before disappearing into the depths of St. Augustine's to "collect information" from her engineering colleagues. Behind closed doors to our left, Tara slept under anesthesia while one of the doctors worked to reactivate her communication implant.

"Are you ready for this?" Caleb asked.

Anything could happen while I'm unconscious, and I'd have no idea. My voice came out less steady than I would've liked. "It didn't occur to me that this would only be possible if *I* got a piece of metal embedded into the back of my head."

"I think they're mostly plastic. But there is *some* metal involved."

"Will it—" I stopped, not wanting to ask the question of someone who'd clearly been through much, much worse. "Will I feel it afterward?"

Caleb slid his left sleeve up, angling his arm toward me. "This doesn't even hurt." He ran a finger along the metallic tracery. "I only notice it's there if something hits my arm hard." He let his sleeve slide down. "You'll be okay. Tara won't let anything happen to you."

"I wish they'd let her go last," I admitted. According to

the doctor, Tara's implant had been easiest to access, and he'd wanted to familiarize himself with the construction before going after Caleb's or implanting mine. "Sitting here anticipating it isn't helping."

"Yeah," Caleb agreed. He bent down and pulled one of the books I'd given him out of his bag. "Here." He passed me the book and leaned against the wall, closing his eyes. "Might as well try to distract yourself."

I KNEW Tara was awake long before the doctor came out to assure us that everything had gone well. The news did nothing to ratchet down the tension building in my heart. By the time she was fully awake and the anesthesia had worn off, my heart was pounding so hard I could feel it in my wrist without putting my fingers on my pulse.

Caleb set his book down. "I think it's almos—Gabe?" He grabbed my shoulder, concern breaking through my panic. "Your eyes are glowing."

I took a deep breath, then another. "Th-they are?"

"Yeah." His face softened. "Do you want me to go next?"

"No, it's okay. I'll—" I forced the panic into the corners of my mind and squared my shoulders against the wall. "I'll be fine. I have to do this."

"That's the spirit." Caleb looked up as the doors beside us swung open.

"Trooper Mendoza?" The doctor who'd overseen Tara's procedure gestured me into the sterile-smelling surgical center. "We're ready."

I stood, my body obeying even as my mind shrieked "don't." As the doors began to swing closed, I looked back frantically. "Caleb?"

"It's going to be okay." The door closed on his words, but the impression he'd meant to convey made it through. *Don't be afraid, Gabriel.*

As I stepped through into the old surgical room, the three nurses stopped what they were doing to look up at me. Whispers filled the corners of the room, the material of what was said filtering through my panic-wracked mind.

Powerful Shattered.

Just like the Commander.

Our next great leader.

"Here, lie down on this." The doctor smoothed a way-too-white sheet across a waist-high table. "We'll do all our prep work after you're asleep."

I ducked my head and obeyed, doing my best to block out everything swirling around the room. My concentration broke as Tara walked into the room, her presence flooding my sixth sense.

Judge's voice echoing around a metal bowl, Gabriel's laughter, Logan's authoritative "Stop!"

I exhaled hard and opened my eyes. "Thanks."

Tara smiled down at me, taking my hand. "I figured if I focused hard enough on the memory, I could snap you out of it. Don't worry, I won't let you feel a thing." She eyed the medical staff with suspicion, and her hand tightened around mine. "And I won't leave your side."

GABRIEL.

My eyelids cracked open. For a second, I thought I was still in the surgical center. Then, I recognized a stain on the ceiling tiles over my head, and recognition flooded back. Sitting up, I looked around at the medical bay in Base 36.

"What—where—"

"Oh, good, she let you wake up." Deadeye handed me a cup of water. In answer to my obvious confusion, she explained, "While you were out cold, some of the command staff started getting all nosy. Tara figured it was better to get you back here before anyone decided to dig around your head while you were unconscious."

I sighed and swung my feet over the side of the bed, making sure everything was still in working order before standing up. To my immense relief, there was little dizziness, and no nausea. "Did Caleb come through his procedure okay?"

Deadeye snorted. "He's fine. Crazy idiot insisted on staying awake."

I'll bet that hurt. Trying not to think too hard about it, I cautiously reached out to see where everyone was in the base. I could feel Bandit in the kitchen, Judge in the Fishbowl, and Caleb and Tara in their room. It felt like Caleb was reading and Tara was sleeping. Returning my attention to Deadeye, I said, "I don't feel any different."

"You won't until we link you through the helmet with this software." She waved a tablet at me.

"Sounds good." I reached up to the spot where the doctor had said they'd insert the device under my skin. Sure enough, a foreign ridge met my fingers, behind my ear and almost lost in my hairline. As my fingers went across it, a dull ache spread to encompass my skull. I dropped my hand, taking a sharp breath.

"Don't mess with it," Deadeye warned. "Our medical tech may be advanced, but the human body hasn't advanced enough to not freak out at something new being jammed into it." She slid the tablet into her cargo pocket and nodded toward the door. "Let's go see if the others are ready to test this thing."

We collected Caleb and Tara from their room and headed to the Fishbowl. Bandit and Judge drifted over to watch as Deadeye lifted the command helmet out of its case and checked it over. "Looks good." She handed it to me.

I settled the helmet over my head, the newly replaced padding cupping my head. Deadeye's voice came discordantly through ears and helmet speakers as she said, "Okay, the connection to the satellite is in place. Toggle it on and let's see if it works."

So far, none of this was new. I brought up the different overlays from the tower atop the base, checking that each interface worked with the display. Inside the helmet, I was immersed as deep in the streams of data as I ever had been. Outside, Judge was getting bored, Bandit didn't quite know how he felt about all this, and Caleb and Tara were nervous. Once I was satisfied everything checked out, I gave Deadeye a thumbs-up. "It looks good so far."

I wasn't paying attention to the moment she switched on the link between myself, Caleb, and Tara, but I didn't need to. The world stretched, blurred, and snapped together again, and for a brief, dizzying moment I couldn't tell which body I was occupying.

Caleb's smile.

Tara's laugh.

A scream out of nowhere.

Fragments of memories, conversations, feelings, and thoughts all swirled around me in a blinding dance. *Which is me? Is any of this me?*

Tara paused on a memory, arresting my tumble through her and Caleb's minds.

"It's always been you. There was never any other question." Only one or two scars traced Caleb's face as he held my hand, slipping a simple metal band around my left third finger. A limitless sea stretched out behind him, sunlight reflecting off the waves as he pulled my face close to his.

A lifetime of knowing each other, and it ends up here. I let go of the memory even as she did, another image slamming into my—our minds.

The wind rushed from my lungs as I pitched forward, catching myself a moment before my face hit the ground. I frantically reached for the knife, barely visible among the books under the sagging couch. A booted foot landed hard on my hand and pain shot up my arm, fear mixing with mortification as tears ran down my face. Around me, the gangsters started laughing.

I'd expected the memory to fade, but the remembered pain ricocheted across my mind as the library morphed into a darkened street. From somewhere outside myself, Caleb gasped.

Abandoning my weapon, I managed to limp back to the dangling cable and stretched out a bloodied hand to grab it. A third blaster bolt sent me to my knees as a fork of electricity arced across the street—targeting not me, but the Thunderbird's engines. The aircraft dipped, plummeting for a heart-stopping moment before the engines caught the air. The cable whisked out of my hand, the sudden force tearing at my shoulder.

I felt him take a deep breath, the fear in his mind coiling and uncoiling.

"Caleb, wake up!" Gabriel's voice floated past my defenses. The memory of sunlight warming my skin pulled

me into the light, and the nightmares dissipated around his voice.

There was my face, seen from someone else's eyes.

I stood there in a vortex of cyan light, my heart feeling like it'd shattered the same way my mind had. "Not again!" A shield formed around me as the vortex collapsed, sending me spiraling into unconsciousness.

It's just like a data stream, I reminded myself, trying hard to hang on to Gabriel in the flow of others' thoughts. *Just a data stream.* I reached as far through their minds as I could, letting the memories flow like the current of a swift river. Tears, heartbreak, joy, pain, hope, and laughter all swirled past and were gone, blurring into a constant fuzzy noise in the back of my head.

Guys? Are you okay? Can you hear me?

Tara's voice was as clear in my mind as her natural voice was to my ears.

We're here.

Caleb's mental voice sounded like his physical one; strong and level, infused with dangerous confidence. *We hear you.*

That was intense. I took a deep breath and let it out slowly. *I don't know if I can do this.* Even admitting it mentally, to the two people I trusted the most, felt dangerous.

It's okay, Tara said. *You got through the hard part. We just dragged you through our most vivid memories, and you aren't a gibbering lunatic.*

Yet, Caleb corrected with a laugh. From inside his head, I could feel the constant fear that dogged his steps, but also the iron will that held it in check.

I circled around that gut-wrenching sensation uneasily. *You really are scared all the time. How do you manage?*

There're more things to life than just fear. As he said it, a rapid-fire succession of emotions mixed with images flicked through our minds; happy dogs with their tongues hanging out, sunsets with Tara at his side, the comfort of a quiet afternoon reading, and the softness of a worn flannel shirt. *I have to focus on those things, not on the fear.* Like a black shadow, the creeping emotion snuck through his thoughts. He pushed it away fiercely. *It gets hard sometimes.*

That's why I'm here, Tara said. *That's why he's here. That's why we agreed to do all this. If we don't do something, more people will have to live with that same type of fear day in, day out.*

I'm still terrified, I admitted. *Even after everything that's happened. I don't want anyone else to have to suffer, but a lifetime of hiding is hard to shake.*

Don't worry too much. Bandit said you were the best person this region could have to fight for it, and I'm pretty sure he's a good judge of character. Tara yawned outside of the link.

You're exhausted, I said as the realization struck. *You were keeping me asleep the entire way back!*

I'm fine.

Don't lie to him, Caleb warned. *You know he can feel when you're lying, right?*

Shut up, Tara told him, then said aloud, "Gabriel, you can open your eyes now."

"What?"

I hadn't even realized my eyes had been closed. I opened them to see the inside of the helmet, and beyond it, Deadeye looking between the three of us. "I wish I'd had a camera for that."

"Be glad you didn't," Tara muttered, one hand going up to her forehead. I knew exactly what she meant as she said, "It's not something you want to do more than once—reliving all those things."

"It won't do that every time, right?" I asked.

"Probably not," Caleb reassured me. "I think it's your mind getting comfortable with ours."

"The more we practice, the more natural it'll feel," Tara said as I reached over to Deadeye's console to disconnect the helmet. The display in front of my eyes went dead, and to my relief the flow of thoughts from Tara and Caleb stopped. "Pretty soon you won't know if we're talking mind-to-mind or through normal comms."

"Well, we don't have forever." I checked my watch. Necessary as the trip to St. Augustine's had been, it had used up an entire day of the two days contained in the Blood Angels' ultimatum. "I'm just glad this worked, because we're out of time."

STAGE NINETEEN

MORNINGS WERE STARTING to get cold, especially in the wee hours before the sun broke the horizon. In the pale light before dawn, I swapped out my regular helmet for the command one. The power indicator in the corner of my vision showed green, and I looked across at Tara and Caleb. "Ready?"

They nodded, taking hands before bracing themselves. This time, the whirlpool of memories and thoughts settled sooner, and I was able to push most of it into background static.

Am I clear?

You're clear, Caleb said, letting go of Tara's hand to adjust his shotgun on its strap over his shoulder. *We'll wait before heading down until you have a good location for us. Just focus on finding them for now.*

Okay... I let the connection to the two of them drop into the background of my mind, kneeling and putting my palms flat on the floor of the abandoned warehouse. Behind us, the others checked over their gear and weapons; Bandit reloading a magazine and sliding it into his pocket, Deadeye watching the screens through the truck's small system, and Judge switching a setting on his monitor cuff.

Closing my eyes, I brought my power to bear, focusing down on the crater below us.

Between satellite images and Shattered power, I could picture the area clearly. Terraced ramps had long since crumbled under the weight of time, leaving the mine looking like a giant had scooped a bowlful of sand out of the ground. A tiny road led out of the pit, switchbacks and retaining walls packed from the crumbling rock and clay. The tailings pond shifted green-blue in the growing daylight, shambling buildings and makeshift chutes surrounding the entrances of several wide-mouthed tunnels. The forms of several human figures could be seen as cyan outlines through my sixth sense, sitting in a truck or congregating in the buildings nearby.

"I think I need to get closer," I said, looking up at Bandit. "I can see the crater, but not tell who individual people are."

Bandit nodded grimly, sliding his handgun into his thigh holster and closing the faceplate on his helmet. "Let's go, then. There's a building overlooking the crater farther along the rim. Let's see if we can reach there."

Moving as a group, we slid between the derelict buildings toward the crater edge. Below us, the Blood Angels came into sharper focus, painting the inside of my mind in lazy vigilance. Most were still sleepy, others resentfully awake after a night on watch. I devoted most of my focus to searching the area for any trace of Josephine and Logan, keeping a small patch of my attention on making sure my feet didn't stumble over the broken asphalt and uneven side-walks as we approached the building Bandit had mentioned.

"Here, get inside." Bandit held open the door for us. "There's a viewing balcony from when this used to be a tourist destination. I'll get on the roof with the infrared."

"Don't bother," I said, grateful that we were still close enough to the truck that helmet comms worked. "I can see them from here without the infrared."

"Can you send that data to our helmets?" Caleb asked. "It might take some of the strain off you."

Clearly, he'd been feeling the headache I was starting. "I don't know how," I apologized. "And I still can't find the hostages, either."

"It's fine," Tara said. She sat down where she could see out one of the windows overlooking the mine. "We'll keep our eyes open up here while you look."

Watch my back, please, I said silently, catching unspoken agreement from both of them as I settled cross-legged in the patch of light under a broken window. *It's just hide-and-seek, Gabriel.* Closing my eyes again, I envisioned the crater below, and the sunbaked buildings surrounding it. *Where are you?*

Somewhere far away, confusion and pain stirred. A brief thread of reassurance came, like a mother's voice shushing an infant in a distant room. Furrowing my brow, I pushed my senses toward that familiar voice, turning my head back and forth until I could tell I was facing the right direction.

"That way." I pointed, certain now. Everyone looked in

the direction I was pointing, relief breaking into concern as I added, "I think one of them is hurt."

"Can you tell who?" Bandit asked, a deadly current of anger running under his words.

Now that I knew where to look, it was easier to pick out individual emotions. "I think it's Logan. They're both scared, but Josephine knows we're here."

"Is there a clear path to them?" Caleb asked, the question coming to my mind a split second before he said it aloud.

"They're underground, like we thought." I pulled my consciousness back from the hostages and let it expand into the ground under us. "Actually..." I stood and went to a rusted door in the side of the building. "Someone help me open this."

Between my muscles and Judge expanding a shield inside the lock, the door opened. Metal-banded concrete steps twisted away from us, the light from the doorway only lasting a little way before everything faded into dusky blackness.

"Down there, huh?" Judge grinned at Caleb. "Have fun, buddy."

"Yeah, thanks." Caleb hunched his shoulders, stemming the tide of fear that had welled up at the sight of the stairwell. "Which way?"

I pointed down. "There's a hallway, about six flights of stairs down. You need to head left."

"Great, and then?"

I sucked in a deep breath. *I can't tell from here.* I repeated myself aloud, ignoring Caleb and Tara's sudden worry as I explained to the others, "I found the hostages, but I can't make out a clear path to them. I—" I settled my shoulders. "I'll have to go with you."

Everyone nodded, and Bandit wrapped me in a brief hug. "We'll head back to the truck. If we have to, we'll create a distraction to keep attention on us."

I stepped free from his arms. "Sounds good." I gave the others a thumbs-up. "Stay safe."

"Get out of here," Judge said laconically. "You're burning daylight."

"Right." I looked over at Caleb and Tara. *Let's go.*

The three of us stepped into the darkened stairwell, turning on our helmet beams as we went. Dust particles danced in my headlight, and even the filter in my helmet couldn't stop the smell of abandoned basement creeping into my nostrils.

Spooky, Tara commented. *Just like old times.*

We came to the end of the hall I'd described, and I paused to let my directional sense recalibrate. *That way,* I said, pointing left. We kept going through the winding tunnels—some hand-dug dirt, others industrial concrete. Far ahead, Logan and Josephine's forms had come into sharper focus, their individual emotions easier to pick out.

Logan is *hurt.* I blinked hard, trying to figure out exactly how badly. Tara's worry overlaid my own as I decided, *I think they shot him.*

All three of us jumped as a Brute howled somewhere nearby.

Where was that?

I pointed at a concrete corridor we'd passed. *There's six of them in a locked-up room. They've built up a bit of a presence here, I'd say.*

Nice. Tara's sarcasm would've been obvious even if she'd been speaking out loud. *Which way?*

This way. I reached ahead, doing my best to separate

hostages from guards. *There's a guard nearby.* Sudden stirring overhead caught my attention. *And we need to hurry. I think someone spotted our tracks out on the creosote flats. They know we're nearby.*

We hurried through the subterranean depths, skirting pipes and piles of crates as the tunnels opened into wider corridors. Ducking into a side hall, I stiffened as Josephine's fear spiked through the roof.

Someone just scared Josephine. We need to go now!

Hurtling around a corner, we almost crashed straight into a pair of guards. One was leaning his chair against the wall, the other coming away from where he'd been talking into the grate on a heavy metal door. Before either had time to yell, Tara had sent an energy bolt straight through the sitting one's forehead, leaving a smoking hole in his helmet. He slumped over, the chair clattering to the floor as Caleb dove on the other guard with silent fury.

Josephine. Logan. Get away from the door if you can.

The locks broke under Tara's power, and the door swung open. I recognized the room from the video the Blood Angels had sent, and my stomach did a flip-flop at the sight of blood splattered against one of the walls. Logan and Josephine were gagged, their wrists bound and ankles tied to the chairs they were sitting in. Logan's flight suit was darkened with dried blood at the shoulder, and his head drooped. Fury spread through my veins as Josephine's fear changed to hope, her emotions driving out any remorse I'd had over the deaths of the two gang members.

Caleb felt similarly. His anger pulsed through my mind as he knelt to untie the ropes holding their ankles. "You okay?"

Josephine gasped as Tara pulled the duct tape off her face. "They're coming for us any moment. Hurry!" She massaged her wrists, pain flicking through her mind as we helped her up.

"They said it was only a matter of time before they'd have all of us dead," Logan said. He winced as Tara put a blue-glowing hand on his shoulder. Dizzying pain pulsed from him, glazing over his brown eyes. "They're not planning on any kind of peaceful exchange."

"I heard them talking," Josephine confirmed. "There're Brutes all over this crater."

"Then let's get out of here." Caleb helped Logan stand with an arm around his torso. "Back the way we came, right, Gabe?"

I put my arm around Josephine. "Let's go."

WE'D JUST STEPPED out of the stairwell in the overlook building when a physical sound pierced through to my ears. *Gunshots.*

"Did you hear that?"

Caleb nodded. "That came from the crater. Sounds like a rifle."

I closed my eyes as a waft of anger came through the edges in my head. "I think something's wrong with the others. Can you find your way to the truck from here?"

He and Tara exchanged a single look, a question and confirmation passing between them faster than I could track. "They'll be fine with me," Tara said. She gave Caleb's shoulder a push. "Go help the others."

Both of us stepped into the blinding sunlight and took off running in the direction of the gunshot. More sounded, both from below and above, and the muffled sounds of a helmet loudspeaker echoed through the air. I was too far to make out the words, but the tone was clear enough. I doubled my speed, skidding to a halt in the shadow of the warehouse where we'd left the truck. Caleb stopped right behind me, his confusion sharp in my mind.

They're at the edge of the crater, I told him. *I don't know why.*

"Bandit!" I yelled as I ran toward the mine, projecting my thoughts as hard as I could. ***The hostages are safe. Let's go!***

"*Mijo?*" Bandit said through comms. "You're back?"

Another gunshot echoed between the rocks as we rounded the corner of a building and saw them—Bandit atop a shipping container, Deadeye crouched behind a concrete barrier at the crater's edge, and Judge standing under a shield in the open. Dark-armored figures scurried about in the crater below.

Casting my senses wider, I was just in time to feel the ground crumbling. *Get back!*

Yells of surprise fell on both ears and mind as Judge and Deadeye slipped over the edge, sliding in a heap of rubble and dirt to the terrace below. Caleb's alarm ricocheted through my mind as the ground beneath our feet also gave way. We slipped and slid in a rush of gravel to come to a halt a little way above the others. Looking up, I estimated that we'd fallen more than fifty feet, the crater wall rising in uneven chunks of rock behind us. *We're trapped.*

"The others?" Deadeye demanded as I regained my feet. Below, the Blood Angels shouted in triumph, bullets spattering against the dirt around us.

"They're safe," I reassured her, raising a shield over Caleb and myself. Judge did the same with himself and Deadeye. "Tara's getting them to the truck. Bandit, Josephine's fine."

"Good." Above us, Bandit's relief was powerful, but brief. "Let's make sure these bastards regret their actions."

An energy bolt streaked from Judge toward the makeshift buildings at the bottom of the crater, setting a roof ablaze and sending the men beneath it running for new cover. "Can do."

A Brute howled, the sound ripping through my mind with the sudden certainty that there were many, many more around the crater than my senses had accounted for.

Caleb felt my panic, steadying me with a hand to my shoulder. *Keep calm. We have to hold them off long enough for the others to reach the truck. Then we can figure out what to do.*

We're almost there, Tara said. *Just give us another few minutes.* As her optimism settled through my head, an air horn sounded. The hail of bullets stopped, and the Blood Angels scattered.

Logan's earlier warning came to the forefront of my mind with a sickening lurch. *I don't know if we have a few minutes.* Just as I said it, the first Brutes crashed through the opening to one of the tunnels, dropping with snarls as Bandit took them out from the shipping container roof. More followed, a handful going after the few Blood Angels who hadn't been fast enough to get into the buildings. Earth flew through the air as another dozen exploded from the far wall. *There's more than we can fight off.*

Below us, the ground erupted with snarls as another

several Brutes burst from the opening of a partially collapsed tunnel. Judge yelled in shock as the already unstable ground crumbled further, sending him and Deadeye sprawling. As she tumbled down the slope, he slammed a force wall in her direction, pushing her up enough that I could reach out and grab her.

"Gotcha." I yanked Deadeye into the shield bubble as Judge regained his feet below us. Terror filled his mind as he collected himself enough to send a handful of energy balls into several of the encroaching monsters. Another fell to one of Caleb's shotgun blasts, and a fifth to a round from Bandit's rifle—but the last managed to dodge both Shattered fire and bullets to clamp its fangs around Judge's shoulder and chest.

Judge screamed, dragged off his feet by the force of the attack as the Brute pulled him toward the center of the crater. Between blinding pain and terror, I felt him rally, sending a bolt of energy through the thing's skull. The monster roared and fell dead, dropping him in a shuddering pile on the ground.

I stumbled forward as Caleb's voice echoed in my head. *Gabe, don't!*

Piercing agony shot through my mind, and I almost let go of the shield. "Judge!" Before I could get any farther, he threw a hand in my direction, freezing my feet to the ground.

"Sorry, kid. My time's run out." Judge's voice came harsh and labored through the comms. His right arm dangled limply as he staggered to his feet, blood coursing down his armor and a cry of pain escaping his lips. I frantically reached out, barely catching fear, pain, and determination before he slammed me out of his mind. "Don't try to stop me, Gabe."

Caleb caught me as my knees hit the ground. *What's going on?*

He's going to do something stupid. I struggled to my feet, raising a hand to cast a shield.

No!

All of us—from Bandit atop the roof, to Deadeye on the slope behind us, to Caleb and myself on the ground—froze in place, our joints locked in the grip of superhuman force. I tried to speak or scream, but nothing came out of my mouth. Overhead, the sky spiraled into a tornado of cyan flames.

Something grabbed in the back of my mind, overwhelming my consciousness. A wash of emotion brought tears to my eyes—battle rage, pain, and the feeling of fire running under my skin, all mixing with—

Love?

A familiar voice echoed in my head, a thousand memories swirling into my mind all at once. ***It's okay, kid. Take care of them for me.***

With an earth-shattering crack, the vortex touched down, exploding outwards in a blast of heat. Around us, the crater shook, tunnel mouths collapsing and Brutes dying under chunks of rock bigger than they were.

Behind me, Deadeye screamed. "Alexi!"

I staggered backward, the fact that I could move again confirming what had happened.

Caleb grabbed my arm. *You okay?*

I'm fine. I swallowed the tears, the last traces of Judge's presence fading from my mind. Below us, a smoking wasteland was all that remained of him *or* the monsters. "It's no good, Reneé. He's gone."

THE DRIVE HOME was dead silent, but filled with enough emotions to resemble the vortex that had snuffed out Judge's life. As we got underway, I yanked off the command helmet and put on my headset, pulling down the screens and turning off my comms. The glowing displays blurred in front of my eyes as I stared meaninglessly into space. For everyone else's sake, I did my best to keep every mental wall I possessed up around the events of the day. Thanks to Tara's memories, I'd seen what a Shattered out of control was capable of, and none of the others needed me to suddenly lose it.

No one else seemed in the mood to pry, either. After a briefly tearful reunion, Josephine fell asleep next to Bandit, his arm tightly wrapped around her. Caleb had volunteered to drive, sitting up front with Tara as Deadeye and Logan took their seats in the back. Even with the bumpy ride, Logan also fell asleep. He'd refused an IV or medication, insisting he'd be fine until we got back to base. I tried not to look in his direction. The way he'd fallen asleep, curled up in the corner, reminded me of how Judge had looked after burning out—

Stop that, I chided myself. *Don't even think about it.* I focused on the screens as the homing beacon for the base came into view. *Just get home. Then you can figure out what's next.*

The bay doors slid closed an hour later, everyone dispersing to showers, bedrooms, infirmary, and kitchen. Even with my best attempts to seal up the shattered parts of my mind, the grief and disbelief floating through the base was thick enough to choke.

Eventually, the screaming silence drove me outside.

Dragging one of our rebuilt targets into the desert behind the bay, I squared up and drew a plasma ball into my palm. When my hand could no longer withstand the heat, I launched the orb straight at the dummy, simultaneously summoning a shield to contain the blast. Lowering my hands, I assessed my performance. This dual casting was difficult at best, and for once I'd been spot-on with the timing. Sighing grimly, I repeated the moves until my hand burned. Each time, the timing got better.

I could never get it right while he was here to coach me. Now that he's dead, it's going to come easily?

I dragged the dummy into the center of the clearing, frustration clearing my head and sending fire through my veins. The sky darkened as cyan light filtered across my vision, tendrils of energy coalescing into a deep blue vortex. My heartbeat pounded in my ears, and my hands shook as they described the same simultaneous movements of releasing and shielding, the vortex thudding into the ground and slamming into the larger shield I threw around it.

After the third time, the dummy flew to pieces, leaving me staring at broken bits of junk littered all over the dusty ground.

Shattered.

I clutched my forehead, dizzy and angry that even with all this practice, I could still feel the pulse of everything around me. *It won't shut up. It won't go away.* The pressure inside my skull mounted as each heartbeat sent both first- and second-hand grief farther and farther through my mind. *It won't go away!*

The dirt stirred around my feet, cyan light spiraling out of the ground and opening into a whirling funnel of sparkling energy. Clenching my jaw, I pushed more energy into the vortex, shoving every bit of other people's emotions into the churning tower of death. Just as the twister reached its peak, my power blinked into emptiness. On the heels of the relief of being alone in my head came the death knell realization—I'd lost control. With a terrified yell, I threw myself backward, knowing the whole time that it was too late.

The bay door crashed open and a shield flew up, just as the combined force of power and grief exploded in brilliant light. The ground shook beneath me as I fell, blinded and deafened with the force of the blast. For a moment, I couldn't tell who had opened the door. Then, Tara's voice came from overhead. "Is he okay?"

Capable hands rolled me to my back, rubbing my chest hard enough to make me groan and start coughing. Bandit answered Tara, "Well, he's conscious at least. *Mijo*, can you hear me?"

"*Te oigo.*" I struggled to an elbow, Bandit's arm coming around my shoulders as I sat up. Dizziness washed over me in waves, and I shuddered in his arms. "It worked."

"I've been watching from the bay." Tara shone a penlight in first one eye, then the other, before adding, "Were you *trying* to burn yourself out?"

Cyan fuzz was collecting around the edges of my vision, but my head stayed blessedly empty of all but my own thoughts. "I just wanted it to be quiet." I knew I should be trying to sit up the rest of the way, but my limbs refused to cooperate. "Now, I'm only tired."

"Sleep, then." Bandit's arms shifted to scoop me up. If I'd been more awake, I'd have objected to him carrying me, but the sensation of being picked up like a small child was comforting enough to send me deeper toward sleep.

We must've gone through the kitchen. Deadeye asked a question, and Bandit's voice rumbled against my own chest as he answered, "Burned himself out. On purpose."

I didn't even need my power to hear the empathy in Deadeye's voice. "Poor kid. Take care of him, 'kay?"

Bandit's response fizzed away into the corners of my brain.

So tired.

STAGE TWENTY

Earth Defense Force Base 36
Gila River Valley
October 19

GRIEF LEFT holes in places I hadn't expected. Sparring with Tara wasn't the same as sparring with Judge, and everything was more solemn without his off-the-wall jokes, wacky T-shirts, and egocentric confidence. Like a tongue constantly exploring the space left by a missing tooth, my mind kept pausing on Judge's absence in my mental checklist of everyone's whereabouts and activities throughout the day. I'd started a new notebook the day after his death, pouring out the memories he'd dumped into my head in his last moments. Sitting over the pages and pages of stories almost a week later, I kept Josephine company as she finished up dinner by reading out a few of the sections.

"Those are some pretty fantastic stories, *mijo*," she commented, tasting a spoonful of *posole* before adding more salt. "Coming from anyone else, I'd say they were making them up. But you..."

"Hey, I wouldn't have believed any of them either." I ran a thumb over the collar of the goose T-shirt. I'd retrieved it the previous day, before Bandit and Josephine boxed up the rest of Judge's things. "But they're all straight from him. I'm writing it down as I remember them—well, as he remembered them. Perhaps there *is* some personal bias."

Josephine's laughter felt odd in my head, but not wrong. After days of grieving, of doing tasks robotically, of quiet meals and subdued practices, it felt good to laugh again.

"Man, that's a good sound," Caleb said as he and Logan came in from a workout in the bay. "How soon is dinner?"

"After you shower," Josephine said, holding her nose. "Shoo!"

I cleaned up my notebooks, returning to the kitchen as everyone else assembled for dinner. Meals together had always been important, but now dinner had become almost a sacred time. Amid the quiet discussion and occasional wisecracks, Bandit cleared his throat and set down his spoon. I had an idea of what he might be about to say. He'd been pacing the Fishbowl with a face like an impending monsoon most of the evening.

"Regional Command sent down new orders this afternoon."

Everyone stopped eating and looked up, their caution mixing with suspicion.

"Are they blaming *us* for what happened?" Deadeye asked.

Logan dropped his spoon into his bowl. "It's not like we could've done anything differently. They had us from the moment the Thunderbird went down."

"Maybe so, but yes, they're blaming us." Bandit looked around the table with uncharacteristic sentiment. "This might be one of the last dinners for us at Base 36. We're all being reassigned."

Disbelief.

"What?"

"Where?" Tara's eyes flicked to Caleb's, and he put his hand over hers.

"How soon?"

"Soon. We're all expected to report by this time next week." Bandit pulled a tablet out of his pocket and scrolled through it. "Josie's going to the hospital in Phoenix. Logan and Deadeye are supposed to take the Thunderbird to maintenance in Texas, then stay there to help train new pilots and techies." He sighed and looked up from the tablet, his eyes finding Josephine's as she came to sit next to him. "I'm going back to training."

Caleb squeezed Tara's hand, silver eyes cautious and mind even more so. "What about us and—"

"You're both being sent to Seattle. Gabriel's being reassigned to Central Command. Someone told them about him using the command helmet, and they want to 'test his capabilities.'"

"We can't let that happen," Tara said, yanking her hand free from Caleb's. Her eyes sparked with cyan light, and a vivid memory streaked across our bond—*Michael's face, worn and exhausted in the glow of emergency lighting.* "They'll use him till he breaks, then throw him out once he's outlived his usefulness. We *have* to do something."

"There has to be some other option," Logan said. "What about the incoming crew? Won't they need a Shattered here?" He leaned an elbow on the table, eyes cunning. "We can say his powers are too tied to this region for him to leave."

Bandit set the tablet down. "There's not another crew coming. The Tucson base is being emptied too." The muscles in his jaw tensed visibly before he said, "Regional Command has decided to abandon this area."

Silence.

I balled my fists against my knees under the table. *The city. They're letting the Blood Angels take control of the city.*

I shoved back my chair and bolted from the room.

Everyone's surprise and concern followed me as I ran out of the bay. A dozen feet away from the bay door, my running turned to sprinting. Finally, I was far enough for the emotions to dissolve into background noise. Breathless and shaken, I stopped in a clearing where a palo verde had stood until being toppled by a storm. Pacing back and forth, I clutched both hands against my temples.

Things are better in the desert. Things are always better in the desert. I settled in a crouch, my back against the trunk of the downed palo verde.

You have a choice, mijo. My father's voice—or was it Bandit's? *You can leave this place and the memories behind, or you can face them and fight for it.*

The city came to my mind—baking in the sun and shimmering with the souls of thousands of people. Bitterness roiled in my gut. That place had held all my pain from childhood onward.

The gangster twisted his boot on my outstretched hand, grinding the bones together and sending white-hot agony up my arm. I bit my lip on my own scream as he applied more pressure.

"Aww, you gonna cry?" The pressure left my hand as he stepped back, crouching to look me right in the eye. "When are you going to learn, kid? No one puts one over on the Angels."

Tears streaming down my face, I looked up at the unfeeling faces around me. Most looked away—at their shoes, the floor, the ceiling—anywhere but at the kid sprawled in terror on the floor.

No one had done anything, and I'd decided it was best to stay hidden from then on. Stay hidden. Don't reach out. Don't draw close to anyone, ever.

Then, the squad had tangled my heart into theirs—only for it to break all over again with Judge's death.

The bitterness spread to encompass my heart, filtering through the broken parts and settling on one thought. *That city has taken the people I love one too many times.*

On the heels of the thought came the sound—or feel—of footsteps. I whirled, energy flickering between my fingers and ready to throw.

"It's just me," Tara said, one hand up. "Don't blast me out of the undergrowth."

I let the energy fade back up my arm. "How'd you find me?"

She pointed in the direction of the base. "Sensors on top of the base still work, even if nothing else does. You taught Logan the screens too well; he found you almost immediately."

I pressed my lips together in annoyance. Tara had the definite aura of someone who had a piece to say, and wasn't going anywhere until she'd said it. "What's going on, then? Why follow me?"

Tara's foot tapped the ground. "Why'd you leave?"

I stepped forward to match her, my height casting her face into shadow. "I'm done fighting to save that city."

Tara's cyan eyes widened, then narrowed. "That's hogwash."

"No, it's not!"

"Yes, it is." Tara crossed her arms. "Look, no one was twisting your arm to get you to agree to this posting," she said, accusation sparking through every word. "I don't think Bandit had to try hard *at all* to get you to come. You're not angry," she insisted. "You're scared."

"Yes! And I have a right to be!" I said, the statement smacking me in the face even as it left my lips. "Every experience I've ever had there was bad." The ground vibrated under my feet, a faint tremor that answered the bitterness in my heart. "My parents disappeared—they left once, and they *never* came back." I balled up a fist, blue swelling between my fingers. "Abuela died protecting me, but the gang *still* didn't leave me alone." My voice built to a yell as I faced Tara, the tremor in the ground building as well. "I spent my entire life hiding and running until I was old enough to escape. There is *nothing* good about that place!" The ground rumbled and cyan light erupted from the dirt, encircling me until I stood under a shield.

"That's not true, Gabriel."

Tara took a steady step forward, putting out a hand to grasp my forearm. A swell of memory came to the forefront of both of our minds.

Prickly pear lemonade, tangy and sweet against my tongue.

Papa's voice, and the press of his uniform against my face —sun-warmed as he came home from a long shift.

Swinging higher and higher on a swing that creaked with age.

Nodding bougainvillea against a blue gate.

The calm light of a single-bulb lamp in a back library room, the smell of old books, and the rumble of a monsoon storm outside.

I gulped back tears as my past—filtered and condensed from what Tara had seen through our linked minds—swept through me. When I opened my eyes, the shield had dropped and Tara was still holding me. "It wasn't all bad, Gabriel," she softly insisted. "And we have a chance to make sure that what happened to you won't happen to anyone else."

I sniffed the tears away, my breath steadying. "Caleb said something similar, once."

Finally, it came together.

Trust me, the exchange is worth it. Deadeye's voice.

Caleb. *What happened to me shouldn't happen to anyone else.*

Take care of them for me, kid.

The last of my tears dried up at the memory of Judge's voice, and I rubbed the collar of his T-shirt gratefully. It hadn't been much time after that day in the library when I'd first heard the stories of the original Earth Defense Force. Over a year followed—of training in secret, of ducking gang conscription, of writing down every story anyone would tell me—until I met the EDF minimum recruitment age. I walked into training with my notebooks clutched against my chest and a single thought burning in my mind.

They wouldn't let their enemies scare them powerless. And they never backed down from protecting the innocent.

"Maybe you're right." A single flame came to hover over

my palm, and I examined it with wonder. "Maybe I've finally found the thing I've spent all this time looking for."

"Oh?" Caution sped from Tara. "You mean power?"

"No." I closed my hand on the flame, the bitterness snuffing out along with it. I looked up at Tara, and resolve settled in my heart. "A good reason to fight back, now that I'm not afraid."

"SORRY, EVERYONE." I went to take my chair again, unbuttoning the last few buttons on my uniform shirt and pulling it off as I sat down. Judge's goose T-shirt looked an even brighter blue in the troubled environment of the room as I apologized. "I had to figure some things out."

"We figured." Deadeye slid a water glass across the table as Tara resumed her seat next to Caleb. "Glad you're back."

"What'd I miss?" I asked Bandit and Josephine.

"Nothing, for the moment," Caleb said. "You weren't gone that long." He balanced an elbow on the table and counted off items on his fingers. "Regional Command is abandoning this region, we're all being reassigned, they want us to report to our new bases by this time next week, and..." He looked at Josephine. "I'm forgetting something, aren't I?"

"And they want to dig through Gabriel's head."

"Right." He raised another finger. "And they want to dig through your head."

Deadeye muttered something in German under her breath.

"What was that?" I asked.

"I *said*"—her head snapped up—"we can't let those cowards get away with this. I didn't spend years fighting to give up this easily."

Logan frowned. "The moment the Defense Force leaves, there'll be violence in the city." He was hiding it well, but sickening worry was filtering out of him. I gently reached past the barriers in his mind to catch a glimpse of a chubby-cheeked toddler, with bright eyes and dusty brown hair just like his. *Guess I'm not the only one with a reason to be afraid.*

"We can't leave the civilians." Tara's eyes flickered before Caleb put his hand over hers. "There are families in the Santa Cruz Valley that deserve protection—regulations or not."

"You're right," Bandit agreed. "But I'm sure we're not the only ones who feel this way. Reneé, do we have any way of talking directly to St. Augustine's? Securely, without inter-ference or eavesdropping from Regional?"

Deadeye's fury had calmed to a simmer behind her good eye. "I'll bet I could rig up some kind of encryption if we patched things through Gabriel's helmet."

Bandit's eyebrows went up. "That could work. Will your contact who listens to cockroaches be willing to help?"

Deadeye smirked. "Benny? Yeah." She frowned. "But he's only a tech guy. We need to get hold of someone impor-tant who'll be sympathetic."

"Dr. Saltori," Josephine said. "You said the St. Augus-tine's base is being closed too?" At Bandit's nod, she explained, "The hospital side of St. Augustine's only shut down a few years ago, but he stayed on as the chief of medical ops." Her eyes glowed with respect and admiration. "He's been a Tucson doctor since the invasion, and if I know him, he'll be furious that we're expected to drop things and run. Forget military stuff—these are his patients he'd be abandoning."

"There's something else we haven't considered."

Everyone looked at Logan as he explained, "The moment we make our intentions clear, Regional will cut off our access to the networks. That's comms, weather, everything. Gabriel will be able to talk with you two"—he nodded at Caleb and Tara—"but no one else."

"Oh yeah..." Tara yanked her hand from Caleb's. "We *all* need active bio interfaces."

"And for that, we actually need to *go* to St. Augustine's, not just talk with them," Deadeye said. "It also gives me an opportunity to have a few choice words with the tech guys." She gave a vindictive smile. "Mark my words—Regional found that cloning facility, and I'm going to figure out where it is."

"If we do this, there's no going back," I said, the pressure of *say something!* becoming too much in my head. *They're throwing away everything they've built over the years.* "I don't want everyone to put themselves in jeopardy over something I got us into."

Tara swiveled toward me, sounding so much like Judge in the moment that a pang of sorrow lanced through my heart. "Gabe, that's the stupidest thing I've heard you say, and that includes what you said outside just a minute ago." She waved her hands around the table. "You *literally* know what all of us are thinking, and you still believe this is something you're *getting* us into?"

I blinked in surprise, following her intense gaze around the table. Sure enough, there wasn't even a touch of resentment directed at me from anyone in the room.

"I didn't realize," I stammered. "I'm sorry, everyone."

"Don't apologize," Caleb said. He allowed some of his mental shields to drop, and I saw the sincerity behind his words. "We'd make this decision even if you weren't involved, just because it's the right thing to do. But because you're involved—" His emotions shifted to something fiercely protective. "It's personal."

I ducked my head, suddenly sheepish at the affection coming at me from all directions. "Thanks, guys. I guess I'm in on this too."

STAGE TWENTY-ONE

ST. Augustine's reminded me of a bee swarm that someone had hit with a garden hose. Even from the vehicle bay, I could feel the swirling eddies of stress, panic, confusion, and grim determination inside the faded-pink tower and adjoining flat-topped building.

Deadeye noticed me holding my head and grimacing as we came to a stop. "You okay?"

I let my hands drop. "I'll be fine." Picking up my backpack and helmet, I explained, "There're a lot of people here, and they're all nervous and scared. It's not exactly pleasant to have all of that bouncing around inside my head."

She nodded, opening the door and letting in a rush of sunlight. All four of us hopped out of the truck, the keys jingling as Caleb stuffed them in his pocket. I instinctively gravitated toward him and Tara, the familiar patterns of their emotions and thoughts as calming to me as the voice of an older sibling is to a nervous toddler.

Tara shifted her bag to her shoulder and looked up, just as the Thunderbird swooped past on its landing approach. "Wow, they sure timed that perfectly."

"Logan knows his aircraft, all right," Deadeye said with admiration. "You know, normally they're supposed to fly with a copilot. He's just good enough that Regional decided to take the risk letting him fly alone."

"I wonder if he's regretting that decision after what happened," Caleb said, leading the way through the over-grown landscaping toward the helipad on the other building.

"If he's not, I imagine his wife is." Deadeye hefted her bag higher on her shoulder. "You guys go meet with the others." The look she gave me was the perfect mix of threat-ening and devious as she added, "Benny once bragged about having a back-door entrance to Regional's files. I'm going to go see how much I can squeeze out of them."

Once, the idea of digging through classified files would have made me nervous. Now, I just nodded grimly. "Good hunting."

After reuniting with the others on the roof, we split up—Caleb and Logan to recharge the power cores, Tara and Josephine to acquire supplies, and Bandit and I to the medical wing. Walking through the halls felt different with him by my side, knowing that I'd soon be able to see the world the way he'd seen it.

Finding the medical wing was difficult. Cornering the doctor who'd performed the surgeries on Caleb, Tara, and I was less difficult, and convincing him to help turned out much easier than I had expected.

Dr. Saltori set down a box of sterile gloves and wiped

his brow tiredly after Bandit explained our plans. For a long second, I thought he was going to turn us down, but finally he asked, "Do you know how long I've been stationed here?"

Bandit shook his head, but I answered almost immediately. The answer had been just at the forefront of the man's mind, wrapped in years of memories both good and bad. "Twelve years. You were here when no one else wanted to be here." I swallowed my nerves and looked him in the eye. "You weathered it through the occupation, the riots, and the hospital becoming an EDF base. This isn't just a workplace to you; it's home. And you're just as angry about the order to abandon your home as we are."

He blinked in surprise several times before nodding, wide-eyed. "Yeah. How'd you—" His gaze dropped to the helmet I was holding under my arm. "Oh, right."

"So, you understand why we're doing this," Bandit said, looking between the two of us.

"Oh, I understand. I've warned Regional that the tactics they use elsewhere won't work here, but they never listen." He raised an eyebrow. "Guess they're about to find out the hard way. Is Captain Fletcher here?"

Bandit nodded. "She and Lieutenant Fletcher both. We were hoping to be able to link our whole team and get back to Base 36 before Regional notices we're gone."

Dr. Saltori frowned. "I can reactivate the interfaces already in your heads, I just can't install any brand-new ones." He nodded toward me. "Yours was sent down special from Phoenix, but there's no way I can requisition two more for Dr. Flores and your Thunderbird pilot without attracting the wrong kind of attention."

He's right. I was saved from having to agree out loud as

Bandit said, "Just Deadeye and myself, then. Can you do that, at least?"

"I guarantee it." The surgeon's eyes flashed with determination as he pushed a button on a device clipped to his collar and said, "Call Rapid Response Nurse." A woman's voice answered, and he commanded, "Tracy, it's Josh. I need Room 8's team prepped and ready to go. We've got an urgent case." After getting confirmation, he turned back to us. "The surgical team's scrubbing in."

Bandit nodded, satisfaction overwriting the nervousness in his mind. "We'll call the others. Gabe?"

I pulled on the command helmet, the tracker in the display reading my retina and pulling up the comms program in a matter of seconds. I dropped into the middle of Caleb and Tara's heads, the initial rush of memories and thoughts catching both of them off guard.

Geez! Caleb said. *Warn me next time!*

Sorry, I said. *I would if I could. Am I coming through clearly?*

You're clear. Tara's mental voice sounded just as annoyed as I expected her physical one would have been after being interrupted. *What is it?*

Can you find Deadeye and bring her over to the medical wing? The doctor's prepping to reactivate her and Bandit's implants, and he'd like you to keep them asleep.

Yeah, I'll find her. Tara disengaged from the conversation she'd been having. *I'll let you know when we're on our way down.*

AN HOUR LATER, Deadeye lay sleeping peacefully under the influence of Tara's power. I was able to stay with her, relaying information passed from Tara to the surgical team as they worked to access the implant in the back of Deadeye's skull. I didn't understand a quarter of what they were saying, and I was glad I didn't. Even the bits I caught about nerves, incisions, and bones made me glad that I'd been unconscious the entire time while getting my bio interface installed. I glanced toward Caleb, watching from the other side of a window with Bandit.

Given his background, I understand why he wanted to stay conscious. It must've hurt like hell, though.

With Deadeye's procedure done, they moved on to Bandit. Josephine's voice shook a little as she explained what was going to happen, her concern stretching deeper than it had for Deadeye.

Before Tara put Bandit under, he reached up to put a reassuring hand on Josephine's arm. "I'll be fine. Don't worry about me."

Inside the helmet, I frowned at how much affection had filled his mind. *Once we bring all these links online, everyone will know how he feels about her. I don't know if he's ready for that.*

The thought dogged my heels as the team worked in quiet, intense concentration to reactivate Bandit's implant. Once his skin had been stitched shut and the device tested, Tara let go of her power, allowing him to wake up naturally.

My head aching, I pulled the helmet off as Deadeye began stirring. Muttering in German, she blinked hard and stared across the room, her bad eye tracking out of sync with her good one.

"Welcome back." I handed her a cup of water. "How do you feel?"

Her gaze settled on me, confusion subsiding at the same time. "Like roadkill."

I had to smile. "How do you know what roadkill feels like?" I handed her the eyepatch that Dr. Saltori had needed to remove in order to work.

She took it with a grateful smile, carefully tying it and settling her hair around the strap. "Gabe, I've seen enough pancaked corpses to have a pretty good idea." As her bad eye vanished behind the patch, she sighed. "That's better."

"How *did* you lose your eye, anyway?" I asked impulsively. "Judge said something about a feral badger when I asked him."

Deadeye chuckled. "I got struck by lightning."

It was a blatant lie. "You did *not*," I accused.

Deadeye ran a finger under the strap of her eyepatch. "Guess you'll never know, then. Sorry, Gabe."

"You're not a bit sorry," I said as I got up. Her laugh followed me as I left the surgical center.

WE GOT BACK to Base 36 a little before dinner, ate in silence, and returned to our individual tasks.

"We'll do what we can to stall, but Command was exact about the date and time by which we had to be out of here," Dr. Saltori had told us. "Once they realize not all of us have left, there'll only be a short window of time in which to act before they decide what the consequences will be." Respect had run clearly through his words as he bade us farewell on the helipad. "Whatever you're going to do, you need to do it fast."

After dinner, I set my room in order. My helmet sat on my table, and the growing collection of notebooks went next to my bed. I closed the closet door on the rest of my possessions, packed into a single duffel bag. Once the room was as clean as I could make it, I took the top notebook off the stack and retrieved a pen. I'd meant to keep writing down Judge's memories, but my mind kept wandering, circling through the base again and again.

Annoyed now, I closed my notebook and went to eavesdrop on Logan and Bandit, who'd spread the blueprints of previously raided xeno facilities across the dining room table. I emerged from my rummage through the cabinets with a handful of stale pretzels, mentally checking on everyone's activities and whereabouts as I closed the door. Bandit and Logan I'd seen. Tara was practicing on her own out on the helipad, Deadeye was fixing an armor piece, and Josephine sat alongside Bandit shuffling around task lists. Out in the bay, Caleb was hitting the punching bag. Dark fear swirled through his mind, pushed back with grim focus.

Must be one of the ways he calms down.

I went out to the bay with nervous energy jittering through my own veins. Caleb didn't acknowledge me as I began practicing energy bolts, containing the power before it could escape and damage anything. He went inside after a while, his conversation with Logan and Bandit echoing past the edges of my subconscious as I kept practicing.

Eventually, my timing slipped. The power discharge rattled the bay windows, knocking me back a pace as I swore miserably.

"Well, that was close," Caleb said. "You okay?"

I hadn't even noticed him behind me.

I let my shield flicker out and picked up my water bottle. "I'm fine."

"Are you sure?" Caleb asked, clambering to his usual seat

on the compressor box. "You seemed pretty upset the other night."

"I don't want to talk about it." I took a drink, grateful, at least, that Caleb was able to keep most of his emotions inside his head and out of mine.

"Yeah, Tara mentioned." He shrugged. "That's why I'm here, and not any of the others."

"Liar," I retorted, going over what I'd felt as his and Bandit's conversation inside had concluded. "You and Bandit flipped a coin, and you lost."

Amusement rebounded first through my mind, then my ears as Caleb chuckled. "Okay, okay. Guilty as charged." He jumped down from the compressor. "Are you trying to burn off your nerves?"

I nodded. "I know everyone's trying to keep a good face on it, but they're all nervous." I put the water down. "That's fine, but having my own nerves multiplied times six isn't helping."

"Well, making yourself sick from burnout won't help either. You need your abilities so we can test these interfaces tomorrow." Caleb dodged behind me, kicking out my knees and twisting an arm behind my back as I hit the ground. He only held on for a second before letting me up, silvery eyes filled with good-natured challenge. "But I'm willing to bet your hand-to-hand skills can use some practice."

STAGE TWENTY-TWO

Earth Defense Force Base 36
Gila River Valley
October 21

THE NEXT DAY, I caught Bandit in the hallway, asking in Spanish, "Hey, can we talk?"

He stopped, looking around the hall. "Here?"

"Outside, actually."

He followed me to the bay, flipping open the tailgate of the truck and sitting down. Morning light filtered through the bay windows, and the air was still cool as he asked, "What's on your mind, *mijo*?"

I sat alongside him, uncomfortable now that I'd begun a conversation I wasn't sure I wanted to finish. "It's this—" I pulled a pen out of my pocket, flipping it between my fingers as I said, "Once we bring the interfaces online later today, we're all going to be seeing into each other's heads. It's not going to be like it was with Michael—he could see into each of your heads, but you couldn't hear or see anyone's thoughts but your own."

"That's right." Bandit's thoughts fuzzed backward, into a memory that I couldn't quite touch. "This'll take some getting used to; everyone knowing what I'm thinking."

"Well, there's something else." I clicked the pen closed and held it tightly. "It's not fair to Josephine that we'll all know how you feel about her, but she won't."

Bandit's mind flared with intensity and protectiveness so strong it sent my stomach into knots. His voice ground low, melodic Spanish threatening. "Gabriel, what are you talking about?"

My stomach churned, but I forced myself to stay the course. "It's clear how much you care about her, and I don't want to be stuck in your head without you addressing it first."

He sighed, the intensity fading to uncertainty. "You think I need to say something?"

"It's not fair to her any other way." I chanced a look at the expression on his face. "And you might be surprised at how she takes it."

For a moment, it was as difficult to read his emotions as it was to keep track of Caleb's. "I'll think about it."

"You'd better think quickly." I pointed at the side of the truck closest to the kitchen door. "She's looking for you, and Logan just told her we're out here."

Surprise jolted from him, and he jumped to his feet. I slid down from the truck and walked into the kitchen, passing Josephine on my way.

"Is Carlos out there?"

"Yeah, he's outside."

The door closed behind her, and I did my best to shut

out the entirety of the bay from my sixth sense. *Let them have their privacy.*

"What's wrong with you?" Deadeye asked from behind the counter. Even with everything up in the air, she'd still insisted on making lunch, and savory smells drifted from the stove.

Remembering Josephine's uncanny hearing, I focused hard and sent the message mentally instead.

I told Bandit he needed to tell Josephine how he feels about her.

The counter shook as someone slammed a door. Tara appeared from the hallway, Caleb a pace behind her. Their faces were a picture of disbelief and amusement.

"You what?"

I crossed my arms defensively. "I'm *not* going to sit in his head with all that in there. I have my limits."

Tara stood on tiptoes to peer out the window into the bay. I felt her embarrassment even before she turned back, face pink. "Well, they're going outside. And they're holding hands. I think we'll be here for a bit."

She and Caleb joined Deadeye and me around the kitchen counter. Within a few minutes Logan joined us too, drawn by the laughter. We fell into talking, and I was so engaged in Deadeye's relating of her university room-mate's hijinks that I didn't notice Bandit and Josephine returning.

"Some veterans you are," Bandit said. "Gabriel, I'm surprised at you. You should've seen us coming a mile away."

All five of us jumped like kids caught in the candy drawer as the door closed behind them. I flipped my notebook shut and stuffed my pen into my pocket, all the while grinning at the happiness coming from him and Josephine.

"Hey, you needed us to be ignoring both of you. I'd say I was doing exactly what I needed to."

Bandit smiled, his arm not leaving its place around Josephine's shoulders. "I guess I'm okay with that." His gaze shifted over to the others. "You're probably wondering what's going on."

"Nah. We'd been wondering what was taking you so long," Deadeye said. "Anyone with one eye and two brain cells could see it."

"Well, that rules you out." Logan elbowed her, and she doubled over with a laugh.

Josephine broke into laughter, wiping away happy tears. "It's been so many years. I'm glad it finally—I mean, we finally—" She buried her face in Bandit's chest as the rest of us smiled.

"It's time to let ourselves move on," Bandit said, rubbing her back affectionately. "Me, more than anyone." He looked up at me. "Thanks, *mijo*."

I didn't say anything, only nodding before putting away my things. After how much sadness had eddied around the base in the last week, genuine happiness felt so good—like monsoon rains on dry ground.

AFTER LUNCH, we all stood in a circle on the practice court in the bay—Bandit, Deadeye, Caleb, Tara, and myself. Josephine and Logan kept to the edge of the court, Josephine with an eye on the readings from the monitors around Tara and my wrists. "Are you ready, Gabe?"

I closed my eyes inside the helmet, glad no one could see my face. *One last moment of my thoughts just being my own.* "I'm ready." I opened my eyes, letting the comms program read my retina and bracing myself for the swirl of everyone else's consciousnesses.

Tara and Caleb's interfaces responded first, immersing me in the now-familiar patterns of their emotions.

Longing.

An adobe house in the desert.

Fierce hope fighting darkness.

Then, with a suddenness that sent me reeling, another presence flooded into my mind.

"Here you go, Reneé." A boy several years older than me lobbed a ping-pong paddle across the table. "Catch!"

I raised a hand to catch, but my reflexes were too slow. The paddle slammed edge-on into my eye, sending instant darkness across my vision. "I can't see!" Panic built. "I can't see!"

Deadeye breathed in and out, her panic subsiding as one of Tara's memories took the forefront of our minds.

Moonlight shone across the inlet waters, my heart content and still for the first time in several months. Flicking a hand out, I tossed a shield bubble to hover in front of the moon. It broke apart into glittering sparkles, raining around my head as Caleb jogged up. "I thought I'd find you here." He stuffed his hands in his pockets, the circuitry in his arm shimmering in the moonlight. His voice filled with wonder. "It's so peaceful."

I tried so hard to stay in the memory of moonlight on water, but all too fast it had whirled away into the blurring background of our combined thoughts.

Mama lit the first two candles placed in the Advent wreath, her hand pausing before touching the flame to the third. "And the third candle—do you know it, schatzi?"

I wriggled impatiently in my seat, eyes drawn to the

plates of lebkuchen *sitting on the red-and-gold tablecloth.* "It's for when the angels appeared to the shepherds."

Angelic messengers, right, Gabe? Deadeye chuckled as I paused on her memory.

Yeah, if you say so, I managed to say before a sudden stab of pain went through both Tara and Caleb—and therefore, me.

"What do you mean, he's dying?"

"Just what I said!" I snapped, my eyes filling with tears. *"I knew it—I knew this stupid power would kill him in the end!" I pressed my hands against my belly, grief tearing at my heart. "It'll take Michael, just like it took my sister, just like it's taken our future from us." Cyan light bubbled and swirled around me before Caleb put his hand on my shoulder.*

I toppled to a knee, Caleb's hand coming to land on my physical shoulder just as it had Tara's in the memory.

"Hey, we'll be okay." He pulled me into a hug, pressing my head against his chest. "Even if it's just the two of us for the rest of our lives, it's still a family."

Josephine muttered under her breath. Something shifted, and the pressure lessened enough to where I could regain my feet. The scene changed, and *the sun beat down against the back of my neck as I drew a handgun and fired a round into the center of a target. Several more followed, the recoil shaking my wrist each time. Once the magazine was empty, I cleared the range and stepped over to the target, breaking into a grin at the sight of a single jagged hole piercing the paper.*

"Woohoo!" Josephine cheered beside me, her wide smile glinting with orthodontia. "One hand and everything!"

I holstered the handgun, prouder than if I'd just won the Olympic gold for sharpshooting.

I'd been coming close to being overwhelmed with the torrent of fragmented thoughts, conversations, and emotions, but Bandit's appearance—protective, wise, and unshakable—helped keep it at bay. Everything subsided into background noise as he said, *That's not something you want to do too often. Is it like that every time?*

It'll get better, I said, thinking back to how Caleb had said the same thing. *All clear, everyone?*

Clear here, Tara said. Deadeye gave me a thumbs-up, and Caleb nodded as he let go of my shoulder and stepped away.

"It's clear," he said aloud. "Don't worry, everyone. It'll be better the more we practice."

WE ONLY PRACTICED for a few hours that afternoon, but all of us became accustomed to the shared thoughts faster than I'd expected. That evening, we spoke with St. Augustine's one more time, everyone crowded around the setup in the Fishbowl.

"Our deadline to report in is day after tomorrow," Bandit said into the microphone at my elbow. "Yours, I imagine, is similar."

"We've already started losing staff," Dr. Saltori said through the speakers. From the echoes in his voice, and the background noises, I gathered that he was in a fairly large room with at least a few other people. "Most of the command here is planning on complying. They're worn out from dealing with an entrenched enemy and tired of losing friends to ambushes."

Electronic garbling cut through his words, making Deadeye swear and hurry to grab a different cable from the conference room. "Cheap, second-rate garbage," she muttered, yanking components free and rearranging them. An anxiety-riddled pause later, she asked, "St. Augustine's, do you copy?"

The background noise returned first, a door slamming and muffled conversation filling the silence before the doctor's voice came back. "We copy, Base 36. You good?"

"A tech issue," Bandit said. "I think we've got it handled, though. What were you saying before we got interrupted?"

"The first flight of personnel and equipment left this afternoon," Dr. Saltori said. From the rustle of paper, I assumed he was going over personnel lists. "That's two of the four Thunderbirds and the transport Regional sent. We're supposed to have the rest of our equipment packed and out of the region by the day after tomorrow."

"Same here," Logan said. He shifted from foot to foot, anxiety plain in the tension across his shoulders. "Once the Blood Angels see there's no EDF presence in Tucson, they're not going to waste a second in taking over."

"We know." This was a new voice, one that I didn't recognize. Bandit did, evidently. He leaned closer to the speakers as the woman said, "Those of us who are meant to close down the base don't plan on going anywhere. We're working on plans now to safeguard the civilians and keep the Blood Angels at bay—your Thunderbird will be very helpful for those." I could hear the desperation in her voice as she said, "It's still going to be a war zone here."

"Hopefully, our taking out the cloning facility in the Ridges will be a big enough blow that they'll pull out of the city," Josephine said. "At the very least, we'll have done what we can to ensure that Brutes stay in nightmares where they belong."

The St. Augustine's commander said something else, but

it was lost in a rush of static. I frowned at the displays. "Deadeye, can you—?"

"I'm trying." She leaned over the desk, hands running across the various cables and connections. "Nothing's wrong here." She grabbed the mic from Josephine. "St. Augustine's, do you copy?"

Static.

Deadeye repeated the question, everyone's anxiety rising as only a few words came in response, broken and garbled before disappearing. It reminded me of what things had sounded like when the Blood Angels took out the first relay tower.

Empty static.

Deadeye slapped the side of the computer. "Come on!"

"Reneé, I don't think it's coming back up." I told the computer to reboot, knowing it wasn't going to make any difference. "It's like it's trying to talk through a brick wall."

"Or maybe something else," Tara said, her voice touched with warning. As all of us turned to look, she pointed at the open door to the conference room.

I slumped in my chair. "Is the transmitter plugged in?"

Logan went to check, only needing a brief glance into the room before his posture told us everything we needed to know. "It's plugged in. And on, but I know I didn't turn it on." He turned around, hands bunching into fists. "I think it's safe to say we're not operating in secrecy anymore."

Deadeye yanked a cord out of the computer, throwing it down with a curse. "Bastards."

"All right, then," Bandit said, his voice dropping. He pointed at the conference room. "One of you, shield that."

Tara nodded grimly and sent a shield to encompass the eavesdropping transmitter. "Now what?"

Everyone clustered around, the circle closely resembling how we'd been standing on the practice court that morning. Bandit ran a hand down his face, the whirling in his mind clear enough that it bled across to mine.

Civilians.

St. Augustine's.

The Ridges.

Regional knows.

I was deep enough in the swirl of planning, caution, and concern that it was a surprise when he spoke aloud. "Regional Command may not know exactly what's going on, but it won't take them long to figure it out. Once they do, they'll be here to stop us." Bandit's level amber eyes looked around the circle of us. "Unless anyone has a good reason to delay, I think we need to move our deployment up by twenty-four hours."

I sucked in a sharp breath. *That's much less time than I thought I'd have.* I ran a hand through my hair, my befuddled mind trying to work out when the new deployment time would be.

Caleb took the guesswork out of things, saying, "That puts us at 1900 tomorrow—you think we can deploy that fast?"

"I don't think we have a choice," Josephine said. She'd pulled a piece of paper out of her pocket; a list of tasks she and Deadeye had made previously. "Regional won't have time to come up with a response team tonight, but even 1900 tomorrow is cutting it *really* close." Looking up from the list, she said, "I think it needs to be even earlier. 1600, if we can swing it."

The general consensus was "not pleased, but deter-mined." As everyone dispersed, I got Deadeye's attention.

"If they could jam transmissions through the network, could they block this?" I pointed to my helmet.

Deadeye spat something in German. By the feel of the word in my mind, I guessed it was a curse. "Of course..." She snatched the helmet and took it to her workbench. "We'll have to get your comms program onto some other device."

"Can we do that?" I asked, standing shakily from my chair. I hadn't wanted to admit it to anyone, but the aftereffects of everything—practice with the mind bridge, talking to St. Augustine's, and the sudden change of plans—were making my head spin.

"Probably." Deadeye added another equipment case to a tottering stack of bins. Various rattling and banging noises punctuated her already hard-edged words. "I have something we can use."

"Um..." I frowned, recognizing one of the items she'd dumped across the worktable. "Is that Judge's monitor cuff?"

Deadeye gave me a nostalgic smile. "Michael's. I kept more than just his helmet." A pile of miscellaneous junk skidded across the bench to crash into a garbage can. "I think I can download a copy of the comms software to it." She looked appraisingly at me as I slouched against the crates. "You're exhausted."

"I'm fine."

"Oh?" Deadeye put her hands on her hips. "When's the last time you slept properly?"

I frowned, trying to remember. *Probably not since before Judge died.*

The pause was evidently enough of an answer. Deadeye gestured toward the Fishbowl door with a snap of her fingers. "Get out of here, Gabe."

TWENTY-ONE HOURS LATER, I stood on the roof looking out at the desert. My old helmet lay at my feet, alongside the backpack I'd carried on all the missions before I'd Shattered. Inside lay my stack of notebooks, containing all the stories collected both before and after the people here had stopped being a squad and become family. *Back when life was simple.*

Behind me, the rest of the squad were loading the last few crates of our belongings and supplies into the Thunderbird. Regional cutting our connection to the satellite hadn't bothered Logan, who said he'd always wondered what it would be like to fly using only instinct and instruments. He and Josephine were headed to Tucson, to join the remaining EDF members in the wake of the region being abandoned.

One way or another, we all knew we weren't returning to Base 36.

Even with the assurance that Logan and Josephine would be fine, I worried. The image of Logan's daughter kept coming to mind—often enough that I knew I was catching flashes of his thoughts as well as my own. Turning my gaze toward the mountains between us and the Santa Cruz Valley, I muttered a prayer into the desert air. "Please, please keep his family safe." Grim foreboding crept through my heart. "Whatever else happens, keep them safe."

The prayer faded into the sky, sunlight catching in the dusty air across the valley. By the Thunderbird, Bandit handed off the last crate to Josephine, calling, "*Mijo*, we're almost ready to go!"

I turned halfway and gave him a thumbs-up before facing the desert again. Digging my recorder out of my pocket, I held it for a long moment before adding one more entry to my personal log.

"It's the kind of afternoon when I can't tell if the stuff obscuring the sky is dust or cloud. And the sun breaking through is casting everything in alternating gold and brown, depending on how many layers it has to get through." I bowed my head over the recorder, my ears catching the raucous call of a raven somewhere out in the desert. "It hasn't rained in almost three months. Everything feels like it's dead, or sleeping until the winter rains come to wake the desert again."

I let my thumb tense on the recorder button, unsure if this was how I wanted the last entry to end. Finally, I depressed the button once more and spoke.

"I don't think I'm coming back from this one. But to whoever finds this, I want you to know it was my choice. Even if this desert never sees rain again, and the cities dry up under the sun with no resources left to scavenge, the people in this region deserve someone who's willing to die protecting them." I took a deep breath. "Even if that person has to be me."

Before I could lose my nerve, I clicked the button off and turned away from the desert, pulling on my old helmet to block out the view of the place I knew so well. Flipping open the monitor cuff on my wrist, I laid my index finger over the login pad Deadeye had jimmied loose from one of the computers. The flood of input from the bio interface surged through my mind, then settled as everyone realized I was there.

You ready? Deadeye asked.

My feet clattered on the stairs down to the bay. Everyone else had already taken their seats in the truck, and the hatch closed behind me with a shudder.

I'm ready. Let's move out.

STAGE TWENTY-THREE

ACCORDING TO THE OTHERS, the wind farm outside the Ridges hadn't always been so desolate. Looking down at it from the jagged rocks at the top of the Ridges, I found that hard to believe. Only a few of the giant windmills still turned in the moonlight; the others were missing fins, rusted tight, or lay toppled in the wake of some cataclysm.

"There was a battle here, wasn't there?" I asked, turning to look at Bandit as he came up behind me.

"Maybe." He shrugged. "I don't remember."

"One of the xeno ships landed here," Deadeye said as she joined us. Below, Caleb and Tara picked their way up the rocky slope. "They made a wind like a hurricane when they took off. If the turbines'd been working then, it would've made enough power to light up the state." She pulled up her map overlay inside her helmet—her thoughts narrowed to just the information before her eyes as she said, "The coords I got from Benny stop here. If I ever see him again, I'm giving him a piece of my mind; he made it sound like there would be a wide-open door or something."

"Watch my back, I'm going to see if I can find it." Pulling off a glove, I knelt and spread my fingers out on the ground. The others' emotions faded out as I allowed my senses to spread farther, deeper, and higher into the Ridges.

C'mon. Where are you?

I knew from previous experience that tunnels were cold and blue, Brutes felt red, and the Blood Angels sounded like Spanish spoken three rooms away. Now, I pushed all that knowledge into the ground beneath us, my sixth sense snapping into place like metal filings jumping to a magnet. Just like that, the place stretched out beneath and away from me. A gasp caught in my throat.

Found it. I swallowed. *It's really big.*

Aww no, Deadeye commented. *How big?*

I looked up, still catching my breath. The others had circled around me, visors obscuring their faces even with our headlight beams. "It's massive. Several layers, and it goes back really far..." I frowned and tried to let my senses find the end of the tunnels. "Really far. I can't see the end. It's like a maze."

"That's a xeno facility for you," Caleb commented, shifting the strap of his gun on his shoulder. "Can you see a way in?"

"Or our objective?" Tara added.

I nodded, turning my attention to things mostly unseen. "There's something farther that direction"—I pointed—"and down. It feels like water and white. There're people awake there, and Brutes nearby. I think that's where we need to go."

And a way in? Bandit reminded me.

I gestured again toward what I supposed was the cloning facility and said with much more confidence than I felt, "One of the corridors ends over there." The area I'd pointed to was down in a valley, near a spot where a few determined trees had managed to stay alive. "That way's our best chance."

"Okay." Bandit shouldered his backpack and rifle. "Stay sharp, everyone."

DEADEYE WAS good at finding hidden spaces. I barely needed to pinpoint the location before she'd rummaged around in the rocks to find a hidden switch. The rocks a few meters away quivered and disappeared, a standard door appearing behind them.

Don't look so surprised, Tara said. *It's a xeno facility, after all. We've been places like this dozens of times.*

Hundreds, Deadeye corrected. She brought her wristband computer to bear on the electronic lock. As it swung open, she chortled, "They didn't even think to update the security software."

"Might not have known how," Caleb mused. He was the first into the gloomy corridor, Tara at his back as they covered each doorway before waving us onward.

Bandit's hand rested on my shoulder before he followed them. Somehow, I could tell that the next words were being spoken only to me. *Gabriel, if all this goes wrong...*

I know. I slipped my rifle from over my shoulder, grateful now for all the missions where I'd had to use it. *You don't have to say anything, Bandit. I know.*

A thought from Caleb interrupted our conversation, such as it was.

Hey, which way?

I gestured to the left, angling my glove down. *That way.* A new presence brushed against my mind, the foreign emotions warning me a split second before the guard walked around the corner up ahead. *Tara!*

Tara reacted fast, but not nearly as fast as Bandit. His arm whipped up, and the echo of a single round pierced the silence of the facility. The Blood Angel fell, redness spreading to match the bandana around his arm.

A flurry of nerves ran through the rest of the squad as Bandit sharply gestured at the next corridor. "Move!"

We pounded through the hallways, passing rooms filled with the rumble of generators and hissing of pipes. Twice, I had to stop our advance to avoid a guard about to cross our path, and Tara took out several more with silent energy bolts.

Eventually, we stopped for a breather in the shelter of a stairwell. Deadeye flipped her visor open to brush sweat from her face, whispering, "I didn't expect this little resistance."

"It is their turf, I suppose," I said. "No one expects an attack on their own turf, but..."

"No, it's not normal," Tara said. Beside her, Bandit and Caleb both nodded, their certainty plain in both body language and thoughts. "A facility this size, this secret, should've had hundreds more people than just the ones you're feeling." A death knell sounded in my head as she explained, "My guess is they've gone to help take over the Santa Cruz Valley."

"He thinks he can fight back."

Crushing pain.

I closed a fist, squashing the memory. "I'm not letting that happen." I pointed toward where something pulsed with turbulent energy—like Brutes, but not yet. "This goes down first. Then we need to get back to St. Augustine's. They'll need all the help they can get."

"Yeah, assuming we get this thing taken out." Tara had been crouching with a palm on the ground. She straightened with a grunt and peered up the stairwell. "Up or down?"

"Down and across." I put my hands up to my helmet more out of habit than anything else, focusing hard on the floor below us. "It's through a storage room off the main hall, with the tanks arranged on either side of a walkway." I frowned. "The ceiling's way too high, and everything's laid out funny."

All of us froze as footsteps sounded on the metal stairs far overhead. Angry voices—muffled at first, but clearer as they approached—echoed through the stairwell.

They found one of the ones we killed, I said. *They're searching the facility.*

Bandit yanked his handgun from its holster. *Move!*

Throwing caution to the wind, we crashed down the last flight of stairs, Caleb throwing his shoulder against a door opening off the landing. The storeroom was more like a warehouse; pallets and pallets of stuff stacked on metal shelving units under stark fluorescent lighting. I barely had time to register my surroundings before the door at the other side of the room slammed open to admit a gust of cool air and several armored Blood Angels. All of us dove for cover, Caleb darting forward and getting a shot off at the first gang member before dodging behind a pallet stacked high with cardboard boxes.

Careful what you shoot, I warned, a lurid yellow hazard sign catching my eye on a shelf nearby.

Fair enough. Tara flicked an energy bolt across the room, an answering scream coming from the Blood Angel she'd hit. *Is the lab next door?*

I blinked hard, my sixth sense momentarily drowning out everyone's voices. A vast, high-ceilinged room opened out on the other side of the wall, filled with the sounds of swishing water and humming equipment. Snapping back into myself, I confirmed, *It's right there.*

There'll be a computer somewhere. Deadeye's mental voice stayed unshaken as a Brute howled on the other side of the wall. *Keep me in cover, and I'll find a way to corrupt every file they've got. They won't be able to send Brutes at us if all the genetic material is scrambled beyond reason.*

Right. I broke from behind the pallet, sending a fireball toward where I could feel two of the remaining Blood Angels. It exploded their cover, sending wood splinters flying through the air as Bandit dropped both of them with quick shots through the forehead.

Do you ever *miss?* Deadeye asked him as he reloaded, the awe in the back of her mind clear even through her sarcasm.

He gave a short laugh. *Be glad I don't.* He pointed at the door. *Control console will be on the other side. Let's go.*

The combination of sight, smell, and feel kicked me in the stomach as I stepped through the door. Chemicals mixed with tinges of growth, decay, viscosity, and humming electricity, the combination making me shudder and check my helmet's bio filters. Lighting banks stretched the length of the ceiling, casting everyone's figures with a weird green hue.

Massive tanks reached over our heads; glass and polymer cylinders sheathed in metal collars at base and crown and connected to a myriad of pipes snaking across the cavernous ceiling. In a few tanks, fully-grown Brutes hung suspended in gently circulating silvery fluid. In others, mere blobs of tissue could be seen, shifting and changing every second. I fought back nausea as we spread out into the room, Deadeye disappearing toward a control console.

Strangely enough, none of the others were as affected by the hideous sights as I was. *Grey goo? Is that what you called it?* I asked Caleb, my eye drawn by a mass of tissue that was sprouting an arm as I watched.

He inspected it for a long moment, revulsion crossing his mind before he answered me. *It was an old video game. The tank fluid looks similar. They had these in other facilities too, just not as many. Must've been a full-scale operation here.*

Deadeye, you find what we're looking for? Bandit asked, alertness sparking through his thoughts.

Deadeye was silent through our link, but I could feel her thoughts humming. My head filled with lines of code and sharp-as-a-tack intuition as she said, *I can bypass the login and get into their files. From there, I think I—Cover me!* she yelled, as shots rang out from the other side of the room. Shouts broke against the pipe-covered walls, Spanish and English blending into the gunfire.

I instinctively dodged behind a tank, firing at every target that presented itself. Casting my senses outward, I could feel the facility above us swarming with activity as the rest of the Blood Angels realized they'd been compromised. Just as I was about to warn the others, a hatch in one of the walls slammed open, howls rebounding off the tanks as the Brutes behind it stampeded out.

Tara swore, her first energy bolt missing a Brute but putting a hole in one of the pipes. Hot water gushed from the broken pipe, sending billowing clouds into the air as more shots sounded.

They can't see through the steam, I told everyone. *Caleb, there's one trying to sneak up on you—left!*

He popped up from a crouch, shotgun report sending a tremor through my bones as I kept relaying information to him, Tara, and Bandit. For a moment, it seemed like we had the upper hand, as Blood Angels and Brutes alike thrashed through the dense fog only to meet their deaths at the muzzle of a gun or crackle of an energy blast.

Then, Deadeye screamed. Reaching toward her, I caught the briefest sight of someone withdrawing a shining blade, now dripping red, before her thoughts blurred into panic.

Several gunshots went off in quick succession from that direction, and the sickening jolt of death made my stomach sink. My heart pounded under my armor as I reached frantically for signs of my squad, then calmed as I felt Deadeye— unconscious, but alive—slumped beneath the console.

Deadeye's unconscious. Bandit's mental voice faltered, and I caught a glimpse through his eyes of blood—far more blood than I had expected. *And she's bleeding. I need to get her out of the line of fire, but she didn't finish with the computers.*

Take care of her. Tara unleashed a blast of cyan light at a pair of Brutes. *Gabe and I can finish this.*

Caleb's shotgun went off twice, and I felt him stand to fire again as Bandit pulled Deadeye out from behind the console. *Get her to the truck. We'll catch up.*

Bandit didn't answer, but all of us felt his acknowledgment as he scooped up Deadeye and ran for the exit. I tracked their path out of the storeroom before a wave of fear overwhelmed my mind and a familiar nightmare-laced scream hit my ears.

Caleb!

Whipping around, I focused on his mind only to find it filled with raging terror and pain. A brief flash of consciousness came from his mind, a man with cyan-glowing eyes looming over him before the stream of his emotions disappeared.

I broke from behind the tank, pounding toward where I'd last felt Caleb. Launching a firebolt at one of the Brutes, I shouted, "Tara, one of their Shattered's here! Caleb's down!"

Fury poured from her, and a blue glow began in the opposite corner of the room. *Where?*

I don't know. I turned my head back and forth. *I can't see him.* As I rounded one of the tanks, Caleb's huddled form appeared out of the steam. He'd curled into a ball, hands wrapped around his helmet as he lay on the floor at the juncture of several walkways. I skidded to a stop next to him, raising a shield over both of us as an energy bolt ricocheted off it. With a *ping*, one of the lights overhead exploded, sending frenzied lightning dancing across the roof. *He's here! Near the center of the room!*

It was a man, taller and broader than me, who appeared wraithlike out of the steam. He raised a glowing hand, fingers twisting cruelly. Memories—corrosive, contaminated memories—slammed into me, knocking me backward.

"Don't try to stop me, Gabe."

"Alexi!" I flung out a hand, my fingers cramping and freezing immobile. Judge stood just out of reach, his voice cracked and breaking with pain as his power held me fast. His laugh echoed through my head, filling me with despair as—

No. That's not him.

I slammed against the power holding me, mental bonds breaking like they had in practice against Judge. Swimming up out of the memory—nightmare—I unleashed a torrent of energy toward my attacker. A curse resounded through my mind as the enemy Shattered staggered backward, his presence fading as a hollow thump went through my stomach. I doubled over, clutching my stomach and coughing as Tara knelt at my side.

"I felt that too. You okay?"

I blinked hard and staggered to my feet. "I'm fine." Anger long contained began pulsing through my veins, energy swirling out of the floor to match it. "But this place has to go."

Tara held out her hand. "For Alexi."

I grabbed her hand, the shield re-forming around us and Caleb as the vortex grew outside it. The combined power screeched through our minds, blurring into our memories until I couldn't tell whose emotions I was feeling. My free hand shook as I raised it, Tara mirroring my actions on the other side. Outside, one of the Brutes screamed with an almost human sound as cyan flames surrounded it, energy swirling to encompass every part of the godforsaken room.

Nausea churned through my stomach, and my limbs shook as memories of everyone I'd lost to this war surged through my mind. Not all the faces were immediately recognizable, and as a sob came from Tara, I knew not all the memories were mine. Fiercely, angrily, I pushed every bit of that pain into the vortex, just like I had the night Judge died.

Bandit's voice echoed through my head from a distance, and I caught a flash of him hauling Deadeye up the stairs with his handgun drawn. *Mijo, don't!*

I swore I could hear Judge's voice as I answered, *Don't try to stop me.*

A tank popped, the contents bubbling and steaming as ooze ran down through the grated walkway. Others followed, a chain reaction down the line and as far as I could see through the swirling energy. Howls echoed through the vast room; panic, terror, and pain blending into the roar of the vortex as Tara and I kept pushing more power into it.

That should be enough. Tara's mental voice was strained. *Let it go!*

For the first time, panic stabbed through my chest. *I don't know if I can!* The roof started shaking overhead, cracks forming and spreading in a spiderweb above us. Cramps spread up my arm, the power pouring out faster than I could contain it.

My last log entry flooded through my mind as chunks of concrete began raining down on the shield.

Everything feels like it's dead.

I don't know if I'm coming back from this one.

I couldn't tell if it was Tara's cry of pain or my own as the shield started flickering, consumed in the tide of our combined power.

This was my choice.

GABRIEL!

Caleb's hand landed on my shoulder. New energy washed across my chest, calming my heartbeat, steadying my shaking arm, and being drawn into the shield like water is drawn into dry ground. The shield flared, then held, as Caleb put an arm around Tara's waist. He bowed his head over hers, pulling her closer into his body. I felt her take a shaking breath.

Hang on, Gabe. We can do this.

I took a similar breath. Four counts in, four counts out. As the last count slipped from my mind, I yelled, "Now!"

We let our grip on the vortex go, staggering backward into Caleb. All three of us crumpled as our worlds turned white.

STAGE TWENTY-FOUR

I'D NEVER BEEN SO grateful for how strong Caleb was. As the vortex collapsed, the energy pouring through our bond was enough to bolster the shield around all three of us. My vision cleared to find me lying a foot away from him and Tara, his hand clamped around my shoulder. Incredibly, the shield still pulsed over us, quakes going through my bones as chunks of concrete and rock hailed down on the glowing bubble. Under, over, and all around us, the facility shook, cracks shooting across the ceiling and fluids spilling every-where from ruined tanks. *The whole place is coming down,* I said, the echoes through my head tinged with nausea as my power flickered. *We have to get out of here.*

Tara pulled herself upright with a groan. *Fast,* she agreed as a shudder went through the floor. Urgency replaced her relief at being alive. *As fast as we can.*

WE CAUGHT up to Bandit on the last sloping corridor toward the surface, the ground shaking beneath our feet as the facility caved in on itself. As the tremors settled, we finally found the exit door and stumbled into the open. Overhead, the rising sun cast the jagged peaks in a wash of red light.

Fighting dizziness with each step, I got to the top of the last hill only to crumble to my knees. The others' confusion and worry quickly faded to subdued panic and resignation as they saw what I'd seen—a Thunderbird, but not *our* Thunderbird, its belly hatch open while over a dozen armored EDF troopers prowled the space between it and our truck.

Thoughts? Caleb asked, letting Deadeye slide to the ground. Behind his exhaustion, he was trying to stir up enough strength to fight his way free.

I managed to stand with Bandit's help, my limbs suddenly feeling like they'd turned to Jello. *If I go with them, it might buy enough time for you guys to get away.*

The combined force of everyone's response almost sent me back to my knees. Tara's adamance was tinged with sympathy as she insisted, *We're not going to let you do that.*

C'mon, mijo. Bandit looped my arm over his shoulders and began walking down toward the troopers. *We're all in this together.*

To their credit, the EDF forces let us walk into their midst unaccosted. Caleb and Tara laid Deadeye on the ground as a woman with a Maltese cross on her helmet knelt next to them, pulling a sealant kit from her bag. The others stirred with something like respect as Bandit and I walked up to the person with command insignia on their armor. The man tipped his head to one side, then pulled off his helmet. With a stab of surprise, I recognized the crisp voice and official manner, even if the eye color was different from the man I'd once known by the call sign of Halo.

"Sergeant Watts," Bandit said. "They promoted you?"

Halo smiled, the tension never leaving his cyan eyes. "Kind of had to." He scanned our company, a hint of recognition coming as his gaze passed over Tara. "Shattereds are hard to come by, especially now." I couldn't be certain with my power at low ebb, but I thought I detected remorse as he made a curt gesture. The troopers leveled their guns in our direction. "Come with us quietly, and no one needs to get hurt."

"Mud sucker," Tara snapped, looking up from Deadeye. "We just took down the Blood Angels' cloning operation, and this is how you're going to thank us?" She spat toward his pristine boots. "I should've let you bleed out in that dust storm."

"It doesn't have to be like this," Bandit said, his hands wide. "We can work this out."

"Regional Command isn't happy with this little stunt you've pulled," Halo insisted. Despite his adamance, I caught a tiny glance between us and our truck as he said, "I have my orders. You lot are facing court-martial, and who knows what else."

Like a gong, realization struck. *He doesn't want to carry out his orders.* I took a deep breath, pulling open my visor so Halo—and the rest of the troopers—could see my Shattered eyes.

"You don't want to do this." I stepped closer to Halo, light swelling inside my curled hand and flickering between my fingers as I held it up. "We just leveled an entire facility and came out alive." *Think of Judge at his most confident,* I told myself. I flicked a curt glance up and down Halo's too-clean armor and ramrod-straight posture, putting as much disdain into my voice as I dared. "You think your training—whatever it was they gave you—is enough to match that type of power? You wouldn't stand a chance."

Halo's face drained of color. The other troopers shifted uneasily, several looking nervously at Tara and myself. Halo noticed their unease too; I could tell. His thoughts churned in a blend of frustration, guilt, and hesitation. When his shoulders slumped, I knew we'd won. "I'll give you a day, Mendoza. Just a day. Then"—his cyan eyes flared with irritation—"I'm carrying out my orders and bringing you in."

"Fine by me." I stepped back, letting the light die in my hand as the troopers lowered their guns. *Let's get out of here.*

Bandit clapped me on the shoulder and hurried to the front of the truck, hopping into the driver's seat. Caleb and Tara helped Deadeye to her feet and into the truck.

I stopped and looked at Halo before climbing into the truck myself, putting as much confidence into my voice as I could. "One day. You promised. Then have at it, but be warned." The truck rumbled under my hand as Bandit started it. "I'm not going to come quietly. This region deserves *someone* to protect it, and you'd better believe I'll do whatever it takes to keep these people safe."

I shut the hatch on Halo's guilt and the relieved troopers. As we got underway, Tara looked up at me with mischief in her eyes.

"Do you even *have* any power left?" She held up her hand, and her fingers shook as points of lights flickered between them. "I know I don't, and your reserve isn't *that* much bigger than mine."

I pulled my helmet off. "No," I admitted, flipping open my monitor cuff and turning off the comms program. The pressure of everyone's minds against mine faded to blissful background noise, and I sighed with relief. "I barely had enough to make that flame. I was afraid I'd actually lose it *while* I was threatening him."

Deadeye groaned, slouching against the wall and covering her eyes. A little of her dizziness washed across to my mind as she muttered, "What a way to start the day. This is going to be the mother of all headaches; I just know it. I don't suppose anyone has any coffee?"

All three of us laughed. As Caleb and Tara explained what had happened in the cloning facility, I let my head lean back to rest against the wall. The bumping of the truck was so soothing that I drifted away to sleep, the hum of everyone else's relief a calming counterpoint to my own.

We did it.

JOSEPHINE'S VOICE woke me a few hours later. Once we'd been properly fed, rested, and patched up—even I had some small injuries that I couldn't remember receiving—she introduced us to the rest of the command staff of St. Augustine's.

Logan crushed me in a hug. "We heard about what you did. You're crazy."

I shook my head. "You're the crazy one. You stayed with us when everyone else left." I took in his flight suit, wrinkled and marred with grime. "Your family—"

"They're safe—oh." A chirp came from the device clipped to his collar. "Duty calls." He gave a cheerful salute. "Rest well. You'll need it."

I was about to ask why when a tremor shook the ground. It wasn't exactly a good instinct, but I looked at Tara first.

"Not me," she said, offense clear in every line of her body. "That came from outside."

I frowned, letting my regenerated sixth sense filter out past the old hospital walls. Something was on fire—I could tell that much—and my heart rate sped up at wondering what else was happening. "What's going on out there?"

Flickers of caution sped between Josephine and the renegade St. Augustine's staff. Dr. Saltori held up a warning hand, stepping between me and the door. "Mendoza, you've had a long day, and—"

He stopped as I pushed past him, throwing the door open and feeling out the hallways to find a path to the roof. With the others close behind me, I ran up the stairs and burst onto the helipad, the rumbling making sense the moment I caught sight of the valley below. The mountains surrounding Tucson were untouched, but columns of smoke had erupted all over the city. Even from this distance, I could feel overtones of panic and uncertainty in the air, lacing the atmosphere like black sludge tainting clear water. To the south, a thick black plume billowed into the sky, another explosion rocking the ground as I stood there in horror.

"What happened?" Tara demanded behind me. I turned as she pulled a fireball into her palm and repeated the question.

"We knew the Blood Angel facility was too empty," I said, taking her hand and closing it to snuff out the fireball. "This isn't exactly a surprise."

Caleb crossed his arms. The sunlight caught in his steel-silver eyes. "We took out their biggest weapon. They're going to be angry." The way he said it—sheer determination crushing the fear in both voice and thoughts—made me straighten my spine and take a deep breath.

"They'll soon find out who they're messing with," I said, shifting to the side as Bandit joined us at the edge of the roof.

He whistled under his breath at the sight. "It's like the riots all over again," he said in Spanish. Switching to English, he said, "I don't know how much manpower Regional is prepared to send after us, or if they'll decide to just let us go. We might not have much time if they decide we're worth pursuing." His voice deepened. "We could end up fighting a war on two fronts. Better make sure we're prepared."

"Yeah, right. Sure." Deadeye sighed. "And here I thought I'd just be getting a cup of coffee." She patted my arm before turning away to follow Bandit downstairs.

Tara and Caleb stood alongside me for another minute, the unspoken conversation between them clear enough that I could catch the gist even without our bio interfaces. It always amazed me how they were able to communicate without any words spoken. Finally, Tara sighed. "I guess our quiet life will have to wait."

Caleb only sounded resigned. "It was too good to last; we both knew that." He put his arm around her shoulders, looking back at me as they left. "You coming?"

I shook my head. "Give me a minute."

Their presence faded as they went down the stairs, and I turned to the city. Even with the smoke casting a haze over the whole valley, I could still see patches of color in the bougainvillea, tiled roofs, mesquite leaves, and red-brick walls. Overhead, the sun was just passing its noonday height, piercing through the smoke and haze with brilliant golden light. I put my hands into my pockets, the slim width of my recorder meeting the tips of my fingers. I pulled out the tiny device and balanced it on my hand for a long moment before clicking it on and speaking into it.

"Well, I survived. But—" The feeling crystallized even as I spoke it. "But some part of me didn't. I guess it was the last part of me that was too scared to fight." I looked past the faded pink walls of St. Augustine's. Below me, I could almost hear the voices of the rest of the squad. "And I came out with more than I had when I went in."

My gaze flicked up to the Catalinas, the jagged edge of a canyon standing out in different colored rocks than the rest of the mountainside. The green from the monsoon had long since faded, but the shades of brown, gold, and grey were beautiful in their own way.

"No one ever cared much about this territory. The aliens didn't." Anger crept into my voice. "And our government doesn't. The only people who care about this region are the people whose roots go too deep to ever consider leaving"— Bandit's fierce protectiveness came to mind—"or those who are trying to hide." Caleb and Tara, just trying to find peace in lives filled by war.

"And me?" I lowered the recorder again, staring up into the smoke-streaked sky before bowing my head and speaking into the log of all my thoughts, fears, and dreams. "I'm here because it's still home. And no matter how awful or hostile a place is, it still deserves someone fighting for it."

Clicking off the recorder, I put it in my pocket and stared down across my city.

Even if that person has to be me.

———

GLOSSARY

From Sonora to Germany
and everywhere in between

ADOBE: A material made from hardened clay, commonly mixed with straw to construct houses and other buildings. Adobe homes have thick walls, which insulate well against both cold and hot weather.

AGUA DE JAMAICA: A bright red, lemonade-like beverage made from dried hibiscus flowers, water, and sugar. Extremely refreshing in hot weather.

BARRIO: The term for a neighborhood within a Spanish-speaking city. These neighborhoods often hold their own cultural distinctions, and function as micro-communities within a larger metropolis.

BIRRIA: A deeply flavored stew typically made with goat meat or beef and garnished with lime juice, onions, and cilantro. The meat is often strained out, chopped finely, and used to fill tacos and quesadillas.

BOUGAINVILLEA: A large shrub, with sharp thorns and large clusters of brilliant magenta blossoms.

CREOSOTE: A short, shrubby bush common to the Sonoran Desert. Blooms with small yellow flowers, and has a distinct smell when it comes into contact with moisture.

DUST SPINNER: Also known as a 'dust devil'. A towering column of spinning air and dust, created when warm updrafts collide with each other to pick dirt up from the ground. While related to tornados, they're not typically dangerous.

HABOOB: An Arabic term used to describe the dust storms preceding some monsoon fronts. Characterized by extremely limited visibility.

JAVELINA: A short, grey, bristly pig species native to the Sonoran Desert, ranging in size between 40 and 60 pounds. Travelling in small to medium herds or family groups, javelina are stupid, aggressive, and possess a musk gland that renders their meat almost inedible.

KARTOFFELPUFFER: German potato pancakes, commonly served with applesauce and/or sour cream.

LEBKUCHEN: A traditional German Christmas cookie, most similar to

American gingerbread. The most traditional include candied citrus peel and finely chopped nuts in the dough, which is then baked on a rice paper wafer and coated in sugar glaze or dark chocolate.

MASA: Dough made out of ground corn treated with lime, used to make tortillas and tamales.

MESQUITE: A native desert tree with twisted trunk and branches, craggy bark, and small, feathery leaves. Some varieties produce edible, protein-rich pods, and wood is widely used in smokers to impart a distinct flavor to meat dishes.

MIJO/MIJA: Term of endearment, commonly used for a younger sibling or by a parent to a child.

MONSOON: A brief July-August phenomenon in which moist air from the Gulf of Mexico combines with hot desert updrafts to create massive thunderstorms. Provides most of the annual rainfall for the desert.

NOPAL: Prickly pear cactus pads, eaten sauteed or grilled as a vegetable. The bright magenta fruit is used to make jellies, syrup, and juice.

PALETAS: Mexican popsicles or ice cream bars, usually fruit-based. Mango, strawberry, and coconut are all popular flavors.

PALO VERDE: A native desert tree with green bark, large spreading branches, and tiny leaves. In late spring, they bloom with a riot of bright yellow flowers, covering the entire tree.

POSOLE: Hominy soup, often with pork or chicken and a tomato or tomatillo-based broth. The Mexican-Sonoran equivalent of chicken noodle soup.

SCHATZI: German term of endearment, like 'sweetheart' in English.

SKY ISLAND: A term used to describe the mountains in the Sonoran Desert. Soaring abruptly from sea level to heights of 5,000 feet or greater, they are integral in helping form the life-giving monsoon storms.

STRUDEL: German pastry, made by stretching a large piece of dough to tissue-paper-like thickness before adding filling, rolling into a log, and baking. Fillings often include apple and nuts, but may also include poppy seed paste or other fruits.

WASH: A dry riverbed, which floods during monsoon storms. Sometimes called an 'arroyo'.

CAST OF CHARACTERS

GABRIEL MENDOZA:

At eighteen, Gabriel is the Technical Surveillance Specialist and youngest of the crew stationed at Base 36. Born and raised in Tucson, he survived the xeno occupation in the care of his grandmother until her death in the riots that followed humanity's victory. A keen observer and collector of stories, Gabriel lives in hope of one day being able to match up to the legacies of his childhood heroes.

CARLOS 'BANDIT' ESPINOZA:

In his late forties, Bandit is a crack shot with handgun or rifle and a deeply intelligent strategist. As commander of Base 36, he's responsible for a growing collection of old friends—and a young technical specialist who reminds him all too much of the things lost to war. Born and bred in Tucson, his roots go too deep for him ever to consider leaving his home.

JOSEPHINE FLORES:

Doctor and Pharmacist assigned to Base 36. After starting a clinic on the outskirts of Tucson in the early days of the occupation, she joined the original EDF with Bandit and stayed after the Commander's death. Six years younger than Bandit, she tagged after him as a child until the age gap narrowed enough for a lasting friendship to develop.

RENEÉ 'DEADEYE' ZIEGLER:

A long-term veteran of the Defense Force, Deadeye combines sharp-as-a-tack intellect with quick with and the aesthetic sense of an artist. As the Communications Specialist for Base 36, she has covert contacts all over Region 520—and a few pieces of contraband tech hidden in a corner. (Just don't ask how she lost her eye.)

ALEXI 'JUDGE' MOROZOV:

After Shattering as a teenager, Judge joined the original EDF and has never left. Now 27, he wields his considerable power as one of the two Shattereds assigned to Base 36. With a mental subtype and a strong affinity for creating shields, Judge balances serious and silly beneath a cocky exterior. (He loves all things pop culture, and has amassed a large collection of silly T-shirts.)

TARA 'BANSHEE' FLETCHER:

Originally from Appalachia, Tara earned her call sign by unleashing a destructive Shattered subtype on occupying xeno forces. Despite her unpredictable reputation, she's kind and caring, and won't back down from a fight to protect the innocent. Tara joined the EDF early in the war, and is half of the most powerful battle pair the Commander had ever seen.

CALEB 'PHANTOM' FLETCHER:

Married to Tara, Caleb's lightning-fast reflexes and level head make him the perfect balance to his wife's Shattered abilities. The path to Base 36 has been filled with sharp moments and heartbreak for them both, but he's never let previous experiences make him bitter. Instead, Caleb is determined to fight—that the horrors of his past may never be the horrors of anyone else's present.

LOGAN MEYER:

Assigned to Base 36 as a Thunderbird pilot, Logan combines technical expertise with sharp instincts to be the ultimate backup whenever the squad gets into a tight situation. A husband and a father to two little girls, he's dedicated to ensuring his family's safety, even if it means being apart from them for a time.

The Homely House
Santa Cruz River Valley

POSOLE

While there are certainly more authentic recipes out there, this dish provides the comfort of a home-cooked meal with fairly true-to-region flavors—and can be made with ingredients easily found in many grocery stores!

For the chicken:

- 2lb bone in, skin on chicken
- 16 oz jarred salsa verde

Combine in slow cooker and cook on high for 5 hours or low for 8 hours, until meat shreds easily. Remove chicken and shred, discarding bones and skin. Reserve 2 cups of shredded chicken and 1 cup cooking liquid for soup, use remaining chicken in another meal (tacos, anyone?).

For soup:

- 12 tomatillos, husked and quartered
- 2 poblano peppers, quartered and deseeded
- 1 tbsp. cooking oil
- 3 cloves garlic, minced
- 1 yellow onion, diced
- 1 16oz can great northern beans, drained
- 1 16oz can corn kernels, drained
- 1 16oz can hominy, drained
- 1 bunch cilantro (stems reserved, leaves chopped)
- 2 tsp. ground cumin
- 2 tsp. dried oregano
- 2-3 C. chicken broth (about two standard cans)

- 2 C. shredded chicken
- 1 C. reserved cooking liquid from chicken
- Juice of 2 limes (about 3 tbsp.)
- Salt & pepper

Instructions:

1. Combine tomatillos, poblanos, the stems of the cilantro, and a teaspoon of salt in a saucepan with enough water to cover. Bring to boil, reduce to simmer and cook until peppers are tender enough to be pierced with a fork.
2. Transfer all saucepan contents to a food processor or blender and pulse until no large chunks remain (you're making your own salsa verde!). Set aside for later.
3. In a large pot, heat cooking oil over medium heat until it shimmers. Add garlic and onion and sauté until onion is translucent, about 6-7 minutes.
4. Add reserved salsa verde to the pot, along with all other ingredients (including chicken and reserved cooking liquid). Bring to a boil and reduce to a simmer, cover.
5. Simmer on low heat for at least an hour and up to three hours. The chicken will gradually break down into smaller shreds, and soup will thicken slightly. After an hour, taste for seasoning and adjust with more salt and/or lime juice if needed.
6. Serve with tortilla chips or cornbread. Best consumed while a rainstorm pounds against the roof.

Notes:

- If short on time, use rotisserie chicken and increase broth to 4 cups.
- Tomatillos and poblano peppers can be found in the produce section of many major grocery stores. If you can't find them, you can substitute a 16 oz jar of salsa verde and proceed with the recipe from step three!

———

ACKNOWLEDGMENTS

The Homely House
Tucson AZ
Spring, 2024

What? We're here? Now?

Yep.

It's funny, but if this book had followed its original trajectory, I'd be spending this week in hibernation after a (hopefully) successful release day. Instead, I'm here with my window open to let in the smell of citrus blossoms and dust— a real Tucson spring if I ever saw one—while my baby daughter sleeps in her crib in the next room over.

We've lost a few things. Gained others. Come to think of it, so have the characters. I'd *never* considered, three years ago, that this story would come to mean everything that it has, or that life would bring me to face so many of the same fears and insecurities that Gabriel encounters...but here we are.

Enough rambling. This story has had a journey, and it's high time to thank the people, places, and non-corporeal entities who've had a hand in its becoming.

First, let's give a shout out to Firaxis Games and the creators of *XCOM* 2: *War of the Chosen*. Y'all created a world and storyline that captured the attention of this very selective gamer girl, and held it through a dozen playthroughs and more reloaded saves than I can count. While The Aftermath no longer resembles the initial inspiration, I still have you to thank for igniting the spark.

Many thanks to my husband, who created the first versions of Deadeye, Bandit, and Judge. The hours of gaming with these characters (remember when you made Judge mind control that chryssalid?) shaped the type of story I wanted to tell in ways I never would have foreseen.

Much appreciation to Celestial Seasonings as the manufacturer of Bengal Spice tea, also known as "what kept me awake during early morning writing sessions".

Immense gratitude goes to the staff of Uncommon Universes Press, not only for giving *The Shattered Ones* a home, but for introducing me to the books that opened my heart to this world of fierce stories written by equally fierce believers.

My thanks to the creators of *Bad Batch*. I've still never seen the show, but from all accounts, the hearts of our stories are similar. Thanks for paving the way (and providing a great comp title)!

In addition to the many beta readers, ARC readers, and general supporters (read: rabid fans) this project has garnered over the years, I have to shed light on the three powerful women who encouraged, convinced, and threatened my wellbeing until I finally believed in myself and this story enough to see it into the world...

Emmy, you believed in me from the start, when you trusted a stranger from the other side of the world to be your NaNoWriMo buddy. Your cleverness is unparalleled, your strength immense, and your heart bigger than the entirety of the distance that separates us. Without you—truthfully!—this series would not exist.

Brittany, my not-agent turned partner-in-crime, how many ups and downs we've had over these years! In addition to your keen mind and ridiculous emphasis on the swoon factor of stories, I've come to rely on you as someone who'll always have my back in prayer. You're priceless, my dear friend.

Laurel…Laurel. There were moments when I was dead set on this series never seeing the light of day, but here we are. And it's because of you—your enthusiasm, your love for the characters, and your ridiculous memes. Thank you.

Last of all (ah, there it is), immense gratitude belongs to the Sonoran Desert and the resilient, unflinchingly loyal people who live here. This whole series is a tribute to you, after all. Thank you for teaching me how to love where I live.

The Homely House
Tucson AZ

Brigitte Cromey didn't plan on falling in love with the desert. After ten years, it's safe to say that it's grown on her. In addition to admiring the glorious Arizona sunsets, praying for rain, and reminding her children not to touch the cactus, she enjoys playing video games with her friends and family, reading entire fantasy books in one sitting, and listening to Christian Reggaeton with the bass turned up. She may forget to drink enough water, but the tea kettle will always be on, and her Homely House in the desert is always open to those seeking refuge from the cares of life.

Tales of Sea and Skies

Book 1: Star of Hope

Book 2: Fires of Freedom

Anthologies

Crowns: A Heartbooks Anthology